THE SABOTEURS

Copyright © 2021 by Sandecker, RLLLP.
Interior illustrations by Roland Dahlquist.
Facing page image: Panama Canal construction by Everett
Collection/Shutterstock.com.
Wheeler Publishing, a part of Gale, a Cengage Company.

LIBRARY OF CONGRESS CIP DATA ON FILE.
CATALOGUING IN PUBLICATION FOR THIS BOOK
IS AVAILABLE FROM THE LIBRARY OF CONGRESS.

ISBN-13: 978-1-4328-8258-7 (hardcover alk. paper)

Published in 2021 by arrangement with G.P. Putnam's Sons, an imprint
of Penguin Publishing Group, a division of Penguin Random House LLC.

Printed in Mexico
Print Number: 01   Print Year: 2021

Panama

GEORGE WASHINGTON GOETHALS Head of Panama Canal Authority

SAM WESTBROOK Canal administrator

JACK SCULLY Canal chief mechanic

JEREMIAH TOWNSEND Canal archivist

RINALDO MORALES Court Talbot's driver

RAUL MORALES Rinaldo's brother

FELIX RAMIREZ Owner of the Central Hotel

ERNST LEIBINGER-HOLTE Swiss businessman

BENEDICT "TATS" MACALISTER Hotel guest

GUILLERMO ACOSTA Argentine civil engineer

WHITTIER AND JULIET WEBB Hotel guests

JORGE NUÑEZ Panamanian guide

DETECTIVE ORTEGA Panama City policeman

RUTH BUSCHMAN Nurse

T.R. in Milwaukee

PROLOGUE

They gave him the gun in New York, he was pretty certain, and he thought some money too. That had allowed him to stalk his prey across eight states, often staying in the same hotels and riding the same train. Most importantly, though, they'd helped him hear the ghost once again. And the ghost gave the same command he'd given eleven years earlier, only John hadn't the strength to act then. Today was different.

John Flammang Schrank spent most of the afternoon in a bar across from the Gilpatrick Hotel, where he knew his target would eat dinner before motoring to the Milwaukee Auditorium to deliver a speech to further his unholy quest. A former bar owner himself, the Bavarian-born Schrank downed six schooners of beer but felt nothing but calm as the crowds outside the

11

nearby hotel swelled in anticipation of getting a glimpse of their hero.

Traitor, he thought sullenly, the weight of the gun tugging at his coat pocket. Traitor and murderer.

He paid the barman and crossed the street. It was close to eight, and light spilled from the hotel's windows. The air was crisp, so people wore long coats and hats pulled down low. Schrank was a portly man, round in the belly, with a friendly enough face dominated by a large, jutting chin. He had little trouble pressing his way through the happy throngs of people.

How could they show such adoration? he wondered. Didn't they know the truth?

That truth had come to him shortly after his target had taken office. It was the ghost's first appearance in a dream, a vivid dream that he'd never been able to shake. And now, with the help of his new benefactors, the dream had returned, only this time his target had been wearing the robes of a priest, but it made no difference. Schrank recognized the usurper at once.

Schrank looked around. People were practically giddy with the thought of seeing their man. The ghost had said their hero had murdered him by placing the Polish anarchist Leon Czolgosz at the Pan-

12

American Expo in Buffalo. The two shots he'd fired to the gut were enough to turn the man into the ghost of John Schrank's dreams.

Schrank recognized a face in the crowd. It was the nice one, the one who listened to him. The other, the taciturn man who demanded and cajoled and demeaned, wasn't at his side as he'd been so many times before when he'd tried to carry out the assassination. This was the omen that tonight it would happen. He moved even closer to the front of the crowd, ignoring the sour looks of people who'd waited some time for their coveted positions.

He felt the hard rubber grip of the .38 caliber Colt revolver deep in his overcoat pocket. He was close to the front row of people. The hotel's door was only a few paces away, and the open-top automobile, with its long hood and sweeping running boards, idled at the curb.

"I can't believe I'm about to see the hero of San Juan Hill," a woman said to her husband a little breathlessly.

"I hear he doesn't like to be called Teddy, but rather TR," said another voice in the crowd.

Schrank fingered the pistol. He couldn't allow him to have a third term. No President had ever had one. George Washington himself had refused, fearing it would turn the presidency into a monarchy like the one America had fought to free herself from. John Schrank saw himself as a patriot, like one of the Minutemen, fighting against the tyranny of a man wishing to become King.

The crowd suddenly erupted in a roar of wild cheering. Teddy Roosevelt came down the handful of steps outside the Gilpatrick and waved to the people who'd waited to see him, envious of the nine thousand awaiting his speech a short distance away at the auditorium. Roosevelt gave them a big-toothed smile, his eyes behind his rimless glasses alight with joy. His walrus mustache twitched.

He mounted the car's running board and lowered himself into the rear seat next to his stenographer, Elbert Martin. Opposite them on the rear-facing seat was another aide, Harry Cochems. The crowd continued to roar and shake the air with their applause. TR gave Harry a knowing smile and got back to his feet, his top hat in hand, to wave once again to the people. They loved him for the gesture, and he loved them for their loyalty and support.

John Flammang Schrank saw his opportunity and lurched a step closer to his target. Without a change in expression, with no real malice at all since he didn't hate the former President but needed to stop him from retaking the Oval Office, he raised the pistol and took aim at Roosevelt's head, just a few feet away.

He squeezed the trigger at the same time someone behind him jostled his arm. The gun went off, a single clap of thunder loud enough to silence the crowd. The smell of burnt powder turned the air acrid.

Teddy Roosevelt staggered just slightly, bending at the knee, before straightening up once again, his hat still raised. Elbert Martin was the first to react. He'd played collegiate football and had lightning reflexes. He dove out of the car and crashed into Schrank before he could fire again. Both men fell to the sidewalk, Martin using his superior size to pin Schrank to the ground while he clamped his hands around the assassin's wrists. A. O. Girard, a bodyguard from the Van Dorn Detective Agency and a former member of TR's Rough Riders, moved in and scooped up the pistol while two of Milwaukee's Finest piled onto the scrum.

Harry Cochems jumped to his feet and asked, "Were you hit, Mr. President?"

"He pinked me, Harry," Roosevelt replied.

15

"Dear God."

The crowd was shouting for blood. Cries of "kill him" and "hang him" rang out.

TR waved his hat and bellowed, "Don't hurt him. Bring him here. I want to see him." The mob could hardly believe their hero was unharmed, and cheers rose up. "I'm all right, I'm all right."

The cops yanked Schrank to his feet.

"Bring him to me," Roosevelt demanded, and the would-be assassin was frog-marched to the side of the idling saloon sedan.

Roosevelt studied the man's face, placing his hands on his head and tried to recall if he'd ever seen the dull-looking creature before. There was no spark of recognition. "What did you do it for?"

Schrank just looked at him, working his jaw but saying nothing.

"Oh, what's the use," Roosevelt said, pain beginning to hone his voice. "Officers, take charge of him, and see that there's no violence done to him."

He sat back into his seat as Schrank was led into the hotel and the crowds booed.

The car pulled away from the curb. Once out of sight of his supporters, Roosevelt opened his topcoat and suit jacket. The fine white linen of his shirt was stained crimson over his right side. His aides stared, slack-jawed, at the amount of blood.

"Driver," Harry Cochems practically shouted. "Get us to the nearest hospital."

"Ignore that. Keep true for the auditorium," Roosevelt countered, and accepted a fresh handkerchief from Elbert to press to the wound. Roosevelt held a hand over his mouth and coughed. He showed his white palm to his assistants. "If I were lung-shot, there'd be blood. I'm going to be fine."

He fished two items from the inside pocket of his jacket. One was the fifty-page speech he planned to deliver neatly folded in two. The bullet had torn a ragged hole through the sheaf of papers. The second item was his leather-covered steel glasses case. It too had been pierced. The bullet had lost enough of its momentum that by the time it struck Roosevelt's chest it merely punctured the skin and lodged against his rib cage.

"Ladies and gentlemen, I don't know if you fully understand that I've been shot, but it takes more than one bullet to kill a Bull Moose."

1

Buenos Aires
Winter 1913

A vast armada of freighters lined the city's busy waterfront, tucked in bow to stern like a wartime convoy. Over them stood the massive grain silos, multi-storied wooden structures with movable spouts from which cascades of golden wheat thundered into their holds. Farther down the quay, special refrigerated ships were being loaded with great slabs of pampas-bred beef destined for homes and restaurants across the breadth of Europe. Other ships were being unloaded with goods from Europe and North America, mostly manufactured items that Argentina couldn't produce herself.

Otto Dreissen hadn't been back in BA, as almost everyone called the Argentine capital, in six months, and it seemed the port was even more hectic than before. Steam tugs were at the ready to tow out a laden ship the instant its holds were filled so another waiting vessel could take its place. Stevedores and longshoremen swarmed like an army of ants, trundling bound bundles of native wool up gangways or swinging barrels of vegetable oils in cargo nets up to the ships where waiting hands were ready to guide the cargo belowdecks.

His steamship passed what had to have been a mile of busy docks before reaching the passenger pier, its horn finally blaring a welcoming blast. There were only a handful of well-wishers waiting on the dock. Like so many ships arriving in South America, the Hamburg Süd-Amerika Line's venerable *São Paulo* was mostly transporting immigrants hoping to find a better life far from the strict social confines of their home countries. Here in Argentina, most were Spaniards or Italians, while Brazil to the north had always been popular with the Portuguese.

Dreissen hadn't made the full transatlantic crossing himself. He normally based out of Panama and had just concluded some business in Brazil and boarded the ship when it put in for coal at Belém on the Amazon River's southern bank. It had been a short cruise for him and his majordomo/bodyguard, Heinz Kohl.

Kohl stood a step behind Dreissen at the top of the gangplank, with a porter waiting behind him with a large, monogrammed steamer trunk on a wheeled handcart. Down on the dock idled a yellow Rolls-Royce Silver Ghost, courtesy of the Plaza Hotel. It was a beautiful summer day, so the luxury car's leather top was down. The driver stood by the vehicle, in gray livery with his peaked cap under his arm, and remained as motionless as a soldier at attention.

The gangway was soon lashed into place, and the ship's first officer was on hand to wish the first-class passengers well. The immigrants in steerage would be let out through a lower hatchway, but only after the better-heeled passengers had disembarked.

"Good to have you aboard, Herr Dreissen," the blond senior officer said. The gold piping on his tropical white uniform gleamed like jewelry.

"I haven't sailed aboard the *São Paulo* since just after the turn of the century. You do her a credit. She's in great shape."

"Our government agrees, Herr Dreissen. They've agreed to purchase her from the line."

"Then I am glad to have enjoyed a final

21

trip on the old girl. Good day."

Dreissen was the first down the gangway and was settled in the Rolls by the time Kohl and the porter had fitted the trunk onto the rack over the rear bumper. It was a short ride to the Plaza Hotel on Calle Florida, but with so much of the streets ripped up for the construction of South America's first subway, it took far longer than normal. They had to detour all the way around San Martín Square and approach the nine-story, Second Empire–style hotel from the side.

The manager himself waited at the entrance and greeted Dreissen with a warm smile and handshake. Like so much of BA, the Plaza Hotel and its staff wanted to make all their European guests feel right at home. The fact that the Argentines chose to copy the Old World more than the American model was a deliberate snub to their neighbors far to the north. Animosity toward the United States dated back to the founding of the nation and the implementation of the Monroe Doctrine a few years later.

"Welcome back, Herr Dreissen. I have your usual suite waiting for you."

Dreissen responded in fluent Spanish, "You're looking prosperous, Raoul."

The hotelier rubbed his expanding belly

with a grin. "These are good times for Argentina, so why shouldn't I grow with our nation?"

A guest of Otto Dreissen's status needn't bother with formalities like check-in. The manager had the suite's key in his pocket, and porters were already swarming over the rear of the hotel's limousine to secure the trunk. Kohl watched the scene and scanned the bustling sidewalks for potential threats.

"If I may be so bold and to ask what brings you to BA, Herr Dreissen?" Raoul asked.

"The *verdammt* British got the concession to supply subway cars to the first lines being built, but we want to build the carriages and engines for the line the Lacroze Company is planning. I have meetings with their senior staff in two days."

The Argentinian frowned. "The English have a near monopoly on all things railroad-related here. I wish you luck."

They took the brass elevator to the top floor, and Raoul opened the suite's heavy door. The windows looked out over the busy streets, but the view was obscured by smoke belching from a steam shovel chewing away at the street for the new underground. Dreissen noted the bottle of champagne chilling in a silver bucket and a bottle of Napoléon cognac on a tray with a cut-crystal snifter.

"Anything else for you, Herr Dreissen?" the manager asked as Kohl and the porter maneuvered the large trunk into the suite. Kohl immediately set about unpacking his master's things.

Dreissen popped the top of the Pol Roger and poured some of the frothing wine into a flute. "Might as well send up another bottle of this. The old *São Paulo* isn't known for her wine cellars."

"Of course." With that, the hotelier and porter departed, well tipped by Kohl for their efforts.

Dreissen ate dinner in his suite and was cracking the second bottle of champagne when his expected guest knocked, and Kohl opened the door. The Argentine Foreign Minister wore a black suit but no hat. His name was Matias Guzman. Unlike the ruggedly built Dreissen, Guzman was willow thin, with a wisp of a mustache and the hands of a pianist. Like Dreissen, he had a formidable mind and was a strategic thinker. Their occasional games of chess usually left both men exhausted.

Dreissen stood from the dining table and strode over to shake his friend's hand. Guzman clasped the German's shoulder in an extra display of affection. "It is good to see you, Otto. It has been far too long since you've come to the Paris of the Americas."

"When you work for my family, you go where they tell you."

They sat, and Dreissen poured some champagne.

"Am I to understand we are celebrating your recent success?" Guzman asked, saluting Dreissen with his flute.

"My success?"

"Rumors out of Manaus say you secured a lucrative contract for all of Don Antônio Oliveira's rubber harvest for this year and next."

"That is true. Essenwerks's new automotive division will now be able to supply all its own tires."

"There was also a rumor that the French representative from Michelin had the inside track for those contracts and that he was found dead, floating in the Amazon River. Rather lucky for you."

Dreissen said, deadpan, "I tend to make my own luck."

That statement, and all its potential meaning, hung in the air for several seconds. Guzman finally said, "What brings you to BA? Your telegram was rather cryptic. And why meet here under a false pretense rather than my office?"

"Does anyone know you're here?"

"Of course they do. My mistress and I had dinner here at the hotel. She's downstairs, sulking in our room, because I left her." Guzman saw a shadow of concern in his host's face. "This is Latin America. Friday nights are for the girlfriend, before you go to the country house to spend the weekend with the wife and kids. Surely you know this."

"I do, but I'd rather no one can link the two of us being at the same hotel together."

"You worry too much." Guzman set his drink aside, then said, "Tell me why all the cloak-and-dagger."

Dreissen ignored the inquiry. "I noticed the port is even busier now than during my last visit."

Guzman leaned back, recognizing early on that their conversation may turn out as exhausting as one of their marathon chess matches. "It is. Exports are up three percent over last year. We are seeing a record number of immigrants coming from Europe to try their hand at a better life here."

"And imports?" Dreissen knew well it was a touchy subject.

"Also up," Guzman said a little tightly.

"And foreign investments? I see the subway is scheduled to open this year. It was built with English money, yes?"

"You know it was. And to answer your question, we receive plenty of foreign capital."

"Do you, though?" Dreissen asked, an eyebrow cocked over a bright gray eye. "Railroad construction is down dramatically because all the profitable lines have already been laid. You are now forced to offer very generous terms to lure investors to install track to the more remote reaches of the interior. The best lands have already been put under the plow and converted to agriculture. Meanwhile, few European investors are interested in bringing manufacturing to your country. You lack indigenous coal or petroleum, so it makes no sense for anyone to open an energy-intensive factory."

The Minister's mouth tightened. "Your point?"

"My point is, your investors have turned Argentina into exactly what they need, a market for their expensive manufactured goods while at the same time a supplier of good-quality but inexpensive beef, mutton, and other agricultural goods. You've gained your independence from Spain, certainly, but your nation remains a colonial state wholly dependent on Europe."

A long moment passed as the two men stared each other down. Guzman was the first to look away. "I don't think I would put our situation in quite those terms."

"Harsh, but essentially true. And now the other proverbial shoe is going to drop, and any hope you have of luring manufacturing here will wither on the vine."

Guzman nodded, knowing he'd lost the opening gambit. "The canal."

"The estimate is, it will open a year from this August."

"At that point they will succeed in effectively cutting off South America from international commerce as Africa had been bypassed by the building of the Suez Canal. You were the one to point that out to me, Otto."

"I recall our conversation. Except for South Africa, there is so little investment taking place there that it will remain colonized and impoverished for generations. The Suez Canal is why my family doesn't have a representative in Africa the way we do in America, Argentina, and in the Orient."

"And you're certain the same will happen here?"

"We've talked about it in the past," Dreissen reminded him. "The newly discovered oil fields around Maracaibo in Venezuela may prove out, giving them something the states of the northern bloc will want, but for the rest of South America, the economies will contract markedly without outside investment. You'll be in a stranglehold from which there is no escape."

Guzman cursed the Americans in no uncertain terms and stood quickly, clearly agitated, for he knew his host was correct. The canal was going to isolate South America as if the entire continent ceased to exist. Clasping his hands behind his back, he paced the suite for a moment. Dreissen clearly saw how much Guzman loved his country, and the Foreign Minister was good enough at his job to see the inevitable failure it would become. He liked that Guzman's passions were so easily inflamed. Such men made an easier mark. He let the Minister pace two full laps across the sitting room carpet before throwing him an unexpected lifeline.

He lit a cheroot and said lazily, "There may be something that can be done to delay the completion of the canal and give you the time you need to attract enough capital to build up a manufacturing base."

Guzman's eyes glittered, and he swept back to the table. "What are you saying? Please don't tease me, old friend."

"At this point, let me just say certain technological breakthroughs have been made that would allow an interested party to severely delay the American construction effort, a matter of years rather than months."

"You can really do it?"

"Not me, but a team of men, trained and determined men. They can prevent the canal from opening long enough for you to strengthen Argentina's economy and ensure a future for your people that's far brighter than it would be otherwise."

"How quickly could this happen?" Guzman asked, knowing the sooner it took place, the better it would be. The canal's construction had been a concern for several potential investors he was currently courting.

"It would take some months to lay the groundwork for the operation," Dreissen admitted. "Security isn't particularly tight, but access is difficult. The Canal Authority is like a nation unto itself."

Guzman took a moment to recharge his glass and calm his nerves. Learning that all may not be lost had let his imagination and ambitions run wild. He gathered his wits, knowing that Dreissen had baited a trap with a bishop or rook while his queen lurked someplace on the board ready to pounce.

He said, "I understand why you want to keep it unofficial for now. I also see why you would bring this to me and, say, not the Brazilians. They are in no position to offer you much by way of compensation. I must ask what it is you want from me in return?"

"The rolling stock for the Lacroze line. I want Essenwerks to build the cars and engines and have exclusive contracts for any additional lines constructed below the streets of Buenos Aires."

"Done," Guzman agreed quickly and started to get to his feet, amazed that it was at such a low cost.

"The rest," Dreissen said, freezing Guzman, half standing, and the smile on his lips, "will be determined by members of our respective nations' diplomatic corps."

"This is something your government is behind?"

"It is something we made them aware of. Companies like Essenwerks and Krupp are so large that we need to keep the Kaiser and his Ministers aware of some of our activities. It is so they can manage the economy with the utmost efficiency. It is a partnership of industry and state. I believe the term is *synergy*. What is best for Essenwerks must also be best for the Fatherland, and vice versa."

"I see." Guzman's earlier delight had cooled. The subway contract covered Dreissen's expenses for the operation. The German government would want far more for giving his nation a future beyond that of an agrarian backwater. "Do you have any idea what the Kaiser wants for helping us?"

"It's not as bad as you think, Matias. I am about to tell you something under the strictest of confidence because it will help you at the bargaining table. When I first proposed this to the government, the Kaiser himself liked the idea of slowing the Americans' progress. He doesn't like their rapid ascent on the world stage since they defeated Spain and took Cuba and the Philippines. He would like to see them slowed in their rise. He tried and failed once before to interfere in their internal affairs and likes the opportunity to try again. My government will want much from you, no doubt, but they also want this to happen so the negotiations will succeed."

Guzman recognized the gift he'd just been given. "Thank you for sharing that."

"I will also share that they think so highly of this plan, they're embedding an agent in Panama to monitor our progress."

"You don't seemed so pleased by that."

"It is the price of working with the government, I suppose. They don't understand the motives of a capitalist. I am in the business of selling machines — trains, automobiles, aircraft. The more customers I can keep, the more my factories prosper. Synergy." He drew on his slender cigar and blew a cloud of fragrant smoke toward the ceiling. "If I may offer some advice . . . With the time this operation buys you, I recommend partnering with the Venezuelans and locking in contracts for their oil. If you have the fuels needed for an industrial economy by the time the canal finally opens, its presence won't matter. Argentina will be a destination port for trade with every civilized nation on earth."

Chase in San Diego Bay

2

San Diego, California
April 1914

As the Coronado Ferry neared the halfway point across San Diego Bay, Isaac Bell turned to look back at the burgeoning city. The skyline was still modest, just a few buildings with multiple stories, but he knew the fate of the city — in fact, the entire West Coast — was about to undergo tremendous upheaval. Los Angeles, this town, and even his beloved San Francisco, still recovering from the earthquake and subsequent fire just eight years prior, were all going to experience unprecedented growth in the coming years.

It wasn't so hard to believe, he mused, that the fundamental nature of the entire country was going to change as a result of what was happening in Central America.

He glanced over his other shoulder at the two warships lying at anchor close to a dry dock facility. Already, the Navy was considering a new base along the California coast, and these two battlewagons, plus others, were exploring all the major harbors. The big, armored cruiser, USS *Maryland,* was over five hundred feet in length and had the distinct pale hull and khaki upperworks of Teddy Roosevelt's Great White Fleet. Her four funnels were as straight as stovepipes, while her hull and turrets bristled with cannons. With her was a smaller escort destroyer, the USS *Whipple.* Around both ships, men rowed sleek longboats to deploy anti-torpedo netting that hung from hundreds of cork floats and dangled to below the bottom of each fighting ship's keel.

There was no fear of an enemy submarine lurking in these waters but rather a thorough test that there were no bottom obstructions to leave gaps in the ships' protective enclosure.

A short while later, the side-wheeler reached the docks of Coronado. The wood pilings stank of newly applied tar. The passengers disembarked before a horse and wagon loaded with silage was led off the ferry. A pair of carriages provided by the hotel waited to take those passengers who were also its guests to their destination. The passengers headed for a day trip to Tent

City, a family-friendly area of amusements and restaurants that had sprung up on the spit in recent years, and either paid the penny for the trolley or walked.

From the ferry landing on 1st Street it was a straight shot down Orange Avenue to Bell's destination. The Hotel del Coronado, known locally and affectionately as The Del, evoked images of every bride's fantasy wedding cake, with walls of white fondant and a red icing roof. The hotel had the ageless quality of a European castle but was so much brighter because of its whimsical turrets and countless gables and dormers and how it sat happily on sand rather than brooding on some mist-shrouded moor.

Bell couldn't help but smile at seeing the Queen Anne–style resort for the first time. He regretted not sharing this moment with his wife, Marion, who loved whimsy.

Off to the right, along the length of the Silver Strand, the spit of land connecting Coronado to the mainland, Bell eyed Tent City. While there were countless tents, many gaily striped, the entertainment destination had permanent buildings as well — bathhouses, restaurants, and wood-framed boardinghouses. A narrow-gauge electric trolley ran down the middle of the main street, its bell chiming merrily to roust pedestrians from its path.

Bell also noticed a boathouse built on pilings over Glorietta Bay. It looked like a miniature version of the main hotel. The carriage driver noticed his interest in the white and red building. He said, "The architect had the carpenters practice the Queen Anne style building the boathouse before turning them loose on the main hotel."

"His idea worked," Bell remarked. He looked back at the sprawling resort. "What an astonishing achievement."

An army of uniformed bellhops appeared when the carriage reached the entrance, and soon Bell and a couple checking in at the same time as him were whisked into the hotel. The lobby was paneled in dark wood that made it feel intimate despite its vast size and lofty coffered ceiling. Registration was to the left, while a large staircase corkscrewing up around a cage elevator was ahead on the right. The buzz of conversation was constant, as guests mingled or made arrangements for the next day's activities with the concierge.

While the rooms overlooking the central courtyard, with its junglelike landscaping, were considered the premier accommodations, Bell requested an outside room so he could sit on the veranda and watch the ever-changing ocean. Not that there would be much time today. Tomorrow was another story. Marion was going to join him for two blissful weeks at The Del, a long-overdue vacation.

A bellhop saw Isaac up to his room. He discussed the hotel's amenities, including the saltwater swimming pool and the fact that each of the hotel's many guest bathrooms featured hot and cold salt and fresh water and that The Del was one of the largest electrified buildings in the country when it was built. He boasted it was also home to the very first outside Christmas tree decorated with electric lights.

After tipping the man and seeing him to the door, Bell pulled a fresh shirt from his leather grip, a towel from the pile of linens, and his dopp kit. He walked down the hall to one of the baths, passing a dark slender man who Bell soon discovered had left the shared washroom a mess. He looked back to see the man enter a room and considered confronting the breach of etiquette but decided it wasn't worth the effort.

At the basin counter, Bell stripped to the waist, then cleaned up at the sink, using warm fresh water, then switched to hot salt water to lather and shave his face. It left his skin feeling tight. He regarded his reflection for just a moment. He was not yet thirty-five but his face looked years younger, with fine features, wide-set blue eyes, and a wave of blond hair he was now wearing slicked back. He worked a dollop of cream into his hair and smoothed it down. He also took a moment to trim his mustache with scissors from his dopp. He checked the Cartier Santos wristwatch that was a gift from Marion. She'd gotten it for him in England following their near-fateful trip aboard the *Titanic.* He quickly donned a fresh shirt.

A tall figure in a tan suit loitered outside his room as he made his way back down the hall. Seeing Bell, the man doffed his boater and held the stiff hat in his hand. He had a lean, eager face, but the suspicious eyes of all Van Dorn detectives.

"Sorry, Mr. Bell, when the bellhop told me you were here, I was at the boathouse."

"Don't worry about it, Renny. Come on in." Bell keyed open his door and held it open for the younger man. "How's everything looking?"

Bell worked on his tie, without need of a mirror, while his advance man from the Agency's Los Angeles office, Renny Hart, gave his report.

"The hotel has been cooperative and allowed me to speak with any of the guests whose reservations were made after Senator Densmore set up this meeting with Courtney Talbot. They're all legit." Bell opened his mouth to ask a question, but the younger man held up a finger. "To be on the safe side, I also checked guests who made their reservation a week prior to Densmore's summit."

Bell nodded. He expected no less from any of the men working for Joseph Van Dorn, the legendary founder of his namesake agency.

He shrugged into the leather shoulder rig with a holster for his Colt 1911 .45 caliber pistol and a separate case for two spare magazines. A snap loop securing the bottom of the holster to his belt ensured it would fit discreetly against his body no matter how he moved. The cream linen jacket he pulled on was tailored so that the weapon's outline was further obscured. Without the shoulder rig, the suit looked ill fitted, but, with it on, only the most sharp-eyed observer would know Bell was armed.

"Where's the Senator now?" Bell asked.

"He's out fishing, on a charter from the marina. That's why I was at the boathouse. Waiting for him to return."

"And the Major?"

"Talbot checked in about an hour before you. He's in his room."

"Okay. This meeting should be a routine briefing. Talbot doesn't know I'm here, but it shouldn't matter. I want you to look at this whole thing as a training exercise. Van Dorns are often hired to act as bodyguards and provide security. Your supervisor says you don't have much experience at either, so stay vigilant but discreet."

"You can count on me, Mr. Bell."

3

One of the hotel's bellhops knocked on Bell's door a few minutes before six. Bell was at the desk, writing in his journal, as he normally did when he had free time. With a life so richly detailed, he found he could remember it better if he first committed it to paper. He set aside his pen and opened the door.

"Apologies, Mr. Bell. Mr. Hart asked that you be informed that the Senator has not yet returned to the property. He has further instructed me to inform you that Mr. Talbot received an order of drinks from room service."

Bell chuckled at such a measured and formal mode of speech coming from a lad who couldn't have been more than fourteen. He fished a coin from his pocket and sent it arcing into the boy's palm with a flip of his thumb. "Thanks, kid. Stay close to Mr. Hart for more updates."

43

"Yes, sir." The boy tipped his cap and stepped away from the door.

By seven, and still with no word of the Senator's return, Bell went downstairs to the bar overlooking the beach for an icy beer and poached fish with mousseline sauce.

A different bellhop found Bell while he was finishing his meal. The bar was filled with laughing summer revelers and music provided by a trio playing some fast-tempo ragtime for the handful of people on the tiny dance floor. Upstairs, in the towering Crown Room, the shining jewel of the Hotel Del, a full orchestra was playing to a more formal crowd.

"Mr. Bell," the boy said. "Senator Densmore is back. There was some boat trouble, and he sends his apologies. He says the meeting is to take place at nine o'clock in the main dining room, when service has ended."

"Thanks," said Bell, and he flipped the kid a coin.

At the appointed hour, Bell approached The Del's dining room. Renny Hart already was sitting in the deserted shoeshine stand, with the evening paper held up to catch the light from a wall sconce. Bell gave the barest of nods as he passed. Just as he reached for the closed door, a figure rushed up and

44

barred him with a raised hand from entering.

The stranger looked like he'd stepped out of central casting at a motion picture studio, lantern-jawed, with sharp, dark eyes and a rugged blue-black shadow of stubble across his cheeks and chin. His nose was aquiline and strong. He wore khaki riding breeches jammed into old but well-cared-for riding boots and matching jacket, replete with pouches and leather shotgun shell loops. A broad-brimmed bush hat with an exotic animal skin band rested on his head.

This, Bell knew, was Courtney Talbot, Major, U.S. Army (ret.). When he was just a sergeant during the Spanish–American War, he'd been among a group of soldiers who'd volunteered to scout landing sites for an attack on an iron fort near the mouth of the San Juan River in Cuba. Once on the beach, they came under withering fire from the fort and from Spanish patrols on foot. Eventually, cannon fire from the gunboat USS *Peoria* bought them room on the beachhead for a rescue attempt carried out by a handful of Buffalo Soldiers from the fabled black 10th Cavalry Regiment who'd come ashore from the steamship *Florida*. Talbot was credited with leading the beach's defense during the desperate battle after the officers were either wounded or killed outright. He'd declined a Medal of Honor so as not to take away those awarded to the four brave soldiers who rescued them off the hellish beach. He did, however, accept a battlefield commission.

According to the bio Van Dorn research had thrown together in the short amount of time they'd been given, Talbot spent the next ten years in various capacities throughout Central America and the Caribbean, usually working out of embassies and often in countries on the verge of revolution. Rumors that he helped stir up said revolutions made him *persona non grata* in much of that part of the world, so he'd then gone off to fight against the Tagalogs in the Philippines, before resigning at age forty. He was now somehow attached to the Panama Canal project, though the people Bell had research his life couldn't find an official title or position within the canal-building Authority.

"Sorry, friend. The dining room is closed for a private meeting." Talbot's tone wasn't threatening, but, in it, Bell heard that he expected to be obeyed.

"I know. I was asked to sit in." Bell thrust out his hand. "I'm Isaac Bell."

Talbot wasn't sure what to make of this,

but he released the door and shook the proffered hand. "Court Talbot."

Bell used the distraction to open the dining room door. The main hall was as large as an aircraft hangar, with an arching coffered ceiling made up of individually jointed glossy planks. The walls were paneled in dark wood as well. The hanging chandeliers were massive affairs, but their glow was intentionally anemic to give the impressive space a sense of intimacy.

Along the far long wall was a raised platform for a band to entertain the diners while they ate, though at this time it was empty. There was only one occupied table and it sat at the opposite end of the dining room under the darkened, almost floor-length windows. It was round and large enough to seat a dozen.

The table was indeed set for a dozen, but there were only two people seated and just one was eating. A waiter in a black uniform hovered close by.

"Gentlemen." Senator J. William Densmore's booming voice managed to fill the cavernous, barrel-vaulted space.

The two newcomers strode through the dining room, weaving separate paths around the countless tables to arrive at the exact same moment. They nodded at each other, for it had been a contest, though one that drew to a tie.

Senator Densmore wore a white suit that was probably sewn by a tentmaker. He was tall, but grossly overweight. His salt-and-pepper hair was thick, and he wore a beard with two silver stripes running downward from the corners of his mouth. His eyes were dark and quick. His nose was bright red from sunburn, but it gave him the cheery glow of Santa Claus. His hands were busy slicing into a tuna steak the size of a dictionary. Bell supposed it was one of the fish he'd caught that afternoon.

To the Senator's right was a young woman wearing a flouncy skirt and buttoned-up blouse under a thin cardigan with *Stanford* stitched over her left breast. Her skin was touched by the California sun, but she was young enough to suffer the embarrassing red welts of teenage acne. Her hair was dark yet shot through with blond streaks from her time in The Del's saltwater swimming pool. Her eyes were as blue as Bell's own, and bright and inquisitive, and they made her rather indistinct features more attractive.

Hands were shaken all around. Bell asked, "And who is your charming companion?"

"This is my niece, Bitsy Densmore."

The girl went red under her tan. "Uncle Bill, now that I'm going to be a freshman at Stanford, I want people to call me Elizabeth. I told you."

"Right, dear, I forgot. Elizabeth Densmore."

"My wife went to Stanford," Bell told her. "She's going to be here tomorrow, and I bet she has a lot of good advice for a freshman coed, like which are the best dorms and who are the worst teachers."

At first, she seemed disappointed that the handsome stranger was married, but then overcame her swift girlish crush and rallied at the prospect of an insider's knowledge of the perils and pitfalls of Stanford University. "Gee, that would be swell. Thank you, Mr. Bell."

"Excuse me, Senator," Talbot said with flint in his voice, "but I thought this was to be a private meeting."

"It was, Mr. Talbot," Densmore said affably. "But then my party bosses reached out and asked for Mr. Bell here to sit in on the briefing. As I want to keep my seat in Washington, I listen to what my bosses ask. Elizabeth says she might want to work for the government when she graduates, so I thought this would be a good opportunity to see how the real world operates. That

49

isn't a problem, is it?"

Bell could tell that Talbot was troubled by the turn of events but also thoroughly outmaneuvered. He now could see how Densmore had enjoyed such a successful political career. The man could turn a situation to his benefit effortlessly. Talbot wiped his palms on his riding breeches. "No, Senator. No problem at all."

A waiter approached and asked if Bell wanted anything. He declined, while Densmore ordered another glass of Napa chardonnay for himself, and his niece ordered a lemon soda.

"That's good," Densmore practically purred. "So, tell me why I need to listen to you and convince my old West Point roommate, George Washington Goethals, that the canal he currently oversees is in peril."

The former military man checked the time on a big wall clock before launching into what was a well-rehearsed speech. "In a nutshell, the completion date of the Panama Canal is in doubt. While it's generally accepted that it will open next year, likely in late summer, something unforeseen has reared up that is slowly grinding work to a halt."

"Is it more disease, like malaria or yellow fever?" Elizabeth asked, to show she wasn't ignorant of the canal's past troubles.

"No, thank God. Both those scourges have been contained for the most part, thanks to Dr. Gorgas and his medical teams, by eradicating mosquitoes from the isthmus and draining the swamps where the infernal creatures bred. No, I'm talking about a local insurgency called Viboras Rojas."

"Can we step back for a moment," Bell interrupted. "I'm newly hired, and I'm not quite sure how the players all fit. Mr. Talbot, who are you exactly and how is it that you can reach out to a United States Senator and convince him that the current head of the Panama Canal Authority is apparently in dereliction of his duty?"

"Let me answer that," Senator Densmore said. "Court was a sergeant in my regiment during the war in Cuba. We were pinned down on the banks of the San Juan River. A shell exploded close enough to blow me off my feet and scramble my brains for the better part of an hour. When I came to, we were still under heavy fire, but I sat there and watched as Sergeant Talbot rallied our defenses and led our men better than any officer. He saved a lot of us that day, me included. I was the one who put him up for a battlefield commission and fought the rest of the war at his side.

51

"I'd spent four years at West Point learning from the finest military minds our country has ever produced and they all pale in comparison to Court's tactical and strategic thinking."

Talbot looked embarrassed by such high praise and mumbled his thanks.

Densmore continued. "Don't get me wrong, George Goethals is a fine man, a brilliant engineer, and a hell of an administrator, but he doesn't have the combat experience or the kind of situational awareness that Court has. If Court says there's a new danger to the canal that Goethals is overlooking, I plan to give him my full attention and endorsement if warranted."

"Thank you, Senator," Bell said. "Now I understand the full picture. Mr. Talbot, please continue."

"Over the past few months an insurgency has arisen on the isthmus. They call themselves Viboras Rojas. It means 'Red Vipers.' Overly dramatic, but effective. In parts of the world where people live alongside jungles, children are taught to fear even harmless snakes because the poisonous ones are all so deadly. I saw it myself in the Philippines, and it's the same in Panama. The local population was at first fearful of the Viboras, but now they are viewed as true

52

Panamanian patriots."

"What do they want?" Bell asked.

"Nothing short of a Marxist takeover of Panama, and they advocate for Vladimir Lenin's form of totalitarian Bolshevism. Are you familiar with him?"

"Russian revolutionary currently in exile someplace in Central Europe," Bell replied.

"Kraków, to be precise," Talbot said. "He's a dangerous character and one I'd hate to see topple the Tsarist regime, even if that group is a corrupt anachronism these days. Viboras Rojas want all foreign influence out of Panama and a Communist system of government installed where all labor is collectivized and all capital is controlled by the state. They especially renounce the Monroe Doctrine, which gives the United States unprecedented influence over Central American affairs."

Densmore grunted. "That's some irony for you. Panama wasn't a country until just a couple years ago. Without the United States, it would still be a backwater province of the nation of Colombia."

"That is true," Talbot conceded. "But because Panama was cut off from the bulk of Colombia by the Darién Gap's impenetrable jungle, they've always maintained a high level of local patriotism and a fierce sense of independence."

"The what?" Elizabeth asked.

"Bitsy, please," Densmore grumbled.

"No, it's okay," Talbot said. "There is an area south of the Canal Zone called Darién that consists of rivers, mountains, and jungle so thick that even the native Indians don't live there. A few expeditions have been able to cross it on foot, but more have simply vanished."

"Back to the Red Vipers," Bell prompted.

"Ah, yes. They want the Americans out of their country, as well as the thirty thousand or so Caribbean islanders working as laborers all along the canal's forty-mile length. 'Panama for the Panamanians' is their motto."

"What kind of insurgency is it?" Bell asked. "Are they targeting civilians?"

"No. They want to win over the hearts of the people, so they are raiding depots belonging to the Canal Authority for supplies that they turn over to villagers and distribute throughout Panama City on the Pacific Coast and Colón on the Atlantic side. That is why the people no longer fear the Vipers but are starting to see them as heroes.

"Few outside Panama realize that the average Panamanian's life has not improved since the canal was first begun. Labor comes from Barbados and Jamaica, and all the skilled workers hail from the United States. The locals get nothing. They don't even sell to the Americans because the Canal Authority limits its workers to commissaries and dining halls they themselves operate. Panama will soon have a path between the seas, as they say, but it has done little for people's lot. Many feel like they're second class in their own land. Therefore, a group of insurrectionists distributing stolen food and fuel are well regarded by the local poor."

"Is that all they've been doing?" Bell asked. "Playing Robin Hood?"

"No," Talbot admitted. "They have begun sabotaging machinery, the big steam-powered excavators and rail lines mostly. The Authority has instituted twenty-four-hour guards in the Culebra Cut, where most of the steam shovels are deployed, and extra sentries along the railroad." He leaned forward to emphasize his next point. "That said, several workers have been injured as a result of their sabotage, and I feel, at best, that this is emboldening them. There are rumors swirling around Panama City that they have something large planned, something that will galvanize the people and garner international support."

"Do they have outside backing now?" Densmore asked.

"Not yet, but I have heard whispers that trade unionists from Europe have been seen in Panama City, so it might be only a matter of time."

Elizabeth raised a finger. "May I ask something, Uncle Bill?" He nodded, and she continued. "Why don't the people building the canal hire more security?"

Bell suggested, "The Army could get involved. Hell, send in the Marines. It wouldn't be the first time in that part of the world."

"That's what we most want to avoid," Talbot said. "Insurgencies are fragile at the early stages, but also so malleable that a crushing force causes them to disperse and then re-form once the Army has moved on. You don't stop them but actually make them stronger. I saw it myself in the Philippines. The war with Spain ended quickly enough, and we took possession of the islands, but ever since we've been fighting the Moro insurgents. That's fifteen years of fighting, and there is no end in sight. We've lost at least five thousand American soldiers. Who knows how many civilians have died. I've heard upward of a million, when you factor in famine and disease."

Densmore wiped his mouth and tossed the soiled napkin on the empty plate in front of him. He nodded to the waiter to take away his place setting. "We can't have that sort of thing on our doorstep, nor can we afford postponing the completion of the canal. We are too heavily invested."

"Precisely," Talbot said brightly. "I want permission from the Canal Authority to lead a small band of local fighters to hunt down Viboras Rojas. I have the men. I just need the consent. Senator, George Goethals just doesn't understand that a war is looming over the horizon, one he can't win but one I can snuff out now. Please contact him and get him to agree to my —"

From outside the large dining room came a sharp shout, and then the closed wooden doors shuddered as a man was thrown against them. A second later, five heavily armed men burst into the cavernous chamber, and the gunfire they unleashed was a hurricane of lead and flame.

4

Renny Hart's cry was all the warning Bell needed. Even as the gunmen were rushing into the room, he was getting to his feet and sliding the .45 Colt from its holster. In the next fraction of a second, before one of the shooters could trigger off a hail of .303 rounds from the Lewis machine gun slung over his shoulder, Bell recognized he was outgunned. Fighting a pitched battle was out of the question. His priority shifted to protecting the Senator's life.

Chivalry may dictate that he protect Elizabeth Densmore, but he knew she wasn't the intended target. William Densmore was the most important person in the room, and Bell knew he had to save his life.

Bell left his pistol in its holster and squatted so he could ram the heels of his hands against the underside of the table.

The Lewis gun erupted, blasting out a tongue of flame and a stitching string of rounds that shattered glass and splintered wood. The weapon filled the room with such a din that even Elizabeth's shrieks of terror were drowned out.

Using the muscles of his legs, Bell heaved the table up on its side. Plates and cutlery and stemware tumbled to the floor as he flipped it vertically so that it presented a heavy shield between the gunmen and their intended target. The waiter fell flat. Court Talbot was struggling to pull a snub-nosed revolver from inside his bush jacket because young Miss Densmore was clambering all over him. She held on to one of his arms while her other arm wrapped around his head. She continued to scream like a steam whistle.

William Densmore had fallen over backward and had gone so red that Bell was legitimately concerned he'd have a heart attack and save the gunmen, doubtlessly members of Viboras Rojas, the trouble.

The shooters were rushing forward and would quickly outflank their position. The table was more than tall enough for Bell to stand behind. The windows were close, but to reach them they'd have to run a dozen feet in plain sight of the shooters. They'd be cut down long before they'd make it.

The table was resting on its edge and two

of its four legs. The other two legs were at head height. Bell shoved one of the legs as hard as he could, and the entire table rotated a quarter turn. Talbot understood what was happening even if he couldn't disentangle himself from Elizabeth's clutches.

The party hiding behind it realized their protective cover was lurching away from them and shuffled on the floor to keep it between them and the shooters.

Bell pushed at the leg now just in front of him, and the table turned another quarter revolution, prompting the party to move again. The waiter stood. He was a big, strapping kid who looked like he could play football for Cal. As soon as Bell flipped the table another partial turn, he was in position to hit the next leg and keep the table rolling across the dining room. All the while, the gunmen continued to rush at them and fire. Their aim was atrocious, thankfully, but rounds still slapped the table, and shards of decorative woodwork rained down from the ceiling.

Their table crashed into another one already set for the next morning's breakfast. The table twisted enough that the party was momentarily exposed. Bell pulled his Colt free from its holster and fired one-handed while yanking Senator Densmore to his feet.

His aim was far superior to the Panamanians', especially the machine gunner. Every time he yanked the Lewis gun's trigger, the barrel rose and pulled to the left. Bell put him down with two rounds to the torso and spiraled another shooter to the hardwood floor with a fatal wound to the throat. Bell ducked back behind cover.

"You're armed?" Courtney Talbot asked incredulously.

A moment later, another of the terrorists had taken up the Lewis gun and let fly. The bullets pounding against the table sounded like it was taking blows from a hammer, but it held. Not even the powerful .303 round could penetrate the stout wood.

Bell fired blindly around the table and dragged a near-catatonic Densmore through one of the shattered windows. Densmore tripped at the last second and pulled Bell to the sidewalk just as a bullet screamed past his ear. Shards of broken glass crunched beneath their tangled bodies.

Bell had seconds. He got Densmore up.

"Run," he shouted to the others, and provided covering fire so they could make their escape through another window. Elizabeth was sandwiched between Talbot and the waiter as they vanished into the night.

The sun was fully set, but there were plenty of lights around the Hotel Del. The midway of Tent City blazed like a carnival, and the raucous toots of a steam calliope carried on the gentle breeze. The air Bell drew into his lungs was sultry and salt-laced. Next to him, the Senator puffed like an asthmatic in full distress. Near to where they stood was a bellhop station. It was unmanned, but a gleaming brass luggage trolley was tucked against the building's flank. Rather than explain his plan, Bell shoved Senator Densmore in the chest so he fell backward onto the trolley. Bell kept his pistol in his hand and threw his weight behind the cart. They began rolling down the hill and away from the hotel, accelerating with each passing second.

"Have you lost your mind?" Densmore bellowed in a panic. "Leave me be, you fool."

"Kindly shut up, Senator. I'm saving your life." Bell chanced a look behind them as they gathered more and more speed. They were almost past the smokestacks of the hotel's dedicated power plant. The gunmen were just now leaping through the broken window more than a hundred feet back. One of them had taken up the Lewis gun from his dead comrade and swapped out the platter-like magazine.

Like all the best hunters, the shooters looked for movement more than anything else and immediately focused on the glimmering brass cart rolling down the hill toward the marina. The streets were full of revelers — couples and families out to enjoy the distractions offered by Tent City. The stream of fire from the Lewis gun would cut through them like a scythe through winter wheat.

The luggage cart was wobbly and awkward. Bell had to keep running behind it in order to prevent Densmore's bulk from accelerating it past a point of no return and crashing. Still, he managed to pull his right hand back enough to point his Model 1911 into the air and fire off the last two bullets in the gun.

People who'd originally thought the hurtling luggage cart with two men aboard was some sort of lark suddenly burst into a panic at the whip-crack report of gunfire. Women screamed, and the men began herding them away from the marina. The groundswell of fear that spread through the crowd likely saved lives.

But Bell taking his right hand off the trolley for the barest of seconds had disastrous results for him and Densmore. The cart listed just a bit. Despite its swiveling casters, it was going too fast and was too unevenly loaded to remain upright.

It flipped onto its side, Bell jumping free just as it fell to the roadway. He hit the ground with his shoulder and allowed momentum to flip him over several times. Senator Densmore stayed with the cart, as it scraped along the pavement, before he rolled clear, his body absorbing the impact with its sloshing waves of fat.

Bell got to his hands and knees, giving himself a second for his senses to clear. He shook his head from side to side and got to his feet. Densmore was on the ground a few feet away, moaning. Bell limped over to the Senator, reaching for a spare magazine. He ejected his spent clip, letting it fall to the ground, and slapped home a fresh one. He racked the slide to seat a fat brass cartridge in the chamber, all the while walking faster and faster. Densmore levered himself onto his backside just as Bell reached him. Bell didn't slow. He dipped and rammed his left arm under the Senator's armpit and hauled the large man from the ground and propelled him forward.

"Unhand me this instant."

"We're not out of the woods yet, sir," Bell

told him. "These Red Vipers are a persistent lot."

The Queen Anne–style boathouse was packed with people enjoying a private party. None of them had heard the shots or seen the cart crash in the parking lot. The waters around the building were thick with boats. Mostly they were single-masted day sailers or large steam yachts, but there were a number of wooden-hulled speedboats.

The air suddenly exploded as the Lewis gun opened up in a roar of fire and smoke and lead. Bell threw Densmore flat just as they'd stepped onto the pier. The shooter had opened fire from two hundred feet away and let the gun's bolt cycle until it was out of ammo. Like before, this man couldn't control the heavy weapon, and rounds ricocheted off lampposts and the ground and streaked harmlessly into the night air. But some people in the crowd were hit.

Bell fired two hasty return shots before dragging Densmore to his feet once again. He'd noted that the other two gunmen were rushing forward while the machine gunner had been left behind to change ammo drums.

"Stay low," the Van Dorn detective cautioned.

Densmore nodded. The Senator was getting over his initial shock.

The throngs of revelers around them had erupted into a mindless mob of screaming and shouting and manic motion. To escape the deadly fire, people surged in ragtag shoals, like frightened fish first sensing a hunting shark. Many ended up falling into the water, while others were pushed to the ground. Bell saw several citizens risk their lives to save those who'd fallen, while others were reaching for life preservers and boat hooks to help those who'd tumbled into the bay. Most others had started running in whatever direction got them away from the carnage left in the wake of the deadly burst of automatic fire.

Bell's eye passed over the array of boats pulled fast to the long pier and spotted the one he wanted. It was a mahogany-hulled runabout with an open cockpit that had just arrived, driven by a dapperly dressed man who was handing over a mooring line to a uniformed dock attendant. Another employee had already helped his stunning companion out of the boat and onto the dock.

The party had all frozen at the sound of the Lewis gun chewing through its drum of .303 rounds, and Bell seized the opportunity. He pushed the Senator into the boat's rear bench seat, just in front of the engine housing, and jumped in after him. The owner swiveled to protest the unauthorized boarders.

Bell showed him the ugly profile of his Colt automatic. "Need to borrow your boat."

The man went ashen but quickly scrambled out of his prized harbor cruiser. Bell ignored everything but getting away from the charging gunmen. As soon as he was in the driver's seat, he reversed the boat away from the pier, slipping the nose around with barely enough room. As soon as the bow was clear, he rammed the T-shaped throttle lever to the stops. The burbling engine changed beat in an instant and snarled like a predatory cat, a rooster tail of water thrown up by its prop dousing the people on the dock with spray as thick as custard.

Bell couldn't hear the crack of the guns over the roar of the runabout's unmuffled engine, but he saw the gunwale at his elbow partially shredded by bullets. Two holes were punched through the windscreen, leaving a spiderweb of cracks that grew and merged as the sleek craft accelerated into Glorietta Bay. It was only sheer luck that saved him from a bullet to the back of the skull.

Moments later, he estimated their speed at better than twenty knots. Bell felt a measure of relief and finally looked behind him to ask the Senator if he was okay. Densmore was sitting up on the leather bench seat and he looked ruffled and foul-tempered but unhurt. Bell didn't bother asking. He saw another boat rocket away from the marina at that moment, and while it was far too dark to tell, years of experience told him the three Panamanians had reached their own motor launch. Bell had unwittingly led himself and the Senator along the gunmen's own preplanned escape route, and now the pursuit was about to continue across the waters off San Diego.

He swapped out his .45's magazine, reseating the one with two missing rounds into his shoulder holster. His jacket flapped distractingly around his torso, so he shrugged out of it and stuffed it behind the back of his seat. Densmore clambered into the seat to Bell's left.

"You are a madman, I tell you," he shouted over the wind.

"You're welcome, but don't thank me yet. They're chasing us."

Densmore looked incredulous. "Thank you? You nearly got me killed."

"You'd be dead right now if it weren't for

me, Senator. They were there to assassinate you."

He closed his slack-jawed mouth. It was clear that such a thought hadn't occurred to him. "I, ah . . . Umm . . . I assumed they were after Major Talbot because of his activities in Panama."

"Talbot's nothing," Bell said, checking over his shoulder the gunmen's progress. They were definitely gaining. "Killing a Senator in his home state would give Viboras Rojas credibility in Panama and, more importantly, gain the interest of foreign powers who aren't too enthusiastic about the United States controlling something as strategic as a trans-isthmus canal."

"I hadn't considered that," the politician admitted. After a minute or so he asked, "What now?"

They had just swung out of Glorietta Bay and were racing across the calm waters of San Diego Bay proper. The city was a yellow glow against the darkness surrounding them. Overhead, the stars shone bright because the moon was but a mere sliver no bigger than an ironic smile.

Off to their right, the two warships were lit with strings of lights running from bow to stern and up to the tops of their towering radio masts.

Bell looked back. The gunmen were in a wooden cabin cruiser much larger than the runabout he'd commandeered. A spotlight attached to the right of the boat's cockpit sent out a probing finger of illumination that quickly found the thick, boiling wake of Bell's craft and soon followed the luminescent path to the runabout. Bell turned away before the light hit his eyes and ruined his night vision. It was painfully clear that he and the Senator wouldn't be able to outrun them.

"Okay, then," he muttered to himself. "Out-think them."

The Panamanians were forty yards back when the machine gunner triggered off a seconds-long blast that stitched the harbor with dozens of tiny geysers. He tried to zero in on the runabout, but his boat was bobbing across the wake. Bell cut some quick zigzags to throw off the gunner's aim even more.

Densmore had the sense to stay low behind the protection of the big marine engine.

They will get closer, Bell thought grimly, and the shooter will open up at point-blank range and demolish the runabout's cockpit. He doubted his .45 would yield much by way of results against the sturdy-looking

70

cruiser running them down like a hunting dog.

As if thinking it made it happen, the driver of the pursuing boat halved the distance, and the Lewis gun barked again. This time, the runabout's fantail came alive with slashing geysers, and several rounds slammed into the transom, some hitting the motor and ricocheting up through the waxed wood of the engine housing.

Bell immediately eased back on the throttle and cranked the wheel hard to the right, using the palm of his hand to spin it faster, and no sooner had they dropped off plane and changed direction, he straightened the rudder and had the engine bellowing at max power once again.

The cabin cruiser's driver wasted seconds before reacting to Bell's quick maneuver. He finally cranked his wheel to maintain the chase but hadn't slowed. The boat canted too far, allowing water to curl over its gunwale and begin filling the large cockpit. In a panic, the driver chopped the throttles to neutral, and the bow dipped and plowed into a creaming wave of its own making. More water flew up and over the windshield, dousing the men with brine.

Bell drove hard for the two white-hulled warships.

A quick glance over his shoulder confirmed what his ears had already told him. There were wisps of gray smoke rising up through the new bullet holes, and more smoke than normal gushed from the exhaust. That last fusillade had hit home. He could hear the change in the engine's beat. The block wasn't cracked — the motor would have seized instantly — but something vital had been hit, and the boat was burning through its finite supply of lubricating oil.

There was no way to know how much time they had, but, once the engine died, they were as good as dead too.

A powerful searchlight aboard the cruiser *Maryland* suddenly snapped on, and it was as if dawn had broken around the massive battlewagon. They were close enough that Bell had to shield his eyes for a moment. Doubtlessly, the sailors had heard the staccato blasts from the Lewis gun and were under orders to investigate. And just as certain, there were other sailors scrambling to man the ship's complement of machine guns and defensive rapid-fire cannons.

Bell glanced back. The gunmen were in pursuit once again, but they'd taken on a lot of water, and their closing speed wasn't what it had been just moments before.

He spotted what he'd been looking for in the water and allowed himself a thin grin. He looked back again. It was going to be tight. He raced parallel to the huge cruiser, running close enough to see sailors on deck in their summer whites pointing at the hurtling runabout with its belching exhaust.

The engine coughed but didn't lose speed. The pursuing boat was bearing down on Bell's craft and seemed to be accelerating. Bell reached the *Maryland*'s knife-edged prow, but rather than cut around it and put the anchored cruiser between him and his pursuers, he kept straight for another fifty yards before smoothly turning the wheel and crossing the bow.

"You've killed us both," Densmore yelled. "They'll be on us in seconds."

The Panamanian at the helm of the other boat must have thought he'd been given a gift. Rather than follow Bell on his unnecessary dogleg maneuver, he sharpened his angle of attack so he'd fly right past the cruiser's anchor chain and catch the runabout before it could race away.

Even with the ship lit up and the searchlight casting its beam, the string of large corks was almost impossible to see. Bell had only spotted them because he'd seen them deployed earlier that evening and knew approximately where to look. The Panamanians had no idea a protective curtain had been strung around both U.S. warships.

The corks bobbed easily as the big cabin cruiser ran over them, but the inch-thick steel cable supporting the anti-torpedo nets sliced into the wooden hull as easily as a cheese cutter through a wedge of brie. Everything below the waterline, and that included the men's legs at the knees, was severed from the upper part of the motor yacht. Fuel lines and, ultimately, the main fuel tank were sliced cleanly. The gush of volatile gasoline hit the open ignition spark before it could be diluted by the flood of seawater. The explosion was as intense as any Bell had ever seen, and the boat's speed made it look like a meteor from darkest space was skimming like a skipping stone across the water. The flaming wreck finally slowed and then sank, a hissing pile of charred wood and dead men.

Bell killed his launch's dying engine and slumped over the wheel. There was silence for a moment before rescue alarms started sounding on the *Maryland* and her accompanying destroyer, the *Whipple.*

Over the din, Bell said, "Now, Senator Densmore, would be the appropriate time to thank me for saving your life."

5

A pinnace sent from the *Maryland* towed the runabout through a narrow gap in the leeward side of the torpedo netting, and the commandeered boat was tied to the stairs that had been lowered from the battlewagon's main deck. Bell had voluntarily surrendered his pistol to the jumpy ensign in charge of the towboat, confident that he'd get it back once this affair was sorted out.

Densmore wisely held his tongue until they reached the ship and were confronted by the captain and first officer. Other members of the crew crowded around the deck in the shadow of the forward turret, with its enormous eight-inch guns.

The ensign handed Bell's .45 to the first mate butt-first. "This was on 'im. The fat bloke's unarmed, Commander."

Bell held out his hand to the taciturn skipper. The man was unusually tall, with a hatchet face and a prominent Adam's apple.

The captain made no move to shake the proffered hand.

Bell withdrew it with an awkward smile. "My name is Isaac Bell. I'm a detective with the Van Dorn Agency. This gentleman is Senator William Densmore of California, and we just escaped an assassination attempt at the Hotel del Coronado."

The captain's gaze remained unmoved. He finally drew air through his nostrils. "What you did is put my ship and crew in jeopardy and for that I will see you arrested and sent to the Navy brig in Portsmouth, New Hampshire."

"See here," Densmore said. He reached for his wallet. "It's true. I am Senator Densmore, and those men were trying to kill us."

He withdrew his congressional identification card from his billfold and held it up for the captain. The man's eyes widened slightly. He asked, "And what were you doing out in the harbor so late?"

Bell spoke for them. "We were ambushed at the Hotel del Coronado, and once we fled the grounds, I commandeered a boat, not realizing the assassins had one of their own. It was how they planned to escape. They were faster than us, so outrunning them wasn't an option. I recalled seeing your nets being deployed earlier this evening, a detail our pursuers didn't know about, so I lured them into hitting them."

"That's how it happened, Captain," Densmore said.

"And for the record," Bell added, "I set my trap so their boat would tear itself apart in front of your ship, rather than straight into your side, to minimize any risk to vessel or crew."

A sailor approached the party but stopped a respectful distance away. The first officer turned, and the two spoke for a second, while the captain continued to look from Bell to Densmore and back again. Bell thought he'd make a formidable poker opponent.

"What is it?" the captain asked when the mate returned to his side.

"Wireless message from the San Diego police requesting our assistance. There was an attack at the Hotel Del tonight, and Senator Densmore is missing. The explosion was noted from shore, and they wanted to know if we have any information."

"Very well," the captain said. He looked back at Isaac. "It appears, Mr. Bell, the civilian authorities have already been alerted to the disturbing events of this evening, and I'm inclined to let them have jurisdiction in the matter. Ensign Armstrong?"

The seaman stepped forward from the crowd of sailors. "Captain?"

"Tow Mr. Bell's boat back to The Del, and see that he and the Senator are presented to the lead investigator at the hotel."

"Yes, Captain."

Bell said, "Sir, if I may be so bold, there are going to be a number of injured people back at the hotel and pier. I'm not sure how long it will take civilian medical services to arrive. I believe it would be prudent to send your ship's surgeon and as many corpsmen as you can spare."

The captain considered Bell's suggestion for only a moment. "XO, round up Sawbones and his staff."

"Aye, sir."

"My weapon, Captain?" Bell asked before the first officer disappeared with it.

"XO?"

The man handed it to the captain, who handed it to the young ensign.

"It will be given to the lead investigator when Ensign Armstrong hands you over."

Bell considered the offer. "Fair enough."

Forty minutes later, the pinnace, with the shot-up runabout in tow, rounded the headland into Glorietta Bay. The marina building was bathed in light from a half dozen cars pulled around it so their headlamps could add much-needed illumination. As the distance narrowed, police could be heard coordinating the crowds to allow a pair of Cunningham motorized ambulances sent by special ferry to approach. They would take to the hospital those most injured in the attack and subsequent stampede.

To Bell's immeasurable relief, he'd later learn that none of the injuries were more severe than broken bones or bumps and bruises, and only six people had non-life-threatening bullet wounds.

As the pinnace drew closer still, a shrill shout rose from a man in the crowd on the pier. "That's my boat."

Bell recognized the foppish owner, in his straw boater and striped knickerbocker pants, as he jumped up and down in place and pointed at the craft following meekly in the Navy boat's wake. The elegant woman with him seemed bored.

The man then spotted Bell, leaning on the pinnace's gunwale, and he yelled again. "And there's the thief. Police. I need the police. That's the man who stole my boat. The blond man. And the fat one too. He's the accomplice."

By the time the pinnace was secured to the dock, two police officers from San

Diego's legendary motorcycle squad were waiting. The owner's outrage reached a fevered pitch when he saw the sorry state of his beloved motor launch and demanded that Bell be hanged for his crime. Ensign Armstrong interceded before Bell and Senator Densmore were clapped in irons. He explained to the cops that he was delivering the two men to the lead investigator and asked who that might be.

While the Navy doctor and his four assistants waded into the crowd in search of patients, and the excitable boatman ranted in increasingly shrill tones, Armstrong and another sailor led Bell and Densmore through the shell-shocked crowds and up the gentle hill they had rocketed down on a luggage cart a short time earlier.

The lobby was full of guests, milling about, most still dressed for the parties that had been interrupted. Waiters ghosted through the throng with trays of whiskey for the gentlemen and lemonade for the ladies, though more than a couple availed themselves of the stronger drink. Uniformed police and detectives in suits were taking statements from anyone who might have been a witness. Bell grabbed two cut-crystal tumblers off a silver tray and handed one to the Senator. The man grunted his thanks.

Bell looked anxiously for Renny Hart but didn't spot the young Van Dorn detective. He guessed where most of the police action was taking place and pointed to the dining room doors. "The chief will be in there," Bell told Armstrong. "That's where the attack started."

The young sailor was overwhelmed by The Del's opulence, but more so by the amount of décolletage on display. "Oh, right."

The vaulted space showed the sheer violence of the attack. Two of the chandeliers had been shattered. Their frosted-glass globes now lay in powdery splinters on the floor like newly fallen snow. Angry bullet holes had chewed up much of the intricate woodwork, leaving raw white scars in the walls and ceiling where chunks of once ornate wood had been savaged by the Lewis gun. On the floor were two shroud-covered corpses. From one, blood had leached through the white cloth and appeared black in the dim lighting.

"Uncle Bill." Elizabeth Densmore was seated at a table with several other men, including Major Talbot and the young waiter. She launched herself from her chair and shouted his name again.

He hugged her tightly. "Are you all right, my dear?"

"Yes, I'm fine. Major Talbot and Beau led me to safety. I've already told Mom and Dad I'm okay, and everything. The police are just finishing taking our statements, and then Beau and I are going to take a walk along the beach. My nerves are frazzled."

"Beau, huh?" Densmore said questioningly. He'd been through this with his own now married daughters.

San Diego's current police chief was Jefferson "Keno" Wilson. He was tall, six foot three, and lankily built. His eyes were a lighter shade of blue than his uniform, and he sported a walrus mustache above his dimpled chin. He had jug ears and long, tapered fingers, and was known as a fair lawman for suspect and victim alike.

Bell went straight to him. At this point, he didn't offer to shake hands. "My name is Isaac Bell. I'm a detective with the Van Dorn Agency. I'd like to know the status of my man Renny Hart?"

Wilson's eyes narrowed. Bell wasn't sure if he was annoyed by the question or approved of him checking the status of a fellow agent before everything else. "Hotel doc checked on him. He has a concussion, but his skull didn't crack." Wilson's voice retained a trace of a Texas accent, from the time he lived there as a boy. "He was out cold for just a couple minutes, tops. Staff took him upstairs to a room. Probably asleep now."

Bell was physically relieved. "I thought the worst when I heard him get slammed into the doors." He held out a hand, and Wilson shook it. "And that's Senator Densmore. This is Ensign Armstrong from the USS *Maryland.*"

The young naval officer offered his hand. "Ensign Frank Armstrong. Like Mr. Bell said, from the cruiser *Maryland,* sir. We rescued these men after the boat chasing them struck our anti-torpedo netting and exploded. My captain asked that they be delivered to you and that I give you the sidearm Mr. Bell carried at the time of his rescue."

"That's fine, son," Wilson drawled. "Always best to tell a lawman that you've got a gun before you show him."

Armstrong handed it to the chief of police, who inspected it closely. "Can't say I much like the look of these," he remarked and cocked a hip. Holstered there was a beautiful Colt .45 revolver with inlaid ivory grips. He gave the automatic back to Bell. Bell rammed it into his holster and resettled his rumpled and ripped suit coat.

The young seaman said, "I'm under orders

83

to help the medical staff we brought ashore."

"Okay, then," Wilson drawled. "Have at it, son."

Armstrong looked like he wanted to salute but wasn't sure if that was appropriate. He finally touched two fingers to his forehead and then strode from the dining hall, his subordinate in tow.

Bell looked over to Talbot and Beau, the waiter. "You guys all right? Sorry for abandoning you like that, but we were so outgunned that I thought my only chance of saving the Senator was through the window."

Talbot had an unreadable look on his face. "Who are you really? And why are you carrying one of the new .45 automatics? You're not some Republican Party hack looking in on a strategy meeting."

"I never said I was. That was your assumption. I'm the senior investigator for the Van Dorn Agency. I was hired by the Republican Party to listen to your assessment of the situation in Panama for them."

"What for?" Talbot asked bluntly.

"I'm not at liberty to say. In fact, the only reason you know who hired me is that the Senator already disclosed it when we first sat down. Is there a problem, Major Talbot?"

The man gave a little shudder as if to

shrug off some emotion or feeling. "I'm sorry. Everything happened so fast, and I knew my .38 didn't stand a chance against those guys, and all of a sudden you let loose with that hand cannon of yours. I don't know, it shook me, is all." Talbot held out a hand to shake. "I'm not used to owing people my life, Mr. Bell, but I owe you mine. Thank you. Thank you on behalf of all of us."

"Hear! Hear!" Densmore said.

Beau chimed in his thanks as well. "When you took off down the hill, I led the Major and Elizabeth around the corner to a service entrance that goes down into the cellar."

"Good thinking."

"So how about it, Bell?" Chief Wilson invited. "I've heard their version of what happened. What did you see and hear?"

Bell laid it all out, surprising Talbot that he'd posted a guard in secret outside the dining room. It was Renny Hart's warning that gave him the time to be ready to defend the group even as the shooters were bursting into the room.

"That alone saved all our lives," Bell concluded. "After we leapt through the window, I loaded the Senator onto a luggage cart, and we more or less rolled to the marina. We swiped some dandy's motorboat, and I thought we were home free. Turns out there was a sixth member of the hit squad — their getaway driver. He was waiting for his companions in a boat that was larger and faster than ours, so they continued to press their attack across San Diego Bay."

"How'd you escape?" Wilson asked. "There was mention of an explosion."

"Yes. I recalled on my ferry ride here that the Navy was deploying heavy-gauge netting around their ships. They're called anti-torpedo nets. From the surface, all you really see are hundreds of bobbing corks, but strung between them is a thick steel cable from which nets dangle into the depths. While they were chasing us, I ran for the big cruiser and took a long dogleg around her bow to avoid the netting. The other driver didn't know it was there and thought he could cut me off and finish the job. Their boat hit the wire at full speed and came apart like it had been dynamited."

"Well done," Talbot said admiringly.

Bell gave a self-deprecating shrug. "There's no heroism in saving your own skin." He turned his attention back to Keno Wilson. "May I inquire about your investigation?"

"Nothing to tell so far. Five Hispanic men

ran down the main stairs and, upon encountering your fella, Hart, they knocked him senseless with the butt of the machine gun, which Major Talbot identified as a Hotchkiss, and proceeded —"

"It was a Lewis," Bell corrected.

"You're right," Talbot said, shaking his head. "I got that wrong. Sorry, Chief Wilson. Bell's right, it was a Lewis gun, not a Hotchkiss. I've been a civilian too long to keep up with modern firearms."

"Either way, it's a poor choice of weapons for an assassination," Bell said and waved a hand toward all the mangled joinery. "The gunman couldn't control it."

"If I had to guess," Wilson said, "I'd think their plan was to burst in here and take you entirely by surprise. The machine gun would keep you pinned down while the other four with revolvers approached and killed the Senator and most likely the rest of you too. Turns out two of the gunmen died in this room. Major Talbot said that was your handiwork."

Bell nodded. "It was."

"Justified, by the way," Wilson told him. "I won't be bringing up charges."

"Thank you."

"That don't mean I want you leaving town anytime soon. There are a lot of questions that need answering."

Bell said, "I believe I can answer one of those questions tonight."

"And that is?"

"How did they sneak a four-foot-long machine gun into a busy hotel without anyone noticing?"

"How?"

"Two of them brought it in in pieces and assembled it in their room upstairs."

"What two men?"

Bell didn't answer Talbot's question. "We need a manager to unlock their room."

"Whose?"

"You'll see." Talbot stuck close to Bell and the police chief while Densmore was content to sit and let a waiter bring him another whiskey. Elizabeth and Beau had vanished on their walk. On the way out of the dining room, Bell paused to pull the shroud back from one of the dead men's faces. Even in the chaos of the brutal assault he'd thought he'd recognized one of the shooters. Now he was certain.

On Wilson's authority, the night duty manager led them up to the second floor just down the hallway from Bell's room.

"Do you know the names of these guests?" Bell asked the manager when they were clustered outside the door.

"Brothers, Mr. Bell. From Mexico. They were here to work on some mosaics for the buildings of the Panama–California Exposition opening next year. I don't recall their names."

"Doesn't matter. They're aliases," Bell said and rapped his knuckles on the door hard enough to rattle it in its frame. He shot a look to Wilson. "One of the supposed brothers is dead on the floor in the dining hall."

"The body you looked at?"

Bell nodded. "I saw him come out of the lavatory earlier today and enter this room. The other brother is dead next to him or on the bottom of the bay."

When no one answered the door, Bell gestured for the manager to open it. Bell pressed the button to turn on the lights. The room was a mess. The bedding had been removed from the two queen-size mattresses and left on the floor. It appeared that's where the two men preferred to sleep. There were dozens of dirty dishes stacked on the credenza and on the nightstands. But the windows had been left open, so at least the air smelled fresh.

In one corner were wooden packing crates, ostensibly for their mosaic tile.

"It nagged at me earlier," Bell said. "I used

one of the lavatories when I arrived. The man in there before me left it a sodden mess. I remember thinking at the time that it looked like he'd never used a public washroom. Turns out I was right. He hadn't, nor did he know enough to let room service take away the dirty dishes."

"Rural boys not used to the city," Wilson said.

"They weren't Mexican artisans," Bell concluded, "but Panamanian peasants turned anarchists sent here on a mission. This is likely the first time either man had ever stayed in a hotel."

Bell crossed over to the wooden crates. Inside was nothing but packing hay. There were no tile cutters or mortaring tools of any kind. One of the crates, he noted, was long enough to accommodate the Lewis gun's barrel. Bell got down on the floor to peer under the beds. He felt around their legs and came out with a wad of cotton. It was stained and smelled of cosmoline, the waxy corrosion inhibitor used to protect their weapons in tropical environments.

He gave it to Wilson. "Not a smoking gun, exactly, but close enough."

"So, these two smuggled in the weapons," Court Talbot stated.

"Right. The other four came to Coronado

on their boat and linked up in here just before the assault." Bell paused. He'd thought of something. "Chief, you'll want to check with law enforcement from surrounding towns for a stolen boat. About thirty feet long, wooden rather than steel, with a big cockpit, and she was fast. They didn't come from Panama in it, so they had to have stolen it. Could have swiped it in northern Mexico, I suppose. Anyway, once the men were together, and their getaway driver was in position at the marina, the guns were passed out and then all five raced downstairs for the ambush."

"That's good to know the details and all," Court Talbot pointed out, "but does it really help? They're dead now, and, like you said, whatever names they used to check in to the hotel are obviously aliases."

"It raises a troubling point," Bell told him, and made sure Chief Wilson was paying attention. "I had my agent make discreet inquiries about hotel guests earlier today. He spoke with all of them who made their reservations after the Senator's meeting time and place became public knowledge."

"Meaning?"

"This room was reserved before anyone could possibly know you were to brief Senator Densmore. Viboras Rojas knew about our conference in advance."

"Wait. What?"

"How is that possible?" Wilson asked.

"I do not know," Bell answered. "But I am damned sure going to find out."

6

Chief Wilson allowed Bell to help him perform a thorough search of the room while the night manager went down to the front desk to retrieve the reservation and registration information. Court Talbot also returned downstairs to check on the Senator, only to find he'd retired for the night.

As Bell suspected, they found nothing of interest — no papers of any kind or any other way of identifying the assailants. The reservation had been made from a telegraph office in Acapulco, most likely when the gunmen were heading north on a tramp steamer. Another dead end.

"Maybe we'll get lucky and there will be some clues on the bodies," Wilson said with little enthusiasm.

Bell gave him an appraising look. "Are you normally lucky?"

The chief gave a mirthless chuckle. They were professional lawmen who understood

93

that smart criminals rarely got caught, and even if these were poorly trained guerrillas — judging by their poor accuracy — whoever backed them knew what they were doing. "Nope. What about where the other four have been sleeping? Boardinghouse, you think?"

"Possible, but if I were them, I'd stay on the boat out at sea. Come morning, I bet we find a small dinghy hidden in the dunes that the three men not staying here rowed ashore while their driver took his position at the marina."

"If they did that, why bother getting a room? Why not launch the attack from the beach?"

"Come on, Chief, you've been here enough times. The public spaces are packed with folks. They'd be spotted immediately. Sneaking down from the deserted guest hallways maintains the element of surprise."

"Not if they just used pistols and didn't bother with a monstrous machine gun. Talk about your overkill, right?"

"That bothers me a bit, but not if you look at it from a propaganda perspective. The notoriety Viboras Rojas would gain by such an audacious assassination more than offsets the cost of a room."

Wilson agreed. "I can see the newspapermen milking that story for all it's worth."

"Headlines for weeks, and not just here but in Panama too. Real shot in the arm for the cause," Bell said. "If you don't mind, I want to check the dining hall again."

"Something bothering you?"

"Well, I don't like being shot at, for one thing, but I want to look at the attack from the gunmen's perspective. It's a technique that helps me see how a crime is committed."

"Suit yourself. I've got to check in on my guys downstairs to see if they learned anything from the guests and staff." Wilson tipped his blue cap and strode from the room.

Bell gave him a moment to get down the stairs and then followed. He imagined one of the gunmen, armed with a pistol, would act as a scout, making sure no one would see the machine gunner walking the halls with the four-foot weapon cradled in his arms. Their room was just a short hallway and two corners from the main stairs. Call it fifteen seconds, at a fast walk.

Once they established their path was clear, the machine gunner would rush down the hall with the others, collecting the scout as they came, with the final man likely waiting at the bottom of the staircase. He'd have to ask Renny Hart about seeing a Panamanian loitering just before the assault.

Bell rushed down the steps, imagining himself cradling the thirty-pound Lewis gun. At the foot of the stairs, they would have seen Renny Hart loitering but would have thought nothing of it until the Van Dorn man reacted. Renny had to have rushed over and managed to shout a warning before he was struck with the butt of the machine gun. The force of the blow shoved him hard against the door, and an instant later they were inside the dining room.

The doors were already open for Bell's reconstructive walkthrough, so he entered the vaulted chamber. The bodies of the two Panamanians had been taken away, though the pools of blood remained as gruesome reminders. The floor was still littered with dozens upon dozens of empty shell casings. The men with pistols had been carrying .38 revolvers, so all the brass belonged to the Lewis. Bell studied the far end of the room where he'd been sitting with Densmore and the others. The range was tricky for a pistol shot unless the shooter was an expert marksman and stood perfectly still. This gave credence to Chief Wilson's theory that the machine gun fire was meant to keep them pinned so the other shooters could get close.

The Lewis gun had left its mark on the far wall. The woodwork was in tatters, and all the windows had been shot out. The bullet holes were all about five feet up the wall, a detail Bell presumed had to do with the weapon's uncontrollable barrel rise when firing on full auto.

The table that had protected the party was another matter. It still leaned drunkenly against the other table they'd smashed into. It had been struck in a cluster in the center of its top a dozen times or more and yet not a single round had penetrated the inch-and-a-half-thick aged oak. Without it, Bell suspected he and Densmore and the others would be on their way to the morgue and not the two shooters he'd taken down.

By the time he was finished scouring the room for additional clues, and possible inspiration, it was almost two in the morning. The lobby was quiet. A different manager was on duty. Bell asked the man if he could reserve a long-distance line for a nine o'clock call to National Studios in Hollywood.

Trying to escape Thomas Edison's draconian rules for using his motion picture cameras and projectors, the major East

Coast studios were slowly migrating to the sleepy town just outside L.A., taking advantage of cheap land, for sets and sound stages, and the almost three hundred sunny days per year, as well as the nearby interesting geographic locations. National Studios was in the process of courting Bell's wife, Marion, to be one of their contract directors.

Movies were mostly being made using classically trained stage actors who were used to overemoting in order for their performance to reach the back of the theater. As a result, their portrayals on-screen tended to be rather exaggerated and campy. Marion instructed her actors to downplay their craft for the more intimate medium of film. As a result, she could draw raw emotion out of an actor better than anyone working in pictures. It made her movies feel more genuine. Despite her gender, she was one of the most bankable directors in the industry.

Bell couldn't just cable her with his change of plan. This deserved a phone call.

He reserved a second long-distance line for nine-thirty. He needed to brief Joseph Van Dorn.

Bell let himself sleep for a couple hours, rousing just before dawn. He'd long ago trained himself to operate on very little sleep for up to three days — the average time needed for a typical stakeout. He dressed and used the washroom before heading downstairs.

The main dining room was locked, as he suspected it would be until everything returned to normal. He went down one more flight to the beach level. The waiters for the casual eatery were just getting ready for early rising guests. He convinced a waitress to combine three bone china cups of coffee in a beer stein and he headed out onto the beach.

The breeze off the Pacific was a cleansing breath that dispelled the fuzziness from only three hours' sleep. With the sun just climbing up from the east, the vast ocean remained dark, like spilled ink, except where the waves curled in on the sugary sand. Seabirds clustered at the tideline, picking at something dead that had washed ashore. A collegian in a USC shirt was just coming back from a barefoot run down the beach.

"Excuse me," Bell said as the student athlete slowed. His face was flushed, and he was breathing hard.

"Yes, sir. May I help you?"

"How far did you just run?"

"Probably three miles down and three back."

"Didn't notice any abandoned boats, did you?"

"Boats? No, sir. Nothing but beach and seaweed."

"Thanks."

Bell started walking in the opposite direction, grateful the young runner had saved him from having to search the beach in both directions. He was fairly sure the attackers wouldn't have risked sneaking past Tent City to the south of the hotel, but having the student confirm it gave him some peace of mind.

Sipping his coffee, Bell set out to the north. It was going to be a beautiful day, and he found himself enjoying the walk. Living in New York for the past few years, he'd forgotten what it was like to be so close to nature. The only sounds were the sea, the wind, and the occasional cry of a gull. He couldn't even hear any ships' horns from inside San Diego Harbor. He wasn't sure how he'd feel if Marion wanted to relocate. He loved the hustle and bustle of life on the East Coast, but it would be a nice change to come west again and take part in California's transformation once the trans-isthmus canal made it more accessible.

He'd covered about a mile when he came upon a thicket of seagrass about thirty feet above the tideline. The beach sand was smooth, but not in a naturally windblown way. It looked like it had been disturbed and then kicked back into place and then raked over with a broom or leafy branch from a tree farther inland.

Bell turned to investigate the tufts of head-high grass, and, just as he'd predicted, there was a small rowboat hidden in the densest part of the little patch. The craft was wooden and poorly maintained. The duckboards were slimy with mold, and rot was eroding the gunwales. The brass oarlocks were pitted from years of exposure to salt air. He checked it thoroughly. There was no name on the transom or any manufacturer's tag. It was just an anonymous boat, but it was doubtlessly the one the attackers had used to come ashore from their stolen cabin cruiser.

He left it alone and began to walk back to the Hotel Del, his now depleted stein swinging from a finger.

7

A bellhop found Isaac Bell eating a breakfast of soft scrambled eggs and smoked salmon with toast at the poolside restaurant. Though it was still early, eager sunbathers were already staking out their spots for when the day warmed. They sat bundled in robes and towels for now, while a handful of children, who seemed to be immune to cold, were already at play in the saltwater pool.

"Begging your pardon, Mr. Bell. Chief Wilson just got word to the hotel that he would like you to meet him at the ferry dock at the base of Orange Avenue."

"When?"

"Now, sir. I took the liberty of arranging a motor taxi."

Without another word, Bell forked the remaining lox and eggs onto a piece of toast and folded it over like a tortilla and wolfed down the first half in a single bite. He settled his hat atop his head and allowed the teen to lead him upstairs and out the main lobby entrance. A black Model T was waiting. The driver was at the wheel, but the door to the rear bench seat was open.

As soon as Bell settled in, the car lurched from the curb and out onto Orange. He shouted to the bellhop, "Cancel my long-distance reservations."

As they sped down the palm-lined street the driver said, "There's no need to pay, sir. My service will be tacked onto your room charge, as a convenience to hotel guests."

"Thanks," Bell said, thinking this would all go onto the bill the Van Dorn accountants would be preparing for the Republican Party. He finished his folded breakfast sandwich.

The ride took only a handful of minutes. The ferry wasn't at the dock, but there was a tubby fishing boat with a small pilothouse jutting forward over her flaring bows. Long trolling poles angled off her stern. Bell recognized Keno Wilson, and another of the cops from the night before, standing just behind the bridge. Exhaust burbled from a vent in the fishing boat's transom.

"I found the rowboat about a mile north of the hotel," Bell said as he approached.

"Well done. Bill, go check it out." The

other cop stepped up off the boat just as Bell jumped down into it.

"It's hidden in a thick patch of seagrass," Bell called after the cop. "Take my taxi, courtesy of the national Republican Party, since they are ultimately picking up the tab."

A deckhand released a line securing the fishing boat to the dock, and the captain at the helm fed in more power. The boat gathered speed, but ponderously, like a dowager trying to swim. They started across the bay toward the white-hulled battlewagons. Bell turned his attention to San Diego's top lawman. "Good morning, Chief. What's the fuss about?"

"Three of the four men killed last night floated up from the sunken boat and were recovered by Navy personnel from the *Maryland.* They're getting ready to send a hard-hat diver down to see if he can find the fourth. I thought you might want to get a look-see at the bodies before they go to the coroner."

"I appreciate that."

"You put a fast end to the worst shooting this city's ever seen," Wilson said, his eyes slit against the wind fanning across the boat's aft deck. "Least I can do."

Wilson didn't seem to have anything more to say, and Bell was just as happy to keep his own counsel. The sun was climbing higher into the sky and throwing lightning-like flashes off the wavelets rippling the harbor. A big gull momentarily hovered over the boat, as it motored toward the heavy cruiser, but soon realized there was no prospect of fish and wheeled away.

They approached the *Maryland* under the vigilant eyes of a half dozen armed men standing watch. After the previous night's brush with anarchists, the captain was taking no chances.

The cruiser's boarding ladder was down, and a sailor in white was waiting on the landing to help Bell and Wilson jump across. They climbed up to the main deck. The ship's second officer was there to greet them. Bell couldn't recall his name. He led them around the forward gun turret, under the enormous barrels of its eight-inch cannons, and back down the cruiser's port side. Just aft of amidships, a crane had been unlimbered and its boom arm maneuvered over the ship's rail. Nearby, a compressor powered by steam from an auxiliary line off the ship's main boilers chugged rhythmically and forced air down a vulcanized rubber hose to the diver standing on a cradle dangling from the end of the crane. Sailors were on hand to feed his umbilical smoothly into the water and to monitor the electric telephone system.

The diver himself was clad in an enclosed canvas suit topped with an enormous brass helmet, with three round viewing ports, and lead-soled boots on his feet. A lead belt was buckled around his waist. Because of the air pressure inside the suit when he was submerged, all the extra weight was needed to anchor him to the seafloor. He had a knife and pry bar attached to an equipment belt.

The dive master threw the diver a salute, which he returned as best he could in the bulky outfit, and the crane started paying out more line. The cradle descended, and the diver was soon chest-deep in the warm waters of San Diego Bay. Then he was gone altogether, leaving only the steady rise of bubbles to give his location.

Bell noticed a Navy rowboat made of gray metal was a safe distance away from the work zone. It was crewed by five sailors, and he understood its grim task.

"Where are the other bodies?" Bell asked the executive officer.

"Come."

He and Wilson were led aft, where the three bodies had been laid out on stretchers under heavy canvas tarps, the edges weighted down with paint cans.

106

"Do you mind if I . . . ?" Bell asked the chief, who had jurisdiction, and knelt next to the first one.

"Help yourself." Wilson had no desire to see the bodies, so he gazed out over the harbor.

Bell lifted the tarp. The man hadn't been in the water long enough for any marine decay, but the explosion and fire had wreaked havoc on his flesh. Not the worst Bell had ever seen, but disturbing nevertheless. His features were Hispanic, with strong native ancestry, and Bell recognized him as the one who'd picked up the Lewis gun after he'd shot its original owner. Like the anarchists he'd inspected in the dining room, he had a slight build but was wiry with muscle, and he had distinct calluses on his hands. The corpse had no legs below the knees.

There was nothing in his sodden pockets and no labels in any of his clothes, but they were rough-spun, so likely bought in Panama.

The other two men were in similar condition and just as uninformative.

Bell joined Wilson at the rail. "I can positively identify these three as part of the squad that attacked us at The Del. I will sign an affidavit, if you'd like."

"Probably should, just to keep everything official. Learn anything about 'em?"

Before Bell could answer there was a commotion farther down the ship. The crew were bringing up the diver. Nearing the surface, his canvas suit and bright helmet began to appear as a light splotch under the murky green water. With no warning, another corpse suddenly surfaced close by, propelled upward by the gases trapped in the stomach.

The body bobbed obscenely.

The diver's brass helmet broached, and moments later he was hoisted clear of the harbor on the cradle, water sluicing off his vulcanized suit and spattering the water beneath his weighted feet.

When the cradle rose over the ship's rail, the derrick swung back over the deck, and he was lowered to where the sailors already had a bucket waiting so he could sit. Standing upright in the heavy suit was a physically draining exercise. Down on the water, the men in the steel boat had rowed over to where the legless body was floating facedown. Rather than haul it over the gunwale, a fifth sailor, not manning an oar, reached over the bow and took a firm grip of the back of the corpse's shirt collar.

It took just minutes for them to row

around the fantail and up to the boarding ladder. Bell and Wilson circled the deck to keep watch. The trawler that had taken them out to the *Maryland* moved in, and the body was lifted from the sea onto her deck. A sailor rushed down from the deck with a tarp, which was quickly draped over the prone figure.

A detail of sailors was assembled to transfer stretchers with the other dead men on them to the fishing boat, so they could be taken ashore. Chief Wilson had mentioned earlier he had horse-drawn hearses standing by on the dock. After the coroner's investigation, they'd be buried in the city's version of a potter's field.

Bell and Wilson thanked the XO and disembarked onto the fishing boat.

Bell checked the hands of the last man recovered from the harbor, the presumed getaway driver, since he didn't recognize his face. Minutes later, the last of the corpses were aboard, and the trawler pulled away from the warship with its grisly cargo laid out on deck. There was barely room for Wilson and Bell to stand.

"What's next for you, Bell?" Wilson asked as they chugged across the bay.

"Panama, I suppose."

The chief was taken aback. "Why? This

isn't your fight."

"You asked me what I deduced from the bodies just before the fourth floated free, remember? Well, here's my answer. Except for the boat driver, who didn't participate in the attack, they all show calluses on the inside of the middle finger of their right hand."

The veteran policeman didn't need long to know what that meant. "Shooter's callus. From the trigger guard."

"Exactly. A very particular callus to develop. These men did heavy training for this mission, enough so they should have been expert marksmen. However, it appeared that they didn't know how to use their weapons effectively, especially the Lewis gun."

"Doesn't figure."

"Right," Bell agreed. "But what if they intentionally fired like a bunch of yokels, for some reason? Recall that my man outside the dining room threw off their timing."

"Okay." Wilson paused, thinking, trying to see how any of this fit together. He finally shook his head. "I don't get it."

"That's just it," Bell agreed. "It doesn't add up. If they were good marksmen, what was the purpose of intentionally missing the Senator during an assassination attempt?"

"Maybe it wasn't an assassination attempt."

"Maybe it wasn't," Bell agreed. "I'm missing a piece to this puzzle and it has to be in Panama."

"Why?"

Bell chuckled a little darkly and looked at the bodies at their feet. "Because I've killed all the leads here in California."

8

Bell was unable to reach Marion when he returned to the hotel but managed to talk with Joseph Van Dorn and brief him on the situation. The veteran detective assured Bell that following the trail down to Panama was the right call, though he wasn't certain the clients would want to continue paying for his services.

"It doesn't matter," Bell fired back. "There are too many inconsistencies for me to ignore. Plus, there's the personal component for me."

"I know, I know. Our contract with the Republicans expires shortly, but we must still protect the man. The agency has a history with him, after all."

"I'll work on my own time, if necessary. We both know this attack won't dissuade him from going to Panama, right?"

"You know him better than I do. He's a close friend of your father, is he not?"

"Very close. He taught me how to shoot a rifle on his ranch in Dakota."

"He's not one to be intimidated, so we'll have to assume his travel plans will remain intact."

"Then tell the Republicans I'll act as an advance man for a security detail."

"Of course," Van Dorn said. "One would hope they'll want to ensure the safety of their candidate."

"I'm heading to Panama on the first boat out of San Diego. The hotel's booking agent is securing passage for me right now."

"Not to pry, old friend, but aren't you supposed to be enjoying a vacation with Marion?"

"Yeaaah," Bell said, drawing out the word and indicating his discomfort. "She's arriving within the hour. With any luck, I'll have a day or two with her before I leave."

"Good luck there."

"Thanks." Bell hung up the phone and stepped out of the glass and brass booth. Across the lobby, The Del's booking agent saw him and waved him over. He was on the phone with another guest and kept a finger in the air to indicate it would be a short conversation.

"Yes, Mrs. Blandon, you're all set. You have a starboard cabin for your journey, and your reservation at the Hotel Sorrento in Seattle has been confirmed." A pause. "Yes, ma'am, it has been our pleasure having you with us. Enjoy your last day here, and *bon voyage* tomorrow."

He settled the receiver on its cradle. Bell felt someone get in line behind him but didn't turn around.

The agent beamed. "Mr. Bell, you are a most fortunate man. There's a cabin available on a steamship heading for New York. It normally doesn't call in on Panama as a regular port of call, but there are more than fifty workers needing passage to the canal so the ship's owners agreed to a detour."

"That's terrific. When does the ship arrive?"

"She's more than a day out of San Francisco, so she'll put in late this afternoon and be gone as soon as her coal bunkers are topped off."

Bell's stomach sank. Marion had always been the most understanding and accommodating woman in the world but abandoning her without warning on the first day of a vacation was a line he shouldn't cross. No one had that much forbearance.

"Is there any chance there's another ship leaving tomorrow or the next day?"

The agent seemed genuinely hurt that his

customer wasn't overjoyed at getting exactly what he wanted. "Is there a problem? You said you needed to be in Panama as soon as possible."

"It's just that my wife . . ."

A sultry voice behind him finished, ". . . was promised a week's holiday at The Del and hopefully she'll forgive me if I stick around for at least a day."

Bell whirled around and was met by an amused and mocking smile. Marion was wearing all white, the only splash of color being a green band around her large hat that perfectly matched the emerald hue of her eyes. Her blond hair cascaded around her shoulders. She was as slender as a teen, willow-waisted but curvy elsewhere, and she always was the most beautiful woman in any room she entered. When asked what she did for a living and she said she was in pictures, everyone assumed she was a starlet and not a director.

She cocked her head, her mouth shifting into a little moue at Bell's stunned surprise.

"Or am I wrong?" She batted her eyes playfully.

"Marion," Bell finally said and took her hands. He leaned in to give her a kiss and she turned her head at the last second so all he got was her silk-soft cheek. "You're here earlier than I expected."

"The train from L.A. caught a tailwind or something. Surprise."

"So —" Bell cut himself off. He saw it then, shining in the back of her eyes. She wasn't mad at all, just having fun at making him think she was. "You minx."

She started to laugh and wrapped her arms around his neck and raised herself up on tiptoes to plant a kiss on his lips that made the travel agent blush.

"I read a newspaper on the ferry on the way over from the mainland. Lead story was about how Panamanian anarchists tried to murder a Senator here at The Del and how an unnamed individual — you, I can only surmise — saved said Senator and dispatched two of the said Panamanian anarchists here and four more following a boat chase across San Diego Bay. The reporter was quite breathless about the whole thing. Me? That's about a five on the Isaac Bell scale of chaos and mayhem."

Marion looked past Bell's shoulder so she could address the agent. "We will be taking that cabin. And could you let the front desk know that we're canceling our stay here? If there is a fee for such late notice, we understand completely."

"What are you doing?" Bell asked his wife.

"As soon as I read that article, I knew you'd want to follow up, and that meant going to Panama. I just want time alone with you. I don't care if it's here at The Del or on a ship heading south. It's us being together that I care about, not where we are."

"I cannot love you more," he said solemnly. "I also can't take you with me."

A storm started brewing in her eyes. "Think very carefully. Are you sure those are what you want your dying words to be?"

Bell had to force himself not to chuckle. "It's dangerous, Marion. There's an insurgency growing in Panama, and the attack last night might be the trigger for a lot more violence."

"I'll make you a deal," she offered. "I come with you, and once we're there if you deem it too unsafe, I'll come home, no argument."

"Promise?"

"Yes. Besides which, you need me."

"How so, more than normal?"

"You don't speak any Spanish, and I speak it practically *con fluidez*."

Senator Densmore had used his office to get a tour of the USS *Maryland* for him and his extended family, so Bell couldn't introduce Marion to Elizabeth. He left a note with the front desk for the Senator and his niece, and he and Marion went up to his room so he could pack. He'd been told earlier that Court Talbot had checked out of the hotel while he was working with Chief Wilson. While he packed, Bell told Marion all the details of the attack and the discrepancies that tugged at his subconscious. Renny Hart came by as he was finishing up. He introduced Hart to his wife.

"I knocked on your door earlier," Bell told him.

The young agent smiled embarrassedly. "The house doc came to my room every hour all night to make sure I didn't have a brain bleed. I finally got some real sleep sometime after five in the morning and just woke up a few minutes ago."

"You feeling okay?" There was a puce knot the size of an egg over his right eye with threads of green and purple around it. He also had a black eye that looked like it was going to linger for weeks.

"Still a little woozy, and the bump hurts like the devil," Hart admitted.

"You on the three o'clock train for L.A.?" Renny nodded. "Marion and I have a ship to catch this evening, but we'll head over early and see that you make your train. I'll cable the L.A. office to make sure someone is there to bring you home."

"You don't need to do all that, Mr. Bell."

Marion piped in, "He does and he did. You saved all those lives."

"She's not exaggerating, Renny. Your warning gave me enough time to flip the table and give us some cover. Without that, they would have killed us all."

The young man blushed and couldn't meet Bell's eye.

Bell zipped up his bag. "Let's enjoy lunch by the pool and then make our way along to the pier."

Hours later, Bell and Marion were in their cabin, unpacking their things, for the six-day cruise to Panama. The SS *Valencia* had once been a luxurious express liner plying the North Atlantic route between New York and Europe, but that had been two decades and four name changes ago. While she was clean and the cabin spacious, her age was really starting to show. The carpets in the common areas were so faded that any pattern they'd once had were now muted smears of indistinct color, and a great deal of the veneer for the paneling was becoming delaminated and curled at the edges.

And when she finally hit the open ocean and her speed began to build, she produced a rhythmic shudder that wasn't quite as bothersome as the clack of a railway carriage, but it was a constant reminder that somewhere deep in her engine room some vital piece of equipment was out of alignment. Also, the smoke from her twin funnels was especially thick because of her inefficient boilers and was so filled with cinders of unburnt coal that standing at the fantail was all but impossible.

Bell and his wife had been apart long enough for them to have other considerations than dressing for dinner and meeting fellow travelers, so it wasn't until breakfast the following day that Bell learned Court Talbot was also a passenger aboard the *Valencia*. He spotted the retired Major at one of the tables along the starboard wall of the main dining salon and wended his way over. Talbot was engrossed in a book.

"Mind some company?" Bell asked as they neared.

"Isaac. Hello. Sit down, please." He then noticed Marion and quickly wiped his mouth with a cloth napkin and sprang to his feet. "Ma'am."

"Court, this is my wife, Marion. Marion, this is Court Talbot, expert on the Panamanian insurgency known as the Red Vipers."

"Viboras Rojas," Marion said.

Talbot said something in Spanish, and Marion replied in kind. They conversed for a moment more and ended with a little laughter.

"Your accent is more Madrid than Central America, Mrs. Bell, but you speak Spanish very well," Talbot said as they all sat down.

A moment later, a waiter in a white jacket with a red sash around his waist poured coffee as black as ink into their cups. Marion added milk and some sugar while Bell drank the potent brew as is.

"We didn't get a chance to see the Senator this morning," Bell told Talbot. "How did it end up between you two?"

"He sent a telegram to Goethals right from the hotel and penned a more detailed letter for me to present to the Canal Administrator once I'm back in Panama. Hopefully, it will be enough to persuade him to let me and my men try to stop this thing before it gets out of hand."

"That's good," Bell said.

Marion asked, "How is it you even have troops in Panama, Major Talbot?"

"Please call me Court, Mrs. Bell."

"Of course, and I'm Marion."

"It goes back to the founding of the Panamanian Republic and the people's revolt against Colombia. There was talk of

121

coups and countercoups at the time. Everyone suspected everyone else's loyalty. U.S. Marines were sent in. Sharpshooters arrived from Colombia. It was a chaotic and very precarious situation, and nobody knew how it would turn out. The first President of Panama was Manuel Amador Guerrero, a friend of mine who knew of my military background. He asked that I establish a small force loyal only to his office. Not him, mind you, but to the Office of the President. I was honored to do so, though we were never called to arms.

"Since then, I have kept regular contact with my men. We drill a few weekends each month for the fun of it. Really, it was more social than anything else. But when Viboras Rojas began to make their presence known, we knew we were in the best position to help. Panama has no army to speak of and can't operate within the Canal Zone anyway while Colonel Goethals purposely keeps the number of American troops to a minimum so the local politicians don't think they are militarizing the canal."

"And you believe you and your men are enough?"

"I do currently, but if the insurgency isn't crushed soon, it will attract more recruits, and then we'll have a slow-boil war on

America's doorstep with the most ambitious project in human history caught in the cross fire."

After breakfast, Marion excused herself and headed back to the cabin. Bell and Talbot moved off to one of the liner's lounges. Talbot produced a well-used pack of playing cards, and he and Bell settled into the new, faster version of rummy, called gin.

After dealing the first hand and going through a couple pickups and discards, Talbot said, "If you don't mind my asking, what are you hoping to accomplish in Panama?"

Bell grabbed the queen Talbot had put down. He now had all four and only needed either the four or seven of clubs. "I have no interest in tramping about in the jungle with you and your men, if that's what you're thinking. I guess I want to get a sense of the situation. There are aspects of the assassination attempt that bother me, and I believe the answers are in Panama."

" 'Aspects'? What aspects?"

Bell pulled the seven. "Gin."

"That was fast."

"You dealt me three queens, so . . ." Bell scooped up the cards and began shuffling. "It's too big of a leap for the Red Vipers being a small-scale indigenous insurgency to attempting an international assassination without some sort of outside influence."

"I believe I mentioned they're inspired by Lenin and his Bolsheviks."

"Inspiration doesn't explain it. There's something else at play."

"I hate to disagree, but if there was some international plot under way in Panama, the local police or the Authority's security squad would have picked up on it."

"I'm sure Panama City has a fine police force, and the Authority have plenty of capable guards, but I'm betting that neither has much in the way of investigators."

"You're barking up the wrong tree, Bell. The Red Vipers are a nest of snakes, but they are a local nest of snakes. I will grant you that they almost got lucky against Senator Densmore. Consider this, though. You alone held off and ultimately killed all six gunmen. You're pretty good in a fight, but are you that good? Or were they in over their heads?"

Bell looked him in the eye. "They pulled off the first successful invasion of American territory since the War of 1812. That means something."

With the exception of one eight-hour storm,

the trip southward was pleasant. The food was decent enough, and staff were all first-rate. Marion found several ladies to socialize with during the day. Bell and Talbot spent a great deal of time together over countless hands of gin. And when the ship rounded the newly constructed breakwater at the Pacific terminus of the canal, they had developed a mutual respect, though both were too restrained to call it a friendship just yet.

Isaac and Marion got their first taste of Panama's notorious rain while the ship was coming into its berth along a pier as busy as any they'd seen in New York City. Cranes were unloading massive pieces of equipment from the holds of freighters twice the size of their ship. Talbot had told him the Atlantic's Port of Colón was even busier, as most of the machinery for the canal came from America's Eastern Seaboard.

The air was oppressively humid, and Bell's linen suit hung on his frame damp and clammy. His hatband was already stained through. Each breath supplied enough oxygen, but somehow it felt like the moisture-laden air was too thick to breathe. Next to him, the fan Marion waved under her chin looked like the wing of a bird flapping to gain elevation. It did little to dispel the sweat dewing her throat.

"This is going to take some getting used to," Bell said.

The sky suddenly darkened, and an ominous charcoal shimmer, like some nightmare optical illusion, raced across the harbor's surface. The effect swept over the steamer, and it was as if the heavens had flooded and were spilling over onto the world. The rain seemed to come down in waves rather than drops. The harbor looked like it had started to boil. Rain pounded the freighter's deck so fiercely that conversation had to be conducted at a yell, and anyone caught out in the downpour was soon soaked to the skin. The docks were made of concrete or wood, but Bell imagined any dirt street beyond in the coastal city would soon be a river of ankle-deep mud.

He had never seen anything like it. The rain was so voluminous that he couldn't see more than a few dozen feet, and any thought of turning his face skyward would risk accidental drowning. Thunder rumbled over the roaring rain, a deeper bass note that he felt in his chest.

Bell and Marion were standing in the doorway of the lounge, looking out over the ship's covered promenade and rail. Talbot came up behind him, peered around Bell's shoulder, and shrugged.

"This is just a light sprinkle," he said and clasped Bell's upper arm. "Wait until the real rain hits. I could have told you about this on the way down, but you need to see it to believe it. And you're going to want to buy a straw hat. That blocked wool thing of yours will be moldy mush inside of a week."

"Thanks," Bell said sarcastically.

"Also, keep an eye on your feet. They won't be dry again until you leave and can develop all sorts of issues." Talbot smiled broadly, enjoying the discomfort of people newly arrived on the isthmus. "Welcome to Panama, Mr. and Mrs. Bell."

There was only one upscale place to stay in the city and that was the Central Hotel Panama on Independence Plaza, not far from the Presidential Palace. There was the Tivoli Hotel, where Teddy Roosevelt had stayed in 1906, but it was within the Canal Zone, for all intents and purposes a separate country, and there was confusion as to whether people who weren't employees could stay there. The Central was located in the Old Quarter of the city and it retained some colonial charm. The small peninsula jutting into the Pacific was actually the second Panama City. The first had been five miles south but it had been sacked and burned by the pirate Henry Morgan in 1671.

Bell had expected heavy Spanish influence on the architecture but noted a lot of French provincial. He realized it dated to their ill-fated attempt to dig a sea level canal some forty years earlier. The three-story hotel had been built at that time and looked faintly Parisian, with dormers along the roof and wrought iron balconies ringing the upper floors.

An associate of Talbot's, Rinaldo Morales, had met them at the dock and given them a lift to their hotel. Despite the heat, the man wore his shirt buttoned to the throat and had on a pair of kid driving gloves. Talbot reminded Bell that he could join in his meeting the following morning with the Canal Administrator, George Goethals. Morales drove the former Army Major away to his house at the base of Ancon Hill, the jungle-shrouded hillock between the city and the canal.

Inside the Central Hotel was an atrium painted a smart, clean white. The floors, however, were muddy despite the staff's efforts. As Bell had thought, the streets of the Casco Viejo district were a mixture of pavement and dirt, and the dirt sections were like quicksand, viscous and impassable, following the storm. The lobby buzzed with a crowd, and Bell noted English was being spoken more than Spanish.

He could just imagine the unprecedented upheaval the country was experiencing thanks to the American effort to bridge the Atlantic and Pacific.

His room was ready, as he'd reserved it while still in San Diego, and the receptionist handed him an envelope with a half dozen telegraph messages in it. To Bell, it was a ritual. At nearly every hotel he visited, upon check-in there were always a number of dispatches waiting that needed his urgent attention.

He turned over their luggage to a bellhop, and they followed the man up to the third floor to their room overlooking the plaza. The décor was spartan, just a bed and dresser with a wash basin, but Marion delighted at the need for mosquito netting. He was aware of the effort during the early years of the canal's construction to tame malaria and yellow fever. Newspapers across America wrote weekly about Dr. Gorgas and his theory that these dread diseases were carried by mosquitoes and how he and his staff had gone about eradicating them by draining the swamps in which they bred and bringing proper drainage and sanitation to the region.

Panama saw its last case of yellow fever in 1906, and malaria grew rarer and rarer, though the threat persisted.

Marion opened the floor-to-ceiling door to the balcony, and they stepped outside. They both marveled at the lawn across the street. Thanks to the tremendous amount of rain the country received each year, the grass covering Independence Plaza was a vibrant green and lusher than any either had ever seen.

While another squall passed over the city, and Marion busied herself unpacking their bags, Bell went through the telegrams. Chief Wilson cabled to tell him that a subsequent dive had discovered the boat's ownership papers in an oilskin pouch. The cabin cruiser had belonged to a couple from Huntington Beach. A check with the local police found that they had been missing almost a week.

Bell didn't need Chief Wilson's speculation that they were dead. He was sure they'd been murdered for their boat and their bodies weighted down and dumped somewhere off the coast of Orange County.

The other telegrams were from Van Dorn about ongoing investigations unrelated to his current mission.

Bell and Marion ate dinner in the hotel and then went strolling through Casco Viejo. He was surprised by the number of bars. It seemed every other business was a saloon of some sort. Some seemed respectable enough, while others were no more than a scrap of canvas strung over the back corner of an alley with a couple stools pulled up to a sawhorse bar. The streets were filled with men in various states of inebriation. Some were out having some fun with their friends and swayed from place to place, others were passed out in gutters and against walls. The second-floor windows of many establishments were adorned with red curtains. In the doorways leading to the stairs up were heavily rouged women making suggestive gestures.

It all reminded Bell of the tales of the Old West. Panama City indeed was a frontier town on the edge of a jungle so thick that very little of it had ever been mapped. Bring in a labor force of some thirty thousand men and they'd seek the same distractions that slaked the appetites of the men who'd built the Great Pyramids of Egypt and the Colosseum in Rome.

As if to reinforce the image of the city Bell was constructing, two men tossed a third out the open door of one of the rougher-looking establishments. He hit the muddy road with a smack but quickly got to his feet, his anger fueled by plenty of drink. He rushed back toward the bouncers, arms flailing. The larger of the bar employees stepped forward, nimbly ducked a floppy haymaker, and put the sot down with a straight right that caused his nose to erupt with blood.

The bouncer shook out his hand and slapped his partner on the shoulder as if to say the next turn was his laying out an overly intoxicated patron. From inside the bar, Bell could hear a pianist pounding out a quick-tempo rag.

He managed to find a clothing store that was still open and bought himself a straw hat that, while made in Ecuador, was called a panama. He also bought a pair of shin-high, well-fitted rubber boots. They were as comfortable as loafers and had a clever venting tube on the inside so his feet wouldn't overheat. His current shoes were already waterlogged, and his feet were white and dimpled from being wet. Unfortunately, they didn't have any boots small enough for Marion, but she assured her husband that she had no intention of traipsing around in the mud.

The last few minutes of their walk was in a downpour every bit as powerful as the afternoon deluge. Bell's head and feet stayed dry, and he realized he was already becoming accustomed to the tropics.

9

The administration building for the Canal Authority overlooked the waterway from partway up Ancon Hill. It was still under construction but was where Goethals wanted to meet. As the Canal Zone was sovereign American territory, there was a checkpoint to gain access. Talbot was friendly with the guard, as he crossed into the zone frequently, but Bell had to present his credentials and have his name written in a ledger.

It truly felt like they had left Panama for the United States. Behind them, French and Spanish influences dominated the architecture and the everyday life. The pace was more languid and without urgency. On this side of the line, the buildings had a barracks-like quality and had been constructed with American efficiency and were diligently maintained. Lawns were well tended and bordered by whitewashed rocks. Roads were perfectly delineated, and the people on them moved with purpose.

Again, Bell was struck by the contrast of the two worlds coexisting side by side and could understand the resentment it could foster in groups like Viboras Rojas.

Talbot's driver took them around Ancon Hill and parked behind the massive building. Half of the roof was missing, as were a number of windows. Scaffolding climbed part of the way up its three-story façade.

The morning sky was a cloudless blue, but the humidity was a physical presence that made everything uncomfortable. Bell felt certain he'd sweat through his suit by noon. Talbot looked more at ease. He wore khakis and riding boots, with his befeathered bush hat on his head. There was just a trace of moisture on his freshly shaved upper lip.

An aide saw them through to Goethals's corner office. The Authority director had a reputation of being terse and to the point. He didn't wear his uniform while in Panama, but there was no disguising his military bearing. He was a little shorter than Bell, with thick silvered hair and a darker mustache.

"Talbot," he said as they entered, and nodded his way. He looked to Bell. "You're

135

the Van Dorn man?"

"Isaac Bell."

They shook hands, and Goethals settled behind his cluttered desk and indicated chairs for his guests. His office was completed down to the stucco walls and wooden baseboards but was so filled with books, maps, rock samples, and other junk that it was hard to tell.

"This is from Senator Densmore," Talbot said and handed over the handwritten page.

Goethals read it through and laid it on his blotter. "Given the attack on you in California, and Bill's telegram, I was inclined to let you and your men loose on the rebels, but then I got a telegram from Washington late yesterday. The powers that be plan on sending down a thousand Marines to put down this insurrection once and for all."

Court Talbot opened his mouth to protest. Goethals silenced him with a look. "I don't like it either. They haven't gotten permission from the Panamanian government to operate outside the zone, which means the Red Vipers will retreat deeper into the jungle after hitting us. I'm sure the diplomats will get the authority for the Marines to chase them, but it's going to be a dog and pony show. Like I said, I was inclined to let you can hunt them with your men, but this negates that entirely."

"May I make a suggestion?" Talbot said.

"What?"

"Let me try to find them before the Marines arrive. How long will that be?"

Goethals lit a cigarette. "It's going to be some time," he admitted. "They need to mobilize them first and then get 'em down here on a troop transport. A month, probably."

"By which time Viboras Rojas will have grown in size and power."

While Goethals said nothing, it was a point he recognized. "That's already happening. We haven't made this public, but when you were in California, they raided a warehouse at Pedro Miguel and made off with a ton of explosives."

"Damn."

"No idea what they're going to use it for, can't be good."

"I'd like to see the warehouse," Bell said.

Goethals blew a plume of smoke up at the ceiling fan. "Think my men missed something?"

"Doubtful," Bell said diplomatically. "I'm the type of man who likes to see things for himself."

A moment passed. "I suppose if you're good enough to single-handedly save Bill

Densmore's life, you deserve some leeway. I'll allow it. However, you'll need an escort at all times."

"What about me, Colonel?"

"You can tag along, if you like."

"Thanks, I would, but what about letting me and my men go after the Viboras?"

"My hands are tied. Unless there's a massive escalation that will convince Washington that we don't have the time to waste waiting for the Marines, you can't search for them in the zone."

"And the local government has no interest searching for them in Panama, so there's nothing to be done."

"That's it precisely."

Goethals's aide knocked and opened the door. "They're here, sir."

"Thanks, Frederick. If you gentlemen will excuse me, I've got to tell some archeologists that the permit they had when this country was part of Colombia is void. Whatever bits and bobs they hoped to find have already been flooded when we sealed the Gatun Dam."

Bell and Talbot got to their feet. "Thank you for your time, Colonel."

"Yes, yes . . . Frederick." The aide popped his head back through the door. "Get these gentlemen passes to be in the zone, and find

138

Sam Westbrook. It's his day off, but I saw him around here earlier." He looked at Bell. "Westbrook's one of my best men. He was the man who discovered the break-in."

"Thank you," Bell said. "That's a big help."

Ten minutes later, they were at the rail station just down from the administration building. Talbot dismissed his driver with some last-minute instructions, and they made it aboard the 10:10 train.

"This is the secret to the whole construction project," Sam Westbrook said, tapping his foot on the floor of the passenger carriage.

It was an old railcar used by workers. The floors were dirty with mud, and the seats were gritty from clinkers thrown from the locomotive's stack. The passengers were all workingmen.

"The train?" Bell said.

Westbrook was not yet thirty, with dark hair and eyes and a strong cleft in his chin. He was handsome enough yet had the unfortunate luck of not even topping five foot four. His handshake had been firm, but his hand was small in Bell's. He was dressed in denim pants tucked into heavy boots and a linen shirt. He wore a panama hat similar

139

to Bell's. He spoke with a heavy New York accent.

"Yes, the railroads. That's the one thing the French never got right. They had decent steam shovels but couldn't get the rock and dirt out of the excavations fast enough."

"Is that your background?"

"New York Transit Authority," he said proudly. "Started when I was sixteen and by the time I left to come here I was first assistant scheduler. We were responsible for making sure every train was on time at every station across the entire system.

"Down here, we use the railroad like it's a giant conveyor belt linking the Culebra Cut, where the lion's share of the excavating is done, to where we need to dump the over-burden. Most went to Gatun, to construct the dam that makes the entire canal possible, while some came here to Panama City to construct seawalls and reclaim land."

"How many trains per day?"

"Five hundred. That works out to be about a train a minute during daylight hours. We're moving more debris out of Culebra in a year than what the French managed in all their seventeen years here. I'll take you to see the cut after I show you the warehouse. You really can't imagine a five-hundred-foot-deep, thousand-foot-wide man-made valley that stretches nine miles. It's something you have to take in with your own eyes."

The train snaked through a jungle so thick that Bell couldn't see more than a few yards into the foliage. The growth oftentimes almost met overhead the railcars, so the effect was like riding through a jade-colored tunnel. They passed an occasional depot or siding, which were the only indications that man had had any impact on the lush landscape.

The heat and humidity were rising the higher the sun climbed into the sky. It was worse than any sweltering New York City heat wave, and Bell imagined he'd welcome the next deluge of rain for the temporary relief it provided.

Even though the train stopped at Mira Flores, the station sat behind some enormous warehouses so Bell couldn't see the giant locks being constructed.

"These here are the double locks," Westbrook said. "There's just a single set at Pedro Miguel, but don't worry, you'll still be impressed."

"How high above sea level will the locks raise the ships?"

"Lake Gatun, and the rest of the canal, will be eighty-five feet above the oceans, so each individual lock chamber raises or lowers a ship about thirty feet."

"And all the water comes from the Chagres River?"

"Yes. It was the reason this isn't a sea level canal like the Suez, which the French originally wanted to build. They arrived in Panama and just started digging at the continental divide with no real plan on how to control the Chagres at full flood. Truth be told, when we first started, we wanted a sea level canal too yet soon realized it was impossible. The Chagres during the rainy season is a beast we simply can't tame.

"Once we'd properly surveyed the possible routes, it was clear we needed locks. I can't imagine the precision it took to set everything at the right elevations across a fifty-mile canal, but that's exactly what they've done. And here's a kicker — because of ocean currents, the Pacific Ocean is a foot higher than the Atlantic and has twenty-foot tides compared to three-footers over in Colón."

"There were so many challenges to overcome," Court Talbot said, "that I had my doubts it would ever happen."

Westbrook nodded. "A lot of people felt that way at first, but John Stevens, the chief engineer before Colonel Goethals, knew what he was doing. He was a railwayman, like me, and had overseen the laying of more than a thousand miles of track in some of the worst conditions America's Northwest could throw at him."

With a blast from its whistle and the clang of couplings stretching out, the train pulled from the station. It was only a short distance to the next construction site on the canal, the Pedro Miguel Locks.

Here, Bell got a better view of the monumental scale of what was being accomplished in the Panamanian jungle. The site stretched for more than a hundred acres. Just clearing that much jungle alone was an enormous undertaking. Then it all had been dug down so that the foundations would be below the canal's eventual bed. And then they built perhaps the largest man-made structure ever conceived.

The concrete walls of each lock chamber were fifty-five feet thick at the base with eighteen-foot-diameter culverts running through them so water from above the locks could be allowed into the structure from below. In this fashion, the boat in the lock wouldn't be buffeted by the force of the water. The lock walls stood eighty feet tall and stretched for a thousand feet. The steel doors were among the largest on the planet, though they were hollow and watertight so their buoyancy meant they could be opened and closed with only a single electric motor.

Each of the two side-by-side chambers were a hundred and ten feet wide, wide enough to accommodate whatever next-generation battleships the Navy built. The outside walls of the chambers were stepped back like the sides of a modern-day ziggurat and would eventually be buried with backfill up to the top, which then would have special train tracks installed on them so electric locomotives, called mules, would maneuver ships through the lock using tow ropes.

All around the site, thousands of men still toiled as if in the shadow of a great cathedral under construction. Four towering cranes built on metal scaffolding and running on rails laid outside the locks carried buckets of cement from a nearby dedicated plant. Welders were at work amid fountains of sparks that cascaded down the lock like fiery waterfalls.

Dwarfed by the massive concrete and steel colossus, the workers looked like ants. But the sound of their endeavors was a throbbing din of train whistles, droning rock crushers, the pounding of rivets with pneumatic hammers, and the shouts of men. Trucks swooped around the site on gravel roads to prevent them from sinking into the mud quagmire of so much overturned earth and rainwater.

As Bell, Talbot, and Sam Westbrook stepped from the train onto the platform, one of the cranes trundled along the length of the lock, an enormous bucket of cement dangling from its two-inch-thick cable. It was lowered to where workers stood ready at some newly built forms. Once it was centered, a lock at the bucket's base was struck with a shovel and the bottom dropped out. The lock wall was too tall for Bell to see, but he imagined the concrete sloshing into the form and completing a few more cubic yards of the structure.

Adjacent to the lock was a small town's worth of buildings. They weren't where the workers lived, that was farther from the site. These were the warehouses, machine shops, and other support structures. A distance away, and linked by temporary rail, was the cement plant, where mounds of rock and sand were delivered hourly by train. The special cars laden with concrete buckets destined for the cranes came out the other end of the plant.

"This level of coordination boggles the mind," Bell said in awe.

Sam nodded. "If just one moving part in

the chain doesn't work, like we miss delivering a load of portland cement, then the whole thing grinds to a halt. Come on, the warehouse that was robbed is this way."

10

Westbrook led them across the busy construction yard, pausing once to let a five-car train carrying gravel from the rock crusher to the cement plant pass by.

"What kind of security do you have here?" Bell asked as they entered a warren of massive warehouses.

"Night patrols, and even though we've stepped up the numbers since Viboras Rojas appeared, as you can tell this place is enormous. We mainly rely on our isolation here. There's only one road in or out, plus the railroad, and the zone extends five miles into the jungle. We actually employ very few Panamanians."

They passed the last of the warehouses and came to a brick-fronted building that had been buried in rubble so that it looked like it had been dug into a mountainside. The door was steel.

"We have explosives bunkers like this all

over the zone. To date, we've gone through about thirty thousand tons of dynamite."

Bell noted how Westbrook used possessives when describing the canal as if it were his. He was certainly proud of his work here.

A guard halted their approach while a bucket brigade of Caribbean laborers moved wooden boxes of explosives from the bunker and loaded them onto the back of a heavy-duty truck. They were watched over by a supervisor, as well as a bookkeeper, who counted each crate and recorded it in a ledger. Once the vehicle pulled away on its journey to wherever the explosives were needed, the three men stepped into the bunker's cool, gloomy interior.

Bell first checked the door's lock. It required a large key but wasn't particularly difficult to pick. "Who has access?"

"Quite a few people," Westbrook admitted. "And I know for a fact that one of the keys went missing a few months ago."

"How?"

"Dropped in the jungle while the quartermaster was answering the call of nature."

It was ridiculous enough to be true, Bell thought, yet that didn't mean it hadn't been found later. "How are relations between the locals and the Caribbean workers? Would the islanders help an insurgency?"

"Some might," Talbot said, wiping the inside of his hat with a bright bandanna. "But mostly the Panamanians are afraid the islanders will stay once the construction is completed so they're hesitant to work with them."

Bell looked around. There were warning signs plastered on the walls not to smoke, and all the lightbulbs had wire mesh cages so they wouldn't be accidentally smashed and cause a spark. Thousands of identical wooden boxes were stacked in orderly blocks, from the earthen floor to just below the rafters. No amount of dirt piled onto the building could contain a blast of the magnitude this amount of dynamite would cause.

"And there are other caches like this?" he asked Westbrook.

"Some even larger, like the ones at Culebra. In fact, we're in the process of closing this one down."

"Any chance they were stolen months ago or that they aren't missing at all and this was an accounting error?"

"No to both questions, Mr. Bell. This is a government run project under the supervision of a military man. Every *i* gets dotted and *t* crossed around here. There are rules and regulations for everything. Heck, there's a prescribed way of shaking out cement bags to get the most out of them."

Bell suppressed a chuckle and said, "That this is a government project doesn't bode well for its efficiency, but I believe in the guiding hand of Colonel Goethals. So I will stipulate that. How heavy are the crates?"

"Fifty pounds each."

Bell did the math for a ton of explosives. "Forty wooden cases of dynamite were removed from this bunker recently, and I can tell you that I know that the boxes are very close to the mechanics' garage. Or wherever you pool your vehicles."

"How could you possibly know that?" Talbot asked, his voice dripping with skepticism.

"That is a bit of a stretch," Westbrook agreed.

"Not at all," Bell continued. "I've observed that the average Panamanian man is slight of stature and build, so chances are it's one crate per man. That's forty men sneaking in here, grabbing a crate each, and vanishing back into the jungle. Not likely your guards would miss such a mob. And even if Viboras Rojas had some real bruisers in their ranks and doubled up on the crates, we're still talking about a crowd of twenty men. Again, unless your guards all suffer from myopia, we can discount that possibility. Therefore, the explosives were loaded onto a truck by a handful of insurgents using the bucket brigade method we ourselves just saw used."

"You're making sense up to this point," Westbrook admitted. "Why is the truck near the garage? Why didn't they take off and hide it in the jungle?"

"No idea why," Bell said. "But I know that's exactly what happened."

"How can you be so sure?" the young engineer persisted.

"It's simple." Bell smiled. "You track everything that moves within the zone, and since no one has reported a stolen truck, it has to still be here, hiding in plain sight. The garage is the most logical place."

The silence that followed was pierced by an angry curse when Westbrook realized Bell's logic was airtight.

Bell sympathized with the younger man. When it came to problems of logic, most people consider themselves smart enough to figure things out. They become truly confounded when they meet an actual expert. It was a reaction Bell encountered time and again.

The garage area sat on a small rise all the way across the massive site. It took them fifteen minutes to reach it. The machine shop itself was corrugated metal, with four mechanic's bays accessible through barn-style doors. Around it was oil-stained gravel littered with empty barrels and castoff vehicle parts. To one side were two rows of trucks with fully enclosed rear beds. The vehicles were showing signs of heavy use in harsh conditions. Bodywork was dented and rust-streaked, and some were missing tires and propped up on jacks. A few had been cannibalized for parts after becoming too damaged to fix and resembled mere skeletons of their brethren.

The chief mechanic saw the party striding toward them at a pace that told him something bad was about to happen. Or already had.

He zipped up his overalls to hide his hairy belly and spit the wad of tobacco from his mouth.

"Have any trucks gone missing?" Westbrook asked as they approached.

"Nope."

"Anything odd happen to any of them?"

" 'Odd'?"

"Been moved without any reason."

"Nope. The ones that run get used and the ones that don't get fixed."

Bell ignored the pointless conversation

and studied the trucks. There were at least thirty of them and they had to be inspected because their suspensions were so stiff that a ton of cargo in the back wouldn't make them noticeably sag. There was an order as to which ones got signed out, and there were obvious gaps in the rows where crews had requisitioned vehicles for their work shifts. They rotated through the vehicles over the course of a week or ten days so that all of them shared the workload evenly and wouldn't require additional maintenance.

There was an extra gap where one of the trucks, out of rotation, had been driven off.

"Hey," Bell called out to get the mechanic's attention.

"What?"

"Where's the truck that should be parked fifth from the end?"

The man scratched at the back of his head. "Don't know. It was there a little while ago."

"You sure?"

"Yup."

Bell looked out across the jobsite. Now that he was concentrating on finding a particular truck, he saw trucks everywhere. Some were parked and seemingly abandoned while others were trundling along to whatever task needed to be done. If the truck they sought had been moved from the garage, the explosives were going to be in play. There were several thousand men clambering over and around the massive lock, and he knew that was the most likely target. From where he stood, he could see several trucks parked along the lock's length.

A sense of foreboding gripped him.

"We need to clear the site immediately," he told Westbrook. "There can't be much time."

The engineer thought for a moment. "There's a signal siren that goes off at —"

The explosion was a catastrophic roar that could be felt at the very base of the brain. It overwhelmed the senses so that the men standing even as far away as they were felt dizzy and disorientated. Next came the shock wave. Bell reflexively turned his back to the blast, but it still felt like he'd taken a half dozen simultaneous hits from baseball bats. He was driven to his knees as he noted the sky going dark. He turned to look over his shoulder. The explosion had gouged a great crater next to the wall of one of the locks, and the mass of pulverized material had been lofted a hundred feet or more into the sky, momentarily blotting out the sun.

And then it all began to fall back to earth in a hailstorm the likes of which no one had ever seen. At the epicenter, larger pieces of rock and chunks of concrete fell like boulders, while across a great swath of the work zone clots of gravel fell from the sky and hit like the pricks from a swarm of stinging wasps. Bell curled himself in a ball, with his hands wrapped around his head, like he was about to be raked by salt from a shotgun.

No sooner had the sky cleared of debris than he was on his feet and running to where the truck had exploded almost directly beneath one of the towering gantry cranes. As he sprinted, he watched in horror as the crane's support structure buckled and began to collapse. High up on the lock's rim, a full bucket of cement had been dangling over a group of workers ready to dump it into a form. The multi-ton crucible slammed down on the edge of the concrete structure so hard that the liquid cement erupted from the bucket like it was lava from a volcano. Two of the men were spared, but three others were hit with hundreds of pounds of mud-like concrete and sent hurtling off the eighty-foot-high perch. Their shouts stopped short when they hit the bottom of the lock.

The crane continued to fall as if its steel

frame had turned to rubber. The empty cement bucket was yanked off the top of the lock by the crane's plummeting and whipsawed toward the ground, where it struck a locomotive pulling a trainload of fresh wooden planks.

The locomotive's boiler was solidly built and could sustain two hundred and fifty pounds per square inch of steam pressure, but it wasn't designed to take such a crushing blow. The boiler split and erupted in a scalding plume of superheated steam that consumed the engineer and his brakeman, plus a handful of poor souls caught nearby, before the cloud curled heavenward and dissipated.

The main body of the crane struck the ground and crumpled under the weight of its heavy wheels and cogs and drums of braided cable. The long boom landed last, folding like paper as it slammed into the earth.

Around the smoking crater, vehicles and equipment had been tossed aside. Several wooden storage sheds were blown flat and set ablaze. Bodies and parts of bodies littered the landscape. Bell knew the death toll would be in the dozens.

Bell wasn't running to offer aid or to help rescue anyone who'd been trapped. That duty would have to fall on others. His was a more deadly pursuit. He'd observed the driver of the explosives-laden truck moments before the blast. Something must have gone wrong because the man hadn't gotten far enough from the detonation.

Bell raced into the swirling clouds of dust, past men who were covered head to toe in fine powder and whose eyes were those of the haunted. The moaning and cries were the stuff of nightmares, and he witnessed every dreadful permutation of what high explosives could do to the human body.

He was still fifty yards from his target and sprinting hard when the truck driver raised himself up off the ground and shook his head to clear it. It was Bell's bad luck that the man possessed the feral instincts of a sewer rat because as he zeroed in on Bell charging at him he instinctively knew he was in trouble and took off running in the opposite direction.

Bell didn't really see the man's face, but he could see that he was young and in shape, for he moved like a thoroughbred, or, more aptly, a steeplechaser. He leapt over any obstacle that got in his way, using his arms for additional leverage. It was almost like he had springs instead of muscles. Bell was having a hard time keeping up, as he had to duck and juke and weave, while his quarry seemed to just glide through the chaos he'd created.

11

The saboteur raced up a flight of stairs hanging on the outside flank of the lock and then leapt off the platform to a towering assembly of wooden scaffolding that rose to the top of the chamber wall.

Bell paused to see if he had a shot with his .45, realized he didn't, and kept after the man. He was breathing heavily in the humid air, and he had to flick sweat from his eyes every few seconds. The driver climbed with the agility of a monkey, while Bell struggled. The top of the lock was some eighty-five feet above the ground, and Bell and the driver climbed all the way up, hand over hand, with feet scrabbling for purchase.

By the time Bell reached the top, his target was running along the lock's great length. Even before Bell was fully to his feet, he pulled the black Colt from its shoulder holster and braced himself in a two-handed shooting stance that gave him far more stability than the one-handed style still popular with law enforcement and the military.

He cycled through the seven rounds in the magazine in three seconds, but the range had grown extreme, and he had zero control over his breathing or the pounding of his heart. It would have been just as effective to throw the bullets at the bomber.

He started running again, changing out the magazine as he went. The top of the lock was wide enough yet littered with construction materials, forcing Bell to weave precariously close to the dizzying edges at times. The lock chamber below him was like the longest, widest, deepest swimming pool in the world, only it hadn't yet been filled. Work was still being done on its concrete floor. For safety's sake, the big holes in the floor that allowed water into the chamber had been fitted with temporary covers.

The bomber ran with the understanding his life was on the line. There would be no slowing, no stopping, no attention paid to sore legs or burning lungs. He had to escape if he wanted to live. Behind him, Bell ran with enough confidence in himself that he wouldn't give up until he had his man in irons or dead. He could block out any amount of discomfort by keeping that singular goal his entire focus.

They ran almost the complete length of the Pedro Miguel Lock. It looked like the bomber was going to run to the end of the tailing that stretched from the lock out some distance from the chamber. It dipped down in a gentle drop, and at the very end of the structure was more scaffolding that he could climb down.

At the last second, the man veered sharply right and took the chase out onto one of the massive steel doors, a towering slab of metal that weighed over seven hundred tons. The doors usually met at an angle to each other to help them stave off the tremendous weight of water they were designed to withstand.

They were currently ajar. That was a relative term, given that each leaf of the mitered gate was sixty-five feet wide.

The bomber didn't hesitate. In fact, he lengthened his stride, hit his mark, and sailed eighty feet above the lock's floor below. He landed on the far gate awkwardly enough that he fell and almost rolled off the edge before catching himself and jumping back onto his feet and continuing. He didn't waste the effort to look back.

Bell raced on, and as he drew closer to the end of the gate, he saw the gap between it and its mate seeming to grow wider and wider. He was at that crucial split second when his mind had to derail his instinctual need for self-preservation and forced himself to jump over the yawning abyss.

He didn't make it.

At least, not all the way. The space between the doors was far wider than Bell had ever jumped. Instead of clearing the far edge, he slammed into it just below his ribs, exploding every molecule of air from his lungs. His pistol crushed against his chest like a full-body punch. He struggled for grip, his hands spread flat against the hot metal, while the toes of his boot found a row of rivets no thicker than suit buttons.

He could feel the void sucking at his heels. His hands began to slide down, leaving trails of sweat on the black steel. A little moan of effort escaped his lips as he curled his toes in hopes of gaining a better hold on the nubbin-like rivets. Still sliding, if only by millimeters, Bell was certain his last mistake had been a fatal one. He thought of Marion's beautiful face and how he would never see her again.

One boot slipped from its rivet at the same time the heel of his hand touched a rough seam in the metal door, a bump no thicker than twenty sheets of paper. He dug his fingers into the seam, curling them so tight that the tendons in his arms raised the skin like the cable stays of a suspension bridge. He didn't panic. He moved his second hand forward and dug in with his fingers and slowly found his foothold once again.

By inches, he pulled himself up until he could shift his body weight enough to roll onto the mitered gate. As much as his body needed to rest, to reinflate his lungs properly and to discharge the adrenaline overload that had shocked his nervous system, he ignored it all and got to his feet. He'd lost precious seconds.

The bomber was already running farther back on the center pier of the lock that separated the two great chambers and had a seventy-yard advantage. He was almost at another set of scaffolding that would take him down to the open chamber floor.

Bell started after him again, each breath a stab of agony. He'd broken ribs before and knew the feeling and, thankfully, this wasn't that. But his pace was off.

The bomber reached the staging and started down without a moment's hesitation. If he reached the bottom with too much of a head start, Bell felt certain he'd lose him in the anonymity of the rescuers hard at work down below.

Next to the scaffolding was an area with benches covered with tools, and a pulley for hauling things up from below. When Bell reached it and looked over the edge, the bomber was nothing more than a shifting shadow lost in the latticework.

He was going to lose the man if he didn't think of something quick. At the base of the wall was a large bucket used to raise tools and materials up to the top. Bell hoped to use it as a counterweight, but it was filled with bags of portland cement, several hundred pounds' worth, and far too heavy for his purposes. They used horses, he realized, as power to hoist.

Instead of holding on to the rope and letting gravity do the work, Bell snatched up a pair of heavy iron tongs, like riveters use to hold hot bolts while they're being pounded into place. The jaws of the tongs closed in a circular shape just slightly larger around than the hemp rope. Had they clamped tight, Bell's plan would have been dashed.

He got a firm grip on both handles and stepped off the concrete wall. Gravity should have sent him plummeting to his death, but his weight and the width of the tongs's jaws meant the rope had to kink sharply as he fell, the friction of metal against the rope slowing his descent to a manageable speed. Still, it was a harrowing drop from the heights of the lock.

The landing was brutal, but he had gained on his man. The bomber was running hard again and ducked out through the opening in the gates they'd leapt from moments before. Bell gave chase.

From the ground level, the doors looked like the enormous portal to some pagan temple, and once again Bell was staggered by the scale of the canal. When he made it through the open gate, he saw the construction site spread out before him. A pair of locomotives sat, huffing steam, on a siding, while a truck raced up the hill away from the site, likely on a mission to bring additional help.

What Bell didn't see was his quarry. He knew he had been close enough that the man couldn't have escaped. There was only one place he could go. Bell rounded the front of the lock and encountered an eighteen-foot culvert, big enough to serve as a railroad tunnel, that ran the length of the lock. It was one of the conduits used to fill the massive locks with water.

The far opening was a thousand feet distant and looked as small and pale as a wafer. Bell drew his pistol again and started jogging. The light faded quickly yet he could hear the bomber running ahead of him and could just discern his loping figure in silhouette.

"Stop," Bell shouted and fired a single bullet down the tunnel but well above the fugitive.

The man kept going. Bell went after him yet again. He raced past an inky black tunnel below that ran across the lock's chamber. Though it was smaller than the main pipe, Bell could have ridden through it on horseback.

Deeper into the concrete structure, the light faded further. Bell could no longer see the bomber's silhouette. He had moved closer to the side of the culvert to mask his location.

Bell passed another dark tunnel crossing below and then a third. He was almost past the fourth when he noticed something different. A bit of light filtered down the shaft from one of the well openings embedded in the floor of the lock. He had a snap decision to make and he'd either be right or the madman would escape. He turned and ran down the side tunnel, trusting his instincts. Cornered rats always take the first way out.

Over the sound of his ragged breathing and the echoing slap of his rubber boots on the tunnel floor, he could hear the bomber running ahead of him. Bell passed under three of the covered round holes in the ceiling, each the size of a large dining room table. It was up ahead, at the fifth and final one, that Bell saw the bomber. He was halfway up a ladder left behind by workers.

Bell would never catch him. The distance was too great. He'd be up on the surface in seconds and he'd haul the ladder up after himself. That would be it.

Bell stopped, raised his pistol so that its weight rested in his left hand and was guided by his right. The shots came in one thunderous tattoo and were painfully loud in the confined tunnel.

No sooner had the man's legs vanished up the tunnel than the ladder was drawn up too.

Bell had failed. By the time he cut back across the width of the lock chamber and made it out the main culvert, the bomber would have vanished. Still, he wouldn't call it fate or bad luck and just succumb to defeat. He ran, as best he could, back out of the giant's maze of piping and conduits. His muscles felt rubbery, his body ached, and he was thoroughly exhausted, but he pushed on at an anemic pace. He didn't stop until he reached daylight.

The scene was as it had been just moments earlier. The trains were there, and a different truck was driving toward the construction zone. Some of the men in the distance moved like walking corpses, while others ran about with frantic haste. Bell saw no one running, or even walking, inside the empty lock. The bomber had either climbed out of the chamber on some scaffolding or just run out the up-channel gates.

He looked more carefully and saw something that caught his eye. He loaded his last magazine into the butt of his .45 and took off at a pained trot.

The driver was barely ten feet from the open hole he'd climbed up through and lay in a lake of congealing blood. Bell understood what had happened as he drew nearer. He'd hit the man in the femoral artery high up his inner thigh. Another round had made a ruin of his face by piercing one of his cheeks. Adrenaline and fear had given him the strength to raise the ladder from the culvert, but the staggering blood loss meant he could go no farther.

Such was the nature of the jungle that flies were already starting to buzz around the body.

12

Bell found Court Talbot in the thick of the rescue work. The scene was like something out of the blackest reaches of Hell. Dead men lay everywhere, while the injured cried out in pain. The air remained fouled by the smell of sulfur, and in odd places were bloodstains where men had been standing when they were blown out of existence. Doctors had yet to arrive, but the Army veteran had seen enough injuries over his military career to triage the most grievous.

"Did you get him?"

"Yes," Bell reported. "He's in the far lock chamber. I want you to verify something about him."

Talbot held up his hands. They were bloody to the wrist. "Little busy right now."

"Where's Westbrook?"

"He went to the telegraph office at the train station to organize transport out of here and to alert the big hospital at Ancon."

The patient Talbot was working on had a deep gash in his right leg. Talbot was trying to fit the injured man with a tourniquet, but he was writhing in such pain that he couldn't form a proper knot in the strip of cloth torn from a dead man's shirt. Bell pressed his weight down on the man's knees. He screamed, but it allowed Talbot to fix the binding and stanch the blood.

Talbot pointed to two workers who hovered close by. They had created a makeshift stretcher out of boards and empty cement bags. "Get this man onto the next truck to the station, and if he starts bleeding, turn the piece of wood I threaded through the knot of the tourniquet to tighten it even more."

By virtue of his natural leadership and calm in the face of chaos, the men responded to Talbot like they were soldiers under his command. It didn't matter that he had no actual authority in the zone, the men simply recognized his leadership and obeyed.

The work went on. Bell acted as litter-bearer and driver and helped corral some of the workhorses and mules that had been spooked by the explosion. It was exhausting work, mentally and physically, but he, like all the others, didn't slow until the last living creature had been tended to.

It was three hours after the blast that the wounded had been evacuated by special train to the zone's principal hospital, where all off-duty staff had been called in for the crisis. The doctors from the small clinic at Pedro Miguel had accompanied the train, though one remained behind for the grisly task of sorting through the dead to get an accurate count.

Talbot, Westbrook, and Bell found a hot metal lean-to just before the inevitable rain began to fall. They flipped over packing cases to use as chairs, and Court passed around Romeo y Julieta cigars from a leather cheroot case made of crocodile hide that he had tucked into one of his bush jacket's pockets. The rain pounding against the tin roof made conversation all but impossible, but these men were beyond the need to talk. They each had their own thoughts on the tragedy and felt no need to discuss their grief. The humid air was soon perfumed by the cigars, and the simple act of sharing a companionable silence helped blunt the worst of the horror they'd seen.

A figure came through the curtain of rain falling across the jobsite so quickly that they never saw him coming. It was Goethals, wearing a dark poncho and a wide-brimmed hat on his head. The fury radiating off his face made the stuffy little shelter feel ten degrees hotter.

Westbrook jumped to his feet. "Colonel."

Goethals waved him down. He shook out his wet things and lit a cigarette, blowing the smoke ceilingward, where it mixed with the clouds from the Romeo y Julietas. He was too agitated to sit, and there was little room to pace, so he stood with his hands clasped behind his back, the white cigarette bouncing between his lips as he spoke.

"Damned savages," he spat. "Twenty-seven dead, and they tell me there's going to be more. Ancon Hospital is overwhelmed with wounded. Worse than the day back in '09 when a premature dynamite blast killed twenty-three."

Bell knew there was something troubling him even more than the loss of life, and the next sentence proved him right.

"And this is going to add months to the construction time. That crane's a total loss, so we'll have to make do with the one remaining on that side of the lock. And once word of this gets back to Jamaica and Barbados, we're going to see our recruitment numbers dwindle to nothing. What a disaster." He looked to Bell. "I heard you shot the bastard."

"He bled to death in the lock."

"I guess that's some small comfort," Goethals said. "Okay, Talbot, it looks like you're getting your wish."

"Colonel?"

"I want you to stamp out this nest of vipers and I don't care how you do it."

Normally, there would be much bravado in such a proclamation, but the Canal Administrator delivered it with tired resignation. While he was an officer of the United States Army, he was an engineer first and foremost. Sending troops into battle was not something he was accustomed to and he did not do it lightly.

"How much do you want?"

"Sir?"

"I expect you want to get paid for risking your life. How much?"

Talbot was taken aback. "To be honest, I hadn't put a number together in my head. Let me see . . ."

Goethals said, "The Marines will be here in a month. I'll pay you twenty-five thousand dollars if you get them in the first week and five thousand less every week after that until the Leathernecks arrive. Once they're here, you're out. Fair?"

"Yes. Very, sir."

"There's a problem," Bell said. He was

speaking to George Goethals, but his attention was on Court Talbot. "I don't recall his name, but the man who blew up the crane, the man I hunted down, he's Major Talbot's personal driver."

Talbot's eyes went wide for a split second. Then he looked doubtful. "Rinaldo? I think you are mistaken, Mr. Bell. Not only have I known him for many years, he is my wife's cousin. He's family.

"I have observed an interesting phenomenon with many new arrivals. When a person is in a foreign country for the first time, it is often the case that most of the locals look alike to you. It's only after you've been here for a while that you focus on the things that make people look different from one another rather than those things they all have in common."

"I'm not wrong," Bell said levelly, though he didn't enjoy being told that he simply categorized people by their race. "There are two parts to my profession, Major. One is merely observing people, places, and things, and I am very good at my job."

The two men held each other's gaze, neither backing off their position.

"What's the second part?" Sam Westbrook asked, cutting the tension.

"Fitting all the parts of what I've seen

174

together to discover which one doesn't belong. Ten times in ten, that's the perpetrator I'm looking for."

Over the sound of rain pelting the metal roof came the haunting peals of a church bell. Almost all the West Indian workers were devout Catholics, and the church the company had built for them was putting out the word that death had struck an especially cruel blow to the congregation.

Goethals lit another cigarette. "We can settle this dispute easy enough. Bell, you said the body is in one of the locks?"

"Yes, Colonel. In the far chamber. I chased him across the site and then down into the tunnels below the lock. He almost got away, but I managed two lucky shots just as he climbed back to the surface. He's near one of the circular water vents."

"If this is true, Major, I will have to rethink my offer."

"Colonel Goethals" — Talbot's tone was somber — "if it were true, I'd have to rethink a great many things. I've known Rinaldo since almost the day I arrived in Panama. He introduced me to his family, and that's where I met my Esmeralda. I would literally not have my wife, and children, without him.

"And I assure you, sir, that he doesn't

have a political bone in his body. His brother, on the other hand, is the family firebrand. He is passionate about how the revolution that created Panama was a sham perpetrated by Roosevelt in order to steal land for the canal."

"He's not exactly wrong," Goethals muttered.

The other three were taken aback by such a forthright comment. While it was public knowledge the revolution was mostly for the benefit of United States's effort to build the canal, it just wasn't mentioned in polite society.

Talbot said, "Raul Morales, the brother, moved to Cartagena about two years ago, but it is possible he came back as an agent of the Colombian government."

"Are you suggesting Colombia is responsible for the insurgency?" Goethals was shaken by the thought.

"No," Talbot said quickly, yet just as quickly amended, "I don't know. On the ship from San Diego, Bell thought there was a behind-the-scenes actor in all of this. While I was thinking European Bolsheviks, maybe Colombia is fighting to win back its lost province of Panama."

"Or I'm right," Bell said, "and that's Rinaldo Morales's body out in the lock chamber, and Major Talbot has been an unwitting conduit into the zone for the Red Vipers."

Like it had been turned off by a spigot, the rain went from roaring downpour to the patter of drops falling off leaves in just a few seconds. It was a little unnerving. By the time the men were halfway to the far lock, the sky had cleared, and the sun beat down once again. Vapor whirled and twisted out of the jungle beyond the cleared jobsite, while rivulets of runoff snaked across the grounds headed for the irrigation ditches. Standing pools of water were breeding grounds for mosquitoes, and every work zone across the isthmus was designed with an eye toward drainage.

The party strode through the open mitered gates and into the lock itself. The scale was overwhelming. A third of the way down its thousand-foot length lay the body of the man Bell had shot. The deluge had washed away the blood that had drained from his corpse and it looked especially pale because of how much of it he'd lost.

They let Talbot take point but stuck close. The Major got down on one knee, heedless of the wet concrete. The Panamanian bomber wore clothing typical of a canal worker. Talbot gently turned the body so

177

they could better see the face. The Major didn't say anything for a second. Bell took note that his bullet had shot through both of the man's cheeks, which would make identification more difficult. He also saw, now that the body had been moved, that another of the rounds had severed the man's left pinkie.

"Well?" Goethals prompted.

"This is Raul Morales, my driver's brother." He stood and then addressed Isaac Bell. "I'm sorry to say, you are wrong. It's an honest mistake. Rinaldo and Raul looked very similar and were only a year apart. Esmeralda's family is going to be disconsolate."

Bell stretched out his hand to shake Talbot's. "I am sorry about the mistaken identity, and I am even more sorry for your loss. No matter what horrible thing this man did, he was still family."

Talbot shook Bell's hand. "Here's some irony for you. Rinaldo is missing his left pinkie, as punishment inflicted by his father — it's a long story, about a disturbed, abusive parent — and now his brother loses the same finger in death."

Bell looked at Talbot critically. He didn't like irony or, in this case, coincidence. "Are you absolutely certain this isn't Rinaldo?"

"The wound to the face makes it a little more difficult, but yes. Besides, you can see for yourself that the hand wound is recent."

"True," Bell said slowly.

Talbot flipped open one of the pouch pockets on his bush jacket and handed an object to Bell. It was a small metal cylinder with a glass end. "Single D cell electric light. Turn it on by twisting the base."

He hefted the ladder lying by the drain opening and slid one end into the tunnel below.

"It's got to be down there."

Bell knew what he meant and turned on the light before descending into the shaft. There was plenty of light below the opening, and while the rainwater had diluted the blood, it still looked pink where it puddled on the bottom of the huge pipe. The severed finger lay about three feet from the opening, roughly the distance Bell expected it would be. He picked it up with a handkerchief from his pocket and examined the stump. The bone showed the expected fracturing from being struck by a bullet.

He climbed back to the surface and once back on top opened the blood-smeared handkerchief to reveal his grisly find. "This is all the proof I need," he announced. "By the way, Court, this is one handy little device. Gives off more light than I expected."

"Sears, Roebuck catalog. Please keep it, I ordered a dozen of them."

Bell thanked him and pocketed the electric torch.

"What does all this mean?" young Sam Westbrook asked. "Was he working for the Colombians or what?"

"This should be a matter for the Canal Authority," Bell said, looking at Goethals, "but with your permission . . ."

He gestured to the body, and the Administrator nodded his approval.

Bell searched the corpse with professional adroitness, not a hiding place overlooked or a motion wasted. The man had nothing on him but some matches in a plain paperboard box and a knife fashioned into a shiv from some unidentifiable piece of metal. The knife had been used to cut an appropriate length of fuse, the matches had been to light it. There were no labels in his clothes and nothing hidden in his boots. Bell took a second to tuck the handkerchief into the dead man's breast pocket.

He got to his feet and said, "It was too much to hope for that he had letters in his pocket from the President of Colombia detailing the plot. Sam asks a good question, Colonel. What will happen if Raul Morales was working with Colombian agents?"

"That's for Washington to decide. They will need something more definitive than our speculation to even inquire diplomatically at this point, but I can see this escalating very quickly." He lit another in his unending chain of cigarettes. "You gentlemen must surely be aware that there is a great deal of sentiment around the world that the United States was in the wrong when it came to the Panamanian revolution. It's said we acted as bullies, and that on the heels of taking Cuba and the Philippines from Spain our colonial aspirations are growing too dangerous."

Bell said, "Ironic, coming from European powers that have spread their tentacles into every corner of the globe and exploited lands and peoples for generations and enriched themselves endlessly from it, but apparently hypocrisy doesn't reflect in the mirror."

"True," Goethals said. "What I am saying is, we've spent half a billion dollars, with a capital *B,* down here and lost better than four thousand men's lives. I don't think we're going to meekly turn over our marvelous accomplishment. I also know there will be a diplomatic firestorm and quite possibly military repercussions if we have to fight the Colombians if it turns out they are behind the Red Vipers."

"We'd risk war," Westbrook said.

"For this?" Goethals spread his arms to encompass the enormous structure in which they stood. "With any and all comers. Mr. Bell, I am very much interested in your continued presence here in the zone, if you are willing to lend a hand. We need answers, and I believe you are the man best qualified to find them."

"Of course, Colonel, I am at your disposal. I already have a first question that demands an answer. Where are the rest of the dynamite crates? That explosion was big, to be sure, and effective, but it wasn't a full ton of explosives." Bell then addressed Westbrook and Talbot. "I believe there was a third option I didn't consider back in the bunker and that's they cached some of the dynamite here and took some of it with them."

"What do we do?"

"We need to search this site from top to bottom, in the unlikely event they left it behind."

"Why do you say 'unlikely'?" Goethals asked.

"No point in splitting your loot if you're

going to leave it all onsite. It doubles the chances of it being discovered."

"Yet halves the chance of losing it all if it were," Talbot pointed out.

Bell shook his head and said to Westbrook, "A ton of dynamite goes missing. What would happen if you found a thousand pounds of unauthorized dynamite in the back of a truck?"

"We'd run an audit of our supply, discover the theft, and then search every nook and cranny until we found the other thousand pounds. If it was here, we'd find it."

Court Talbot could find no fault in the logic. "You are rather good at this, Bell. Go on."

"Point two is that they have already struck here. If I were trying to sow unrest, I would spread my swath of destruction far and wide. That's why I say it is unlikely they left the remainder of the dynamite behind. They took it with them and will use it to strike elsewhere."

"Where?" Goethals asked.

"I don't know, but we need to find out before they attack again."

13

Goethals remained at Pedro Miguel for another hour, then had to return to Ancon on his private train, nicknamed the Yellow Peril because of the carriage's yellow roof and because he used it for surprise inspections up and down the canal. Court Talbot returned with him, while Bell remained at Pedro Miguel to personally oversee the search for the missing explosives. Sam Westbrook, with nothing more exciting planned for his day off than to hang out at the YMCA, offered to help.

Once workers understood what was at stake with the search, there was no loss of volunteers. Bell gave the hundred or so Americans and Caribbean islanders strict instructions not to touch the crates if they found them and to come find him immediately. Men combed every square inch of the sprawling construction site, inspecting all the trucks and trains, searching every foot of tunnel under the two massive lock chambers, and rooting through every warehouse, shed, lean-to, and tent. They sifted through mountains of coal waiting to be used in the locomotives, and a pair of equipment operators checked the crates in the unlikely chance they were hidden high atop the surviving gantry cranes that were the men's kingdom. Bell detailed other men to search a fifty-foot swath of jungle near the explosives bunker in case the missing dynamite had been hidden there.

As Bell had suspected, they found nothing. He did get a consensus from having conversations with men knowledgeable on the subject and who'd witnessed the blast that it had been produced by about a thousand pounds of explosives, and possibly more, but certainly not less. Again, this fit with Bell's own hunch that the perpetrators made off with additional crates of dynamite after loading the truck.

The sun was about a half hour from setting, and the shadows were growing long and hard-edged. Sam Westbrook found Bell standing at the base of the ruined crane. He was tracing the curve of bent and torn steel struts as if the ruined metal could give him some clue. Sam handed over a cooled bottle of beer.

Bell thanked him, and his brows shot up when he realized the bottle was chilled. He didn't realize how thirsty he was until the mild beer hit his lips. The bottle remained upright until the last of it was drained, Bell letting out a satisfied sigh.

"You might have just saved my life."

"If you want to see the Culebra Cut, work crews are getting ready to head in to fix whatever got broken today and replace bits on the big rock drills and the like. This means it's a little quieter, and there's no restrictions on movement because the blasting is suspended for a while. It's a great time to see the cut for yourself."

"Anything to distract me from this mess. Let's go."

Westbrook took one of the trucks from the motor pool, and they drove northeast on the road that paralleled the double tracks of the Panama Canal Railway. At another station and company town like the one at the Pedro Miguel Locks, Westbrook parked, and they walked to the edge of a narrow valley that stretched for miles in either direction.

On each side of the valley, the land had been contoured into steps like those in the photographs of Asian rice paddies Bell had seen, but these tiers were enormous. On many, two sets of train tracks had been laid. The upper steps were devoid of any activity, while toward the valley floor, as they watched, a train loaded with ore pulled away while another slid into its place. Each train included twenty-one open-sided flatbed cars hauled by a single locomotive.

Westbrook said, "When the trains reach their destination, a three-ton plow blade is placed at the back of the last car. It's attached to a winch between the first car and the locomotive. Power from the locomotive drives the winch and drags the plow over all the cars, scraping the dirt off to one side. That way, we can unload an entire train in about ten minutes."

What fed the rock and earth onto the flatbed cars were machines that looked like they'd sprung from the era of iron dinosaurs. These were the ninety-five-ton Bucyrus steam shovels. They were longer than the locomotives and belched black smoke from a single stack in the middle of their broad backs. Men fed coal into the boiler at the rear of the machine, which provided the motivating power, while at the front was a forty-foot riveted boom that supported a mechanical dipping arm capped by a shovel bucket that looked to be the size of a bedroom.

Bell watched, rapt, as the operator swung the boom to the side and dropped the dipper so that the bucket faced the mountain of dirt ahead of the machine. The dipper then slid forward and upward, the bucket tearing a great gash in the ground. Even as the operator raised the bucket up, he was swinging the boom to the other side so that the bucket was in position to dump its contents onto a train without wasting a single second. With the throw of a lever in the cab, the bottom of the bucket fell open and the mass of rock and dirt tumbled onto the flatbed. And then the boom was in motion again to let the bucket rip out another eight-ton chunk of the Culebra Cut.

"And how long have you been widening this valley?"

Westbrook shook his head as if disappointed. "That's a common question from first-time visitors. And when I tell them the answer, they're even more impressed."

"Okaaay," Bell said, drawing out the word a bit.

"There was no valley, Mr. Bell. We dug it all. Eight miles long, fifteen hundred feet wide in places, five hundred feet deep in other places. When we finish, we'll have pulled a hundred million cubic yards of rock out of the cut."

Bell looked back with even deeper appreciation at what he was seeing and the enormity and audacity of the herculean undertaking. Everywhere he gazed he saw the monstrous excavators swinging their booms back and forth, filling train after train, while ahead of them teams of men worked around mobile drilling vehicles bigger than any truck he'd ever seen. They drilled close-knit clusters of holes that would be packed with dynamite. Long, rolling detonations would echo across the artificial canyon as the blasts pulverized rock into manageable chunks for the steam shovels. There was even room for laborers by the thousands, with picks and shovels and hand drills, all trying to feed the insatiable appetite of the excavators.

"At the height of digging," Westbrook added, "we had more than one hundred steam shovels, four thousand ore cars, a hundred and thirty miles of track, which could be shifted as the work progressed, and more than nine thousand men. With the spoil, we built the Gatun Dam, the longest in the world, plus a three-mile breakwater at the Pacific terminus of the canal, and thereby reclaimed five hundred acres of the Pacific that will be a new town and military fort. And there is still so much overburden that we have a bunch of dumpsites in the jungle."

"I had no idea," was all Bell could say.

Westbrook smiled knowingly. "No one really does."

Bell pointed down the cut to where the wall of the valley bulged. "Why have you left that big pile of rubble on the valley floor?"

Now the young engineer grimaced. "That's a landslide. One of many we've encountered. The biggest is at Cucaracha and is about two million cubic yards' worth of headache. Eventually, we're going to have to flood the canal and clear it by dredge."

"What causes the slides?"

"Rain is a big factor, but really it's just that the weight of the material we've removed kept the earth stable. When we dig it out, the ground needs to find its equilibrium again. The geologists say that this will be a problem for a hundred years or more, and dredging will be a constant part of the canal's maintenance.

"But to get back to your original question, we've been digging here pretty much nonstop since crews first arrived in Panama in 1904."

"Truly amazing," Bell said.

"That's the thing about the canal. Its three

principal components — the locks, the Gatun Dam to create a navigable lake, and the Culebra Cut — are each in and of themselves the largest and most daunting engineering challenges ever undertaken. Here we managed to undertake all three simultaneously in hundred-degree heat, ninety percent humidity, and under the constant threat of tropical disease."

"I had some thoughts about the changes coming to America's West Coast as a result of the canal's completion without really thinking through what the canal means for the rest of the country and the world. I believe we are at the dawn of the American Century, where we take our place as a world power."

"There's a lot of talk like that down here," Westbrook agreed. "The great Ferdinand de Lesseps, the architect of the Suez Canal, came here and failed miserably, practically bankrupting his nation and losing twenty thousand men in the process. But we're about to finish it, Mr. Bell. Little upstart America is going to do what the mighty French could not. We see it as a sort of baton pass, like in a relay race. We're all mighty proud of what we've done, which makes the likes of the Red Vipers doubly vicious. They're killing our men while also trying to kill our dream."

"Today was a big escalation on their part."

"I'm not sure what that means."

"It doesn't fit the pattern. They've been small-scale, so far, thievery and sabotage, with just some incidental, rather than deliberate, injuries. Then came the attack in California, and now the bombing. Outright murder. What changed here in Panama that led them to such an attack? Their message is out there and spreading. They are garnering allies among the local population, so things are working in their favor for the time being. And time is something they have on their side. Construction will likely carry on for another year, meaning there's plenty of opportunity to press their case."

"I hadn't thought about that."

Bell shrugged. "And maybe this fits their timetable exactly and I'm talking out of my hat."

"Let's head back. I can drop you at the Tivoli."

"I'm actually staying at the Central."

"Better choice," Sam told him. "Tivoli tends to be temporary workers and Washington types, skulking around. There's usually some interesting characters at the Central."

14

Fresh from a shower and wearing a cream linen suit with a dark tie and proper shoes rather than his rain boots, Bell slipped into the Central Hotel's dining room with Marion on his arm. She wore a yellow dress and the smile of a woman who'd just won an argument. Bell had failed to convince her to return to home in light of the bombing.

Bell scanned the space on the off chance he'd recognize someone and immediately spotted Court Talbot at a table with a handful of people. A few of the other tables in the brightly lit room were occupied, but the level of conversation was muted. People were still reeling from the news about the bombing. Ceiling fans stirred the warm smoky air.

Talbot waved Bell to his table. "Ah, the Bells. Join us, please."

"No. We haven't eaten yet and all of you have."

193

"It doesn't matter. Sit." He summoned a waiter. "Bring two bowls of sancocho for my friends." He pulled out a chair for Marion as he explained. "Sancocho is the national dish. It's a kind of chicken soup with corn, yams, and fresh cilantro. It's also good in the morning if you are hungover. What are you drinking?"

"What do you recommend?"

Talbot called to the retreating waiter, "Juan, two rum and lime sodas, *por favor.*"

"*Sí,* Señor Talbot."

"I'm here most Friday nights just to meet new people passing through the city," the former Army Major explained. "Let me introduce you around. That lovely woman seated next to the luckiest man in the world is Mrs. Juliet Webb. Her husband is Whittier. Next to him is Felix Ramirez, and on the other side is Herr Ernst Leibinger-Holte of Zurich. And the last gentleman is Guillermo Acosta from Argentina." Rather than reach awkwardly across the table to shake hands, Bell nodded to each person in turn. "It's too bad you missed the famed aviator Robert Fowler, Isaac. He has just left Panama. Anyway, my friends, this is Isaac Bell, of the Van Dorn Detective Agency, and his charming wife, Marion. In case any of you don't know, Isaac is the man who killed the fiend responsible for today's tragedy."

Bell noted that Talbot did not mention his tenuous connection to the bomber.

"Bravo, Mr. Bell," Juliet said. She was raven-haired and maybe thirty years old, dressed in stylish clothes that gave no concession to the rain or mud. Her white skirt was long but amazingly unsullied. Her husband was a few years younger with a look Bell knew well. Whit Webb was the son of privilege. It was in the indolent way he held his mouth, to the hooded eyes, to the way he dismissed Bell as being nothing more than a tradesman.

Then he studied the man a little closer and realized he was a plaything for his wife. Bell noted he wore no class ring, so wherever he was schooled wasn't worth bragging about. He was drinking a dark wine with fish, and his shoes, though a little muddy, lacked the underlying shine a gentleman would expect no matter what the circumstances. She was obviously well-off. Her diamond necklace alone cost as much as a Model T. But it was definitely her money, not his, and that would certainly be the dynamic of their relationship.

"You did Panama a service today, señor." Felix Ramirez was as sleek as a cat, with slicked-back black hair and a thin mustache.

His eyes flashed with both intelligence and cunning and were crinkled at the corners, which made him look over forty but not yet fifty. He was dressed well, though Bell could see where a button had been poorly resewn onto his shirt, and there was fraying around one jacket pocket. He wasn't as successful as he wanted people to think he was. He smoked a cigar with his left hand while his right played absently with a gambling token with the dexterity of a street magician.

"A harrowing thing, I should imagine," said the Swiss gentleman, Leibinger-Holte.

He sported a dark worsted suit that had wilted in the tropical heat, and his shirt was stained around the collar by the day's sweat. He wore a severe expression, yet behind his wire-rimmed glasses his blue eyes were friendly. Bell sensed a conflict between who he presented himself as and who he really was. He was seated so there was no way to determine his height, but he had a slight build, with long, tapering fingers, and a network of veins on the back of each hand.

Bell guessed his age as fifty.

"Sorry I'm late, what?" a man said, coming up behind Bell. His accent was pure Eton and Oxford, with just enough of a country undertone to make one think of England's charming villages and impart the impression his family likely had several on its estate.

"Tats," Court Talbot said, smiling at the new arrival. "Finally back from the Colon? I mean from Colón. Too much Spanish in my English?"

Bell saw by the flush on Juliet Webb's cheeks and the way she'd parted and moistened her lips that it meant the unseen man behind him was as handsome as his voice was cultured.

"Mr. and Mrs. Whittier Webb and Mr. and Mrs. Isaac Bell, may I present Lord Benedict Hamilton Macalister. Tats, you already know Felix and Ernst."

"I do. Gentlemen, always a pleasure." He grabbed a chair from a nearby table and wedged himself in with the group. "To have not one but two beautiful women gracing our presence gives some amount of pleasure on an otherwise dreadful day."

"Why do they call you Tats?" Juliet Webb asked.

The Englishman gave a self-deprecating little chuckle that was as practiced as his story. "I made an unfortunate wager that I could beat Christ's College's fastest rower in the Wingfield Sculls race on the Thames. It turned out that I could not beat him, and, as a result, his winning time was tattooed in such a place that I preferred not to sit for a few days afterward. There were no others at Ox with such a decoration and so I was given my nickname."

His tale got a round of laughter from the people at the table and a fresh flush on Juliet Webb's face.

Macalister was in his mid-thirties but had the self-possession of a much older person, one who was making his way through life and finding success and joy at every turn. His hair was sandy blond and cut longer than fashionable so that a cowlick was always threatening to cover his long-lashed eyes. He was slender without being gaunt, and his white suit was impeccably tailored. Marion would have cast him in one of her movies the moment she laid eyes on him.

He was seated next to Bell, so they shook hands.

"Nice to meet you, Mr. Bell." Macalister indicated to the waiter that he wanted a rum and lime soda. "What brings you to Panama?"

Court Talbot answered before Bell could. "He happened to be with me and Senator Densmore of California when we were attacked by Viboras Rojas. Like today's terrible event, Mr. Bell was there to save the day, as it were. So, it comes as little surprise

198

he's an investigator for the Van Dorn Agency."

"Ooh," cried Juliet, her eyes shining. "That must be an exciting job."

Bell made a dismissive gesture. "Not as much as you would think. A lot of it is just waiting and watching for your target to do something stupid so you can prove your case."

"Ha," Talbot said, braying. "I've known you a week, and you've thwarted an assassination attempt and brought a mad bomber to heel."

Bell laughed. "Let's just say this hasn't been a typical week. What about you, Lord Macalister? Why are you here?"

He shot Talbot a scowl. "I'm afraid Lord Macalister is my father and eventually to be my eldest brother. Court continues to believe he has a sense of humor because we're all too kind to tell him otherwise. As I will not be a lord, and since our family had to give up their serfs eons ago, and thus our unlimited wealth, I must make my way in this world in any manner I can. There are always opportunities at the beginning of any great enterprise, and currently there is none greater than the canal."

Bell noted that Macalister's response wasn't really an answer. He asked the same of the Argentine, Acosta.

Felix Ramirez answered instead. "I am sorry, Mr. Bell. Señor Acosta speaks very little English. He is a civil engineer here to learn dam-building techniques to take back to his native country. They have tremendous hydroelectric potential in the highlands."

"Ahh."

Macalister addressed Court Talbot. "Did the old man give you the okay?"

"He did right after they hit the crane at Pedro Miguel."

"Awful business, that," the Englishman said. "More than two dozen dead, and for what? Do they really think at this late stage that you Yanks are going to stop work, pull up stakes, and bugger off back to America?"

"We would never," Juliet said with patriotic fervor. "Right, Whit?"

"Absolutely." As if he would ever disagree with his wife. "The more someone pushes us, the harder we push back."

"We are a proud people and have not had a hand in our destiny for a long time." This from Felix Ramirez.

"Surely you do not agree with these" — the businessman from Switzerland, Leibinger-Holte, struggled to find the right word — "monsters?"

"No, of course not," Ramirez said quickly.

"But there are those who believe that Panama should be for Panamanians."

"Was that the belief before there was a canal?" Marion asked.

While it could have been a provocative question, Ramirez was too smooth to rise to the bait. "It was a much quieter aspiration back then, Mrs. Bell. However, the belief that we are different than those living on the other side of the Darién Gap is as old as the country itself."

A waiter arrived with more drinks and the bowls of stew for Marion and Bell.

Tats then asked Talbot, "How will you proceed from here?"

The veteran soldier said nothing for the few seconds it took for the waiter to finish his delivery and retreat. "Can't be too careful."

Felix laughed. "You think the waiter could be an agent for Viboras Rojas?"

Talbot said, "I actually think anyone can be. They managed to pull off a sophisticated attack here and in California. That means they have connections inside and outside the zone. And Tats, as to my plans, surely you know I can't discuss them with anyone outside my squad."

Bell and Court Talbot exchanged a brief look. They hadn't forgotten that the Red

Vipers had possessed advanced knowledge of the meeting in San Diego. The leak had to have come from here rather than Senator Densmore's office. That meant one of his troopers was talking to someone he shouldn't.

Bell believed there was a very real possibility that Talbot's driver, Rinaldo, had inadvertently passed information to his brother, not knowing he was Viboras Rojas.

Unfortunately, Talbot had given Rinaldo permission to travel north to break the news of Raul's death to his parents before Bell could stop him. It would be telling if Rinaldo returned or if he ran. Even if he did come back to the city, a likely sign of innocence, Bell had every intention of interrogating him.

"Good luck to you, Herr Talbot." Ernst Leibinger-Holte raised his glass. "To a successful hunt."

"Hear! Hear!" the others echoed.

Bell asked the Swiss about his interest in Panama.

"Business, Herr Bell. I represent a firm that specializes in precision gauges and electric control systems. We had hoped to sell some of our wares to the Canal Authority, but they are using American-made products almost exclusively. I am now working with representatives from the national railroad. There is interest in what we manufacture."

"And you, Mr. Webb?" Tats Macalister asked. "Surely you didn't take your lovely wife on such a tedious business trip?"

The man looked sheepish because that's exactly what had happened. "Jules's father's company made all the glass insulators for the power lines coming from the hydro works at Gatun. There was a problem with a few batches, and they sent me down to sort it all out. Jules isn't the sort of woman to say no to an adventure and decided to come along."

"Good for you, Juliet," Marion said. "It's the same for me. Isaac didn't want me along because he thinks there's some danger, and I reminded him of the danger he'd be in if he didn't change his mind."

The table laughed at Bell's expense, not knowing the tale wasn't exactly true.

Leibinger-Holte asked Whit, "Herr Webb, have you solved your insulator problem?"

"Days ago," Juliet answered for her husband. "My clever boy. He noticed the trains down here rattle far more than the ones back home. There wasn't enough cushioning material in our packing crates to handle the extra shaking, and a lot of the insulators chipped and cracked."

"Ach, and you now return to America?"

"Yes," Juliet said, allowing defeat to creep into her voice, "but this has been ever so much fun, and I really don't want to go back home."

It was the way she said that last line that made Bell realize that what she really wanted was to not have the kind of life a wealthy father had mapped out for her. That's why she was with her husband. Despite the fancy-sounding name, Whittier wasn't someone her family would have chosen. He was an act of defiance just like her coming to Panama was. Her father obviously indulged her — otherwise, she wouldn't be here — but that must be coming to an end.

The old man doubtlessly wanted an heir for his insulator company sooner rather than later.

Whittier Webb added, "Unfortunately, there are no suitable boats back to the States from Colón. Plenty of ships heading to Barbados and Jamaica to bring workers back to their home islands at the end of their contracts, but they just won't do. We're stuck here until a ship from the North Star Line arrives."

Leibinger-Holte said, "For myself, I will

take the first ship sailing away and not remain in Panama one day longer than necessary. The rain is miserable and the heat intolerable, and I have seen spiders as large as a dinner plates." He shuddered theatrically.

"Not to mention the snakes," Felix Ramirez added.

Court Talbot leaned forward, to make sure everyone was listening, and said, "A few years ago, I was on the Chagres River as it was subsiding following a late-summer flood. We were in a dugout canoe that wasn't very stable and we wanted to stay close to the riverbank, where the current was more stable. The problem was the floodwaters had driven all the snakes in the area into the trees. Every tree was wreathed in them, enormous coils of them, thousands upon thousands, hanging over our heads as we veered toward shore.

"Ones that lost their perches fell into the water and either swam to another tree or drowned. For a time, it looked like it was actually raining snakes, so many of them fell from the branches. Some that dropped close enough tried to slither into our dugout. We had to beat them back with our paddles. One bushmaster viper — they're poisonous, mind you — had to have been twelve feet long and as big around as my arm. I'd never seen a more disturbing sight in my life."

This time, everyone shuddered involuntarily with revulsion.

Juliet turned to her husband. "I take back my earlier reluctance to leave. I have no desire to see a snake storm. Let's go home."

The others at the table started discussing the hardships of living in Panama and didn't hear her say to Whit, "This means we'll never solve the mystery of the humming clouds either."

Only Bell seemed to have heard her statement. "Excuse me, Mrs. Webb, but what are humming clouds?"

"Oh, it's something our guide to old Panama City told us about. Jorge is his name. The hotel arranged it for us. He's a retired teacher. He says it's a phenomenon that some villagers on the other coast have discovered. They say that at night they can hear clouds humming in the sky. He'd never heard of such a thing before."

Court Talbot had caught her story and said, "I bet it's connected to the filling of the Gatun reservoir. I've spoken with geologists who say the weight of that much water will actually deform the land underneath it. I imagine submerged pockets of swamp gas being expelled under pressure are the cause of the humming."

"That makes sense," Whit said, nodding to his wife for her agreement.

"I suppose," she said, slowly warming to the idea. "Truth is, I was hoping for a less mundane answer. It sounds so fantastic, you know?"

Bell said, "That's why you thought being a detective is interesting. You have a strong imagination and you want to believe there is something fascinating amid the everyday."

"I can't believe none of you are talking about the other big story of the day," Tats said.

"What other story?" Court asked him.

"It will doubtlessly be out in tomorrow's paper. Your former President Roosevelt is planning on stopping in Panama on his way to South America to see the canal's progress for himself."

Marion had been with Isaac long enough to never react to news that had even an indirect connection to a case he was working, so she didn't move even a muscle when the very reason he was on this case was blown wide open in public.

Outwardly, Bell also remained unmoved by the bombshell revelation even as, inside, he was seething with rage over the stupidity of politicians who didn't understand that secrecy was their first line of defense against assassination plots, and old TR should know more than most since he'd been the victim of one himself.

They managed to stay for one more drink before Bell and his wife excused themselves and returned to their room upstairs. It took a good bit of his will not to slam the door, the rest not to raise his voice.

"I can't believe he'd do something so reckless," Bell said. "The Republican Party hired Van Dorn to sit in on Senator Densmore's Panama briefing to report back to them my thoughts on the situation down here on the chance — chance, mind you — that Roosevelt would want to see the canal on his way to Brazil. Now the bloody fool has announced to the world and Viboras Rojas that he's coming."

"To be fair, Isaac, Teddy doesn't know the Republicans want him to run for President again under their banner. So he knew nothing of your investigation."

"He has to be aware there's an insurgency. The attack on Densmore made headlines across the country. Van Dorn has probably spoken with him as well." Bell took a breath. "Come to think of it, knowing there's an additional element of danger is likely why he's coming. The man's never backed away from a challenge in his life."

Marion could see her husband was regaining his composure and said, "As I'm sure you remember, he gave a ninety-minute speech after being shot two years ago."

"He was campaigning for President then and had bodyguards who foiled the assassin's aim. As an ex-President, he no longer has protection, and now there's a whole guerrilla army potentially gunning for him."

"Oh, Isaac, what are you going to do?"

"Ask again that you leave for the States, for starters."

"And after that doesn't work?"

He grinned wryly, knowing she wasn't about to budge. "Cable Joseph in the morning for instructions but with the understanding that I'm staying on here in Panama and continuing to work the case."

"What is the plan now, exactly?"

"Stop the Red Vipers from further damaging and delaying the canal, and make sure President Roosevelt isn't walking into an ambush."

"How?"

"Not sure yet, but I think one or more of our dinner companions isn't who they say they are."

While Marion was used to such unexpected proclamations, this time she was incredulous. "I didn't get that sense at all. I really like Juliet."

"I actually think she's on the up-and-up, and her husband and Court Talbot of course. It's the other three. Because the Canal Zone is so self-contained, there are precious few prospects here for a career opportunist like Tats Macalister. The Swiss guy, Leibinger-Holte, should have known before leaving Europe that an American canal-building effort would use mostly American equipment, and Felix Ramirez has con man written all over him."

"Sure you're not being a little paranoid?" she teased.

"Trust me, this case is going to require a lot of paranoid."

15

By the owner's standards, the house south of Panama City overlooking the beach from a low hill was a hovel, but by the standards of the country it was one of the finest residences in the nation. It was built of whitewashed limestone blocks with a great many windows so the sea breezes could cool the interior. The roof was red tile and had a clerestory for additional ventilation. There were a half dozen bedrooms and appropriate areas for entertaining. Electricity and hot water were provided by a separate steam-powered generator in an outbuilding far enough from the main hacienda that it couldn't be heard.

By comparison, the Dreissen family's ancestral home, Schloss Werdener, outside Essen in Germany's Ruhr Valley, was a century-old, four-story manor house with eighty rooms sitting on over a hundred hectares of fields and forestland.

The grounds here were lush and meticulously groomed. The lawn sparkled like a sheet of emeralds. Ringing the leeward side of the property was one of the best natural defenses in the world. The manchineel tree, with its innocent-looking green fruits, was a native of Central America and the Caribbean islands. Stands of them guarded the back edges of the lawn and ran along the crushed-coral driveway coming from the closest road. The tree produced so much toxin in its leaves, fruit, and bark that to stand under one in a rainstorm guaranteed burned and blistered skin. Contact between the eye and the tree's milky sap will produce unendurable pain, and eating the fruit will cause a half day's worth of intestinal misery and agony.

The windward side of the property was open to the beach and the Pacific Ocean beyond.

The visitor arrived a few minutes early in a private car he'd rented for the day. He was one of the men who'd had drinks with Bell at the Central the previous evening. An attendant in white livery opened the hacienda's door as he climbed the three steps up from the drive.

"Guten Morgen, mein Herr," the butler said in German. A little deeper into the house

lurked Heinz Kohl. Kohl recognized the visitor and drifted back into the shadows without needing to conduct a search.

"Morgen," the guest replied and handed over his hat as well as a calling card. Both items were placed on a table just inside the entrance.

"The master is expecting you." The butler turned and led the way across the tile floor and out onto a back terrace with a view of the sea framed by swaying palms. The surf was gentle, and the sound it produced hypnotic.

A table had been set as a buffet, with chilled juices in dew-kissed glass carafes, piles of fruits of every hue and shape, as well as baked delicacies that glimmered with sugar and spices. There were silver salvers with sausages and Bavarian ham, in addition to bowls of diced and seasoned potatoes and traditional goetta.

Otto Dreissen sat at separate table with a bone china coffee cup and a slender ledger and his fountain pen poised to make a notation. He and his two brothers had inherited a vast enterprise upon the death of their father, himself an only child who'd inherited only a modest industrial empire from his. It was implied that the three brothers would turn Essenwerks into a colossus.

He was in his forties but kept himself in shape, so there was no paunch at his waist-line or jowls under his chin like so many of his fellow countrymen his age. He was hawk-nosed yet handsome, with his finest feature being his eyes. They were sharp gray and could hold sway with a mere glance.

"*Guten Morgen,* Herr Dreissen," the visitor greeted as he stepped past the butler and onto the terrace. A canvas awning dyed tropical colors kept the veranda shaded from the sun and cool.

"*Guten Morgen, mein Freund,*" the industrialist said and stood to shake the newcomer's hand.

The conversation continued in their native German, though both men were fluent in several languages as demanded by the international nature of their professions.

"You've heard?" The visitor sat opposite his host and accepted coffee from a maid. "Goethals isn't waiting for the Marines to go after Viboras Rojas."

"Yes, I did. Certainly took some convincing," Dreissen replied. "A lot of men died at Pedro Miguel. Will the attacks end?"

"Hard to say. The loss of life is tragic, but that isn't really our concern."

"I suppose you're right. And the crane's destruction buys additional time, should we

214

need it."

"And we likely will. A complication has arisen in the person of Theodore Roosevelt, the former President of the United States. He is paying the Canal Zone another visit in just a few days."

Dreissen went very still, his gray eyes clouding, as his formidable intellect plotted out move and counter-move in a game he played in his mind, looking at all combinations and permutations, attacks and defenses. He carefully wiped his mouth.

"I am going to take you into my confidence and reveal a secret few outside Berlin know."

Dreissen's guest instinctively leaned in as if there were listeners hiding in the hydrangeas.

"What do you know of the American electoral system?"

The question wasn't expected, and the man muttered for a moment before calling up the information. "They hold elections every four years for their President, and I think every two or six for their Congress. There's something about a 'college' that never made any sense to me."

"For the purposes of our discussion, the 'electoral college' is irrelevant. The other point that need be brought up is that they have a two-party system. The Democrats and the Republicans. Each has a distinct way of seeing their country and different paths for taking it forward."

"I have heard of the parties."

"The last election was different. Theodore Roosevelt challenged the incumbent, President Taft, at their party's convention for a chance to retake the White House for an unprecedented third term. The party bosses refused and renominated Taft to run against the Democrat challenger, Woodrow Wilson."

"Who defeated Taft and is now the President."

"Correct. Here's the interesting thing. There is nothing in the American constitution that forbids a third presidential term, just tradition. Instead of tucking tail, Roosevelt formed a third party, the Bull Moose, and ran for office once again. Roosevelt and Taft, men with similar agendas, managed to garner more ballots together than Wilson did by himself. The electoral college was a landslide for Wilson, and while he technically won the popular vote against his rivals individually, he didn't if their numbers were combined."

"An interesting lesson in American civics, but what does that have to do with us now?"

"After their loss, the Republicans knew

they made a terrible mistake not giving Roosevelt the nomination. He remains wildly popular in America, and his diverting more than half of traditional Republican voters away from the party's nominee sank their chances to remain in power.

"There will be another national election in 1916, and the Republicans are desperate to regain the White House."

"You believe they'll ask Roosevelt?"

"At this point, I do. Things may change between now and then, yet he is who they would most likely want to run. His charisma and popularity would surely lead to Wilson being a single-term President."

Dreissen paused to light a cigarette from a silver case.

His guest said, "I still don't understand the relevance of this to our current mission."

"Because I haven't yet brought you into my confidence. You know, I have an older brother in New York who oversees Essenwerks's business in the United States. Like me, he also has contacts high up in our government and does occasional favors for them. Like what I am doing here with the canal." There was no need to mention the Argentine angle — the guest had no need to know. "Last year my brother was asked to help on a secret project, one that would destroy relations with the United States if it ever came to light."

"Go on," the guest said eagerly.

Dreissen would have never divulged what he was about to say if he didn't think Berlin would authorize another mission that would by necessity involve his visitor at the very highest levels.

"The Kaiser and his Ministers believed that even with three men in the race for President, Roosevelt would win, and that he would continue raising America's profile among the nations of the world. They already have the world's largest economy but lack the diplomatic clout to assert their dominance. Our leaders speculated that the United States would take a world leadership role and eclipse Great Britain and Germany if he was returned to the White House for a third term."

"What did they do?"

"They sent a doctor well versed in suggestive hypnotism and pharmacology from Germany to New York. My brother, who put him up, used his contacts to find a suitable candidate, someone weak-willed and easily manipulated. The man they found was Bavarian by birth and had once been a saloonkeeper in the city before selling his property and immersing himself in Christian fundamentalism, which has grown popular in America. He'd become a traveling preacher, who'd often wander at night, muttering to himself. He happened to be in New York City at the time and was taken to a secure facility outside the city on September fifth, roughly a month after Roosevelt began his campaign.

"The man's name was John Flammang Schrank," Dreissen continued. "Over the course of the next two weeks, the doctor kept him in a near-constant state of hypnosis using multiple techniques including drugs. They shaped an already disturbed man by feeding him new delusions to occupy his mind. While the drugs were doing that, the doctor was making him forget he was under any kind of care.

"By the time they were done, Schrank believed that Roosevelt was trying to establish a monarchy in America by running for a third time. The doctor also convinced Schrank that Roosevelt was responsible for William McKinley's assassination in 1901, which resulted in Roosevelt becoming President in the first place."

Dreissen's guest knew enough about recent history to realize where the story was heading and couldn't believe his nation had a hand in it.

"They stayed with Schrank as he stalked the President while he was on the campaign trail. They monitored his mental state and fed him more drugs and more sessions under hypnosis if he showed signs of wavering. My brother told me that it really wasn't necessary. By this point, Schrank was delusional and believed himself on a sacred mission to protect the United States from what he called a 'third termer' and to avenge the spirit of President McKinley."

"Schrank caught up to Roosevelt in the city of Milwaukee, if I remember right."

"Yes. In the state of Wisconsin, in what they call the Midwest. As you know the assassination attempt failed. The bullet hit Roosevelt in the chest but had to pass through his fifty-page speech and eyeglasses case first. It punctured his muscles yet not his chest cavity. Schrank never got off a second shot because Roosevelt's security detail was so quick. Roosevelt famously went on with the speech, and later doctors determined that it was safer to leave the bullet lodged in his chest than remove it."

"What happened to Schrank?"

"He was declared insane following a series of hearings and sessions with a lunacy commission. He was committed to an insane asylum, probably for life."

"Mein Gott." The guest was taken aback by the casual cruelty of using an already unbalanced man and warping him into an assassin and then leaving him abandoned in an asylum.

Dreissen mistook his expression for one of admiration. "The best part is, even if Schrank somehow recalls the sessions with our doctor, no one will believe him. They will assume it's just a new delusion that further proves his original diagnosis. Our doctor was on his way back to Germany days after the shooting, and Schrank never knew he'd been held in the basement of my brother's country house."

When his guest didn't speak, Dreissen deduced the truth and said, "For the greater glory of *das Vaterland,* it is nothing to us to sacrifice the freedom of a simpleton. When the war with France finally comes, Germans must be willing to sacrifice all, even their lives, to ensure our nation's future. Don't be so squeamish. Now, let's get breakfast, and I'll explain what I think should happen."

The men rose and loaded plates at the buffet. There was enough food to feed a dozen, but it had been laid out for just the two of them. Neither paid the monumental waste the least notice.

"Nothing has changed since that last assassination attempt. Roosevelt remains wildly popular, and if he is the Republican nominee, he will certainly win the Presidency once again, something no one in Berlin wants to see. He's vulnerable here. Viboras Rojas have already demonstrated they're willing to go after American politicians, so it makes perfect sense they will try here."

"Why is he coming, then?"

"Ego, my friend. He thinks he is bulletproof, for one. More important than that, I think he wants to see his canal. I have no doubt that he will insist on ascending the Gatun Locks and cruising on Lake Gatun, now that it is high enough to float in a shallow-draft boat. He can't resist. This is his crowning achievement, more than the trophy hunting or charging up San Juan Hill in Cuba. The Panama Canal is the most transformative engineering feat in history, and he will not be able to resist seeing it with his own eyes now that it's almost completed. A man like Roosevelt can't resist, dangers be damned.

"I am going to cable Berlin through my brother's offices in New York and get approval to kill him, but we need to step up our timeline immediately if we are to have a chance at him."

"Do we tell the others this?"

"No," Dreissen replied forcefully. "This is for us alone. We will say that the engineers reconsidered and believe we need a second string of explosives to be successful. We will lay the first row now and the second after the excitement of Roosevelt's brief visit has died down."

His visitor nodded.

Dreissen went on, "We're only pushing up our timetable by a couple weeks. Our recent deployments of the *Cologne* have been great successes. Though the crew would like more practice, they'll follow orders."

"Of course."

"We had better start moving material into position. Not tonight or tomorrow, let's plan for the following night. I'll radio my people and let them know. So much of this is weather dependent. We have to make only six trips, but we need near-windless nights to make them."

"We will just have to hope for the best. Have they found a suitable spot?"

"Yes, it's perfect," Dreissen assured him. "It's close enough to the dam yet still remote, with hills — well, islands now, I suppose — to protect it on two sides so no one will see what we're doing."

"Excellent," the visitor said as he finished his meal. "There is one more thing we need to discuss. Isaac Bell."

"Bell?"

"The Van Dorn detective."

"Right. The man with the nine lives of a cat."

"That's the one," the visitor agreed grimly. "I had the chance to speak with him last night. He has absolutely no idea what is going on down here, but his instincts and intuition are uncanny."

"He worries you?"

"Yes. My impression of him is that he is skeptical of everybody and everything until he's proved to himself that things really are as they seem. There are so many moving parts of our operation that I'm concerned we overlooked some minor detail, something no one else would think to question."

"Except Bell would question it, *ja*?"

"He already has. And he's not satisfied with the answers he's being given."

"And you think we should eliminate him?"

The visitor nodded. "I didn't think his survival of the attack in California would prove to be of any consequence, yet no one imagined he'd come nosing around here in Panama. I fear he could find some lead, that one detail we neglected, and expose our operation."

"Do you propose we kill him and pin the blame on the Viboras?"

"The Viboras wouldn't know his identity or reason for being here. They have no reason to kill him."

"But he is an investigator. Wouldn't they be concerned he'd find out information about them?"

"If he was getting close to unmasking them, certainly. But he has only just arrived. He hasn't learned anything about them to get himself killed. I think it better that Isaac Bell should meet with an accident. Panama is a dangerous place. It will be easy enough to see him die in an automobile crash or something equally mundane."

"Can you arrange it?"

The visitor slung an arm over the back of his chair in a relaxed pose. "It's already done."

16

Because it was the weekend, and Rinaldo Morales wasn't expected back from his home village until Monday, Bell had some time on his hands. Marion's knowledge of Spanish made things easier, but she didn't have any knowledge of the local politics that Bell needed if he was going to understand Viboras Rojas. He hired Jorge Nuñez, a retired teacher whom the Webbs had hired through the hotel as a guide to the city. Marion was spending the day shopping and sightseeing with Juliet Webb. Bell felt certain the Viboras would lay low after such a spectacular assault and was comfortable leaving his wife for a few hours.

"At first, people thought the Viboras were a joke," the bespectacled academic said. His face was nut brown and deeply wrinkled, and he barely reached to Bell's shoulder. His straw hat was more like an Old West Stetson than a panama, while the cane he used was just some gnarled root. "Who could possibly stand up to the Americans? Their power is undeniable. We just need to look at how they transformed our country to realize they are an unstoppable force."

"But then?"

Bell and Nuñez were strolling along Panama City's streets with no real destination in mind. When they walked past some building of significance, Jorge would briefly explain its history and then they would move on. The day was hot and humid, as they all were, but at least there was no rain.

"They had some success in their attacks and grew bolder. When they derailed a supply train and managed to steal some canned food that they gave away, people started taking them to heart. The story of Robin Hood was on everyone's lips, though I don't recall ever hearing it before Viboras Rojas."

"So, they have a propaganda wing?"

"I don't think I understand what that means," Nuñez said.

"It means they made certain the people knew who had provided the food and taught them context by way of a well-known legend. This is the hallmark of a very well-organized force. I voiced my concerns to Court Talbot. Do you know him?"

Nuñez nodded quickly. "Ojo Muerto?

227

Everyone in Panama knows the Major."

"I think there is a professional behind this group, someone well versed in how revolutions are supposed to work."

Nuñez seemed to take exception to this. "Do you think so little of my people that we need an outsider to tell us how to fight? That we are incapable of helping ourselves? Remember, we cast off Bogotá's shackles just ten years ago."

Bell held up a hand in a defusing gesture. "I mean no disrespect, Señor Nuñez. Talbot told me that the Viboras are motivated by Marxist doctrine. That's an economic system for an industrialized country with a strong class structure, not an agrarian society where the majority of the people are subsistence farmers. Communism is a very Europe-specific ideal. The chance that someone here is well versed enough without outside tutelage doesn't seem likely. You were an educator, surely you understand that the brightest pupil still needs a teacher to reach his full potential, yes?"

The older man couldn't fault Bell's logic, as it appealed to his very core. "I can see why you'd reach that conclusion. Go on."

"I guess my question is, have you heard any rumors about some Europeans backing the Viboras or even just a group of foreigners in the country with no real reason to be here?"

"Not that I've heard. Almost all the white people here work on the canal in some form or another. We sometimes get missionaries trying to spread Christianity among the indigenous peoples. I suppose that could be a cover story for Bolshevik agitators."

"Is there any way to track them?"

"Not once they clear customs."

"Would you know anyone who could get me a list of foreign nationals visiting Panama in the last, say, three months?"

"I know people in the government, so I can ask around, but it's doubtful they will share anything without some kind of legal precedent."

Bell reconsidered. "On second thought, don't bother. There would be too many names, and any of them could be an alias. I would need an army of investigators to back-check each and every one."

"No doubt for the best."

"What about the leadership of Viboras Rojas? What do you know about its head?"

"Nothing. And no one else does either. They've never said who he is, though the people call him Tío. That is Spanish for 'Uncle.' "

"Usually, these kinds of things are started

by someone with charismatic charm and a vision. The central figure is key, like Lenin or Simón Bolívar."

"Maybe maintaining their secrecy is the key," Nuñez countered.

"I don't know. Movements like this are ultimately about the power to control other people's lives. It takes a certain type of personality to want that, and all the autocrats throughout the ages had one thing in common — massive egos. They liked to wield their power on a personal level. They didn't hide in the shadows."

What concerned Bell was that the leader of the Vipers would finally show himself in some spectacular fashion, some unifying act that would generate a spontaneous uprising. During dinner the night before, Talbot had shown proper discretion to not ask about the search for the missing dynamite. There was no sense in fanning the flames of rumor over the explosives' whereabouts, but their eventual use was very much on Bell's mind. Blowing up the crane had been an act to slow the canal's construction, a tactical attack in a way. What Bell feared now was a strategic move, something bold and unexpected.

He wished Archie Abbott was along for this particular ride. Abbott was another Van

Dorn agent and Bell's closest friend. At times like this, he liked to have another investigator he could bounce ideas off of without jeopardizing security. While he doubted Jorge Nuñez was a risk, Bell made it a habit to keep his own counsel around all but a select handful of people.

"Perhaps," Nuñez said after a couple minutes of walking in silence, "the Vipers' leader will show himself when the time is right, build anticipation first, make the people long for his presence."

"I was thinking along those lines myself. Only I have no idea when that will be. It's no secret that Colonel Goethals requested a Marine division for additional security. Once they're here, the Vipers will have a much harder time striking. They have to act before then. They also must know that Major Talbot has permission to hunt them down, meaning the smart play is to lie low."

"A tricky balance."

"Exactly," Bell agreed. "To succeed with their plan, they are going to need perfect timing." He then added, with some recrimination, "I don't understand their strategy, the escalations, their goals. I understand nothing, really."

"I can tell that is a situation you find most displeasing, my friend."

"You have no idea. But I find motivation in frustration. And now I have to add President Roosevelt's visit to the mix."

"What will be your next step?"

"What I always do, Señor Nuñez, keep poking around the problem until I find that one thread that doesn't fit and tug on it so the whole ball of yarn comes unwound."

The Panamanian teacher nodded. "I can tell by the tone of your voice that you are deadly serious."

"Criminals always make mistakes. It's because they're human. Investigators joke about how there can't be a perfect crime so long as there is a victim, because once you identify him, you can trace back what was done to him and by whom. Viboras Rojas has yet to leave any overt clues in their wake of destruction, but that doesn't mean they won't."

"And you will find them?"

"We have a saying about how Van Dorn agents always get their man, always. None of us has ever failed. And I certainly don't intend to be the first."

The following day was Sunday, a day reserved for prayer and contemplation, but nothing was more sacred in Panama than the completion of the canal. The work never slowed.

Bell was surprised to find Felix Ramirez at a corner booth in the dining room when it opened for breakfast. A cheroot smoldered in a cut-glass ashtray at his elbow, and strewn across the tables were dozens of ledger pages and loose receipts. He sipped from a tiny cup of espresso produced by the domed La Pavoni coffeemaker behind the bar.

"Morning."

"Ah, Señor Bell. Good morning. Join me, please." He swept the papers into a neat pile and set it aside.

"Thank you." Bell slid into the booth opposite Ramirez, setting his panama hat on the table next to Ramirez's. Rather than a tie, Ramirez wore a yellow-patterned cravat tucked into his collar.

"Where is your wife?"

"Still asleep," Bell said and then pointed to the tiny cup in front of the Panamanian. "Is that actual espresso?"

"You know about espresso?"

"I've had it in Europe. I can't find anyone in the States willing to buy one of the machines. Devilishly expensive things."

"I know."

Bell cocked his head, putting together

subtle clues from the night before. "Wait, do you own the hotel?"

"Not own, exactly," Felix replied vaguely, "but I have an interest in it, thanks to a card game some months back. My first order of business was ordering an espresso machine. I lived in Rome two years ago and fell in love with strong, bitter coffee."

"Rome? Nice. Do you speak Italian?"

"Italian, French, some Portuguese, and of course English and Spanish. Oh, and some Tagalog. I was once stranded in Manila by a sea captain who didn't want to pay his gambling debts." He signaled the barman for two more demitasses of espresso.

"You seem to live off your wits, Mr. Ramirez."

"I think that is why we like each other, Señor Bell. You do the same, no?"

"Differently, but close enough."

"Hah. I can tell by looking at you that you're formidable at cards. I know you're married now yet I imagine there were countless youthful indiscretions in your past, and I bet you can outfight, outshoot, and outdrink any of the ruffians who drift in and out of this lawless place looking to make his fortune."

Bell laughed at the flattery and said, "My 'indiscretions,' as you call them, weren't countless. I know the exact number."

Ramirez laughed appreciatively. "I really do like you. May I call you Isaac?"

"By all means, Felix."

"How was your time with Jorge?"

"I had hoped to gain a local's insight into Viboras Rojas, but he really couldn't add to what I already know. Nice enough fellow, though."

The chrome coffeemaker on the back bar was snorting and belching and producing bursts of steam as it prepared tiny cups of ultra-rich espresso.

"What about you, Felix? Any insights you'd like to share?"

"I learned long ago to never give my opinion. Anyone listening is also judging and could eventually use what you've said against you."

"Keep your ears open and your mouth shut?"

"Precisely. But in this case, I will make an exception. Let's be honest with each other. The American government backed a bogus revolution in order to break Panama away from Colombia in what was essentially an illegitimate annexation. They dispatched Marines and gunboats to send Colombia's forces back south with its tail between its legs.

"What's at stake here is money. Millions upon millions of dollars in revenue over the decades the canal is going to be in operation. My opinion is, the Colombians want some of that for themselves. Either a lump sum payment or annual payoff. If they can get that, they will stop telling the rest of the world about what an awful thing the American Imperialists did to their poor and downtrodden people."

The barman brought the steaming little cups, and the two men took some time to appreciate the aroma and enjoy a couple of sips. At length, Bell said, "You think Viboras Rojas are part of a covert Colombian operation to pressure the United States into handing over reparations?"

"That's my theory. To me, the group's supposed goals are ridiculous. I can't see anything stopping the canal's completion nor do I envision a mass uprising to seize control of it once it's done." He leaned closer. "I wouldn't be surprised to learn of backchannel negotiations being carried out between Bogotá and Washington. Your people will pay the Colombians, who, in turn, will act like they are negotiating with the Viboras to lay down their arms. Everybody gets what they want and nobody loses face. You know that expression?"

"Chinese in origin. It means 'to avoid humiliation.' " Bell could find little fault in Ramirez's theory, with the exception the guerrillas had gone too far by targeting a United States Senator on American soil. For that, they would be brought to justice, and the cost be damned. He said as much to Felix.

"Ah, there you might have a point," Ramirez conceded. "I formulated my theory before that particular attack, and now with such loss of life at Pedro Miguel, maybe I should rethink everything."

"I haven't been able to wrap my mind around their exponential escalation in violence. It's like there's a deadline looming over their insurgency."

"The Marines are coming," Ramirez reminded Bell.

"But it was the Viboras's actions that triggered them being sent in the first place."

"Timing? The canal is nearing completion. Probably less than a year away."

Bell shook his head. "I don't believe that's the answer. Or the entire answer. There's something else. Something I'm not seeing yet."

"I have confidence you will find what you seek," Felix said with his slender cigar clamped between whiter-than-white teeth.

He gathered his papers and stood up. "In the meantime, have some breakfast. And as many espressos as your nerves can handle."

17

Isaac Bell had no idea how many times he'd traversed continental America by train, but he was quite certain he'd never done it in a little over two hours. That was how long it took to get from Panama's Pacific Coast to the Atlantic. The rail line was about fifty miles long and rose only a couple hundred feet in elevation. The difficulty for its builders was hacking through an almost impenetrable jungle with little more than hand tools.

The original route followed the Chagres River Valley, but with the river now dammed at Gatun, and the world's largest artificial lake continuing to expand across the land, the line had to be rebuilt so it would curve around the lake's eventual shore. They also had two sets of tracks so trains could run east or west simultaneously. With a hundred and thirty ore trains coming out of the Culebra Cut on a daily basis, the Panama

Railway was mostly a freight-carrying line. However, until the canal was completed, passengers wishing to avoid the perils of the Drake Passage around Tierra del Fuego used the rails as a middle leg in their oceangoing journey from New York to California.

Bell and Marion had a seat in a carriage meant for travelers rather than canal workers, so it was nicer than the car he'd ridden in out to the Pedro Miguel Locks site. They sipped at a glass of blended tropical fruit juices he'd bought at the Panama City terminal and enjoyed their ride across the continent. In most places, the jungle was little more than arm's length from the carriage windows, while there were other places where they had an expanded vista. Bell saw dozens of crews tasked with picking up rocks that had fallen out of the open-sided ore cars. He imagined if such maintenance wasn't performed, the rail line would be choked off in a matter of days.

Marion cried with delight when they passed a tree filled with red-furred monkeys with wizened faces like old men.

"I believe they're called tamarins," Bell said.

"They're adorable."

The train rolled across the Chagres River

on a low trestle bridge, and Bell got his first look at what essentially powered the Panama Canal. Since this was the rainy season, the river was swollen and surged with such power that it was like a living thing. The surface was muddy brown and littered with branches and boughs and entire trees it had torn from their roots as it eroded its way down from the highlands.

The train made several stops as it meandered across the country, exclusively at building sites affiliated with the canal's construction. Few people got on or off, and the train left the stations quickly.

The Port of Colón, unlike Panama City, had no colonial history. It had been built in the swamps of Manzanillo Island on reclaimed land made possible by stone quarried nearby. It was meant to be the Atlantic port for the railroad. Thus, the city was not yet seventy years old when Bell handed his wife down from the train carriage onto the bustling station platform. Opposite were the freight yards, where machines and material shipped from the States were transferred to trains. Bell could see the harbor through a forest of electric-powered cranes and derricks. There seemed to be an armada of merchant ships in Limon Bay awaiting their turn to have their cargos unloaded.

Just at the limit of what Bell could see, a line of Jamaican men was boarding a two-masted schooner. Having seen the hellscape of the Culebra Cut firsthand, Bell could only imagine these men were happy to be heading home.

Colón was tidy, compared to Panama City, and logically laid out, more like New York than Boston, Bell thought. The streets were paved, for the most part, properly pitched so that water didn't pool in the gutters. He found a taxi outside the station and instructed the driver to take them to the Gatun Locks. He showed the driver that he had a pass to enter the Canal Zone. Marion didn't need one because she was with him.

The ride took only a few minutes.

The stage of completion at Gatun was ahead of the work at Pedro Miguel. The locks had already been backfilled to make access for mechanics installing the mitered gates easier. Here, rather than a single chamber, there were three locks strung together in a row that rose up the slope of an artificially constructed hill. In essence, it was a concrete and steel sculpture stretching for more than two-thirds of a mile and climbing eighty-six feet to what was to be the final depth of Lake Gatun.

This was Marion's first visit to a lock, so

Isaac took time to explain how they worked and the function of each piece of equipment.

As impressed as Bell had been at Pedro Miguel, the audacious scale of this structure was even more amazing. At a distance, the men laboring around the locks were Lilliputian, the vehicles delivering parts and supplies like toys. The small electric locomotives, called mules, had already been installed and really did look like model trains. The seaward door to the bottom lock was open so water had filled the thousand-foot chamber. Bell could picture a giant battleship or elegant ocean liner being drawn into the lock by one of the plucky little locos. He could see the doors close, the water level inside the lock raised by the inundation coming through the maze of pipes and culverts, as the ship made its journey up through the next two chambers and ultimately out onto Lake Gatun.

Bell had the driver park for about ten minutes while he watched the work and studied the site. "Okay," he finally said. "Take us to the dam."

Roughly six miles from where the Chagres River met the Caribbean, an earthen dam stretched some seven and a half thousand feet across the river valley. The measurements for its other dimensions were equally impressive. At its base, the Gatun Dam was a half mile thick, tapered to four hundred feet at the waterline, and was just shy of one hundred feet at its top. The structure was built using spoil carved out of the Culebra Cut, and other parts of the canal, deposited in two parallel rows and sloping inward to meet at the top. The hollow cavity between these two walls was then filled with a slurry of clay and water that, when dry, hardened into a core as solid as concrete. The downstream slopes had already been grassed over, so the mammoth dam already looked like part of the landscape.

Only at the dam's center did it look like the work of man. A semicircular concrete spillway had been built next to a red-tile-roofed hydroelectric power plant. The spillway prevented the annual floods from overtopping the dam and eroding it away, while the electricity produced from water flowing through the turbines supplied all the electrical needs of the entire canal.

Because Lake Gatun was still filling up behind the dam, the spillways were dry, but water was flowing through the plant and wending its way down to the sea.

There wasn't much for them to see. Bell

had the driver cross the bridge over the spillway and go up to the far side of the dam so he could get out and look to the water. Beyond the dam, Lake Gatun continued to grow at a rate of about one hundred thousand cubic feet per second. It sounded like a lot of water, and it was, but it was feeding into a lake that would soon be some one hundred and sixty square miles.

"I can't hear any humming," Marion said. "Remember what they said about ground pressure causing mysterious noises?"

"I can't imagine it's a constant thing," Bell replied. "I bet it's localized in pockets of weaker soil."

"It's odd to think this lake isn't natural. It looks like it's been here forever."

What were once hilltops surrounding a lush jungle valley were now isolated islands dotting the lake's tranquil surface. In just one year's time, it would be the transit route for countless ocean liners and freighters. Bell truly understood what an accomplishment this was and how transformative it would be for the United States.

While his idle chat on that topic with Court Talbot and Senator Densmore back in San Diego had been speculative, seeing the canal with his own eyes brought the feat into sharp focus. Bell now understood what was at stake, and he understood the canal's vulnerabilities too. No matter how far the workers here had come, they weren't done yet, and it could all still come to a crashing halt.

He told the driver to take them back to the station. Bell had seen enough. He didn't know where or when the Red Vipers would strike again, but after seeing the rest of the canal, he understood their tactics, and that gave him his first advantage in the game.

18

Monday started out with the kind of rain the locals knew would last all day, a thin drizzle without any wind to lend the patter of drops striking the ground any variation in tone. A monotonous rain, in every sense of the word. Bell ate early at the hotel, and would have enjoyed Felix Ramirez's company, but the man was nowhere to be found. Marion had awoken with him, took one look at the rain through the balcony doors, and scampered back to bed.

"No thank you," she'd said and pulled the covers to her chin. "See you when you get back."

Sam Westbrook had managed to scrounge a vehicle from the Authority's motor pool for Bell's use. It was a three-year-old Gramm-Bernstein two-ton truck. Instead of a traditional cargo bed, the big vehicle had a large cylindrical tank for hauling water to feed the insatiable thirst of all the steam boilers in the Canal Zone, especially those powering all the mechanical shovels chewing their way through the cut. The truck was well used. One of the fenders had been torn off and replaced with a replica fashioned from an old oil drum, and the water tank had a deep dent from being backed into some obstacle.

On the passenger's seat sat a bucket of dirty water and a sponge on a stick. Bell quickly realized it was to clean the spray of mud the poorly fabricated fender didn't prevent from being splattered against the windshield whenever the truck slogged through a turn.

The town of Gamboa sat where the Chagres River debouched into the canal just to the north of the Culebra Cut. It sat just three miles from the abandoned town of Las Cruces, which had been the starting point for the Spanish Conquistadors' El Camino Real de Panama, a four-foot-wide cobblestone mule path that remained in use until the construction of the railroad in 1855.

The town was purpose-built on cleared land by the Canal Authority for workers and support staff, mostly Caribbean islanders living in identical bunkhouses. Many of the town's other buildings were nothing more than old boxcars that were beyond repair for use as rolling stock. At the water's edge were some storehouses and a dock. A little way off was the temporary earthen dike that prevented the slowly rising waters from flooding into the still-dry Culebra Cut. The lake's water level was low compared to what its final depth would be, leaving the dock looking awkward on its tall, creosote-coated pilings.

The journey from Panama City was approximately twenty-five miles, but the road was in rough condition because of the heavy rains. The potholes were spine-jarring at any speed, and Bell had to traverse many areas where inches-deep water sluiced across the gravel track. Despite the truck's weight, several times he felt the Gramm get caught in the wash and slide sideways. He kept it on the road each time, yet there were a few close calls, with the vehicle right up to the edge of the road and teetering. Things got worse when he came upon the tail end of a caravan of trucks all heading in the same direction as he was. They were lumbering cargo haulers, and their progress was plodding at best. With few opportunities to pass, he had no choice but to ride along behind the vehicles, which were like circus elephants marching trunk to tail.

Whenever the snaking road ran parallel to

the train tracks, he got a sense of how the railroad was essentially a continuous loop conveyor belt of fully laden ore cars coming out of the cut and empty ones returning. He was also afforded some spectacular views of the cut when the road meandered closer to the rim. Once filled with water, it would lose much of its grandeur, but since it was still dry it reminded Bell of looking out over a massive canyon.

Bell arrived in Gamboa a little past ten and threaded his way through town to the harbor. As this was a work camp, there were few people wandering the streets, but those that did wore wide-brimmed hats of woven grass for the rain and didn't bother with shoes for the mud. A few men stood under an awning attached to a building housing a commercial kitchen that also was used for dining. The tables were overturned barrels, and they didn't have chairs. Bell could smell the jerk seasonings as he passed.

He parked in a gravel lot between warehouses just shy of the dock and took a moment to dump the sludge from his windshield washing bucket and leave it out in the rain to refill. On the quay were a group of men handing bags and crates down to others on a boat too low to be seen from the parking lot.

Court Talbot broke off from the men when he saw Bell approaching through the veil of drifting rain. Around his waist he'd strapped a leather belt with a holster for a Webley top-break pistol. The bottom of the holster was secured to his thigh with a leather thong. They shook hands and sought cover in the open entrance of one of the warehouses. Inside, wooden boxes were piled to the ceiling. Workers moved crates on steel-wheeled trollies under the watchful eye of a supervisor. Out through the open doors on the opposite side of the warehouse, Bell could see boxcars being loaded with crates and steam coiling from a waiting locomotive. At least there was a roof over most of the platform to protect the men from the dreary weather.

"This is your secret plan?" Bell asked while Talbot lit a cigar. "A boat?"

"The only powered boat on all of Lake Gatun. I had her laid up here in Gamboa when they started blocking off the Chagres. I had hoped to hire her out to the Authority during construction. During Stevens's time in charge, there wasn't enough water in the lake to use her, but now, with plenty of it, Goethals wouldn't give me permission to move her."

"Until now?"

"Correct."

"So how do you propose fulfilling your contract with Goethals?"

"The way I see it, the Viboras can't operate out of the city. Too many people would see them. That means they have to base their operations in the jungle yet close enough to be effective. Only there's so much traffic in the zone that the likelihood of them being spotted is the same as if they were in Panama City. That leaves the lake, and that's where I think they're hiding. There are so few locals using it now that they can cross it with impunity."

"But you said Goethals banned traffic on the lake."

"He stopped me. Locals have been fishing the lake since it was deep enough for their pirogues. I think after the Vipers raid a train or hijack a truck or placed that bomb at Pedro Miguel, they head back to the lake and vanish in one of the countless islands or along its shore. Remember, this is now unexplored territory. A couple years ago it was all impenetrable jungle. With Gatun filling, a whole new world is opening up."

Bell nodded. Talbot's logic was sound. "The lake has to be about a hundred and fifty square miles. How do you expect to cover that much territory?"

"They have to stay close enough to this side to be effective. That cuts the search area down significantly. Because there are no other people out here, if we see any smoke from cooking fires, we'll have them dead to rights."

"You've thought this through," Bell said with some respect in his voice.

"From the very first attack. That's why I wanted to put pressure on Colonel Goethals to let me go after these savages." He added bitterly, "If he'd given permission when it all started, we could have prevented a lot of bloodshed."

"Speaking of which, did your man Rinaldo return from his village?"

"Of course," Talbot said as if it was never in doubt. "He's on the boat. Let's go. We can talk in the cabin."

Talbot led the way back to the jetty. The last of the gear had been handed down, and the men had come aboard to stow it properly.

The boat was about forty feet long and extra-beamy. Her aft deck took up two thirds of her length, an open space for freight, with a hand-cranked derrick mounted in one corner. The deck was half covered with dozens of identical fuel cans. A tubular frame enclosed the cargo deck, and a timeworn canvas cover was tied to it to protect the deck from the rain. Forward was a short flight of steps that rose to the enclosed bridge that sat atop the main cabin. The crew's area was accessible through a separate hatchway tucked under the bridge stairs. A large engine was buried in the guts of the workboat, exhaust coiling from a slender stack mounted along the outside of the wooden superstructure. Over her fantail dangled a little rowboat that could be lowered into the water.

The craft was hard-used. The deck was severely scarred from years of work, and the railings were slick with a patina of mildew. A crewman was scouring the green slime with a pumice stone, another leaned over the rail to scrape the hull, letting the flakes of peeling lead paint fall into the water. The only things that looked new were the dinghy's bronze oarlocks.

There were a great many guns lying about with casual negligence, leaning against gunwales or hanging by slings from hooks, with little regard to the rain.

"Rinaldo, hey," Talbot called as he climbed down a ladder to reach the deck. His driver was on the steep little steps leading up to the bridge.

"Sí."

"Mr. Bell needs a minute." Talbot dropped the last couple feet, his boots making a satisfying smack when they hit the deck. It gave Bell the impression he was very used to spending time on boats.

Bell reached the deck and studied the chauffeur. The man looked nothing like he had when Bell had first seen him. "You shaved your mustache and cut your hair."

"*Sí*. For Raul's funeral." His expression was unreadable. "*Mi madre* would have been very unhappy if I didn't show proper respect."

Talbot led them down into the space below the bridge. It was utilitarian, with just metal walls painted white. The main part was a salon with a small galley kitchen and a dining table large enough to seat six. On the port side were three doors. One was open, and Bell could see unmade bunk beds and a footlocker. The other was to a second cabin, and he guessed the third was the head.

Talbot indicated that they should sit at the table while he got to work making coffee in the tiny galley.

As sincerely as he could, Bell said, "I am sorry about your brother. It wasn't my intention to kill him, only to capture him."

"Nothing you can say makes any difference, Señor Bell, so it is wisest not to say anything, okay?" His eyes narrowed, and there had been a flintiness to his voice.

The message was clear, and Bell simply said, "Fair enough. I do have some questions for you."

Morales waved a hand to indicate Bell should proceed. Bell noted the missing pinkie. The skin at the stub appeared white and callused. An old wound.

"Did you talk to your brother about your work with Talbot and, specifically, his trip to the United States?"

"I did, but I didn't know he was part of Viboras Rojas. He told me he had come back from Colombia to help take care of our mother."

"Did his arrival coincide with the rise of the Viboras?"

"I do not know the word *coincide*?"

Talbot uttered the Spanish translation.

"Yes. It was only a short while later that the attacks started." He then admitted, "I should have made the connection. He hated what had become of Panama, and especially how the Canal Authority treats the locals while hiring outsiders from the Caribbean by the thousands."

"Is it possible he was the leader of the Viboras?"

"I don't know. My mother said that he never left our village since his return, so he couldn't have gone out on any of the raids."

Bell could see there was more to it than that and said, "And?"

"She did say that men would visit him in the night. They would talk in whispers and then they would leave again. She, ah . . ."

Bell slapped the table. "Out with it, man."

"She said she also found a bag of cash. American bills. She wanted to show it to me when I went back for Raul's funeral, but it was gone."

Bell looked to Court Talbot. "He had a backer."

"My bet is the government in Bogotá. The Colombians are the only people who have a legitimate grievance with the canal's construction, and Raul must have been their agent in Panama."

"If he was the moneyman and organizer, why was he at the locks last week?" Bell asked, then answered his own question. "This was a major escalation for his group, and he would want to make certain everything went as planned. I'd do the same if I were in his shoes."

"So would I," Talbot added.

Bell turned his attention back to Morales. "Is there anything else? Did she recognize any of the men? Would she be able to provide descriptions?"

"My mother's eyes are not so good."

"Did your brother mention names or addresses? Anything specific?"

"Not to me, señor, or *mi madre.* I am sorry."

Bell leaned back and took a sip of the coffee Talbot had set out in tin mugs on the table. The rain made the cabin stuffy, and his shirt's collar chafed his neck.

"Can I get back to work?" the Panamanian asked.

"Yes. Thank you for answering my questions."

"What do you think?" Talbot asked after Morales closed the cabin door behind him.

"Not sure," Bell admitted. "I was half thinking it really was Rinaldo who I shot at Pedro Miguel, and you were covering it up to distance yourself from him in Colonel Goethals's eyes."

"Not the case," the former soldier said. "And I'd take offense at the insinuation, if it wasn't a theory I would have come up with, were I in your shoes."

Bell continued, "I'd like to know what happened to the money. It wasn't on the body when I searched it."

"Probably moved to a new hiding place

that only Raul knew. Probably lost forever."

"Or already disbursed to carry out the next attack. Don't forget the dynamite we haven't accounted for."

"You think the Viboras will keep fighting?" Talbot's tone was doubtful.

"You don't?" Bell countered. "Insurgencies need money, sure, but they are driven by ideology. That hasn't changed, and if you're right about the Colombian government being behind all this, then the masters in Bogotá will hear of Morales's death through whatever backchannel communications system they've put in place. They'll send another bagman with another sackload of money. And I think, ultimately, that's what Morales was, a go-between."

"Really? You sure?"

"Absolutely. I believe the head of the Viboras is still out there. I think he's someone known to both Morales brothers. Otherwise, how could the insurgency have started so soon after Raul's arrival from Colombia?"

"Surely it's a friend of Raul's, not Rinaldo's."

"In order to have the level of trust necessary to launch something like this, the chances are the Viboras's head honcho is someone Raul grew up with. You mentioned their village is pretty isolated. If one brother knew our guy, so did the other."

"You didn't question Rinaldo about it?"

"No point. It could be any one of a dozen childhood friends or even a relative. I'm alone down here without the resources to track down that many people. You're in a position to roll up the fighters out in the jungle, their leader especially. I want to disassemble the Colombians' network inside Panama and make certain they don't try a stunt like this again. There are serious diplomatic ramifications to this whole affair. Our government is already sending troops. I can imagine scenarios where they sail right past Panama and invade Colombia via Cartagena."

"Let's hope we can contain this thing before it goes off the rails," Talbot said and got to his feet. He had to adjust the holster at his hip.

On deck, all the gear had been stowed properly. Several fighting men lounged under a canvas tarp that was sagging in the middle under the weight of the steadily falling rain. Others were in the pilothouse, getting ready to start their search and destroy operation.

Bell and Talbot shook hands at the base of the ladder bolted to the pier's wooden piling. "Good luck, Court, and be careful."

"Always. What's your next move?"

"It's time I get to know some of the diplomats stationed here." Talbot's expression showed that he didn't understand Bell's answer. "Joseph Van Dorn taught me years ago that any gossip worth knowing comes from Foreign Service types because every one of them, from office boy up to Ambassador, is a spy, and their bread and butter is information. If Colombia — or anyone else, for that matter — is trying to exert influence in Panama, the diplomatic community will know all about it."

"Then good luck to you too."

Bell didn't need luck. The truth is, he needed about ten minutes with Colonel Goethals and he'd have the whole affair wrapped up and the way paved for Teddy Roosevelt to inspect his canal without fear of attack.

19

It took several minutes of tinkering to get the tanker truck fired up for the ride back to Panama City. He'd watched Talbot's boat pull away from the dock and head out across the lake. It was quickly swallowed by distance and the mist until even the rumble of its engine muted entirely. His bucket for washing the windshield had refilled with rainwater, so he set it on the passenger's seat and climbed behind the wheel.

If Isaac Bell was entirely honest with himself, he didn't have all the answers just yet. There were some loose ends. He was sure he knew the who of the case and the why, but there was still the question of the backer. Bell liked the theory that Colombia had a hand in the insurgency, yet he felt there was another layer to the plot, someone as yet unseen pulling the strings. Their goal was to delay the canal's completion since it could never be permanently halted. He needed to think, remembering that classic Latin question detectives ask themselves with every case. *Cui bono?* Who benefits?

Who had the resources and desire to delay the canal's construction? It couldn't be an exceptionally long list, but at the moment Bell couldn't add even a single entry to it. It had to be someone wealthy enough to be a player in all of this, and also someone who would be made wealthier still by the canal not opening on time. The more he thought, the more of a disconnect he found between those two points. It wasn't like there were private construction bonds that could be sold as a short. The United States government was footing the entire bill.

There was another angle he just couldn't see yet.

A spine-jarring pothole tore him from his reverie and reminded him to focus more on his driving. The road was a soggy quagmire, and he passed several vehicles pulled to the verge because of the conditions. Though it was only early afternoon, the storm and the shadow of the encroaching jungle made Bell's view of the road murky at best. The truck had oil lamps, but he doubted he'd get them lit with the constant pattering rain. He hunched over the wheel and steered into the gloom. He halted at the swiftest wash yet, where rain poured out of the jungle and swept across the road in a shallow river.

He considered turning back, but he wouldn't without at least trying to cross the hazard. He eased out into the water. The truck's tires were two inches of solid rubber around wooden-spoked wheels, so they offered little resistance to the current. The front of the truck, with the heavy engine and Bell's own weight, remained solidly rooted to the road. It was the back end that swayed and skipped drunkenly, forcing Bell to crab the vehicle like an airplane caught in a crosswind.

Even though he kept the speed steady, as he reached the far side of the watery hazard the road dipped so that the level of the water rose dangerously fast. The tail of the truck slewed hard, and he had no choice but to gun the motor, dashing from the trap like a hippopotamus launching itself from some African river. The truck bellowed and snorted and didn't let him down. He was soon out of the zone of danger and on gravel once again.

A short distance later, the jungle to Bell's right vanished as the road began to run parallel to the rim of the Culebra Cut. The huge earthen dam back in Gamboa prevented the rising waters of Lake Gatun from flooding the works, yet Bell had been told by Sam Westbrook that it would be blown up in the autumn by President Wilson pressing a button in the Oval Office. The remainder of the excavations within the cut would be carried out by floating dredges.

The left side of the road remained an impenetrable wall of tropical trees, bushes, and creeping vines.

Bell was reaching around the edge of the windshield with his sponge-tipped stick to clean mud from the glass when he spotted something on the road. Though at first it looked like a narrow channel of water cutting across the dirt track, he soon realized it was a downed tree. He straightened and slammed his foot on the brake, the big truck's tires cutting deep grooves into the muddy roadway.

In the seconds until impact, he considered turning the wheel but wisely kept it straight. Hitting the foot-thick trunk at an angle would likely flip the water carrier. Its rear end started to slip sideways, as he slowed, and he steered the vehicle through the skid. It straightened and came to a stop a few feet from the downed tree. Had he hit it, the wooden-spoked front wheels would have come apart and the front of the truck would have collapsed. Bell had seen such accidents before. The driver invariably went through the windshield like he'd been launched from a catapult. Survival was a fifty/fifty proposition.

He shook out his hands because they were clutching at the wheel tightly enough to have gone bloodless and white. Leaving the motor sputtering, he swung down from the truck, his attention on the fallen tree. The rain had intensified, the sound of it falling through the jungle was like standing next to a waterfall.

He hadn't gone even two steps when there came a roar from the jungle, and a truck much like his own burst out of the foliage in reverse so that it led with its big water tank. Bell had no option but to leap back into his truck, and he managed to wedge himself into the foot-well with the gas and brake pedals by the time the other vehicle slammed into his.

It hadn't built enough speed to stave in the side of Bell's cab yet had the momentum to shove his truck bodily across the road to the precipice of the Culebra Cut. Bell clutched the underside of the steering wheel. He knew he was going over.

Geology dictated how steep the sides of the cut had to be. In areas where there was solid rock, the workers shaved the walls so they were near-vertical cliffs. In other places, where the soil was particularly soft, the earth had to be gently sloped so that it didn't break free and ooze into the canal like the Cucaracha slide that had vexed the French effort and still defied the Americans.

The ambush to take out Isaac Bell had been laid in a spot that was a mixture of both. The ground was solid enough, but not so stable that there wasn't some degree of slope.

When the two outside tires went over the edge, it felt like the truck was going to remain upright for a joyride down to the bottom. And then they hooked, and the heavy truck fell onto its side. Bell felt like he'd just been mule-kicked in the chest.

Had Westbrook lent him any other type of vehicle, what happened next would have seen the truck barrel-roll down the quarter-mile hill, shedding bodywork with each ever-accelerating tumble, until there was nothing left but the chassis and engine, spinning like a dervish. Bell's lifeless body would have been jettisoned from it like a rag doll long before it came to rest in the muddy mess at the canal's bottom.

But the big, round water tank was like a toboggan on snow. There was little friction between its smooth metal sides and the watery mud. This allowed the truck to slide down the slope with barely any resistance. The cab dug in a little, causing the vehicle do a slow pirouette as it went down the hill. But it remained on its side, and Bell continued to cling tightly to the steering wheel as he understood that this delicate balance could shift, and the truck could begin to flip at any moment.

That didn't come to pass, and the truck slid sedately to the bottom of the canal, where pooled rainwater quickly flooded the footwell where Bell sheltered. He scrambled up to the seat and then had to hoist himself out of the cab using the steering wheel as a foothold and climbing out the passenger's side. He sat in the window of the door with his legs dangling into the truck. The engine pinged and popped as its block cooled in the water with steam venting from a crack in the radiator.

Bell was shaken, and the adrenaline spike left his mouth dry and his stomach knotted. It took a few seconds to remember he was still a target. He rolled off the side of the truck and dropped to the soggy ground. He pulled his .45 from a slender holster at the small of his back and looked around the truck's torn fender. The rim of the man-made canyon was several hundred feet above him and at least a thousand feet away. For an expert marksman, the shot wasn't a challenge, but there was no one above him peering down through a telescopic sight of a sniper rifle. He saw no one at all. The truck that had forced him off the road was gone.

Wary, Bell watched for several minutes, checking left and right to see if someone was trying to outflank him. There was nothing, just the constant rain. Behind him, the far rim of the canal was too distant for a marksman to make an accurate shot in these conditions.

He turned back to where his truck had been shoved off the road and was looking at the exact spot when the explosion came. The earth along the ridge lurched upward like a muscle in spasm. And then, in a line stretching many hundreds of feet, the ground erupted as a string of explosives linked by a fast-burning fuse were touched off. Seconds later, Bell heard and felt the concussive whoomph of the simultaneous blasts.

What followed next was the true horror. A slab of the hill detached itself from the earth and began to rumble down into the canal in an avalanche of mud and dirt and rock that looked as thick and wide as the horizon itself. It thundered toward Bell with the force of a tsunami and the throaty roar of a hundred locomotives.

When it hit, he would be smeared like paste and buried under twenty feet of rubble and muck. He couldn't outrun the wall of accelerating debris and thought he had a better chance bracing himself behind the truck. But he knew that was a losing proposition. The avalanche would strike the tanker like a sledgehammer on a child's toy.

Then came inspiration born out of desperation. While the truck would tumble and rattle and likely get broken up, there was a chance the water tank would survive. Bell scrambled around the vehicle, trying not to think about what was coming. The cap for filling the tank was located on top of it and was big enough to feed a large-diameter hose through it, like those for locomotives.

The landslide had a deeper rumble than the storm, a sound like the growl of a predator on the hunt, and it seemed to fill all five of Bell's senses.

He undogged the filler cap's locked lid and dove inside. Gravity slammed the lid closed, and Bell had just seconds to jam the pistol into the front of his pants and ball himself around it while lying in the residual water pooled at the tank's bottom. Moments later, the wall of mud and rock hit the bottom of the canal, gushing outward and slamming into the overturned Gramm-Bernstein. Bell crashed into the rear bulkhead, taking the impact with his feet and backside.

Unbeknownst to him, the tank was ripped from its mounts by the initial blow. The wave of earth buried the rest of the truck, tearing it apart so thoroughly that it looked like it had gone through a woodchipper.

But the tank was somewhat spared. Its volume of air meant that it was lighter than the surrounding muck so that as it was borne along, spinning and tumbling, it also rose up through the quagmire with each passing second.

Bell took the pounding of his life. He was flung like a puppet, bouncing off the walls, and was battered by the sloshing water like he was caught in a hurricane at sea. It was all made worse because of the darkness, an inky black deeper than any night. Had he left his gun in its holster, the pummeling his body was taking would have driven the weapon so hard into his kidneys his urine would be red for months. Through it all, he kept his hands cradling the back of his head and never uncoiled his body.

That was until a particularly hard tumble

dashed his forehead against the water tank, and he lost consciousness.

The big cylinder finally came to a rest as the tidal wave of mud and rock lost its momentum by spreading across the bottom of the cut in a two-story pile of debris that covered dozens of acres.

Bell didn't awaken for more than an hour, and, when he did, he wished for a coma's sweet embrace. He ached. Everywhere. His head and neck especially. He lay in the pooled water, soaked through to the skin with a depth of cold that seeped into his very bones. He was shivering in an absolute blackness that felt as heavy and cloying as molasses.

He touched the lump on his forehead. His hand came away wet, to be expected, warm and sticky and smelling like an old penny. He was bleeding. And he had no idea where he was. He was in a metal tank of some sort, but beyond that . . .

He had no idea how he'd gotten here. He remembered nothing.

The panic hit, sending a jolting shock across every nerve ending in his body. For a moment it felt like he had the worst case of sunburn in his life. His heart rate accelerated dangerously as adrenaline flooded his system with a near overdose of chemicals.

He breathed in rapid gulps that filled his lungs but provided no oxygen.

He'd lost his memory. He didn't know where he was or who he was. Total amnesia.

But then he fought the panic, forced himself to regain rationality. It was okay that he'd lost it for a second, he told himself. He was only human, and the reaction had been a natural one, but now he had to focus. He got a handle on his nerves, his skin cooled, his heart slowed, and he took slow, even breaths.

He now knew his name and said it just to hear if it sounded right. "Isaac Bell."

Yes, that was it. It sounded natural and right. He was Isaac Bell. He was a detective, and he had a wife named Marion. He was currently on an assignment in Panama. He remembered leaving his hotel that morning, Marion staying in bed because of the rain, his herculean effort not to join her under the covers. After that, there wasn't much. He had no recollection of how he'd gotten himself inside a metal cylinder.

And then it started to come back to him. Or parts of it. He remembered driving the truck, the crash, going over the side of the Culebra Cut. Maybe there was another vehicle. And some explosions. He vaguely remembered seeing a boat swallowed in the mist.

His truck, the one he'd been lent by Sam Westbrook, was a tanker for supplying the steam shovels and other boilers needed along the canal with water. He was inside its tank. That had to be it. He had no idea why he'd climbed into it, but at least he knew where he was. The panic attack subsided further.

The tank was almost perfectly level, with about eight inches of water pooled at the bottom. He regretted not bringing the little flashlight Court had given him. By feel, he found his submerged pistol. He drained it, pulled the magazine, and blew water from the weapon's inner workings. He racked the slide a few times, shedding even more water, before returning the magazine and securing the Colt in his holster.

He wondered why the water was so cold. The truck sat in the sun all day, every day. The water should be hot. Even with the day-long rainstorm, the tank's contents would at least be lukewarm. The water here was icy almost. And then the answer hit him. Bell realized that the water had cooled to the ambient surrounding temperature. The truck wasn't lying on its side out in the open. It had been buried.

He slapped at the steel walls and they returned a dull tone in response. There wasn't one place that gave even the faintest hollow echo to indicate that it wasn't covered in dirt. While he had no idea how deeply he was buried, at this point it didn't matter.

He located the filler cap. Using the puddle as a guide, since his own sense of balance was still recovering, Bell found the cap was only halfway up one wall. But its metal lid was jammed, and no amount of pushing would get it open.

Isaac Bell was well and truly buried alive.

20

While Bell was not a man to give in to panic, the past little incident notwithstanding, he had to admit his current predicament was more than a little unsettling. He took stock of the things he could control. He had enough water to last him a week or more, though it probably was teeming with parasites. He had no food, but that wouldn't be a problem for a while. He stripped out of his wet clothes and laid them out on the tank above the waterline. His body couldn't generate enough heat to dry his clothes. It was best to let them air-dry.

Then came the realization that sent his heart back into overdrive. Water and food meant nothing if he couldn't get air. He had no idea how long he'd been out, but there was only a finite amount of oxygen in the tank and no way to dispense with the excess carbon dioxide.

He allowed himself two deep, calming

breaths and then regulated his breathing by allowing himself small sips of air only. He knew his only hope was a quick rescue.

Had anyone seen the accident? Would they come to investigate? Even if a survey team came out to assess the damage, the tank was somehow buried. They wouldn't be able to reach him until it was dug up, and that could take weeks. He had hours at most.

Bell popped the magazine out of the .45 and offered a silent apology to John Moses Browning because he was going to use the pistol's butt like a hammer against the tank's interior. It hit with a dull thud. Not the sound he needed. There was a narrow flange around the filler cap. He rapped it with the gun and it delivered a satisfying chime.

For some reason the only song that came to mind was the popular rag "Sailing Down the Chesapeake Bay," and so that's what he tapped out again and again, pausing only after two hours to get into his still-damp clothes. They weren't perfect, yet he soon felt warmer.

He switched arms regularly and tapped out the tune again and again. A hundred times, five hundred? He didn't know, but he could tell the air was growing more fouled. His mind grew fuzzy, and while he couldn't see anything save Stygian darkness, he felt his optic nerves constricting as if his vision were fading.

He didn't know he'd nodded off until he woke with a start after just a couple seconds. He hit his gun against the flange. He couldn't remember the tune he'd been playing, so he began tapping in Morse code. Dot-dot-dot. Dash-dash-dash. Dot-dot-dot. S.O.S.

It was never an abbreviation for anything, merely a Morse phrase that was easy to remember and transmit, but many believed it stood for "Save Our Ship" or "Save Our Souls." For Bell, it was a plea to whoever was out there.

Search Out Survivor.

He blacked out several more times, yet as soon as he yanked himself back to consciousness he'd begin tapping again, though any semblance of code was soon lost. He could no longer remain upright enough to reach the flange, so he lay on his side, just above the murky water, and tapped the Colt's butt against the tank wall, a sound that grew weaker and weaker until it went silent altogether.

Isaac Bell awoke in Heaven. The light was painfully bright, and the creature hovering over him was too beautiful to be anything other than an angel. He could open his eyes just a fraction of an inch. This particular seraph had cascading blond hair, eyes as bright and sharp as colored glass, and such a look of worry that tiny wrinkles had formed between her brows. He immediately believed it was the power of her concern that brought him back from the abyss.

He wished, though, that he'd returned in a better state. His head pounded, and his body felt like he'd gone twenty rounds with the current bare-knuckle-boxing champ. Surely he should be at peace.

Maybe this wasn't Heaven. It couldn't be. He hurt too damned much. But the angel . . .

He drifted off again before the angel realized he'd awakened.

The next time Bell clawed his way to consciousness it was dark, but he could see the moon's glow through a gauzy curtain. He was thirsty and sore yet somehow knew he was safe. He was in a bed, the sheets were crisp and the blanket smelled of detergent. The pillow beneath his head was like a cloud, and that thought brought memories of the angel. While he wanted to get up and search for her, struggling to turn his body even a little was too much and he gave up the idea and let sleep envelop him once more.

When he came back the third time, it was early morning. The light was soft, and the angel was there once again, dabbing his head with a cool compress, her hair tamed in a ponytail that snaked down over her shoulder and almost brushed the bed.

She saw he was awake and cried out his name as he croaked hers.

"Isaac."

"Marion."

"I've been so worried," she said as joyous tears welled up in her deep green eyes. She leaned over to kiss his face, and he could taste the salt on her lips.

"I don't understand." And he didn't. Marion should be in Los Angeles. And then a sickening thought rushed in on him so hard and fast that he levered himself upright and grabbed her arm. "How long was I out?"

In their relationship, it was Isaac who usually had all the answers, so for a moment Marion delighted in having information he did not. But she couldn't let his questions go unanswered for too long. That would just be cruel.

"Not even a day, my dear." She handed him a glass of water, which he drank spar-

281

ingly despite his obvious thirst.

Then he almost spit it out. Bell was defined by logic. It was the underpinning of his life, yet right now nothing made sense, and he felt suspended back between wakefulness and sleep. "What? How is that possible? What the devil is going on here?"

"Easy, Isaac. I came to Panama with you, remember? You promised me a getaway at the Hotel Del, but then you had to come here, and I joined you."

Bell took some more water and looked around. It was clear he was in the private room of a hospital, maybe the big one on Ancon Hill. The gauzy veil he'd noted the night before was mosquito netting that had been draped around his bed. It was pulled back now, and Marion sat in a straight-backed chair at his side.

Out the window he could see the serrated fronds of some palm trees.

"Right," he finally said, recalling the voyage and their room at the Central overlooking the unnaturally green lawn.

"Felix Ramirez found me last night having dinner with the Webbs when word reached the city that you'd been rescued from an avalanche. He stayed with us all night and only left earlier this morning because of his work at the hotel. He said he would try to come by later."

"Wait. An avalanche? I was in an avalanche?"

"That's what they told me."

"I don't remember that at all." He pointedly touched the gauze-swathed lump on his forehead. "I don't remember much at all, actually. What happened?"

"I'll let someone involved tell you all about it. Give me a moment."

She rose. She was wearing an all-white outfit that was open at the throat and with wide sleeves so she wouldn't overheat in the tropical climate.

Bell stared out the window as the sun slowly crept over the distant hills. He tried yet couldn't recall details of the day before. While his brain rarely failed him, all he could recollect was eating breakfast alone and driving for a bit. He didn't know his destination. Marion related that Felix had said he had a meeting, but he couldn't remember where or with whom. He didn't know if he'd kept the appointment. And he certainly didn't remember any avalanche.

Bell felt an icy panic grip his stomach. His mind was everything. What if . . . .

Two men came into the room with Marion. One was Sam Westbrook, the young railroad scheduler, and the other was a doctor, judging by the white lab coat and stethoscope coiled in one of its pockets.

"Mr. Bell," Sam said earnestly, his panama hat held in his hands in front of him. "Boy, is it good to see you. That sure was something."

"Just a moment," the doctor said. He was a ginger with a thick beard who looked like he knew his way around a gymnasium. "Mr. Bell, I'm Dr. Hamby. How are you feeling?"

"Beat up but okay."

The doctor stepped between Bell and the window and peered closely into his eyes. Bell held still while Hamby moved his head to the side, allowing the light of the rising sun to strike Isaac in the face. Both pupils contracted at the same time and the same amount.

Bell winced and turned away quickly.

"Good. Very good," Hamby said and moved back toward the door. "Sorry about that, but it's the most accurate way to tell if you're concussed. How's your memory?"

"He doesn't remember the crash," Marion answered for her husband. "Is that common?"

"Actually, yes," the doctor reassured her. "There's a French psychologist by the name of Théodule Ribot who's written on the subject. It's called retrograde amnesia, meaning one forgets things on a gradient from newest memories to oldest. Oftentimes, the victim of a trauma doesn't remember the trauma itself and sometimes bits and pieces of its immediate aftermath. Does that sound like what you're experiencing?"

"I . . . I think so," Bell said. "I remember being in a tank of some sort. It was utterly black in there. But I don't remember an avalanche or . . . . Wait. The tank was mounted on the truck you let me use, Sam."

"That's right. Colonel Goethals granted you carte blanche within the zone, and I got you a truck, one of the surplus water carriers."

"What happened to me?"

Before Sam could tell the story, Dr. Hamby said, "I've got rounds right now. I'll come check on you later for a more thorough exam. As I understand it, retrograde amnesia is usually temporary. In a day or two it all should come back, though, if it doesn't, there's no real danger."

"Thank you, Doctor."

"Rest now. And consider yourself the luckiest man in Panama."

"Hello, all," Tats Macalister greeted the room cheerfully as he slid past Hamby.

The Englishman wore riding breeches and

285

a gaily striped muslin shirt stained with sweat around the collar and under the arms despite the early-morning hour. His eyes swept the room and immediately returned to Marion. "Felix told me you were up all night. If I may be so bold, you don't look it at all."

"Thanks, Tats," Marion replied to the flattery. "You're an accomplished liar."

Macalister greeted Sam by name and shook his hand before angling his face toward Bell, still lying on the bed. Tats's smile now touched his eyes. "I shudder to think the premiums you pay for life insurance, Isaac."

"While it's a group thing for all Van Dorn agents, I do think Joe had to get a special rider so I can be covered too."

"I would have come last night, but I was engaged with some engineers from General Electric who thought us limeys don't know how to play poker. I'm glad you're okay." Tats looked quickly to Marion. "He is okay?"

"Yes. Just sore, with a nasty bump on his head, and a little amnesia."

"Amnesia? Awful, old sport. What do you remember?"

"Almost nothing. Sam was about to fill in some details."

286

"By all means continue."

Marion slid off the chair and perched herself on the bed so that she could rest a protective hand on Isaac's leg. Sam remained standing, and Tats turned Marion's chair around so he could rest his wrists on its back as he sat astride.

"The doctor wasn't wrong," Westbrook said to start his tale. "Isaac, you are the luckiest man in all of Panama. There was a survey crew working the far side of the cut opposite of where you went off the road and down into the canal. You are also the unluckiest, because as you went over the edge, you triggered a string of explosives likely planted last spring when we were working that section. Sometimes when we have a large shot, some of the dynamite doesn't go off. Maybe a fuse gets cut. We don't realize explosives have been left behind at the time, then it all goes off weeks or months later."

He added grimly, "Usually, when some poor sod is working right above it."

"I drove over the edge of the canal and right on top of an old string of dynamite?"

Sam nodded. "One of the men on the crew said it looked like the truck slid a little sideways off the road and tipped on its side before tobogganing down to the bottom of the canal. Seconds later, the charges went off, and a big chunk of the slope came down after you. They saw you dive into the water tank just before it was hit and then they lost sight of the truck.

"It turned out the avalanche carried you another eighty or so feet from where you'd first came to rest, though they didn't know it at the time. All they saw was the wall of mud hit you and then you had simply vanished. When the avalanche finally settled, there was nothing to see, just a new field of mud and rock blocking half the channel. It'll take months to dig all that slop out again."

"How did you find me before my air ran out?"

"Near thing. You were as gray as a corpse, and just as stiff, when you were pulled free. The survey crew, having seen everything that happened, knew you were down there. While one of them took their truck to bring help, the other three slogged their way across the new landslide and started looking around, hoping to see part of the truck sticking out of the ground. They could estimate where the truck finally ended up but couldn't find anything.

"An hour or so later, a crew of about fifty men arrived in a convoy. I was part of it because when I heard it was a water truck that went over, I figured it had to be you. You would have been on the road from Gamboa about then."

"Gamboa?"

"Yeah, you had a meeting with Courtney Talbot in the morning."

Bell shook his head, frustration furrowing his brow. He didn't remember meeting with Court.

A concerned look came over Marion. "Maybe we should do this later, Isaac. You need to rest."

"No, I'm fine." But he knew he wasn't fine. Not being able to rely on his wits was a disorienting shock that he could neither comprehend nor accept. At length he said, "You're right, but let's hear the rest of the story first."

"And then straight to sleep."

"Yes, Nurse Bell."

"Mr. Westbrook, please keep it brief."

"Yes, ma'am. Like I said, there were fifty of us, mostly islanders used to heavy shovel work. They hammered metal rods into the ground to try to locate the truck, but it was no use. There were so many boulders in the dirt that the rods either couldn't penetrate very deeply or were deflected. Finally, it was a man who'd dropped his tobacco pouch who heard you first."

"You heard me? Was I shouting?"

"No. You were tapping with something metal inside the tank. He'd been standing right on top of you, yet with all the banging and hollering and general hubbub of our rescue efforts no one heard it."

A split-second flash of clarity raced across the synapses of Bell's brain. "My .45? Where's my pistol?"

"Your stuff is in the bottom drawer of the nightstand," Marion said as she leaned forward to open it.

Some hospital staffer had laundered the clothes and folded them neatly. Bell's boots were next to the wooden stand and they'd been cleaned too. Sandwiched between his shirt and pants were his undergarments and holster. She handed him the weapon, and Bell examined it. The magazine was missing. He assumed it had been removed and put in the holster. The butt plate at the bottom end of the grip showed numerous scratches where he'd tapped it repeatedly against the flange around the tank's filler cap.

He showed the others. "This is what I used. I remember that now."

"See," Marion said, beaming. She'd noticed her husband's disquiet over the retrograde amnesia. "It's already coming back."

"The funniest part is, you were tapping out a song, and one of the workers knew it. Pretty soon, he'd taught all the others the lyrics. Darnedest sight I'll ever see is fifty men, stripped to their waist, in the rain, digging into the muck and mud and singing 'Sailing Down the Chesapeake Bay' over and over again." He then sang in a surprisingly good voice, " 'Come on, Nancy, put your best dress on. Come on, Nancy, 'fore the steamboat's gone.' "

Isaac and Marion joined him, though Tats Macalister stayed quiet, as he'd never heard the tune.

" 'Everything is lovely on the Chesapeake Bay. All aboard for Baltimore, and if we're late they'll all be sore.' "

Bell laughed for the first time since regaining consciousness.

"The men swear you kept perfect time for the first hour, though by then a lot of them were joking about you taking requests because the song had become repetitive." Westbrook turned a little somber. "The jokes dried up when the tune trailed off, and you started tapping out Morse code. I told them that S.O.S. was a dire call for assistance, and, damn, if those men didn't double their pace. I don't think if we'd laid track and gotten a steam shovel on-site that more dirt would have been moved.

"We figured out the orientation of the tank as we excavated around it by noting where the mounting brackets had been torn free from the truck. We concentrated where we knew the filler cap would be. The men tore into the ground like savages, and when they came across a boulder that they could wrest out by hand, a few would act as riggers to secure it to ropes, the rest would pull it out like they were draft horses.

"You had become more than someone needing to be rescued, you became an inspiration in a fight they refused to lose. The softer you tapped your gun against the tank, the harder they worked because they knew you were dying and they were failing. In the end it was only a couple minutes after you stopped tapping that we could wrench open the tank and get a man inside to pull you out."

"I had no idea," Bell breathed. Everyone had been moved by the story, but him most of all since it was his life that they saved.

Marion clutched her husband's hand. "We must do something for those men."

Sam looked suddenly uncomfortable.

"What is it?"

"Once we got you out of the tank, I drove you straight here. The workers scattered.

I'm sorry to say I don't know who any of them were, and there's no real way to track them down."

"That's the canal in a nutshell," Tats Macalister said. "A heroic task undertaken by faceless men whose effort will be remembered but whose names were never known."

"I'll ask around, if you like," Sam offered.

"Please do," Bell said and tried to stifle a yawn.

"That's our signal to go," Macalister said, straightening up from his chair.

He and Westbrook shook Bell's hand — Tats looked away at the last moment as if a little overcome by emotion at Bell's survival — and bade their good-byes to Marion.

"I like them," she said when they were alone. "Sam has been a real sweetie since he learned I was your wife. And that Tats Macalister — boy, could I make him a matinee idol in no time."

Bell remained silent, his mind elsewhere.

"Stop thinking about what all those men did for you," Marion said ardently. "You don't need to feel that you owe them. They did it because they wanted to and because it was the right thing. You do the right thing all the time and never expect any kind of acknowledgment. You're not in their debt, so quit brooding."

He chuckled. "You can read me like a book."

"One I am particularly fond of, so please stop trying to destroy it. Seriously, you could have died out there."

"I think that was the intention."

Her concern deepened. "Do you remember something?"

"No, but you know me and how well I drive. There's no way I lost control on my own."

"You were on an unfamiliar road in the middle of a storm in a truck you've never driven," she pointed out. "Even you can make a mistake."

"But I'm also on the trail of a violent insurgent group whose moneyman I killed a couple days before. I can well imagine they'd like their revenge."

"Why such an elaborate trap?"

"If there were witnesses, it's easier to explain away a road accident than standing over a dead body with a smoking gun in your hand."

"But it could still just be an accident," Marion persisted.

"Until my memory resolves itself, I have to be extra-careful and assume the worst, otherwise I'm leaving myself vulnerable." Bell tried to lean over to reach into the nightstand, but the rush of blood to his head made him almost lose consciousness again. He flopped back onto the pillows. His face had turned the color of old ash.

"What do you think you're doing?"

"The magazine of my .45 should be in my holster."

"I don't think —" Marion stopped when she saw the determined look in her husband's eye. She got up and perused the holster in the drawer, then handed him the loaded magazine.

He slipped it into the magazine well, quietly racked the slide, and then thumbed down the hammer. He slid the gun under his pillow. "Thank you."

"You're welcome."

"Can I ask another favor?"

She smiled. "Of course."

"Leave Panama."

The smile vanished.

"You heard me, Marion. You shouldn't be here. It's too dangerous, and I'm in no condition to protect you."

"I don't need your protect—"

He cut her off. "You do. You're a target now because you're my wife. That makes you leverage. I can't continue my investigation knowing you could be kidnapped or worse. You're a distraction. A lovely, beautiful, wonderful distraction. And one I can't afford."

Her face bore a mask of utter frustration. He'd laid out a logical argument that she could not refute. Marion took another tack. "Let's both get out of here. You're in no shape to continue investigating. You hardly remember the past twenty-four hours. What can you hope to accomplish?"

"I can't let some two dozen men die without getting justice," he said.

She watched him for a moment. "This is your way to balance the scales, isn't it?"

He didn't reply.

"Don't you see that it doesn't, Isaac? Finding the killers will make no difference to the men who dug you out. It won't repay the debt you feel you owe them."

"There's also Roosevelt's visit, and the attack in California," he said, then added, "You know I can't leave this alone."

"I do. Your dedication is one of the things I love most about you, but . . ."

"But there's a price to pay. And you're the one who pays it the most."

"It's okay." Her smile was a little wan. "If I wanted a worry-free life, I would have married an accountant."

Guilt rippled across Bell's face. He loved Marion desperately and knew he caused her anguish with every case he took and every madman, anarchist, or murderer he chased down. It wasn't that she didn't know and understand his job before they married, yet he could tell that she worried more now as they both recalculated their mortality.

"I know that I know something," he said at last. "I just don't know what I know. Does that make sense?"

"It does," Marion said, her voice softened by concern. "I also see that it's killing you."

"There's a hole in my memory, a black void I don't know how to fill." Coming from Bell, this was an admission of doubt and weakness. "I've never experienced anything like it, Marion. It's like my brain has let me down. Or I've let myself down. Or something."

"Don't torture yourself like this. You've been injured. It will take time to heal."

"What if it doesn't?" he asked. "What if the blow caused permanent harm? As you've so often pointed out, I live by my wits. Right now, I feel like a half-wit."

Her grip on his hand tightened, but she said nothing.

"I'm not sure how well I can look after myself here in Panama and I'm certain I can't protect us both. I also know I can't leave. I have to see this through to the end."

"For your sake, I'll go," Marion said. "Me being here puts too much on your plate. You need to focus on yourself and the case. I accept that. I don't like it, but I accept it."

Relief washed over him, and the somber cast in his eyes brightened. He kissed her as tenderly as he ever had. "Thank you."

"You're welcome. I was talking with some nurses last night when you were still unconscious. A few of them are at the end of their contract and are steaming back to San Francisco the day after tomorrow. I should be able to book passage on the same ship."

"Perfect."

"What are you going to do once you're cleared to leave here?"

"I was told I was driving back from Gamboa after meeting Court Talbot. I don't remember our get-together, but I have a vague image in my mind of a boat heading off into the mist. I think Talbot's out hunting the Viboras on Lake Gatun. I need to talk to him about our meeting and, hopefully, jog loose whatever it was I understood before the crash."

"Sounds to me like you're thinking straight."

"Thanks. In the meantime, I'll see to it that Dr. Hamby thinks it's a good idea to have another bed dragged in here until you're safely out of the country."

Her cheeks pinked and her eyes narrowed knowingly. "If we put extra pillows under the blanket, it'll look like I'm actually using it."

21

Bell was released from the hospital the next morning. His head was feeling clearer, though the retrograde amnesia persisted, and the knot above his brow was noticeably red. In addition, he had bruises on his arms, legs, and shoulders. None of his joints were impaired, thankfully. He wasn't in top form, he freely admitted, but he could function.

It was on the drive from the Ancon Hospital to the Central Hotel that Bell began to sense rising paranoia in himself. Not knowing what had happened on the road from Gamboa made him feel vulnerable, and that made him imagine danger lurking all around. He no longer saw people walking the streets as they went about their business. He saw potential threats.

If he'd become a target of the Viboras, he realized that they could come after him at any time and any place and in any manner they chose. The passenger in the car next to him, as they idled at a crossing for a train to pass, could pull a gun and shoot him without warning. There was a man selling fruit juice, from a big brass urn strapped to his back, on the sidewalk outside the hotel. He could knife Bell, as he passed, then vanish in the crowd. There could be a sniper on just about any rooftop or window within a three-block radius.

That was the power of an insurgency, Bell knew, its ability to blend in and carry out attacks without provocation or warning. How does one fight an enemy you can't detect until after they've struck? He thought about the guerrilla war grinding on in the Philippines and knew a long occupation doesn't work. To end this, Bell had to think of some other way or the body count would continue to rise.

"Are you okay?" Marion asked. She was seated next to him in the hired car.

Sam Westbrook had been apologetic but resolute about Bell's not borrowing a second government vehicle. He was already on the hook for the first truck's loss and had to find a way of hiding it from the accountants. He did arrange for Isaac to rent a car from a friend who was laid up with a broken leg and couldn't drive.

"Yes, I'm fine."

"You seem a little jumpy."

"Vigilant," he countered. "Not knowing who my enemies are is making me see them everywhere."

"Isaac, you can't go on like this."

"Don't you see? I've gotten to them. I think that's why they tried to kill me." He paused, then explained. "Every time an insurgency reveals itself, be it an attack or just graffitiing their name on a wall, they risk exposure. They must balance that risk with the reward. Understand?"

"Yes."

"For them to expose themselves and try to kill me shows I am a danger to them, even if I'm not sure why."

"I don't like this, Isaac," she said, unable to stop herself. "I manage to keep myself together when you're on a case because I know how clever you are. But, right now, you're not yourself."

Bell knew not to offer her platitudes. They were too closely connected for that. "You're not wrong, but that doesn't change the fact more people are going to die if I can't solve this. I wouldn't be able to live with myself if I walked away."

"I know." She touched his cheek. "And I appreciate your honesty."

Bell parked in front of the Central Hotel

302

and sent a bellhop up to the room with Marion to fetch her things. He found Felix Ramirez in the bar, talking with his head chef. As soon as he saw Bell step into the deserted room, he dismissed the white-aproned chef and rose in greeting.

"You look none the worse for wear, my friend. I'm sorry I couldn't visit in the hospital. I had a problem with overbooking." He caught himself. "What do you care about my problems? What matters is you. How are you feeling? Tats reported you had some memory loss?"

"Still do," Bell said. "I don't remember driving to Gamboa, let alone back. The whole day is pretty much a blank."

"Most distressing. But otherwise?"

"Beat up, but not knocked out."

Felix threw him a toothy smile. "That's the *yanqui* spirit. Does that mean you're staying?"

"It does. I want to meet up with Court Talbot again. I hope talking with him will help with my memory."

"You do remember he is out on the lake hunting the Viboras?"

"Sam Westbrook reminded me. Has there been any word?"

"No, nothing. But it is a big lake. Let me do this. I have friends in Gamboa. As soon as Talbot returns, I will have them call me, and I will drive us both to meet with him at the dock."

"Thanks for the offer, I already have a car."

"Suit yourself. Want an espresso?"

While Marion was a fast packer, Bell felt he had the time. "Love one. Anything happening since I went for my joyride?"

"Nothing much. Tats is trying to work out how the canal's opening is going to affect the region and how he can profit from it. He knows the Authority will look after the needs of its workers, yet he feels that there will be ships lingering at both ends of the canal waiting their turns to transit. He's looking for an angle there, and he may be onto something. If he can get goods out to the ships on small boats, the captains won't have to pay dockage fees or deal with customs."

"Smart. I assume the Webbs are still awaiting a ship to New York, but what about Herr Leibinger-Holte?"

Felix hesitated as if he'd just remembered something. "Sorry, what? Oh, I haven't seen much of Ernst. He's been holed up with the railroad people over in Colón, trying to make a sale. Last he told me was, if he isn't successful, he's being ordered to Brazil to pitch their electronic switches for a new hydroelectric dam being built near São Paulo."

"And what about old Jorge Nuñez? I really like him."

"He's a good man, our Jorge. I'm glad you got along. For the past few months, he's been trying to get a permit to work in the Canal Zone as a tutor for some of the workers' children without any luck. He mostly takes jobs as a tour guide for visiting Americans or acts as a translator down on the docks. Apart from Spanish and English, he speaks Portuguese, Italian, German, and French."

"Perhaps I can put in a word," Bell offered. "If I get Viboras Rojas sorted out, Colonel Goethals will owe me a favor."

"Damned decent of you," Felix said with genuine surprise. "It's refreshing to see someone look beyond the surface and appreciate the depths below."

Bell said nothing and took an appreciative sip of his strong espresso.

"I like your wife, Isaac. She's a true beauty."

"Thank you. And thank you for escorting her to the hospital."

"Of course. I felt bad I couldn't stay to see you wake up. But then, I'm sure you preferred seeing her face when you awoke rather than mine."

Bell chuckled. "For the first few seconds, I thought I was in Heaven, looking at an angel."

"Had it been me, you would have been certain you were in Hell," Ramirez said and roared at his own joke. "I look forward to discussing her career over drinks tonight, before dinner."

"I'm afraid that's impossible," Isaac said to the obviously crestfallen hotelier. "I'm sending her home. She's too tempting of a target. Kidnapping her would be as effective at stopping me as if the Viboras had put a bullet in my brain."

"You do not think as a *latino-americano*, Isaac." Ramirez took true exception to Bell's inference. "We treat all women as if they are *abençoada Maria*, the Blessed Mary herself. No matter how badly the Viboras would want to hurt you, they would not harm your wife."

"I hate to disagree. Just like there is no honor among thieves, there is no chivalry when it comes to insurgents. If an act will advance their cause, they will strike. They just indiscriminately killed almost thirty men at Pedro Miguel, and in San Diego they fired off a Lewis gun around crowds of

306

women and children. I am not taking any chances."

"*Sí*. I get your point. If I had a wife as beautiful as yours, I would want her home safely too. Are you then not concerned while she is at sea?"

Before Bell replied, the front desk clerk entered the dining room and beckoned Felix.

"Duty calls." The hotelier smiled. "Forgive me."

"Of course."

"Who's going to sea?" Tats Macalister had approached from behind, as silent as a cat. He had a half-eaten piece of fruit in one hand.

"Hmm? Oh, my wife. After my ordeal, she's agreed to head back to the States."

"Today?"

"That's right. There's a group of nurses rotating back home. Marion's going to bunk with them as it's all on short notice."

"Ah, the *Spinster Express.*"

"Pardon?"

"It's what some of the men call the ship taking women who didn't find husbands here back to America. The vessel is actually named the *Spatminster,* a Belgian liner contracted by the Authority to transport miners from California."

Just then, Marion swept into the room, carrying a scarlet hatbox in one hand and a wicker basket in the other. Her boater had a peacock feather stuck in its hatband that matched the emerald sparkle of her eyes. "Good morning, Mr. Macalister."

"For me, that is not the case, Mrs. Bell, for your husband just informed me that you are leaving us."

"I'm afraid so," she said. "On those rare occasions when he uses reasoned arguments for wanting me out of his hair, sometimes a girl has to listen. Isaac, my ship leaves in a few hours, and I want a picnic." She held up the woven basket. "Cold chicken salad, French bread, a perfectly ripened avocado, and fruit tea. It's the least you can do."

"I guess it is," Bell said. "Where'd you get the food?"

"Chef whipped it up while you gents were chatting. It only took me about a minute to pack, after all."

"You are a lucky man, Isaac Bell," Tats said with an admiring grin. "Take her to the overlook near Ancon. It is the best spot from which to see the canal."

"Good idea," Bell agreed.

They ran into Jorge Nuñez, Bell's guide, just outside the Central's front door.

"Meeting clients, Jorge?" Bell said by way

of greeting.

"Hoping to get some business if I loiter in the lobby, Mr. Bell."

Bell gestured that Marion should see to her luggage in order for him to have a private word with Jorge about the case.

The bellhop already had Marion's matching valises in the small bench seat behind the car's open cockpit. She handed over her hatbox and picnic hamper and let him buckle the securing straps. Bell walked over and tipped the man and accepted his offer to crank the engine while he worked the throttle and choke controls.

He had use of a three-year-old Renault AX roadster. Under its distinctive coal scuttle hood was a 1000cc, two-cylinder motor capable of delivering a top speed of thirty-five miles per hour. It was painted green, with faded gold striping, and while it was lovingly maintained, the ravages of its tropical home were apparent. The leather upholstery was brittle and had black mold in its creases. The brightwork was showing pitting. Like with the water truck Bell had totaled, the fender flaring over one of the front wheels had been crumpled and then beaten back into shape. At least the wheels were in good condition, though where a spare tire was supposed to be attached to the chassis, there was nothing but clamps.

The car was right-hand drive, which Bell was getting used to, and they were soon on their way out of the city.

Marion had already been to Ancon Hospital, so she knew almost immediately that Bell had another destination in mind.

"Where are we going?" she called over the sound of air rushing past and the burble-pop of the two-cylinder engine.

"What's your biggest complaint about California?"

She thought for a second and remembered something she'd said when they'd arrived in Los Angeles. "The beaches are beautiful, but the ocean's too cold," she said and then clapped her hands like a little girl. "You know a beach?"

"My new friend Sam Westbrook told me about a spot south of the city when we were walking around a few days ago. Very secluded."

"But I don't have a swimming costume."

"Like I said," Bell replied wolfishly, "very secluded."

22

They made it to the pier with just moments to spare. The *Spatminster* was a white-hulled ship with yellow funnels that had two purple bands ringing them at the top. She had a three-decked superstructure sand-wiched among forests of derricks, booms, and masts. Her main deck was so covered with air scoops to ventilate the interior spaces, she reminded Bell of tubas in an orchestra's brass section.

The gangway was still down, but the docks were mostly deserted. The stevedores and truck drivers had moved down a couple berths to see to the unloading of another ship, a vessel that had made the long run around the cape.

Passengers lined the *Spatminster*'s railing, and when Marion alit from the Renault, a clutch of women at the top of the gangway shouted and waved. A pair of them came down to greet her, while Bell caught the attention of a porter to hustle Marion's luggage aboard.

"You made it," one of the women said. She no longer wore her nurse's uniform, but Isaac recognized her from the hospital.

"Just, right? Jenny, you remember my husband, Isaac?"

She smiled warmly. "You look a lot better now than when I first saw you, Mr. Bell."

"Thanks to the care I received at your hospital," Bell said, tipping his hat.

"And Isaac, this is Ruth Buschman. She's going to attend the medical school at UCSF in the fall."

"Congratulations," he said. His next words were drowned out by a throaty blast of the ship's horn. The porter was already coming down the ramp with an empty hand truck, having delivered Marion's luggage to a steward. It was time. "If you ladies will excuse us for one second . . ."

Isaac turned aside and took Marion's hands. "Thank you for doing this for me."

Her eyes were glassy wet. "You be careful. Lay as low as you can until your memory comes back. I mean it."

"I'll do my best." It was as close to a promise as he could make. "Stay close with your new friends. I can't imagine the Viboras have had time to plan anything aboard the ship, but be careful. I've made the line aware of your situation."

"Isaac, there is no 'situation.' It'll be fine."

"Okay, sorry. You know me. Couldn't care less about my own safety yet I hate the thought of you crossing a street unescorted."

"My knight in shining armor."

Bell picked at his damp, clinging shirt. "In these conditions, I'm afraid the armor's all rusty."

They kissed, and the horn trumpeted again. A ship's officer ahemed to get their attention. "Ma'am, please."

They parted reluctantly, but, as with so many of their partings, they just smiled, and then Marion turned and went up to the main deck with Ruth and Jenny in tow. At the top, she turned, her blond hair catching the light like a mirror, and waved one last time.

Bell scanned the docks, looking for anyone showing extra interest in him, but saw nothing out of the ordinary. Workers bustled around pallets of cargo, horse teams with trailers conveyed crates and burlap sacks, laden trucks were driven off the docks to wherever their loads were needed. A few seagulls were perched atop some bollards.

The skies were threatening more rain.

He turned back to the ship and spotted

Marion at the rail, a tiny figure three stories over his head, and waved his hat. She saw him and waved back. He could imagine the smile on her face. She blew him exaggerated kisses and he pretended to catch a few. But then the horn blew again, and heavy smoke coiled from the ship's funnels, as her twin screws began to churn the water while a tug helped pull her from the dock. Bell waited a few minutes more, then returned to his car.

With rain threatening once again, Bell deployed some wooden braces and unfurled the leather top over the coupe's open cockpit. He drove to the lookout atop Ancon Hill. There were a couple cars in the newly laid lime-shell parking lot and a scattering of tourists looking down into the yawning mouth of the Panama Canal. A canopy had been erected by the Authority to protect visitors from the sun or rain, depending, and a few benches to sit on and rest their feet.

Bell parked and walked over to where a man was sitting alone on one of the benches, Isaac's shoes crunching the bed of crushed shells.

"Anything?" he asked.

"A quiet morning," Jorge Nuñez said. "A couple cars with gringos, looking at the excavation, and a flock of parrots flew by. What'd you expect?"

"Just that, actually, but I needed to be sure." Bell pulled some cash from his wallet.

"I feel guilty taking it from you."

"Don't. You've done me a huge service."

"Is this how an investigation goes?"

"Typically." Bell handed the money to Nuñez and indicated that he would give the guide a ride back into Panama City. "Hour upon hour of boredom and ten minutes of action."

"Can you explain why you wanted me to watch this particular parking lot?"

"Because my wife and I had the day to play tourists, and this is where a tourist would typically come. Tats even suggested it. If the Viboras were going to pick up my trail, this would be a good place to start."

"You're a clever man, Mr. Bell. You were elsewhere yet would still know if someone is trying to follow you."

"Exactly. Now that my wife is safely away, I can use myself as bait to draw them out."

"Is that wise?"

"No, but at least I saved a few hours of boredom that were part of my job."

Bell spotted the tail as soon as they drove out of the zone. The car was a Model T, and in it were three men. He would have picked up on them anyway, but they were so unprofessional that they actually pointed out Isaac's car as he and Jorge passed. Traffic was moderate, but he slowed enough to give them time to merge onto the two-lane road.

It was time for those ten minutes of action.

23

As soon as the pursuing Ford had bulled its way into traffic three cars back, Bell said, "Jorge, we've picked up a tail. Don't look back. It's a Model T with three men in it. Its top is down. I suspect the men are armed. I wish I had time to drop you off before they tagged me, but it wasn't in the cards."

Jorge resisted the urge to look over his shoulder. He had stiffened, though, and his eyes had gotten larger and rounder, as fear began to affect him physically. His breathing went a little shallow and rapid. "What are we going to do?"

"I'm going to lure them into a trap," Bell said, swinging the nimble roadster across a plaza and down a street lined with three-story buildings.

The Model T gained two car lengths. Bell knew that there was a problem with his plan. The Ford had a four-cylinder engine and was capable of close to fifty miles per hour. It would be slower because of the weight of the driver and passengers yet would still have a speed advantage over his two-cylinder Renault.

The car jounced over the cobbled streets, and Bell felt the tonneau cover overhead the back passengers' compartment luffing like a sail in the wind and slowing the car down even further. "Pop out the roof's support frame on your side."

"What?"

"We need to ditch the soft top. Pull the locking pin and yank up on the support strut."

Bell did the same on his side, fumbling over his shoulder to yank out the varnished wooden hoop that stiffened the leather cover. When it popped free, the top remained inflated by air rushing into the cockpit, but once Bell popped a few of the grommets holding it to the windshield, the leather cover pulled free and collapsed into the tiny rumble seat behind them.

They gained an extra mile or two per hour. Not that it mattered much. The Model T quickly passed the vehicle remaining between them and accelerated into the Renault's bumper. Had they hit at an angle, the bigger sedan would have spun the

French roadster, but they hit flat against its rear. Both men lurched upon impact.

Bell swung the car through a ninety-degree corner, the wooden-spoked wheels straining at the lateral load. Bell's face reflected concern. He had seen such violent maneuvers snap spindles and crumple wheels on much better maintained cars.

This new road was little more than an alley, so the Tin Lizzie was stuck behind Bell. They took the opportunity to use the Ford like a battering ram. Three times they struck the little Renault, and would have hit a fourth time had the third impact not wrenched their bumper askew and accordioned their hood a little.

The alley opened into another plaza, one with a fountain at its center topped by a statue of some past person of importance. Bell didn't have time to care. He mashed the accelerator and squeezed the horn's bulb like a Highlander going into battle blowing his bagpipes. Pigeons and people scattered. He threaded the car through a stream of traffic crossing the plaza on a diagonal road. The Ford stayed on his bumper as it rocketed through a gap of horrified drivers amid an off-key symphony of car honking and shouted oaths.

With virtually no effort, the Model T

swung around the Renault and pulled up alongside. The driver watched the road while his passenger leered at their quarry. It was the guy in back, wearing simple peasant clothes but with a bandanna tied over his nose and mouth, who pulled a sawed-off shotgun into view. The mouths of the twin barrels looked as big around as silver dollars. He seemed confused, for the smallest fraction of a second, that the roadster's driver was on the opposite side of the car.

That hesitation was all Bell needed. He braked hard, waited to bleed off enough speed to slide behind the Ford, even as the shotgun roared and a storefront window disintegrated into a million glass chips.

The Ford's driver hadn't expected Bell's maneuver, and by the time he started slowing, Bell was around again on the other side and racing past. That was his one advantage. The much-lighter Renault could out-accelerate and out-brake the heavy sedan.

"We can't play cat and mouse with them," he said, turning down yet another street. The Ford lost a good twenty seconds as it lumbered back up to speed.

"We're only a few blocks from a police station," Jorge told him. His hands were so tightly clenched, his knuckles were white.

"That's not how this is going to end," Bell

said as he worked the car around the worst of the puddles on this new street. The houses were little more than run-down shacks crammed in so tightly they held one another upright. Women doing chores on the stoops watched them race by with indolent eyes. Stick-thin children pointed.

Bell then said, "At the next cross street, I'm going to make a hard left turn. I need you to get out."

"What?"

"We're going too slow with you in the car, and I can't risk them blasting away at us with that shotgun. Don't worry, I'll be going slowly enough. Just open the door and hit the ground jogging."

"But my leg . . ." Jorge protested.

". . . is functional enough for this. The alternative is a double load of buckshot to the head." Bell lined up on the next corner, stealing a glance behind. The Ford was almost on their bumper.

At the last second, he downshifted with a grinding of gears and hit the brakes hard. The spoked wheels warped slightly as the car skidded across the muddy street in a power drift its designers had never imagined it could handle. Bell hit the gas, even as the car was still fishtailing through the corner, and managed to reach across a terrified

Jorge Nuñez and throw open the passenger's door.

"Go."

The Ford shot past the intersection, its rear slewing dangerously from side to side as the driver overcompensated for his mistake.

Jorge leapt from the Renault, his short legs pumping for all they were worth. To his credit, he stayed upright until he tripped over some broken cobblestones and fell, sprawling into a mud puddle deep enough to safely absorb his momentum.

Bell put him out of mind, noting the car picked up speed now that it was carrying only one man. The Ford lost a minute backtracking through the intersection and taking up the chase once again. It took several minutes and many blind turns for Bell to begin to recognize where he was. The overloaded Ford was barely keeping pace with his nimble little car.

But then Bell came to a near-complete stop. A wagoner was trying to maneuver a two-horse team on a street that was far too narrow. The wagon held barrels, most likely Caribbean rum, as there seemed to be nothing but bars and cantinas lining this particular road. The Ford came roaring up behind him. Bell didn't bother with the horn. It was useless with city horses. In his haste to jump free, Jorge had left his knobby cane in the car. Bell took it and rose slightly in his seat to deliver a backhander to the one horse's rump as sweetly as an eight goal handicap polo player.

The horse reared up, causing its yoke mate to do likewise, their front hooves pawing the air, and giving Bell the room he needed to sneak past the traffic snarl. Barrels fell from the wagon as the horses' initial panic became self-sustaining terror. The driver hauled at the reins while crowds of men who'd been paying for drinks in the bars and cantinas suddenly had a lake of free booze glugging merrily from broken casks.

The Ford was stuck while Bell pulled away, but his pursuers maintained the line of sight and saw him take a sweeping turn that led to the coast road where he'd earlier taken Marion. He knew they would be after him quickly, so he poured on the speed. He had to reach a specific spot on the road with at least a minute ahead of the Viboras.

The Renault gave him everything it had, the little engine puttering away as smoothly as an electric sewing machine. The city quickly gave way to suburbs, and then civilization fell away so just a few huts clung to the shoulders of the road. Minutes later, he was barreling close enough to the beach to hear the surf crashing onto the sand, while the western sky was darkening with fresh storm clouds. To his left were a few driveways where wealthy Panamanians enjoyed ocean views. Backing the homes were some low hills covered with more of the country's impenetrable jungle.

Bell found the cove where he and Marion had enjoyed their picnic. He couldn't see the Ford but had to trust it was still behind him. There was no real turnoff, just a slight widening of the dirt track. Bell wrestled the car through a three-point turn and had it racing back the way he'd just come.

In less than a minute, a speck appeared on the road ahead of Bell, and it quickly resolved itself into the boxy shape of the Ford Model T. The gunmen never suspected a thing until the last moment, when the sharp-eyed driver recognized the green Renault.

Bell saw his eyes go wide, and just before they raced past each other at a closing speed of eighty miles per hour, Bell gave his wheel the tiniest tug, twitching the roadster just enough for the approaching driver to react and then overreact.

The Ford slid, its back end whipping

around so quickly that it almost flipped onto its side. The outside rear wheel collapsed in a shower of wooden shards and rubber chunks, and the car dropped heavily onto its suspension, the de-wheeled axle gouging a furrow in the road.

Bell watched the accident unfold over his shoulder and slowed his car to a safer speed, a satisfied expression on his face. He hadn't expected the wheel to come apart like that and he wasn't displeased. He had more time to get into position and camouflage the Renault.

Two miles closer to town, Bell came to a stop and carefully backed his car off the coast road onto an overgrown track that gave access to the beach fifty feet behind him. Opposite was a driveway with a gate drawn across it to prevent anyone accessing the property. The track was little more than a footpath for the homeowners to make their way to the water's edge. This was another feature Bell had seen on his earlier visit and it had given him the idea of how to turn the tables on whoever the Viboras had sent to attack him.

He'd originally planned to simply back the Renault into this nook and wait for the hunters to pass. He would then begin to tail them, but with the gunmen stuck, changing out their ruined wheel, he had time to rake the side road clean of his tire tracks and drape some fronds over the windshield and hood.

It took them a solid thirty minutes to replace the tire. Had the car not suffered a breakdown, the Model T would have raced back toward the city still in hot pursuit of Bell's Renault. But the Viboras's return was one of ignoble defeat. They knew their quarry was long gone. Bell watched them approach from behind some dense bushes.

A light rain began to patter the leaves and impact the dusty road with micro-sized explosions.

The Ford was doing less than thirty miles per hour, maybe not even twenty-five. Bell noted that the spare wheel wasn't in great shape. He recognized the driver and his accomplice in the front seat. They were natives, with dark skin and hair. The shooter in the back, the man whose features remained hidden behind a red bandanna, looked tense, like a man who dreaded having to deliver bad news to his boss. Bell had a fleeting familiarity with the man, the way he held his head, perhaps. More likely, it was Isaac's mind hoping this would be the spark to trigger a flood of memories that didn't come.

Bell began to uncover the car. In a jarring flash, the vague feeling he'd had earlier of some boat vanishing into the mist solidified into the solid image of a poorly maintained cargo vessel from which Talbot planned to scour the lake for the terrorists. The detail his mind focused on was the dinghy hanging off the back of the craft. He remembered bright bronze oarlocks.

It was the first concrete memory he had of that fateful day and it felt like he'd reached a turning point. He was now confident that the floodgates would open soon and the rest would come back too. He felt his resolve sharpen as he cranked the engine and climbed behind the wheel. He edged the Renault back onto the coast road. The Model T was out of sight, but Bell could see its tire tracks in the newly spread mud layer.

He accelerated hard enough to catch up, and in less than a minute he could just make out the Ford ahead of him. The falling rain helped keep the vehicle indistinct, which also meant it would be near impossible for the men to see the much smaller roadster in their wake.

A few minutes later, Bell realized the Ford was growing larger, from his perspective. The rain hadn't slackened, so it meant the

Model T was slowing. He parroted the move, bringing the Renault to a standstill. Where the dirt road veered away from the shoreline and thick jungle lined both sides of it, the Ford made a left-hand turn. Whoever had a house on this side of the road would have uninterrupted views of the beach and Pacific Ocean beyond.

Bell had expected they would return to the city to report their failure, yet they had turned down the driveway to one of the big haciendas. He made no assumptions about what was unfolding, but his pulse quickened with the potential of a new quarry. There was no cover to hide the Renault like he'd done before. Instead, he backed about a quarter mile up the road and trusted that the Viboras would continue on to Panama City.

Before abandoning the car, he used the dagger he kept in an ankle sheath to cut away the roadster's leather top and fashion it into a makeshift poncho. He sliced off the two cargo straps from the rear rumble seat and made them into a belt to keep the poncho in place. He wished he had his rubber boots, but they were back at the hotel.

Like in so many of his investigations, he had no idea if he was going to be rewarded with answers or left with more questions.

24

In the deepening gloom and worsening rain, Bell jogged up the coast road to the driveway where the Ford had turned. There was no gate or gatehouse, and the main house was far enough back that he couldn't see it from there. The driveway curved through the lush landscaping and coconut palms. The rain would block out the sound of an approaching car, so Bell couldn't follow the drive directly. He moved off into the thicket a good twenty feet and made his way parallel to the gravel track. The going was slow. This place was professionally landscaped and maintained yet still felt like virgin jungle. He had to use his dagger to cut his way through some of the denser vines and creepers.

Five minutes after starting out, Bell reached a clearing. He crouched down under the cover of a canopy of trees. The grand house was in the center of a vast lawn sprinkled with beds of flowers and stands of trees like isles in a green sea. The Model T was parked in the driveway in front of the entrance portico. Its top was up against the rain, and the driver's elbow rested on his door. Occasional bursts of cigarette smoke blew from the interior and were shredded by the rain.

The house was whitewashed limestone blocks with a red, barrel tile roof, and it made Bell think of some colonial-era plantation. The railings, the window trim, and the double front door were all made of a tropical wood so dark that it looked black in the watery light.

Bell adjusted his poncho and felt a needle-like sting on the back of his hand. He thought it was some insect bite, but when he examined it, it was just a red weal left by a milky splatter of rainwater that was now growing painful. He looked around and recognized the leathery yellow-green leaves, as described by Court Talbot. He'd blundered into a solid wall of manchineel trees. One night on the voyage from California, when Court was on a roll describing all the horrors Panama had to offer, he spent a good amount of time describing the highly acidic plants.

At Bell's feet were dozens of small, lemon-sized fruits. Court called them *manzanillas de la muerte,* "little apples of death."

Another drop of sap-laden water fell from the brim of his hat and hit the back of his neck. It felt like someone had held a smoldering match to his skin. Rather than panic, Bell went very still. He sat more upright so any water falling from his hat landed on the poncho. He pulled his hands under its leather and held them close to his body.

Court had especially warned him not to let any of the toxin get into his eyes. The blindness that caused was only temporary, but the pain was some of the worst imaginable. He'd once been forced to shoot a horse that had broken two legs when it had thrashed in pain after such blinding. He'd been with men who'd begged for the same release.

There was no other cover Bell could reach, with the car sitting in the driveway, and he couldn't risk backing out of the dangerous grove because any movement would heighten the chances of severe burns across his face and in his eyes. He'd been lucky getting this far through the thicket, but the oozing sap from the leaves and bark and fruit turned the falling rain into a veritable shower of acid. He could not go forward or back without exposing himself to the caustic deluge.

And so Bell sat as still as a statue while a naturally corrosive liquid dripped and dribbled inches from his face. He reduced his breathing to shallow sips of air, fearing that the sap would easily be dispersed during storms. The only positive of his situation was that local wildlife avoided the noxious plants. He didn't have to worry about snakes.

Bell crouched under his poncho with his hands now resting on his knees. After just five minutes his legs and back began to ache, but he dared not move. At the ten-minute mark, his muscles were screaming for relief. And after fifteen, he was contemplating a course to get him out of this minefield of toxic trees when the hacienda's front door opened, and a figure, hunching under the rainfall, dashed back to the car. Last drags of cigarettes were taken and butts were hastily tossed onto the drive. The passenger jumped to open the rear door for the team leader and then rushed around to the front of the car to crank the four-cylinder engine to life.

Moments later, the Model T looped around the circular drive and headed back to the coast road. Bell levered himself to a standing position, his knees protesting like he was an eighty-year-old man.

It had grown dark enough that lights were turned on inside the big house. Bell stepped out onto the lawn, moving slowly to his left to circle the house on its darker side, where he assumed most of the bedrooms were located. The poncho was perfect camouflage against the dark trunks of the manchineel trees. He reached a back terrace and could sense the vastness of the Pacific stretching out behind the mansion. He could see the blurry lines of white surf curling against the beach. Palms swayed in the stormy breeze while rain continued to fall. Bell's shoes were soaked through and squelched with each step.

He found cover behind a planter and watched the hacienda's interior through multiple pairs of French doors. The back of the house was essentially all glass. An elderly servant in dark livery glided across the airy living room with a silver tray in hand that was holding a heavy cut-crystal tumbler filled with amber liquor. The man reached the door and was about to knock. Bell could see through the glass doors that the servant had approached the study, where the master of the house was at work at his desk. The furniture in the home office was heavy and dark, more befitting Old Europe than the

New World. There were few books on the towering shelves, and Bell imagined that without proper conservation the pages of any volumes would disintegrate quickly.

Bell saw the owner's head rise from his work at what had to have been the knock on the door. He heard a muffled response, and the study's door opened inward. The majordomo stepped in to place the drink within reach atop the massive desk. They spoke for just a moment, and the butler backed out. Bell tracked his progress back across the living room. The man vanished through a set of doors Bell assumed led to the kitchen.

Bell shifted his position, finding cover behind another planter that afforded him a better view into the study. He couldn't see what the man was working on, and the tall back of his desk chair prevented Bell from seeing the man himself. Bell could only see his arm, in a billowy white shirtsleeve, his hand plucking the glass off the blotter and returning it seconds later with its level noticeably lower.

The homeowner worked at his desk for another thirty minutes and then suddenly started closing up the ledgers strewn around him. Bell leaned forward to adjust his aching legs and bumped into the planter, which scraped against the stone flooring of the ter-race. The storm more than covered the sound of the light clatter. At least for the man.

A dog had been curled, unseen, at its master's feet and leapt up at the sound, pressing its snout to the glass door and barking madly. It was sleek and black, with cropped ears and a mouthful of teeth like those of an industrial saw. With its front paws pressed high up on the window, it stood almost as tall as a man.

Fifteen feet and a tightly closed door separated Bell from the dog, but for a fleet-ing moment Bell was sure he could smell its breath and feel its angry heat on his face.

Knowing what was coming next, Bell backed away from the planter and then off the patio entirely. His best hope was reach-ing the ocean and waiting out the animal in the surf. The homeowner stood, and Bell caught a glimpse of a large-framed man several inches taller than himself. He opened one of the French doors, and the dog, a breed Bell had never seen before, shot out like a rocket, its ears erect and its mouth wide, powerful haunches launching each smooth stride.

It raced for the exact spot where Bell had been crouched behind the planter. Bell was still in motion and had another thirty feet of beach to cover before reaching the surf. The dog would track his scent and cover that distance in half the time it would take Bell.

The animal put its nose to the patio and suddenly began yelping in pain. Bell stopped and watched as the poor dog bowed its head down so it could swipe at its longish snout with its paws, all the while crying pitiably.

The manchineel, Bell realized. The rain had washed the rest of the toxic sap off his poncho and the concentrate that pooled at his feet had burned the canine's sensitive nose when it tried to pick up his scent. The animal sneezed several times and seemed to get the worst of the toxin out of its nose, but its enthusiasm for chasing the intruder had died. It high-stepped back to the study door and sat, waiting for its master to open it, sneezing a few more times for good measure.

The owner reemerged and spoke to the dog for a few seconds before letting it back in the house. Bell had remained on the beach in the water, so all he heard was low murmurs.

He waited twenty minutes, now hidden in some sedge grass, before returning to the patio. On one side of the study was a formal living room, on the other was a dining room large enough to seat a dozen guests. Its white walls were hung with colorful, locally dyed fabrics in simple wooden frames. The table was of a honey-hued wood and styled more in keeping with the hacienda's tropical setting. The homeowner ate by himself, though his butler made frequent forays into the dining room with additional dishes and refreshed drinks.

Bell had a better view of his quarry. The man had dark hair and an unlined, Central European face, putting him closer to forty than fifty. He couldn't get a read on him because of the distance and angle, but Bell could imagine his anger at tonight's failure to either capture him or, more likely, kill him. Bell had no doubt that this stranger was the person behind Viboras Rojas, the puppet master secretly pulling the strings. He also had no idea what the man would gain by sabotaging the construction of the canal.

Questions and answers. The ledger for those wouldn't balance out until the case was solved.

After his meal, the homeowner returned to his study to use the telephone on the desk and then sat in the living room, listening to Richard Wagner operas on a gramophone and smoking a cigar. His taste in music led Bell to believe he was German.

A short time passed before the man rose from a sofa and lifted the needle from a gramophone disc and made his way to his bedroom. The dog stayed close to its master. The butler appeared a few minutes later, bustling about the living room to tidy it up, and then he vanished into the servants' quarters.

Bell circled the house twice, moving slowly and always locating his next spot for cover before doing so. There was no additional security, and all the lights were off. On his second sweep, Bell located a clutch of outbuildings. One was a garden shed, another housed an oil-burning steam boiler and an electric generator. The former emitted only the soft glow of its pilot light under its insulated main tank, while the generator itself was quiet. The equipment wouldn't be needed again until morning.

By his estimation, forty-five minutes had elapsed since the homeowner had gone to bed. The servant too was surely deeply asleep. Time to move.

The lock on the study's French doors took less than fifteen seconds to pick using the tools Bell always carried. Before entering the house, he pulled off the rain-slicked poncho. There wasn't much he could do about his wet shoes, but at least he wouldn't drip an obvious amount of water on the floor. The door swung out silently, and Bell slipped into the room. He flicked on the battery-powered lamp and held it so that his fingers blocked all but a tiny ray of light from shining through.

Bell went straight for the desk, sweeping the light across its broad surface and committing the location of everything on it to memory so he could put it all back when he was done. Riffling through some of the ledgers and other books, Bell learned his man was named Otto Dreissen and that he was part owner of a large family business concern called Essenwerks. He knew of the company, not its owners. They were a manufacturing, smelting, and coal mining concern and looked to be mostly profitable.

For ten tense minutes he sought some clue as to Dreissen's ultimate goal in Panama. There was a great deal about the collieries they owned, and he found a dossier on some of the equipment they manufactured. He saw designs for a biplane that appeared to be able to shoot twin machine guns through the spinning blades of its propeller. There were sketches of a submarine that was as sleek as a shark, others of robust-looking trucks that ran on metal belts rather than wheels and were shown towing large field guns. Still others detailed motors that were meant to be lightweight and more powerful than anything Bell could imagine, and a control room for some unknown craft that looked decades ahead of its time. There was a drawing of an aerodynamic pod whose function was a complete mystery. It was like he was looking at the work of some futurist rather than a contemporary.

Everyone knew Europe was heading to war. The storm clouds had been building for years as alliances were formed and stiffened to the point that a spark would set off a continent-wide conflagration far deadlier than any in history. Bell could see that Dreissen's company was positioning the Germans to have vastly superior equipment for when the shooting finally started.

He needed to pass this on to some friends with Army Intelligence, but he couldn't see what any of this had to do with the canal.

He was about to open a new file folder titled *Cologne,* with a sketch of what appeared to be a cigar, when a floorboard creaked just outside the closed study door an instant before the door itself was thrown open.

Bell doused his light, but a man Bell had

never seen before was carrying a flashlight in one hand. His other was gloved in dark leather and balled in a fist. A night watch-man making his rounds, was Bell's first thought. He had the look of a grizzled veteran, tall and strong but past his prime.

The man's eyes widened for just a second upon seeing Bell, an intruder, before he took two quick paces forward. Bell stepped back, edging closer to the French doors and escape. The broad desk was between them and it was far too wide to reach across. The guard had to go around it, and by the time he could, Bell would be dashing across the lawn.

The man rushed for the desk and swung a punch with his left hand. It looked awkward, and the range was far beyond his reach, but his fist smashed into Bell's face anyway. It was a glancing blow yet one that stunned Bell for the long moment it took his brain to process the possibility of being struck.

The guard took that opening to leap on the desk and chop down with what Bell now realized was an artificial arm, one fashioned several inches longer than its flesh-and-blood partner in order to serve as a weapon of surprise.

The distraction had so rooted Bell to where he stood that he barely got an arm up to protect himself as the man tried to stave in his head. The power of the blow struck him with enough momentum to drop him to his knees, and his forearm went numb.

The guard jumped off the desk, aiming his shoes at the back of Bell's neck.

Bell rolled just before the impact, hooked a hand around the man's ankle before he had centered his weight, and yanked him off his feet. He crashed to the floor hard enough to rattle the house. The dog began barking in another room, and its claws scratched frantically as it accelerated through the house to investigate the disturbance. Bell got to his feet and pushed through the French doors and back out into the storm. Its glass shattered in his wake as the guard swung again with his elongated prosthetic arm and it met nothing but the elegant door.

Bell retrieved his poncho as he ran. The dog was after him like an arrow and would have sunk its jaws into his thigh before he reached the patio's edge had it not detected the strong scent of manchineel again.

It kept barking and running alongside Bell, but it wouldn't commit itself to attack. Bell ran hard for the manchineel trees, flipping the poncho over his head as he plowed into the toxin-laced forest. The storm had diluted the trees' potency, yet any water touching his skin still felt like fire. The dog managed to get tangled between Bell's feet. Bell and the dog both fell to the ground in a jumble of limbs. The animal's coat was short, so its skin was poorly protected. It let out a yelp when its belly hit the forest's litter of wet leaves and it scrambled to its feet before Bell had even come to a full stop.

Torn between its duty to protect his master and its instinct of self-preservation, the dog raced back toward the house in an inky black streak.

Bell got to his feet, careful not to use his hands when levering himself upright. He adjusted both his hat and poncho to give the most protection and set off again, much more mindful of his surroundings.

He steered clear of the driveway, knowing that with the dog returning to the house so soon, the guard would go search for him in an automobile. Minutes into his hike back to the Renault, a long-hooded saloon sedan drove by slowly. Bell paused and sank to the ground until the vehicle was past. He could tell the car was turning toward Panama City when it reached the end of the drive. Bell tore through the jungle to get to the road and ran as hard as he could in the opposite direction to where he'd left his car. He figured the guard would check the roads for no more than a mile or two before doubling back and investigating the coast road past the estate.

Bell reached the Renault in record time, but he was breathing so heavily that he wasted precious seconds doubled over trying to get his breath back. He set the throttle and choke to the proper settings and worked the hand crank a quarter turn to prime the carburetor. Then he pulled the throttle, making sure the car was in neutral, before returning to the crank once more. It took six tries for the now cooled engine to fire. In that time, a glow had emerged down the road, a vague aura that grew in brightness as the stately saloon drew closer.

Bell hopped back into the sodden driver's seat and put the Renault in reverse, steering by looking over his shoulder so he didn't waste time turning the car around. He didn't bother with the headlights.

He backed down the road as fast as he dared, and all the while Dreissen's car was growing closer and closer. He was still far out of range of the German's lights, but every second their corona became brighter. He'd gone at least a mile in reverse and suspected the engine was overheating, as no air was getting through the radiator. He had to spin around or the car would die.

By what silvery light made it through the storm clouds from the half-moon, Bell judged the best spot to sling the car around. Near one of the other hacienda driveways, the gravel track was a bit wider. Bell steered the Renault as close as he could risk to the verge and then stomped the brakes and powered the wheel hard over. The roadster slewed around so quickly that the front wheels lost grip. Bell had the transmission in first by the time the hood was lined up with the road once again. He popped the clutch and mashed the throttle so the engine would stop the car from spinning out and into the ditch.

He was quickly up to thirty miles per hour, and while Dreissen's automobile kept gaining, the driver never got close enough to spot Bell ahead of him. After three miles or so, Bell saw the other car's headlights diminish, as the guard slowed, and then go dark when he turned the big car back toward the hacienda.

Bell took his foot off the gas and let the Renault coast until it stopped on the side of the road. He took a few breaths. As close calls went, this one wasn't even in the top fifty for him, but his nerves still needed a moment, and he needed to think through the information he'd gained and its context for his investigation.

He came to the conclusion all too quickly that knowing Dreissen's identity and the connection between him and Viboras Rojas was not the same as being able to prove anything. Bell needed more. He turned around once again to return to Panama City.

Heinz Kohl found his employer in his study when he returned to the hacienda. The Panamanian house servants were putting hurricane shutters over the smashed windows on the outside. The broken glass and water had already been cleaned up. Dreissen was wearing baggy pants and a sleeveless white singlet. The suspenders pulled over his shoulder were decorated with hunting motifs. A lit cigarette sat in the ashtray, blue-gray smoke coiling into the thick air.

"He got away," Kohl said.

"That's the second time tonight I've heard that," the industrialist said angrily. "I assume it was Bell, yes?"

"He fit the description," Kohl told him. "And he was in the area. He doubled back on our men after they lost him on the coast road. That's how he knew to come here to the house." Kohl pointed at a crystal decanter sitting on a small side table beneath a painting of Dreissen's blond wife.

"Help yourself," Dreissen said and took a sip of the Napoléon brandy he'd poured earlier.

Kohl pressed the decanter against the wall with his prosthetic left hand in order to pull out the stubborn stopper. He splashed some of the golden liquor into a snifter and reinserted the plug. He gulped half the drink in a single swallow and loudly exhaled the fumes.

"What did you think of him?" Dreissen asked, his voice full of contempt.

"He has fast reflexes." Kohl set his drink down and began unbuttoning his left sleeve. All his shirts were custom-made so he could slide his right hand through the cuff without assistance. The left arms all had buttons running up past the elbow and were cut extra-long to conceal the fake limb. "When I throw this hand at someone the first time, he takes a long time to process what he's seen, enough time for me to take him out. Bell understood what had happened in the blink of an eye. Fast reflexes and a fast mind."

"Considering how he took out six men in California and killed Morales, that's something we already knew."

Heinz Kohl had worked for Dreissen for a decade and still insisted on asking permission from his employer. He asked to sit, and Dreissen waved him into a chair. For his part, the industrialist also insisted on being asked permission. They were not friends yet were closer to each other, in a way, than they were to any other human being. Heinz Kohl would lay down his life for Otto Dreissen and Otto Dreissen would certainly let him.

"How do you want to proceed?" Kohl asked while tugging on his artificial limb.

"Bell will get no traction with the local police, we've got them bought off. But he certainly will have Goethals's ear."

"He has no power outside the Canal Zone."

"He has clout, and that may be enough to override the bribes we've paid to the police and to people in the Justice Department."

"Why don't you let me kill him? We can pin it on the Vipers."

"No. It's important that Viboras Rojas lay low while Court Talbot is hunting them on the lake. We can't kill Bell anyway. I didn't tell you, but I received a cable this afternoon. Berlin has authorized the assassination of Theodore Roosevelt. Bell is

Roosevelt's point man for his visit. If Bell is murdered, there's no way he'll come to inspect the canal."

"We hadn't thought of that before."

Dreissen nodded. "Good thing the avalanche failed. There is something else. We don't know how much time Bell had to go through my papers and what he will report to the Americans about Essenwerks's weapons development. He may even know about the *Cologne,* even if he doesn't know it's here. We need to sweat that information out of him. A man like Bell won't easily break under physical torture, but I have an idea how to break him psychologically."

"What do you need from me?"

"Phone Detective Ortega. Tell him we want Isaac Bell arrested for breaking into my house. He's bound to show up at the Central Hotel sooner or later. I'm going to radio Captain Grosse and send him on a little errand."

"Won't that delay —"

"One night won't matter," Dreissen countered before Kohl could finish.

"Of course."

"This should work out quite well." Dreissen took a final drag on his cigarette and crushed it in the ashtray. "If Bell is merely arrested, Roosevelt will still come, and we'll make up for a past failure. Heinz, this will raise our company's profile with the Kaiser. I can see Essenwerks getting more and more government contracts, work that would have gone to Krupp or Rheinmetall. It'll be ours. And when the war comes, our factories will be the busiest in Germany."

"An amazing opportunity," his man agreed. "I will call Ortega now in case Bell goes straight to his hotel. Good night, Herr Dreissen."

"Good night."

25

The two nurses, Jenny and Ruth, stood at the rail of the *Spatminster* with Marion Bell until her husband walked off the docks and headed back to the parking lot. They stayed out until the breakwater, built of rock and stone wrested from the Culebra Cut, was off to the port side, and the liner began to roll with the long Pacific waves.

"Come on," said Ruth Buschman, "Jenny and I have already unpacked. We'll show you the cabin, and we can get changed for dinner. We're scheduled for the early seating."

Their shared cabin was one deck up from the main deck, which meant they had a private entrance from the promenade and a real window rather than a single porthole like the accommodations in the liner's hull.

The room had bunk beds, tucked behind the door, as well as a standard bed. There was a washbasin, with hot and cold running water, but no *en suite* bathroom. That was down the hall and shared by five other cabins. The walls were paneled in wood veneer, and the carpet was surprisingly plush.

"We left you the big bed, Marion," Jenny Sanders said. "At the hospital, we had old cots we joked were left behind by De Lesseps, so the bunk beds are going to feel downright extravagant to us."

"We should draw straws for the bed," Marion protested. "It's only fair."

"Don't worry yourself," Ruth said. "After a year in Panama, this is the pinnacle of luxury. Right, Jen?"

"Right."

"Well, thank you both," Marion said and set her hatbox on the bed. Her other cases were stacked in one corner. "Tell you what, I didn't bring a whole lot of clothes with me, but let's all three of us get dolled up tonight. Borrow anything you'd like."

The two nurses exchanged a look. "Deal."

At dinner, they talked about how Illinois had recently passed women's suffrage, making it the first state east of the Mississippi to grant the vote, and how that boded well for national passage. Marion told them she'd had friends who'd been at the disastrous rally in Washington, D.C., ahead of

President Wilson's inauguration, and how the police did nothing to protect the women marchers, two hundred of whom were injured.

"I'm afraid it will be a few more years yet before we all have the vote," she concluded.

"Maddening," Ruth said. "I'm going to medical school in a couple months. I'm going to be a doctor and yet I can't vote for the people passing laws that affect how I do my job."

"Makes no sense," Jenny agreed.

"Oh, it makes perfect sense," Marion said with a devilish look in her eye, "from the perspective of inferior men who can't grasp that women can be smarter and more capable in everything we do."

That got a knowing laugh.

After dinner, they stayed in the parlor, listening to a pair of passengers take turns at an upright piano. People sang along with the songs they knew, and a few of the other ladies aboard accepted invitations to dance from gentlemen passengers and crew alike. Marion declined at least a dozen offers.

It was almost ten when they returned to their cabin. The *Spatminster* had left a storm far to the south. The moon was a bright half circle, and the seas had flattened. The ship's forward movement meant there was a nice breeze running the length of her wooden deck, and now that she was many miles from land, the humidity was tolerable.

After readying themselves for bed, they wished one another good night, and Marion switched off the electric light. She drifted off worrying about Isaac and his memory issues.

She awoke in the middle of the night, unsure what had roused her from slumber. The cabin was noisy, in the sense she could hear the wind blowing past and also whistling through the ventilation louvers, and then there was the deep rumble of steam engines grinding away deep in the ship's guts.

But then came a tiny rasp, barely perceptible. It was as soft as a mouse's paw on a metal floor, but it had been enough to wake her. Though not quickly enough.

The intruder had finished manipulating the pins inside the cabin door's lock and snicked it open just as Marion was coming to realize what was happening. Uniformed men burst into the cabin in a wave, each holding an electric flashlight and a Luger pistol with a silencer attached to the barrel. They had to have known in advance the number of passengers in the cabin because there were three men, plus one more who appeared to be in charge.

Two of the men went for the bunk beds while the third lunged across the room at Marion. When he tried to get his hands around her throat, Marion managed to pull her right hand free of the covers and connect with a solid blow to his jaw before he could grasp her.

She wanted to kick free of the bedding, but her attacker's weight had pinned her legs. Her punch had done little more than stun him, and he was soon on the attack. Because he was still above her, he had enough leverage to elbow the side of her neck. It was an expert strike. The muscles around her carotid artery contracted at the blow, cutting off the flow of blood to her brain, and Marion Bell fell unconscious.

While the two men had no trouble subduing the two terrified nurses, Marion came back around just as a hood was about to be pulled over her head by the third man. She roused in time to bite her attacker's hand hard enough to draw blood.

"Scheisse," he said.

Filled with determination and rage, Marion kicked free from her blankets and stood up on the bed in a fighting stance. She struck her attacker, slamming the heel of her right foot just below his sternum. Air blew from his mouth in an explosive whoosh that left him doubled over and gasping as his diaphragm spasmed and refused to refill his lungs.

She jumped off the bed in a swirl of nightclothes and went after the men tying gags around her new friends' mouths. She swept up her purse, hoping to retrieve the .22 caliber pepperbox derringer she carried when she traveled. She didn't get more than a step when the boarding party's leader leveled his pistol at her and pulled the trigger. Even with a silencer, the 9 millimeter was as loud as a sharp handclap. Expecting crushing pain, Marion cringed, but the shot had been an intentional miss, though it had whizzed by so close to Marion's head she smelled singed hair.

"Enough," the man said tightly.

He switched his aim and pressed the gun's hot muzzle to Jenny's temple. The sneer he gave Marion told her that this man wouldn't care one way or the other if she compelled him to pull the trigger. Human life meant nothing to him.

Marion deflated. If it was just her, she would have fought all four to the death. But she wasn't alone. She wouldn't put her new friends in any more danger than they were already facing. She dropped her handbag and allowed one of the men to bind her wrists with rope and another to gag her mouth. The black hood came next. She was thrown over one of the bigger men's shoulder like a joint of meat and bustled from the cabin. The boarding party made its way aft. At this late hour, the *Spatminster* was like a ghost ship. The decks were deserted, and any lookouts would be studying the seas ahead of the liner and not be looking over her fantail.

One of the boarders tugged on a tow rope tied to an all-aluminum boat bobbing in the ship's wake. Two of his compatriots climbed down to keep the craft stable. Marion felt a hemp line being looped under her armpits, and then she was spinning and dancing like a plumb bob as she was lowered to the skiff. Waiting hands guided her the last few feet. The rope was untied, and she was shoved to the floor.

The night air was warm, yet the aluminum hull was chilled by the sea and dripped with condensation. Her silk gown was quickly soaked through, and she began to shiver. She also began to think. She already assumed these men were tied to Isaac's investigation and that her kidnapping meant they were going to use her as leverage with him. The leader spoke English, but the other had cursed in German. So they were likely Germans, validating Isaac's theory that there was a European influence over the Red Vipers.

As the remaining boarders climbed down from the three-hundred-foot liner, Marion Bell vowed to keep fighting. She expected no less of herself, even if in one corner of her mind she wasn't shivering just because of the cold.

The line securing the boat to the *Spatminster* was cut, and the skiff vanished into the night.

The only evidence of the assault were the two ropes hanging off the fantail and the two bound and gagged nurses and a beaten-up purser locked in a closet who'd been forced to disclose the location of Marion's cabin. The kidnapping went undetected until Ruth Buschman worked herself free of her rope and gag six hours after the assault.

The *Spatminster* didn't carry a Marconi radio set, and she wasn't scheduled to make landfall until the colliery in Rosarito. The captain was torn as to where his duty lay. On the one hand, he had a schedule to maintain, but, on the other hand, he needed to report this brazen act of high seas piracy.

He decided the best course was to detour to the closest port that he knew had international telephone service, Acapulco, in Mexico. From there, he could contact the authorities back in Panama.

By then, though, the kidnappers would have an insurmountable head start.

26

Bell had to assume that Otto Dreissen had phoned his people stationed in Panama City and that by now it was open season on his life. The Viboras would be combing the town for him, which meant he couldn't go back to the Hotel Central. He spent the night in a seedier section of town, in a run-down rooming house on a street full of bars and brothels. He'd paid for a broom-closet-sized room above a cantina and was overcharged by the night clerk, who knew desperation when he saw it.

He'd washed up in the lavatory as best he could. In the silvered mirror over the basin, Bell could see the manchineel burns on his face were barely noticeable, but the lump on his head from the avalanche was a sickly-looking purple. He stood in his undershirt while he wrung out the linen oxford he wore under the poncho. A double whiskey sat on the edge of the sink.

Back in his room, he draped his wet things over a chair and hoped the night air would dry them by morning. The room's lock was a joke, so he placed his wallet and .45 under his pillow. Ignoring the raucous singing and tuneless piano coming up through the floor, Bell was asleep in seconds.

He awoke to sunshine and recalled dreaming about a great-aunt he'd stayed with when he was a boy who'd punished him by making him swallow a spoonful of castor oil. He hadn't thought about it in years yet still could feel the greasy emollient on his tongue.

His clothes were damp but wearable. He found a cheap restaurant near the cantina and sat in the far back. The food was simple — eggs, over thick corn tortillas, and a sweet green fruit he didn't recognize — but the coffee was excellent, and the waitress came by often to refill his mug. The clientele were locals, who eyed him for a moment, then left him in peace.

Bell had parked the Renault a few blocks from his room in case its description had been passed on to the Viboras. He found a vantage point from which to watch the car, or, more accurately, watch if anyone else was watching it. After ten minutes and a careful assessment of all the open windows above the establishment-lined street, he approached the car. He got it fired up in record time and lit out of the rough neighborhood.

After filling the tank at a gas station next to Ancon Hill, Bell took the road back toward Gamboa. He'd thought that traveling it again and seeing where he'd been buried alive might jog some memories.

Seen from above, the landslide looked enormous, though it was nothing compared to some of the bigger ones slowing the excavation. A great tongue of soil and rocks stretched from the canal's rim at Bell's feet almost halfway across its breadth. In the middle of the rubble field, he could see where the workers had excavated around the water tank that had saved his life. The tank was still buried, but he saw the piles of dirt that had been shoveled from the hole and some large rocks that had been levered out of the way to give them access.

Bell was moved by the dedication his rescuers had shown — the amount of rubble they'd excavated was impressive.

Looking down the artificial valley that was the canal, he spotted work crews already laying a fresh set of tracks to reach the avalanche. They were a mile away or more, but he could see a large mobile crane, which was capable of swinging prefabricated sections of rail in place, atop the gravel bed, the men swarming it tamping each rail flat. When the track was completed, a steam shovel would be brought in to tackle the slide. The debris would be hauled out on a separate rail spur, while the ore cars would remain on the main line to haul out the overburden.

It might take them months — or, in the case of the Cucaracha slide at Panama City, years — to undo the damage, yet they went about their job undeterred.

What Bell didn't get was the spark that coming here was supposed to ignite to make him remember additional details of that day's events. While it was a gap of only a couple hours he couldn't remember, Bell felt a hollowness he could not fill. He lacked trust in himself, his mind, his instincts. He could see yet felt like he was blindly groping, stumbling and lurching when he should be walking easily. Isaac Bell had never been defined by his memories but rather by his ability to recall them so readily. The chunk of missing time was a reminder that he was no longer himself.

He spent ten minutes scouting the area around where he'd left the road. Just beyond the grass verge, he did spot a twenty-foot-long log. He didn't know its significance. Had it fallen off a lumber truck and forced him off the road? Had it been deliberately laid there as a roadblock? Given the attempts on his life, the latter seemed the more likely option.

Too much time had passed for any subtler clues to have remained. The rains here were so intense, they dissolved footprints and tire tracks in minutes.

Bell saw no point in clambering down the hillside to get a better look at his temporary prison. Not only did he not need to see the oversize and inky black claustrophobic tank, he had no idea if the ordnance disposal team had made certain there weren't more undetonated charges littering the slope.

Rather than return to an uncertain future in Panama City, Bell continued to the company town of Gamboa. Sam Westbrook told Isaac about meeting with Courtney Talbot there, and Bell recalled a boat being involved. He also recalled the bronze oar-locks. However, driving into the drab town brought back no new memories. There were warehouses near a train station, and a few bunkhouses for workers, plus a handful of dilapidated railcars that had been pulled from the line and left in a field. They housed more workers, and one was a general store.

Bell parked the Renault in an alley between two warehouses. He leaned a pair of rotting cargo pallets against its grille, and, from even a few feet away, it looked like a pile of scrap left abandoned and out of sight.

He double-checked his .45 and crossed the tracks, heading away from the speeding Chagres River to a small field, where he found a makeshift restaurant. Outside, there were no chairs, and the tables were empty barrels set on end. Men stood as they ate. The ten or so watched Bell approach. He didn't sense hostility, but rather a surprised curiosity. Gamboa was populated exclusively by West Indian islanders. Bell crossed under the awning and stepped into the restaurant proper. That was a misnomer. Inside was just a serving line that separated the entrance from a large commercial kitchen built inside a tin shanty.

"I think you lost, yes?" said a lady at the end of the counter. She was accepting paper scrip from the workers to pay for their meals. She had a heavily lined face, which told of a hard life, but laughing eyes. When she moved her plump arms, bracelets made of twisted copper wire tinkled faintly.

"Not if your food tastes as good as it smells," Bell replied.

She liked his reply, and a smile creased

her face even more. "It taste even better, love, but you ain't a company man so I can't feed you." While her accent was thick, her grasp of English was good.

"Tell you what." Bell pulled a dollar from his pocket. It was almost enough to get a filet mignon at Delmonico's. "What say we pretend I'm a company man just for today."

The bill vanished into a pocket of her voluminous apron. "Best if you eat out back."

The irony wasn't lost on Bell, but he thought it was probably a good idea.

"Go out and sit yourself down, and I'll bring you a plate," she told him. She motioned to one of the women tending the stove inside the kitchen. She came out and took over the till while Bell's new friend went to get him lunch.

Behind the makeshift restaurant was a small garden with meticulously straight rows of lettuce, tomato plants, and all manner of herbs. Some chickens scratched at the ground, and in the distance was a rickety bamboo pen with two goats in it. They rushed the fence when they saw Bell, hopeful he was bringing food. When Bell sat on an over-turned bucket next to a covered coal locker, the goats lost interest.

A moment later, the restaurant's back

screen door banged open, and the woman came out with a metal plate mounded with rice and chicken stew. She handed it to him, pulled a spoon from one apron pocket and a bottled beer from the other. "It's either this or our water, and you don't want our water."

"Thank you. It's fine. Can I ask you something?"

"Your dollar still buyin', love."

"Do you know Major Courtney Talbot? He left a few days ago in a boat."

"We all know him," she said guardedly. "What you want him for?"

Bell couldn't get a read on her. He wasn't sure if she was protecting Talbot or was suspicious of anyone associated with him. He said, "I met with him just before he left. I want to know if he's come back."

"You talk to Jimmer. Him run the store. He and Ojo Muerto are . . ." She meshed her fingers together to indicate the two were tight.

"Thanks."

"You trouble, man?"

"Like, am I in trouble or do I cause trouble?"

"Both, I think," she said cryptically and then returned to her job. Bell was grateful for the beer because the stew was fiery hot but delicious. When he'd scraped the plate clean, he returned it to the kitchen, catching the woman's eye when he set it and the empty bottle on a shelf just inside the door. He nodded his thanks.

He went to the town's store in the abandoned railroad car. The wheel trucks had been removed, leaving the box portion of the car resting on the ground. Rot was slowly making its way up the walls because the wood wicked moisture from the ground. Inside, shelves fashioned from wood scraps had been built along all four walls and were stocked like this store was the jungle version of a five-and-dime. There were gallon cans of lamp fuel, bolts of cloth to make clothing, boots in several sizes, plus socks, and flour, cornmeal, and lentils in five-pound sacks. Bell saw pouches of tobacco, hand-forged tools, tins of condensed milk, fishing line and hooks. He didn't see things like soap or shampoo, or any luxury items.

"Help you, sir?" the proprietor asked. He was about the same age as the woman at the commissary, but he was rail thin, and while his hair was silver, his face was smooth.

"I'm looking for Courtney Talbot."

"He ain't here."

"I know that. I saw him off a few days ago.

I was wondering if he'd come back."

"He tell Gemma 'n' I he comin' back this afternoon."

"Gemini?"

"Gemma and I," he said slowly and pointed to where a woman — his wife, presumably — was coming in from the back storeroom carrying a big pot of yams.

Bell couldn't believe his luck. Then he reconsidered. It was likely he did know of Talbot's return but had forgotten it as a result of his amnesia. Yet on some deeper level the knowledge lingered as only a hunch, and that's why he'd driven to Gamboa.

He wondered what else his lapsed memory was trying to recover. More than his conscious, for sure. Gemini? He admonished himself. The shopkeeper had clearly said "Gemma and I."

Bell thanked the storeowner and returned to his car. The shadow from one of the warehouses fell across the passengers' compartment in back. He stretched out as best he could, adjusted his hat so the straw brim better covered his eyes, and napped through the hottest part of the day.

He was awakened by a train chuffing into the Gamboa depot, steam boiling around its four drive wheels, its bell chiming merrily. He would have awoken in a few minutes, as the sun had swung enough to put its light and heat inches from where he lay. No one was waiting to board the train, and no one descended from any of its carriages. It didn't need to take on coal or water, so no sooner had the wheels stopped than the locomotive began to pull away again, its schedule fulfilled.

Bell left the car and cut around the warehouse so he could stroll across the gravel expanse fronting the harbor. Men were standing at the edge of the pier. He picked up his pace. When he got close enough, he recognized Court Talbot's silhouette. One of the Major's men pointed past his shoulder and he turned. He froze for the moment it took to recognize his visitor.

"Bell, how are you?"

"Good. How was your hunting trip?"

"A disaster."

They shook hands.

"Did you find the Viboras?"

"No. Instead, we discovered twenty or thirty different family groups living on rafts all along the lake's shore. The first time we saw the cooking fires on one of them, I was certain we'd caught the Vipers — remember how I said that was how we were going to get them? It turned out to be a false alarm, just a family of fishermen, two brothers and their wives, an *abuela* and a handful of kids. And for the next few days, and the next twenty or so fires we spotted, it was false alarm after false alarm. Maddening. Wait. What's with the lump on your head? What happened to you?"

"Long story involving an avalanche and me impersonating laundry inside a washing machine. Spent the night after our last meeting in the hospital, and people had to tell me the story because I remember nothing from that day."

"Nothing?"

"Nothing of any significance. The doctor calls it retrograde amnesia. He said it's not uncommon for people with head injuries. I don't even remember what you and I spoke about."

"You had some questions for Rinaldo about his brother. You came to the conclusion that Raul was working for the Colombians. You left here wanting to talk to diplomats back in Panama City." Talbot glanced over Bell's shoulder. A group of workmen had opened a warehouse door to give them enough room to reorganize the jam-packed interior.

"There's more to it than that," Bell said.

"You suspected another player? A European connection, perhaps?"

"That's what I'm working on now."

"Do you have anyone in mind in particular?"

"At this point, I'd rather not say."

Talbot just about begged. "You've got to tell me who. I just spent days chasing my own tail out there in malarial swamps with nothing to show for it. Can't you give me something?"

Bell ignored his plea. "What are your plans?"

Talbot recognized it was prudent to drop the subject. "Refuel, restock, and return."

"You're going to keep hunting them?"

"What other option is there? Every day I don't get them is less money in my pocket and that much closer to the Marines showing up and Colonel Goethals kicking us out. They have to be hiding on the lake."

"When do you plan on leaving?"

"Few hours."

"Enough time for me to get to Panama City and back?"

Talbot nodded. "We could wait for you, sure."

"Okay. I need some place to lay low for a while, and malarial swamps sound perfect."

27

Bell parked three blocks from the Hotel Central. He approached slowly and cautiously, watching windows and doorways, alleys and idling cars. He saw nothing suspicious. The street had its normal amount of hustle.

He wasn't going to take any unnecessary risks. He avoided the main lobby door and sidled around the block to a loading dock at the rear of the hotel. Its big door was up. Inside was a platform for workers to stand on to unload directly from the back of trucks or horse-drawn wagons. A couple young men in bellhop uniforms sat with their feet dangling while sharing a cigarette.

They spoke to him in Spanish as he approached. He knew the context of their phrases, if not the actual words. This was a restricted area, and he shouldn't be here.

"Señor Ramirez is *mi amigo*. It's okay."

He brushed past them without giving

them time to react further. That was the other key, he knew. Act like you belong, and people generally accept you being there. He climbed the steps up to the loading dock and went through the double doors into the hotel. He found himself in a utilitarian space used for the storage of dry goods as well as a place where the housekeepers parked their cleaning carts when they weren't making their rounds.

Bell took the service elevator up to his floor and dashed down the hall to his room. The brass key slid into the lock and turned smoothly. He held his .45 low and inconspicuous. He let himself in and closed the door behind him. That's when he realized he wasn't alone. A man in a suit jacket, but without a tie, was sitting on his bed. Another had been behind the door, while a third was close to the window. These two men wore the blue uniforms of the Panama City police department. Bell guessed the man in civilian attire was the lead detective. He saw this in the first fraction of a second and it was enough to tell him he didn't stand a chance of escaping. He released his grip on the pistol and let it dangle from his index finger.

"Isaac Bell?"

"Wouldn't it be ironic if I was someone else here to rob his room?"

The officer behind the door had come up behind him with a pair of heavy handcuffs. His partner stepped closer and pulled a wooden baton from his belt as an unsubtle threat. The cop took the Colt from Bell's finger and handed it to the detective before slapping on the cuffs. At the last second, Bell bent his wrists backward, as the manacles were cinched, to enlarge the circumference of his wrists. The metal dug into his flesh until he relaxed his hands, then the cuffs were loose enough to no longer be painful. One of the many tricks he'd learned from the cons he'd arrested over the years.

"Droll, Señor Bell. You have wasted a great deal of my time." The man's English was good. He was older, in his fifties, with a veteran cop's wariness and weariness. He had more Spanish blood than native, his skin being on the lighter side, and his hair was brown and wavy with a few strands of silver in it. "After our first hour waiting in the lobby, Señor Ramirez insisted we leave and that he would call us when you returned. I trust him less than I trust you, so we came to this compromise. I knew you would come back sooner or later."

"Am I allowed to know your name and what I'm being charged with?"

"I am Detective Ortega, and you are

charged with trespassing and attempted burglary."

"Where and when did this supposedly take place?"

"Otto Dreissen is an important man here in Panama, Señor Bell. We take his complaints seriously. He caught you in his home last night, attempting what he called" — Ortega read from a small notebook he pulled from a pocket — " 'industrial espionage on behalf of his American masters.' Those were his exact words."

Bell knew his only chance was to get ahead of this thing now before it got worse. "I am here on behalf of the Canal Authority to help them stop the attacks by Viboras Rojas. This can be confirmed with Colonel Goethals and Courtney Talbot. In fact, he's waiting for me in Gamboa right now."

"Do you deny being in Dreissen's house last night?" Ortega asked archly. "Before you answer, know that he gave a very accurate description of you and noted that you ran through manchineel trees and likely got burned. I can see the red marks on your hands and face, just as he predicted."

"I think maybe I shouldn't answer that question at this time," Bell said.

Ortega got off the bed and moved so his face was inches from Bell's. His breath smelled of the rum he'd had at lunch. "But you will answer it."

He nodded to the officer behind Bell, and the man rammed a fist so deeply into Isaac's right kidney that the pain dropped him to his knees. That put him in the perfect position for Ortega to drive a fist into Isaac's cheekbone and collapse him to the floor. He wasn't out completely, but his brain misfired for a few seconds.

Orders were given in Spanish. Bell was lifted from the floor and held upright on rubbery legs by one of the officers. All his possessions had been packed in his valise, which the other cop carried when they followed Ortega down the hall to the main elevator.

Outside, one of the uniformed patrolmen ran off and returned in a car a few minutes later. Bell was taken to a nearby police station. He wasn't formally charged with anything. Or told anything, for that matter. While Ortega vanished into a side office, the other two escorted Bell through a central workroom abuzz with activity and the clacking of typewriters. At the far end was a heavy door that had to be unlocked with an enormous key. Beyond was a whitewashed hallway with individual cells along the right-hand wall. The paint was peeling badly and speckled with drops and smears of what could only be blood. There were no bars, just solid brick walls and steel doors.

Bell was shoved into one of the cells and its door slammed shut behind him. The only light came from the dime-thin crack under the door. The lock clanked home. Bell sank to the floor, his back against a wall. The stench was unimaginable.

He hadn't seen this coming and had no plan. His surroundings were so bad, he found himself overly grateful for that razor slash of light coming from the hallway. It was something, a ray of hope perhaps. But then a switch was flicked, as the cop left the cell block, and the fixtures in the hallway went dark. Bell couldn't help but feel the claustrophobic dread of being trapped in the water tank all over again.

He had to order his thoughts. Dreissen was playing games, Bell realized. He knew full well why he'd been at the man's house, so this was just a stunt to involve the police and ramp up the intimidation. As soon as he thought it through, Bell had already considered his options and figured out a way to completely turn the tables on the German.

The big *if* hanging over his plan was the level of corruption within the Panamanian police. Ortega was obviously in Dreissen's pocket, and, to a lesser extent, so were the two uniformed cops. Bell needed to talk to someone higher up, someone who couldn't be bought or, if he had been, wouldn't do the Hun's bidding once he realized the truth.

There was one other tack to take, but it again depended on how deep the police corruption ran. If it was as bad as he feared, Bell's only other option was to hope Court Talbot and Colonel Goethals could somehow spring him.

He estimated two hours had passed when he heard the squad room door creak open in the cell block and the lights turned on. The little aura seeping under Bell's door was a welcome sight, though he understood the techniques at play here. The deprivation was meant to soften him up.

Fat chance.

He pretended to be asleep when his cell door was wrenched open. He acted like they'd startled him awake and he blinked owlishly. The same two cops stood outside his cell. "Oh, hey, fellas. Morning already?"

They yanked him off the floor and frogmarched him down the hall and into the big reception area. This time, they had him climb to the second floor to a windowless interrogation room. There was a table, with two chairs on the side closest to the door and a single chair opposite. That's where the men dumped him. The psychological tactic on display here was that for him to gain his freedom, represented by the door, he had to get past the interrogators. The only thing missing was a one-way mirror set into the wall so Detective Ortega could judge how his prisoner was faring.

Bell folded his hands on the table and waited. If they didn't have access to one of those new mirrors, then there was a peephole someplace for spying. He guessed that Ortega was watching him now and would keep checking in on him for a while. For the next hour, other than the slow blinking of his eyes, Bell didn't move a muscle.

It was his way of telling the Panamanian officer that petty little intimidations were wasted on him.

At the two-hour mark, the door opened. Ortega strode in and took a seat followed a moment later by a strongly built man in a white tropical suit. Bell's eyes widened a fraction when recognition hit. It was Otto Dreissen.

"Your accuser wanted to meet you, Señor Bell," Ortega said. "Señor Dreissen said he might let this matter drop if the two of you can come to an understanding."

Bell cocked his head. Dreissen removed his hat and sat down. He had a slim file folder in his hands that he set in front of him on the table. The antagonism he showed Bell was instinctual and instant. Dreissen knew he was facing an adversary, and from the squint of his eyes to the tension carried in his shoulders, he let Bell know it too.

"A compromise entails each party wanting something from the other," Bell said blandly. He'd faced far tougher men than Otto Dreissen. "How can I possibly help you?"

"Detective Ortega was kind enough to inform me when they had arrested the man who broke into my house." His English was accented, his voice deep. Bell had to admit that the man had a commanding presence. "The detective also mentioned you are in Panama under the auspices of the Canal Authority to help them hunt down the insurgents plaguing the construction efforts."

"That's true," Bell admitted.

"So perhaps you aren't a spy looking to steal trade secrets from Essenwerks after all, that maybe your presence in my home was a mistake."

Bell nodded, playing his role, for Detective Ortega, in this bit of theater. "You are correct and have my sincerest apologies," Bell said. "I had intelligence that the leaders of Viboras Rojas were headquartered in a hacienda on the coast road. I got carried away in my quest to hunt the vermin down. Again, I am sorry for the fright I must have given you."

Dreissen turned to Ortega. "Detective, would you excuse us for a moment. I need to ask Mr. Bell the specifics of what he might have seen in my office. There are important patents involved that need to remain secret."

Ortega stood and straightened his jacket. "I understand, señor. I will be right outside, should you need me."

"Danke."

When the door to the interrogation room closed behind the detective, and the two men were alone, Bell and Dreissen dropped all pretense of civility.

"What are you getting at?" Bell said, snarling.

"Proving to you that you are in far over your head, Herr Bell. Goethals and the Americans hold sway in the Canal Zone. Out here, I'm more powerful than you know. With a snap of my fingers, I can see you stuffed down a hole so deep and so dark you'll wish I'd had you killed instead."

In one fluid motion, Bell pulled the knife from his ankle sheath, the one the police hadn't found because, foolishly, they'd not frisked him after he gave up his .45. He was over the table with the blade against Dreissen's throat before the businessman had time to react. "Feel powerful now?" Bell snapped.

Dreissen groped for the folder he'd brought into the room. He flipped it open and held up the single photograph it contained.

Isaac Bell's brain had been through a lot in recent days, so it took him an extra second to understand what he was seeing. The woman in the glossy held that morning's edition of the *Canal Record* newspaper, the local weekly. She couldn't read the broadsheet's headlines because she was blindfolded with a narrow strip of black cloth. Worse, she also couldn't see the Luger pistol and the out-of-frame man aiming it at her temple, its hammer cocked and his finger on the trigger. What took so terribly long for Bell to grasp was that the woman he saw in the picture in such helpless peril was supposed to be safely aboard the *Spatminster*. Somehow, Otto Dreissen and his Red Vipers had kidnapped his wife.

The picture was of Marion, and the bastard across the table held her life in his hands.

Bell fell back into his chair. His entire world collapsed into uncertainty. He couldn't get his mind around this unexpected twist, and it felt like a knife had cut through his very being.

With unmatched arrogance, Dreissen took a moment to adjust his tie and check to see if any blood came from where the razor-sharp boot knife had been pressed to his skin. There was a single claret droplet. "Yes, Herr Bell." His lips pursed in a smile. "I feel especially powerful now."

Bell found an anchor amid his swirling emotions strong enough to hold him steady. "What do you want?"

Dreissen used his foot to drag over the knife Bell had dropped so he could pick it up. "Originally, I wanted you on the next ship out of the country, with the understanding that you would never return. Once you were back in the United States, I would release your wife."

"How do I know you just wouldn't kill her and be done with it?"

"You don't, actually, but I think under those circumstances you would hunt me to the ends of the earth."

"You think I won't anyway for what you've already done to her?"

Dreissen's eyes narrowed. He could tell that Bell's words weren't an idle threat. He matched the deadly tone. "Her time with my men can be very easy on her or very hard, do you understand? She can be returned to you without so much as a hair out of place or she'll come back a shattered husk of her former self, a living corpse that has endured the unendurable."

"If you —"

The German cut him off. "Never counter a threat with another threat when you have no leverage. Agree that this ends now, that there will be no reprisals in the future, or your wife will pay a price far higher than your desire for revenge."

Unable to speak because of the rage coursing through his body, Bell nodded.

"That wasn't so hard, was it?" Dreissen's arrogance was growing in step with his confidence. He slipped the photograph of Marion back into its folder and stood. "I need to know what you saw in my office, Bell. A man like you can't be trusted to tell the truth, which is why I needed your wife as assurance you will cooperate. I will give you a few days to consider the balance between her fate and your commitment to duty."

He opened the door. Ortega was leaning on the wall on the opposite side of the corridor. He straightened and approached.

"Detective, I am sorry to say that we couldn't come to an understanding after all. I want this man held on all charges. Also, he threatened me with a knife that your men failed to find." He showed Ortega the thin weal on his throat and handed him the blade. "I would consider it a personal favor if you held him for a while."

The wad of cash Dreissen handed over vanished into a jacket pocket. Ortega's smile was greasy. "I think there is no judge to hear any arraignment for many days."

"Perfect." Dreissen gave Bell a condescending glance.

"What about my wife?" Bell shouted at him.

"What indeed, Herr Bell? What indeed?" He moved off down the hallway and out of view.

Bell leapt from the table to give chase. He knew he could blow through Ortega easily enough even if the man had his knife. But then his two henchmen stepped into view, wooden batons at the ready. Bell stopped short and held up both hands. "Okay, boys.

It's all okay."

It wasn't okay.

They went after him with the nightsticks. This too was a psychological ploy, as was so much of what the police did to suspects and prisoners. The beating wasn't personal, it was just to show the prisoner that he no longer had rights, not even freedom from harm — especially not that. Bell's shoulders and arms took a savage number of blows as he fought to protect his head. Through it all, he thought nothing of himself and only of Marion and her uncertain fate.

28

The beating finally stopped when one lucky blow glanced off Bell's temple, tearing skin and opening a patchwork of tiny veins and arteries. Blood welled from the wound, looking far worse than it was. Bell hadn't lost consciousness, but the gore was enough to satisfy the cops' lust for violence.

"Alto," Ortega said.

Bell was certain that once he was back in a cell, he wouldn't see freedom for weeks. Ortega didn't care who he was, never even asked how Dreissen knew Bell's identity. The detective had his own part to play in the sham and now he would fulfill whatever promises he'd made to Dreissen. Once they had Bell caged, it was over. He had to make a move now. Acting like the blow had affected him more than just bloodying his face, he rolled his eyes back into his head and crumpled to the dirty floor.

Ortega said something that could have

been an admonishment, that his men had gone too far, Bell wasn't sure. The detective issued an order and left. Each man taking ahold of a wrist, Bell was dragged out of the interrogation room and down the hall to the stairs. In a move that had been perfected by frequent repetition, they spun Bell so that his boots dangled over the top step and began pushing him down feetfirst. They had to tighten their grip on his wrists to take the weight, but in no time they reached the ground floor, where they spun Bell around a second time and continued to drag him behind them.

The outer door to the cell block was open, so there was no need to pause. They kept going, past several cells, until they reached the one Bell had been tossed into earlier.

The instant the guards released Bell's wrists, he clenched his abdominal muscles with every ounce of his strength to jerk his torso off the floor, the heels of his hands pumping upward for extra power. The right hand landed squarely at the juncture of one guard's legs in a crippling blow that sent him staggering back and clutching his agonized groin. The second strike was off target and mostly hit the guard's thigh and barely made an impression. Bell continued up off the floor, twisting his body and sweeping a leg as he rose to knock the uninjured cop off his feet.

Bell spun once more, building momentum. The closest guard was on his back and already trying to get up. Bell leveraged the weight of his body behind his fist, slamming it into the man's face with everything he had. The nose exploded and head and body crashed backward onto the cement floor. The man's eyes fluttered for a moment, then he was out.

The second guard, still clutching his crushed manhood, sensed the danger he was in and tried to draw his baton. Bell was on him like a wraith. He pulled the stick from the cop's hands and whipped it around his throat, choking off the flow of blood to his brain. The man struggled, but Bell's fury could not be matched. The cop's movements slowed, and then the man went limp in Bell's arms. He let him fall.

Just eleven seconds had elapsed.

Bell removed the Sam Browne belt from the officer closest to his size and tugged the man's arms out of the sleeves of his blue uniform coat. Bell's own pants were a close enough match, so he didn't bother swapping. He ripped a swath from the man's shirt to clean the blood from his face. Once he had the jacket on, he cinched the belt and pulled the cop's visored cap over his head at an angle to cover the wound.

He was running on pure instinct now and didn't know if trying to disguise himself was worth it. He grabbed the ring of keys, stepped out of the cell, and broke its key off in the lock.

Imitating the cop's leisurely pace and slouch, Bell left the cell block and immediately turned his back on the main room beyond in order to lock the outer door. He'd swept the squad rooms with his eyes as he'd turned and noted everyone's position. Two uniformed cops were just leaving the building, two others in plain clothes were at their desks, one typing a report, the other taking a statement from an overwrought woman in a black dress. There were three more people, talking, at a round table in a corner near a bunch of filing cabinets.

The doors to the offices along the left-hand wall, through one of which Ortega had vanished earlier, were all closed.

Certain of his route, Bell turned and started ambling through the police station like he didn't have a care in the world. No one showed even the remotest interest. To maintain as much distance as he could from the others, Isaac walked along the left side of the room and could only hope none of the higher-ranking members of the city's police force chose that moment to step from his office.

A door did open, and a shapely woman's backside appeared. The secretary continued backing out of the office, muttering something to the superior inside. She closed the door and straightened. In her hands was Bell's shoulder holster with the .45 nestled inside. An evidence tag dangled from one strap. She also had his boot knife.

Without thinking, Bell took the items from the stunned woman's hands and kept walking. *"Gracias, señorita."*

"Hey," she shouted indignantly, and all the attention in the room swung to Bell and the woman.

Bell ran out of the room. He'd pushed his luck too far. He should have just made his way out the door and onto the street. The typewriters had gone silent, and he could hear chairs scraping back as officers rose to get a better look at the disturbance.

The desk sergeant happened to be out from behind his counter and talking to a couple kids waiting on a couch while their mother was giving a statement. He was older, rounded, yet he had good reflexes. And he wasn't fooled by the uniform. He tried to stop Bell, as he raced for the front door, grabbing at one of his arms. Bell easily twisted free, but the veteran cop was on his heels when he burst out onto the street.

A police car sat at the curb. Bell couldn't tell if the engine was running, but there was a driver in the front seat, with another cop leaning in the window, chatting.

Bell turned right and kept running. He looped an arm through the shoulder holster strap to keep one hand free. At the end of the block, he slowed just enough to look back. The sergeant was jumping into the backseat of the patrol car. It accelerated from the curb, its horn honking to make room in the traffic. They would be on him before he made another block.

As a truck was just about to roar past, Bell ran into the street, trying to keep pace with the vehicle. The two-ton Mack had an open bed with tall wooden stakes along the sides. Able to match its speed for barely a second, Bell leapt and managed to grab two of the stanchions just behind the cab. His feet hung dangerously close to the spinning rear wheels. He pulled and groped and climbed to get his legs clear of danger.

The truck went around a corner, and Bell's grip was almost broken as his legs swung out away from the vehicle. When the truck was back on the straightaway, the centrifugal force dissipated, and Bell slammed into its side. He was forced to tuck his legs to keep them from being torn off.

A second later, the police car careened around the same corner, its driver honking the horn furiously. The sound was muffled by the din in the street and the truck engine's noise.

Bell clamped the blade with his teeth and straightened himself out a bit, climbing high enough for one foot to find purchase and free up a hand. He transferred the knife to its sheath. From his perch, clinging to the outside of the truck, it felt like they were rocketing down the street. In fact, the police car chasing them was much faster and would overtake the Mack in just a few more seconds. Bell noted the truck's cargo contained tidy ranks of small wooden barrels. Hand over hand, he clambered to the rear of the vehicle and swung himself over the single length of chain that acted as a tailgate. He landed atop the barrels and rushed to unhook one side of the chain. It dropped free, twisting and rattling on the rough road like a snake.

He kicked one of the two-foot-tall pony kegs off the back of the truck. It smashed onto the ground hard enough to crack some of its staves, and a thick black fluid oozed out. It was either engine grease or molasses.

The police car slowed in plenty of time to swerve around the obstacle and continue the chase. When it drew closer, Bell unleashed another projectile. He kicked the second barrel much harder this time, causing it to land farther behind the truck and nearer the pursuing sedan. The driver had to brake hard before jerking the wheel over to avoid the keg.

Bell did this two more times before the cops decided they didn't need to close in on the truck again but seemed satisfied to tail the big Mack for as long as it took. They thought ahead and knew the driver had a destination for his cargo and would reach it at some point. All they had to do was stay behind it.

For a moment, Bell sensed that he was trapped. The .45 hanging under his arm wasn't an option. There was no way he was going to open fire on the police. If he somehow made it into the Canal Zone, he doubted Ortega would launch a formal protest over some trumped-up charges. But if Bell took potshots at the police, he imagined Colonel Goethals would be compelled to turn him in.

He was contemplating jumping out of the moving vehicle when inspiration hit. He dumped two more barrels haphazardly to give himself some working room. The police car dodged them with ease. Bell then lined up four barrels at the very edge of the cargo bed, but rather than kick them off one by one, he lay down and wedged his back against them and waited until the opposite lane was choked by traffic. Against the barrels' combined two hundred–plus pounds of deadweight, he pushed with his arms and legs. The barrels dropped in unison, and all four split open and stuck fast.

The lane was effectively blocked. Bell dusted off his hands in triumph as the cops had no choice but to stop. It would be several minutes before there was a hole in the traffic, buying Bell enough time to improvise the next part of his escape.

The policeman didn't hesitate. He swung the wheel and took the cruiser up onto the sidewalk, scattering pedestrians and smashing apart the wooden boxes of vegetables displayed outside a greengrocer's. The car dropped back onto the road past the gooey barricade, and this time kept coming. The sergeant leaned out the window, a revolver in his hand.

Bell wormed his way into the remaining barrels to protect himself. The gun roared. Bell heard the bullet hit close by.

Unbeknownst to him, the truck's driver had a second man in the cab with him. At the sound of gunfire, the man looked back to see a police car on their tail with one officer brandishing a weapon. He yelled at the driver to stop.

The truck slowed rapidly, its brakes squealing and the barrels shifting so that Bell felt their weight pressing in on him from all sides.

Traffic in the other lane also came to a quick stop. Horns began to sound off, mimicking the noise of a flock of angry geese.

Bell got to his feet as the police were about to get out of their car. He climbed to the top of the truck's staked side and jumped down onto the roof of a car idling in the other lane. He leapt from there to the hood of the next car, scrambled up its windshield and dashed across its roof too. Twice more he did this until he found himself at an intersection. Right at the corner was a livery stable with the horses penned close to the street.

He jumped from the last car roof to the top of the split-rail fence, fought to keep his balance, and then launched himself across the corral, stepping his way across the backs of five horses, moving swiftly yet softly enough that the animals barely had time to react. He reached the far fence rail, and from its top he jumped astride a horse that had just been saddled for its owner — a local farmer or *ranchero,* by the look of him.

"Sorry," Bell said, shaking out the reins and putting a heel to the horse's flank. "I'll have it brought back within the hour."

Because the horse had been saddled, it was primed to ride even if Bell's style of mounting wasn't what it expected. It started off at a decent trot. The owner had been too stunned to move for a second, but he quickly gave chase. Bell drew his .45 and pointed it back at the man. He stopped and cursed at Bell until he'd ridden out of earshot.

There was no sign of the police. He'd given them the slip.

He made note of the street, so later he could pay someone to deliver the horse back to the stable, and then rode aimlessly for several minutes to fully get his bearings.

As much as he wanted to race straight to Dreissen's house and beat the man until he divulged Marion's location, Bell knew not to give in to the urge. Dreissen would have been tipped off the minute he'd escaped. Either the German would leave or turn his house into a guarded fortress. Probably both. Bell's best course of action if he wanted to rescue his wife was getting to the Canal Zone as quickly as possible. If Ortega got his hands on him again, Bell suspected they'd kill him outright, and to hell with any consequences.

He couldn't risk encountering a police barricade on the main road into the zone. It would be Ortega's first order even before freeing his men from the cell. Bell didn't have the time to wait them out or try to sneak past that night, so he rode toward Ancon Hill, the six-hundred-foot, jungle-covered peak that partially overlooked the section of the canal where he had met the tour guide Jorge Nuñez.

The side of the mountain facing the city wasn't as developed as the canal side. Once across Martyrs Avenue, Bell had to bushwhack his way up the hill. To its credit, the horse seemed more than game and exploited the tiniest opening between the bushes and shrubs and knew to keep its head down to avoid the vines draped between the trees like so many Christmas garlands. It was amazing how the humidity shot up under the jungle canopy and how the light became weak and gauzy.

Both horse and rider were drenched in sweat when they burst out of the undergrowth without knowing they had reached their destination. Before them stretched the dazzlingly white observation point's parking lot with a motor bus disgorging a troop of tourists. It was a jarring transition from primordial jungle to modernity in just a few steps.

A dazzling kaleidoscope of images and an array of scents and feelings flooded Bell's nervous system, almost causing him to fall from the horse.

He remembered.

He remembered it all. Everything came back. All the memories. The truck slamming into the water carrier and sending him over the edge of the Culebra Cut. The creeping despair of being buried alive. And especially his conversation with Court Talbot and Rinaldo Morales.

"Yes," he shouted triumphantly, eliciting some startled looks from the tourists across the parking lot.

He had never felt such a tremendous sense of relief in his life. He'd felt like his mind had betrayed him, but now that the memories had returned, he knew that wasn't the case.

He also understood two more things, one of which he'd deduced earlier but forgotten, the other was something new. He had the answer to the mystery of the humming clouds many locals had reported. And he'd figured out that Viboras Rojas, his very reason for being in Panama, didn't exist.

29

Bell had made it safely to the Canal Zone. He was beyond the reach of the Panamanian police. That gave him some measure of satisfaction yet did not lessen the urgency of his mission. He wanted to race down to the administration building, but his mount was in no condition. The horse had given its all to get him to the summit of Ancon Hill, and that was as far as it would let itself be ridden. No amount of coaxing changed its mind.

He dismounted and led the horse down the other side of the hill along the winding road the tourist buses used. The horse plodded along, its head down and the sweat drying on its flanks. When they finally arrived at the soon to be completed building, Bell uncoiled the *reata* that was secured to the bridle and tied it to a tree in the middle of a lawn so the horse could graze.

"You can't leave that animal there." The

speaker wasn't any sort of guard, just a man in shirtsleeves and an accountant's green visor.

"I'm late for a meeting with the Colonel. Care to join me to explain why I was further delayed?"

Between the little-veiled threat and his noticing the big pistol hanging below Bell's left arm, the busybody decided his interest lay elsewhere and moved on.

Bell mounted the steps to the sprawling building. Workers moved purposefully around the site, some administration types, others tradesmen, such as carpenters and plasterers. He spoke to a construction worker installing some wooden moldings just inside the entrance to get directions to which parts of the building were already in use. Moments later, he found where Sam Westbrook worked and located the young man in the open office space. He was standing up behind his desk to give himself a bird's-eye view of the hodgepodge of papers covering its blotter.

"Hey, Sam."

"Mr. Bell." His jaw dropped when he saw Bell's battered appearance.

"We've been through enough together for you to call me Isaac, and I'm afraid our adventures aren't yet done."

"Of course. What on earth happened to you?"

"Where to start," Bell said rhetorically. "First of all, I owe a horse some tender loving care. Is there someone here who can return it to its stable over on Avenue Peru y Calle?"

What Bell especially liked about Sam was that nothing seemed to faze him, not a terrorist attack or a bizarre request. "Sure. I'll get one of my clerks to do it. Where's the horse?"

"Tied to a tree out front." Bell then hesitated, as if he wanted to say more.

"Something to add?" Sam asked in a teasing tone.

"I . . . Yes. I stole the horse and I need to make some sort of restitution to its owner, but my wallet was confiscated by the police."

Sam took that news in stride as well. He opened a desk drawer and pulled out a metal strongbox, which he opened with a small key on a ring of keys he kept in his pocket. He took out a rumpled five-dollar bill. "Petty cash."

He called over a teenage junior clerk from the office across the hall. "There's a horse out front that needs to go to that stable on Peru y Calle. Do you know it?" The towheaded lad nodded. "The owner is going to be ripping mad, so give him the money. Tell him it was taken on a drunken bet, or something."

The kid threw a questioning look to Bell. Bell shrugged. "I sober up fast."

When the clerk scurried out, Sam took a seat at his desk and indicated Bell should pull up a chair. "Police custody? Let me guess — you stole the horse to escape jail."

Bell remained on his feet. "I stole the horse to escape being railroaded, shanghaied, and Count of Monte Cristoed. But that's nothing but a distraction at this point, Sam. They have my wife."

"What? Who?" Sam shot to his feet as if he were gearing up for action.

"Do you know Otto Dreissen?"

"Never heard of him."

"He's a German businessman who has a big house on the coast road south of the city. He had her kidnapped off the *Spatminster* and is holding her someplace here in Panama."

"Do you think in his house?" Sam suggested eagerly.

"He wouldn't be that stupid," Bell said. "And Detective Ortega, his man on the police force, would have gotten word to him as soon as I escaped. Dreissen's long gone. In his place is a trap set for me in case I go there looking for Marion. Maybe cops. Most likely Viboras Rojas."

"The Viboras? This Dreissen is involved with the Viboras?"

"He's bankrolling them," Bell told him.

He was about to drop a real bombshell revelation when the shouts of men rushing through the building overwhelmed their conversation.

A wide-eyed clerk rushed into the room, breathless. "Do you fellas know where the Colonel is?"

"He left this morning for the power plant at the dam," Sam said. "What's going on?"

The kid was already rushing out again. He shouted over his shoulder, "The Red Vipers hit us again."

"What?" Sam and Bell said in unison. They took off after the clerk, who was racing for the telephone exchange's office. Other office workers were already there, milling around outside the closed door. Someone had beaten all of them there with Goethals's location and was in the exchange having a call placed to the power station. The mood of the crowd was ugly, anxious, and more than a little fearful.

Sam grabbed the elbow of one of the men he knew and drew him away a little from the mob.

"What do you know, Billy?"

"Not much. They say one of the big steam shovels down in the cut exploded. They say a bunch of guys were killed and that it was the Vipers that did it."

"How do they know it wasn't an accident?" Bell asked sharply, almost like an accusation. "Steam engines explode all the time."

"Not the shovels, Isaac," Sam said. "Those machines are babied by a team of mechanics. For all the years they've been digging, we've never had one blow. Men have been killed on 'em, and by 'em, but not like this."

"I need to see." Bell said it in such a way that it wasn't a request, it was an order.

Sam Westbrook nodded. "Fastest way is if we take the Donkey."

"Donkey?" Bell said with skepticism. "Surely horses would be quicker."

"Not this donkey." He turned to his friend. "Any idea where the attack happened?"

"The base of Gold Hill."

Bell said, "Call the hospital, have a doctor meet us at the, er, Donkey." He asked Sam if they would know where that was and was assured any doctor would.

"Do you want a change of clothes?" Sam asked. "You look like a bum and smell like an old nag that's on its way to the glue factory."

"We've got to do this on the jump, Sam. Clues could be compromised."

"Right. At least I can get you some decent boots."

They found the beast parked under a tin-roofed lean-to near the rail marshaling yards. It had started life as a one-ton truck with an open flatbed behind the cabin. The bed had been fitted with rows of seats like a bus, and a canvas cover stretched across a metal frame kept out the rain and blocked the sun. What made the truck so unusual was that the suspension had been modified to run on four heavily treaded tractor tires. It required some ladder rungs welded to the side of the truck to get in the cab. A small platform secured to the bumper for the driver to stand on could be unfolded to provide the proper leverage to crank the six-cylinder engine.

"That is one monster of a truck," Bell said.

"The only thing, other than a train on tracks, that can move around in the muck at the bottom of the canal."

Sam climbed into the cab, while Bell got in position to fire the engine. It took more tries than expected, and Bell's shoulder was screaming by the time the motor caught and the crank jumped so hard it almost broke his hand. A doctor and two orderlies arrived moments later, each carrying a bag of medical gear. They knew the drill, obviously, because they came running and immediately climbed onto the cargo bed.

Sam drove the Donkey fast but not recklessly, keeping to the main road for much of the journey. They passed the construction sites at Miraflores and Pedro Miguel and finally came to a turnoff that allowed access down into the Culebra Cut on a narrow track that had been carved into switchbacks to make it easier for pack animals. About a mile distant was the massif of Gold Hill, the tallest promontory along the canal route that had to be whittled down. This was the exact center of the continental divide.

The bottom of the cut was a flat, open plain with multiple rail lines heading southeast toward Panama City and its ocean reclamation project for the spoil. Like mechanical dragons wreathed in steam, the big excavators chewed eight-ton bites out of the earth, turned their booms like animals swinging their necks, and dumped the rocks and dirt onto the ore cars that slowly trundled by but never stopped. Gangs of men worked with picks and shovels, others tended the tall rotary drills for coring holes in the rock for dynamite.

As wide as the canal was there, its two sloped banks still seemed to focus the heat like a lens. It was easily a hundred and fifteen degrees, with no shade to speak of. And the noise. From the rim, it had sounded like construction going on in the background, a presence but not a problem, while down among the machines the constant clanking of trains and screams of whistles, the thunder of rubble crashing in the hopper cars, was an assault on the senses louder than at any site Bell had ever been. His ears ached.

One steam shovel sat dormant while all the others Bell could see were hard at work. The men killed were friends of the men toiling away, brothers in arms in their struggle to dig the Panama Canal, and yet the work continued. Always the work continued. There would be time for mourning later on that night, off the company clock. For now, there was nothing but the constant need to feed the ore trains chugging through the cut.

"Damn," Sam said when they got close enough to see the serial number on the back of the machine.

"What is it?"

"That's Lyle Preston's rig."

"You know him?"

"Not personally, but he and his crew hold all the records for moving dirt. He was the best by far. I bet the Vipers knew it and targeted him."

Bell said nothing.

There were some men standing around the idle digger, moving about aimlessly, unsure of what to do. After a train loaded with ore had gone past on its way out of the Culebra Cut, Sam crossed the tracks and parked a short distance from the damaged Bucyrus steam shovel.

Bell was staggered by its size, now that he could see the machine up close. The rotating platform was on double sets of bogeys as tall as a man, and the cabin behind the boom, called a house, was as big as one. Keeping with that analogy, it was a house that had been caught up in a West Texas tornado of particular savagery.

Much of the corrugated metal sides of the cabin had been blown out when the big boiler erupted, exposing the excavator's dizzyingly complex innards of crankshafts, pistons, bull wheels, gears and cams, and still other industrial equipment parts he couldn't identify. At the rear of the platform was a coal bunker for the fireman to access to stoke the boiler. The eruption of high-pressure steam had blasted the coal from the bunker like a broadside of fired grapeshot. The coal lay scattered in a fifty-foot arc stretching out from the scene, and within its radius lay two corpses with their heads and torsos hastily covered with draped work shirts. They had been cut down by the flying coal.

Nearer to the steam shovel was the body of the stoker. He was covered head to toe with a filthy scrap of canvas tarp. The bodies of the two men who worked the business end of the excavator had been left in their seats, one in the forward section of the cabin behind a candelabra-like clutch of mechanical levers, the second man in his perch halfway up the boom.

The lead operator had taken shrapnel from the exploded boiler and had been cut almost in half. Exposure to steam had turned any skin not protected by clothing the color of an overripe apple. The guy in the boom had been spared having his body punctured, but the steam and the tremendous force of its wall of pressure had ended his life in a fraction of a second just like the others.

Bell climbed down from the big truck and strode toward the big excavator. His approaching caught the attention of the roughly half dozen men milling around and they turned toward him expectantly.

"Gentlemen, my name is Isaac Bell. I am the lead investigator for the Van Dorn Detective Agency and I am here with the permission of Colonel Goethals himself. This is a potential crime scene, and I must ask all of you to please stay at least fifty feet back. I need to talk to any of you who saw the explosion or anything else you think might be important." He saw most of the men nod and only a couple frown at being shooed away. But they did comply. "Thank you. I'll talk to you once I've had a chance to look around."

The doctor and his orderlies ran to where another, smaller group of men were attending to two figures lying inside a tent that was used as a temporary zone office.

Five dead and two wounded, Bell thought. Not as bad as at Pedro Miguel, but a high butcher's bill nevertheless.

He circled the excavator in ever-tightening rings, looking at the ground, the sprayed pattern of coal. He looked for footprints or trash or anything that shouldn't have been there. He lifted the shirts covering the faces of the two West Indian islanders who'd been struck by flying coal. Both men had fist-sized indentations in their foreheads and multiple other places.

Bell knelt over the body of the stoker, who'd been blown fifteen feet from the excavator, and gently pulled back the tarp. The force of the blast had stripped him of all his clothing, and the scalding heat of the steam explosion had stripped him of all his skin. He looked piebald and boiled. The only small mercy was, death would have been instantaneous. Bell settled the shroud back over the corpse and continued his preliminary inspection.

The only thing of note, and he wanted to know if it was unusual, was that the giant boulder they were trying to dislodge with the shovel's iron bucket seemed too big for the machine to move.

He gave himself fifteen minutes. Any longer, and the witnesses either would drift away or they would start to misremember the incident. He'd heard of controlled experiments where witnesses to a single incident were asked about it in differing increments of time — minutes, hours, and days of the week — and the accuracy of their recollections faded sharply while, at the same time, their imaginations created details that hadn't occurred.

Before talking to the men, Bell sought out the doctor and gave him permission for he and his men to retrieve Lyle Preston and the bodies of his crew from inside the excavator and asked that an autopsy be performed. The doctor said he'd planned on it anyway as a formality.

Bell spoke to each witness individually, breaking from the group and walking a short distance away. He kept his questions vague enough so that the men gave rambling answers often tending to fill in subtle details. It was another investigator's trick. Yet, in the end, he learned nothing. The boulder would have put a strain on the steam shovel, but it could handle it. There was no warning before the blast, no whistle or unusual jet of steam or odd color to the smoke coming from the stovepipe funnel atop the digger. It had been a typical work-day, unremarkable in every way.

Bell cut any worker off who wanted to discuss how Viboras Rojas had managed to sabotage the Bucyrus. He had no interest in conjectures or theories.

He had two more men to interview as Colonel Goethals's private train arrived. It slowed just enough for its passengers to jump free since there was a long ore train behind it, and nothing, not even the Canal Administrator, could slow the work. Bell cut the witnesses loose as Goethals led a two-man entourage straight for the damaged steam shovel. The Colonel wore a tropical suit, while the men in his party were in grease-stained overalls. Mechanics, Bell assumed. The older was a fireplug of a man and the chief, obviously. The other, younger and taller, was his protégé. Bell desperately needed their cooperation and had no idea how to get it because he was about to accuse them of gross incompetence.

30

Bell gave Goethals and the others a few minutes to inspect the wreckage before walking over. Sam joined him.

"I'll figure it out, Colonel," a voice said in a rasp from inside the ruined husk. Bell assumed it was the chief engineer. "I'll know by nightfall how they sabotaged my girl here."

"I expect nothing less," Goethals replied, appearing from behind the boiler. He saw Bell and Sam Westbrook standing at the base of the ladder. The Colonel spun so he could back down the iron rungs. They shook hands. "Bell, I'm glad you're here. Did you find anything?"

"Nothing definitive, but I have my theories. We should talk back in your office. First, I need a word with your engineer. What's his name?"

"Jack Scully. Be quick about it. Looks like rain's coming. The Donkey can't handle the ground down here when it rains."

"It'll only take a second."

Bell climbed up onto the Bucyrus steam shovel and moved aft to where Scully and his assistant were on their hands and knees, peering into the guts of the blown boiler.

"Mr. Scully?"

"Who's asking?" the man barked without climbing out of the boiler's tank.

"My name is Bell. I'm a Van Dorn detective working with the Colonel on the whole Red Viper mess." Bell could hear Scully and his aide talking, their voices muffled yet echoing inside the hollow cylinder. He was being ignored. "Sir?"

"I heard you. You haven't said anything I give two bits about."

"It's just that I want to ask that you not jump to any conclusions as you determine the cause of the explosion."

Bell had just poked a hornet's nest with a very short stick. Scully scrambled from the boiler and rushed over so he was standing just a foot from Bell's face. While Bell had seven inches on the engineer, that didn't slow him one bit. His face was as flushed red as a boiled lobster. "Listen here, mister whoever the hell you are, the cause is sabotage. Those snake bastards destroyed one of my machines. I'll find out how, don't you worry none about that, but I tell you, here and now, that this was no accident."

Bell opened his mouth to speak.

"You even think about saying this was our fault, that our maintenance wasn't good enough, that she blew because of negligence, I will knock your block off." Scully raised a fist so that it was under Bell's nose. His hand was the size of a sledgehammer and looked just as hard.

"I'll be with Colonel Goethals," Bell drawled, unconcerned by the threat. "We'll be at his office waiting for your report."

Goethals was sitting in the Donkey's cab next to Sam, so once Bell'd cranked the engine to life, he climbed onto the rear deck and took a seat with the doctor and his orderlies, plus the two wounded islanders. The five bodies were laid out on the floor between the last rows of seats, each swathed in a white sheet the orderlies had brought. No one talked during the long drive to Ancon Hospital. The engine was too loud, and the mood too dark, for conversation.

Bell sat alone with his thoughts after the others had been dropped off and the bodies removed so they could be taken to the morgue. The upcoming conversation with Goethals was critical. Bell's arguments had to be irrefutable if he was going to convince the Colonel of the truth. The problem was, he had no evidence to present, nothing tangible. It was all conjecture, supposition, the very thing he wouldn't tolerate from the witnesses back at the Culebra Cut.

Goethals was a practical man, a West Point graduate who was one of the finest civil engineers in the country. He didn't build the canal using guesses and instinct. It took facts to build something like that, accurate maps, engineered schematics, detailed plans.

Isaac Bell had just one thing going for him and that was unshakable confidence that he was right.

He and Sam waited for two hours outside Goethals's office as he made arrangements with a string of assistants and secretaries who paraded in and out of his inner sanctum as their boss dealt with this latest setback. Sam didn't have a role to play, and should probably get back to his own job, but Bell was glad his friend stayed on. Bell used the time to compose a quick cable to the Van Dorn office in New York, asking for any known information on Otto Dreissen. Before handing the note over to Sam to send, he added a footnote, "Ask A. O. Girard."

As the last secretary left, Bell heard Goethals say, "While we can replace the ruined machine with one of those we idled earlier this year, it was the hardest-working digging crew in the cut those bastards killed."

"Yes, Colonel."

"Send in Westbrook and the investigator."

"Yes, Colonel." The man opened the door and, gesturing, beckoned Sam and Bell.

A pall of stale cigarette smoke as thick as a London fog hung in the office. The windows were open, and a ceiling fan whirled high up near the ceiling, but neither made any headway with the rank cloud. Goethals was a chain-smoker, and the stress had upped his intake to the point his glass ashtray was overflowing, and it had been emptied just that morning.

"Sit down, you two," Goethals greeted them without looking up from the folder on his desk. "Damn. These are recruiting figures for getting workers from Jamaica and Barbados. Down eight percent from last month, which was down four from the previous." He looked up. "This is before the Red Vipers targeted the lock at Pedro Miguel and today's attack. The zone will look like a ghost town in a few months."

"Once we flood the cut and start working off dredges, we won't need as much labor," Sam said, trying to be optimistic.

Goethals ignored him. "What do you

think, Bell? You said you had some theories about how they took out one of our excavators. Let's hear it."

"Your engineer, Jack Scully — I provoked him earlier by asking him to keep an open mind about what caused the explosion. He took it as a bold accusation that his negligence killed those men."

"Not a wise thing to do, Bell. Jack Scully is quick to temper and lets his fists do their fair share of the talking."

"I could tell that just by looking at him," Bell agreed. "I needed him mad at someone other than the Red Vipers, so he stays focused on where the evidence leads him and not the preconceived notion that everyone currently has about what happened out there."

Colonel Goethals looked at him warily. "What are you saying?"

Bell caught and kept his eye. "I am saying that Viboras Rojas didn't attack that machine. If he's as good as he looks, Scully will find that it was a tragic accident, plain and simple."

"And how can you be so certain? Are you suddenly an expert on rail-mounted steam shovels?" His voice oozed wary sarcasm.

"No, Colonel. I'm an expert on people and their motivations. The Viboras didn't hit the excavator because that organization doesn't exist. And determining the explosion was an accident will be my proof."

Smoke jetted from Goethals's nostrils in a dismissive snort. "You claim to have recovered your faculties, Bell. I say you hit your head harder than you let on. What do you mean they don't exist? I've got plenty of acts of sabotage, as well as dozens of dead men, that says otherwise." Goethals crushed out the cigarette and turned his attention to Sam Westbrook. "You buy this nonsense? I thought you had a better head on your shoulders."

"First I've heard of it. Isaac told me a connection to some German guy, but not this."

"Explain yourself, Bell," Goethals demanded, "and don't waste my time doing it."

"I'm not saying attacks didn't take place, Colonel," Bell replied, "but they weren't carried out by a nativist insurrection whose goal is the overthrow of the government and, subsequently, to nationalize your canal. Viboras Rojas was fabricated by Court Talbot for the sole purpose of gaining him unrestricted and unsupervised access to Lake Gatun."

Goethals looked at him for a long moment, lit another cigarette, and said, "I've heard enough. Get out. Both of you."

"No, Colonel. You have to listen to me. Talbot and his men are the Red Vipers. I know this because of the identity of the bomber at Pedro Miguel."

"Raul Morales," Sam interjected, in case Colonel Goethals had forgotten. "Talbot's driver's brother."

"No. It wasn't Raul," Bell countered. "It really was the driver. Rinaldo."

Goethals asked, "How can you be so sure?"

"That was the biggest thing I forgot when I had amnesia. Rinaldo is Talbot's most trusted man, right? They are always together. For the sake of argument, let's say Talbot was behind the Red Vipers. He would want his best and most trusted operative, Rinaldo, to carry out their most destructive act yet, one so heinous you would have to let him pursue the Viboras onto the lake."

Goethals remained silent, doubtful.

Bell plowed on. "What he didn't expect is me tracking and killing the bomber after the explosion. Right away, he had to distance himself from his driver, and so he told us it wasn't Rinaldo but a brother named Raul. Do you recall in the lock chamber how Talbot pointed out that the corpse was missing the same finger as his driver?"

"I do," Sam said. "You found it down in the tunnels under the lock."

"Talbot had more than enough time to get to the body and shoot off the pinkie and toss it in the tunnel."

"Why?"

"Because Rinaldo isn't missing a finger, his brother Raul is. Rinaldo always wore these nice kidskin driving gloves, so I never saw whether it was one way or the other. We all just took Talbot's word for it that Rinaldo was a finger short, and finding the body with the severed finger felt like proof the bomber was Raul and not Rinaldo. Talbot thought through and executed his plan while we were working on rescuing any survivors. He acted fast, lied cleverly, and fooled everyone."

"But now you claim you weren't fooled at all?" Goethals asked, one bushy eyebrow cocked.

"I was, at the time," Bell conceded. "It was later, when I interviewed Morales on the boat in Gamboa, that I figured everything out. Even though I'd seen Rinaldo Morales on only two brief occasions, I have made my living on my powers of observation. The man Court Talbot presented as his driver was an impostor. Talbot claimed they were a year apart. He lied. Rinaldo and Raul were fraternal twins and closely matched to be sure, but I could tell right away that it wasn't Rinaldo. The fact Talbot was peddling this charade was proof he was the mastermind behind the Viboras and all their attacks. I was going to come straight here after my meeting with him to tell you, Colonel, when they ambushed me on the road and almost killed me."

"Any physical evidence of all this?"

"None, but I know what I saw."

Goethals looked far from convinced but he hadn't sent Bell packing. "You said earlier that Talbot wanted access to Lake Gatun. Why?"

"I don't know that yet. I do know he has the only workboat on the lake, and that you hadn't allowed him to leave Gamboa since the Chagres River was dammed up. And this isn't really about Courtney Talbot either, Colonel. There's another angle — well, two really — that I haven't mentioned. I believe Talbot is just hired muscle working for a German industrialist named Otto Dreissen. The company he owns is called Essenwerks, and they have their finger in a lot of different pies."

"I've met him at a couple receptions in the city," Goethals said. "Typical cold fish

Teutonic type."

"He's the one bankrolling this."

When Goethals was about to ask the obvious question, Bell stopped him with a raised hand.

"I don't know what he's after, but it comes down to getting Talbot's boat away from Gamboa and out on the broad lake. I do know that Dreissen is involved because I followed someone who tried to kill me out to his house on the coast road."

George Washington Goethals was Army through and through, a West Point graduate and a man who governed by rules and regulations. Bell's instincts told him that if he revealed he'd broken into Dreissen's house, this interview would be over, so he lied.

"Armed with the address, I learned Dreissen's name from a British expat here named Macalister. While I knew nothing of the man or his company, I was looking at that time into a possible European agent being behind the Viboras, and this man fit the bill. I cabled my office in New York for a biographical and business dossier.

"I believe the scheme played out like this. Dreissen wants access to Lake Gatun, for some unknown reason. Court Talbot has the only workboat on the lake, Dreissen hires

427

him. You won't just give him permission, so Dreissen and Talbot invent a fake insurgency that only Talbot can destroy. They create a backstory, a narrative, that is elaborate enough to begin taking on a life of its own. Remember, Talbot is well versed in guerrilla tactics because of his time in the Philippines fighting the Moro uprising. When the low-level stuff like robbing depots and derailing trains doesn't get your attention in the way Talbot wants, he ups the stakes."

"The business in California?"

"Yes, sir. Talbot went after your old West Point roommate, Senator Densmore. The plan was to have it look like the Viboras assassinated him, goading you on to the point where you would let Talbot out on the lake to hunt them down. The whole thing was a setup from the beginning, and had I known Spanish, I would have picked up on it sooner. Did you know Talbot has a nickname with some of the locals?"

"I didn't."

Sam Westbrook provided the name as he was familiar with Talbot's legend. "He's called Ojo Muerto, 'Dead Eye.' He's a crack shot, with a pistol or rifle."

Bell continued, "When we were attacked at the Hotel Del, Talbot didn't expect me or Senator Densmore's niece to be in on the meeting. I believe the original plan was for Talbot to murder the Senator while the gunman shot up the dining room to make it look like a brutal terrorist assault that he miraculously survives. The gunmen vanish into the night, and Talbot returns to Panama to exact your vengeance on your friend's killers.

"It didn't work as intended, obviously, but I noted that after the attack much of the Panamanians' initial fire had been aimed well above our heads. They weren't aiming at us initially because they didn't want to hit their boss, Talbot, who spent much of the battle in the clutches of the Senator's terrified niece and could do little until he'd disentangled from her. It wasn't until I nailed a couple of them that they started to defend themselves and fire at me. The interesting thing is, the only shot that came near the Senator was fired just as he tripped going out the window. Had he not, it would have killed him. Dead Eye Talbot had a pistol in his hand, and the niece and the waiter had turned away. I believe he took that shot, only he missed. After that, the Panamanians tried to complete the busted mission by gunning for me and the Senator."

The look on Goethals's face told Bell he

remained skeptical.

Bell knew he had one last chance to convince the Colonel or he was going to be shut out entirely, and Marion's life would be all but forfeited. "I know what I've presented to you seems convoluted and contrived, but my conclusions are based on known facts and solid observation.

"Viboras Rojas acts like no other insurgency in history, and the fact it has no named leader is unprecedented. Its stated goal of stopping the canal's construction and nationalizing it once it's completed are farcical. Neither thing could ever happen. Yet even though it has no source of income, it somehow supports a small guerrilla army in the field.

"These three things alone make their very existence suspicious. What makes more sense is, they are an army of mercenaries hired to do a specific job under the guise of a nativist uprising because that makes them look more legitimate. The fact that Court Talbot is so hard-pressed about going after them makes me think of Shakespeare's lady who doth protest too much. He wants unfettered access to the Canal Zone for reasons other than those he professes. Otto Dreissen is involved, I've seen it with my own eyes, and he likely is the financier and ultimate beneficiary of their plot."

"Or," Goethals said slowly, "a decorated war hero is lending a hand to a project of vital national importance by stopping a gang of murderous though, yes, delusional thugs from preying on its company and workers."

"Sir, I —"

"Save it. I know Talbot a bit. The man's a patriot. Bill Densmore vouches for him. That's good enough, in my book. I don't know you, Bell, but I do know you've taken a pretty bad crack to the skull and I don't think you're squared away just yet. Check yourself back into the hospital. Rest for a few days. Jack Scully is going to come back with evidence of sabotage, and you'll come to realize the real truth. You can't tell the difference between one Panamanian brother and the other because, as you said, you'd met only one of them briefly. That's what your story hinges on, the misidentification of a stranger . . . Sam, take Mr. Bell back to Ancon and see that he gets a quiet room."

"Yes, Colonel."

"And one more thing, Bell. On my way from Gatun to the cut, I stopped in Gamboa. Court Talbot was back for supplies. He told me he'd engaged the Viboras on an inlet on the lake's western side and showed me the bodies of the two men they'd killed, along with a couple guns and ten pounds of dynamite. I let you spin your tale out of respect for what you did at the Hotel Del and here at Pedro Miguel, but that's enough of that. You need help."

Isaac Bell was not used to being ignored, patronized even. He wasn't mad, at least not yet. He was shocked. He had laid out everything as simply and logically as he could and yet Goethals didn't believe him. It was a strange experience, coming so closely after his amnesia, that Bell felt the first worms of doubt creep into his mind.

He remembered feeling certain that Court Talbot was trying to pass off Raul Morales as his driver Rinaldo. What if that wasn't it? What if he was certain about something else, and his mind was playing tricks on him? What if the damage to his brain caused by his tumble inside the water truck's tank was far worse than he'd imagined? The implications sent a bolt of cold terror through his heart.

Just then, someone knocked on Goethals's door, and Isaac about jumped out of his seat, he'd been so wrapped in his own, desperate thoughts.

"Come."

An aide opened the door and came in, something clutched in his right hand. "Sir, a courier just brought this from Culebra. It's from Chief Engineer Scully." He handed a scrap of paper to the Colonel and set a small round object on the desk.

Bell couldn't tell what it was.

Goethals grunted as he finished reading the note. He set it aside and picked up the object. It was a round stone a little larger than a child's marble. "Jack found this lodged inside the boiler's pressure relief valve. He said that when the operator called for extra pressure to lift the boulder that was in the dipper's bucket, the valve wouldn't open. When he then backed off to get a better grip on the rock, the pressure skyrocketed and the boiler blew. Jack says there is no way a stone this size could get inside the system because of the filters we use, both when water is pumped into the haul trucks and on the excavators themselves. He said it was placed in the boiler's intake intentionally."

He tossed the stone to Bell.

"Scully also had some rather unkind words for you, Mr. Bell, that need not be repeated. There you have it. You were certain it was an accident. You were wrong. It was sabotage. The Viboras are still out there and they remain a deadly threat."

Bell knew he could argue no further.

Outside the administrative building it had grown dark, but at least the rain that had threatened earlier had held off. Bell and Sam Westbrook headed for the railway station and walked the short distance in silence.

"You okay?" Sam finally asked.

"I'm not sure," Bell admitted. "I'm not used to being dismissed like that."

"He's a tough old bird, our Colonel Goethals. Pragmatist of the first order. If it isn't right in front of his face and he can't see it, feel it, and study it, he won't pay it any attention."

"That describes me as well," Bell said. "Or it did. Do you believe me, Sam?"

"Let's just say I believe that you believe it."

"You think I made it up?"

"No. Honest. Still, I think your noodle got more scrambled than you thought."

Bell stopped so that they faced each other. "Here's the thing. I'm not wrong about any of it."

"Come on, you heard what Jack Scully found. The excavator was sabotaged just like everyone figured. Maybe you're right about Court Talbot being in on this thing, but you're wrong about the Vipers no longer attacking us."

Bell shook his head. "I'm actually banking on Mr. Scully to prove me right. I just hope he does so soon."

"You're not making much sense. You just heard Scully's final report to Colonel Goethals."

They started walking again.

"I'm good at reading people, Sam. Very good, in fact. I had Scully pegged as a perfectionist the moment he jumped down from Goethals's little yellow train. He won't be satisfied until he's taken that steam shovel down to its last nut and bolt."

"And you think he's going to find it was an accident?"

"Yes. And when he does, and Goethals believes me, I can tell him the rest of what I've learned."

"There's more?"

"Yes. Dreissen had my wife kidnapped at sea using an airship."

31

Bell didn't go to the hospital, as Goethals had recommended. Sam Westbrook's roommate had rotated back to the States a few weeks earlier, and no one had been assigned his place in the company's austere housing for bachelors.

They ate together, and, afterward, Bell cleaned his clothes in the sink in the communal bathroom and took one of the longest showers of his life. He thought back to his conversation with Goethals, viewing it from all angles to see if he could have done better and convinced the man that he was right. He doubted it. A trained engineer, an Army one at that, would demand tangible proof, not supposition.

Back home, Joseph Van Dorn trusted whatever tale Bell spun from the evidence he'd gathered because they had had a decade of working together and Bell's theories about various crimes, no matter how farfetched or implausible they seemed, eventually proved correct.

To Goethals, Isaac Bell was a stranger with no basis for credibility other than the fact he was good with a gun. This is why he didn't push the conversation harder or bring up Marion's kidnapping. Without any ally other than young Mr. Westbrook, Bell didn't have a leg to stand on. He had to wait until Jack Scully came to his rescue.

Meanwhile, Dreissen had Marion. Bell tried not to dwell on what the German would do when he learned he'd escaped police custody. He believed Dreissen still wanted leverage over him, so he wouldn't kill her but his talk of making her captivity difficult sent his mind racing down dozens of unpleasant avenues.

Bell twisted the tap to its coldest setting to stop himself from thinking like that. It didn't work, the water never got cooler than tepid because of the tropical climate, so he was left with a vivid image of Marion in the hands of a bunch of sadists.

That thought faded only when his rage grew too intense.

After breakfast the following morning, Bell accompanied Sam back to his office. Bell wanted to look at the maps the Authority had commissioned, especially of the

Lake Gatun basin. They weren't stored in the unfinished office building. For access, Bell had to travel to a warehouse about a mile away.

The building was like every other one within the zone, clapboard and wood-framed with a roof pitched enough to shed the prodigious rain the country endured almost daily at this time of year. An older man sat at a desk in the reception room. He wore a banker's green visor and had garters holding up his sleeves. His clothes looked thirty years out of fashion. He looked up, his eyes big and owlish behind thick-lensed spectacles.

"I suspect you're lost, young man. I haven't had a visitor here in a long time."

"If you're Mr. Townsend, then I'm in the right place," Bell said.

"Jeremiah Townsend at your service, Mr. . . ."

"Bell, sir. Isaac Bell. I'm a detective with the Van Dorn Agency here to help sort out the Red Vipers."

"And you can do that by looking at a bunch of dusty old maps?" he asked with a teasing twinkle in his eye.

"I believe that I can, actually."

"Okay. Are you a coffee drinker, Mr. Bell?"

"I am."

Townsend had a metal thermos bottle on his desk next to a big ceramic mug. He unscrewed the bottle's top, which doubled as a cup, and un-stoppered the flask itself. He poured steaming black coffee into the cup and then topped off his own mug. He handed the cup to Bell, they saluted each other, and each took a sip. It was the weakest, most burned cup of coffee Bell had ever had, but the old guy was so happy to have company, Isaac made the appropriate grunts of appreciation.

"How can I help? What exactly do you need?"

"I'm not sure," Bell said. "I guess I'm looking for someplace secluded along the shores of Lake Gatun where I can hold a secret rendezvous."

"Between . . . ?"

"A fifty-foot workboat and a Zeppelin, let's guess, four hundred and fifty feet in length."

To his credit, Townsend didn't send Bell away. Or maybe he was so bored and lonely, he welcomed the lunatic's request. He sat still for a few moments before asking, "And these meetings are taking place now or sometime in the past? Remember, the lake continues to rise, so its shoreline is constantly changing."

"Currently taking place," Bell assured him.

"Okay, then." Townsend stood. "Come with me."

The old archivist led Bell down a short hallway, past a closet-sized washroom and through a door at the back of the reception room. Beyond was a vast, open space, with exposed wooden beams and V-bracing columns. Light came from tall, narrow windows, as well as from electric bulbs. The room was filled with waist-high metal filing cabinets with wide but very shallow drawers for storing maps flat. It looked like there was enough space for tens of thousands of plats and charts.

Bell was overwhelmed by the task he'd set out for himself.

"The upstairs is more of the same. It's said that Panama is the best-mapped place on earth, and I'm not one to argue with that. There are two other buildings like this one for storing all the engineering drawings done for the canal, all in metal file cabinets to protect them in case of fire. Those facilities are still busy because we're still building stuff, but all the site work's done. No real need to look at the maps any longer."

"But you've kept them?"

"This is a government project, which

means everything must be accounted for."

"Job security?"

"I've been here since the beginning almost," Townsend said proudly. "Any chance you can narrow your search some? The lake's pretty big, even if it has another year to reach its full size."

In Bell's experience, the most convincing lies always contain a bit of the truth. It's easier to remember and comes across as more trustworthy. Talbot had lied to Goethals about killing two Viboras Rojases. The dead men were no doubt hapless fishermen in the wrong place at the wrong time. But he'd said they'd been found on the lake's western side, a detail mentioned to make the lie feel authentic.

"Let's concentrate on the western side of the lake for now."

"Easy enough."

Bell followed Townsend as he wound his way through the maze of filing cabinets until he stopped at one as anonymous as all the others. He opened a drawer about halfway down and pulled out a map that was four feet by four. He set it on top of the cabinet, studied it for a second, then slid it back in its drawer. He pulled another map from one drawer higher up and set it on top of the cabinet.

"We're looking for hills that became islands when the lake rose, Mr. Bell. Hills big enough to hide a dirigible hovering close to the water. Is that how you envision it?"

"Yes, I believe so."

"What you're looking at is not a map, per se, but a projection of what the shoreline around Gatun should look like this month, give or take. It could be off by several feet because rainfall actuals are likely to be different from the early estimates. It's still good enough to get us in the ballpark. You a baseball fan by any chance?"

"I was born in Boston, so baseball is in my blood."

"Think the Red Sox will win the Series this year?"

Bell smiled. "In my line of work, we try not to predict the future, but, in this case, I'll make an exception and say we may not win it this year, but we're going to do quite well in the next few years. After that, who knows?"

"As a Cleveland Naps fan, I hope you're wrong." He pointed at the map, all official again. "This is an overview, a reference for us to pick some likely candidate. See all those boxes?"

The map of the Canal Zone and surrounding jungle was divided up into hundreds of separate little blocks, each with a reference number too small to read with the naked eye.

From an inside pocket of his vest, Townsend pulled an ivory-handled magnifying glass. "Once we have some choice spots picked out, we'll pull the corresponding topographical maps, the ones with elevation notations, to see if the hills are high enough to hide your airship."

"Mr. Townsend, I don't think I could do this without you," Bell said gratefully.

"You could, I'm sure. You seem like a sharp fellow, but it might take you a couple weeks."

"Months." Bell laughed.

Together, the archivist and the investigator pooled their talents and pored over dozens of maps, discussing the merits of various locations, discarding unlikely places, and holding aside the topographical maps of possibles. They worked as they shared Townsend's lunch, a ham sandwich, on stale bread, with fiery mustard that made Bell's eyes swim, washed down with the dregs of the cold, watery coffee.

Bell's eyes were gritty, and his back ached from stooping over so many maps, by the time they had narrowed it down to two potential places where Court Talbot could be meeting Otto Dreissen's airship. Both had been deep valleys before the lake began to fill them and now they resembled Norwegian fjords with enough breadth for a massive dirigible to maneuver in. Townsend allowed Bell to keep one map, to annotate it with navigational directions and waypoints, provided he filled out a receipt and promised to return it.

A Model T passed Bell on his walk back to the administration building, and he would have thought nothing of it if he had not looked over his shoulder and seen it slow to a stop in front of the map building's front portico. He turned and started heading back, instinct raising his hopes. As Townsend said, no one came out to his domain anymore, so the odds were slim that it would happen twice on the same day. Bell suspected the driver was looking for him.

The driver, a lad still in his teens, was exiting the building just as Bell reached the stairs. Isaac's chest heaved from trying to draw oxygen out of the hot humid air. "You looking for me?"

"Are you Isaac Bell of the Van Dorn —"

"I am. Did Goethals send you?"

"Yes. And Sam Westbrook asked me to give you this." He handed Bell a folded slip of paper.

It was a cable response from Van Dorn. "Researching Dreissen. A. O. Girard reports that late uncle of John Schrank employed by Essenwerks. Stop."

Bell read it twice, then nodded, grim-lipped. "Let's go. On the jump."

Jack Scully refused to sit in Goethals's office because he'd come straight from the cut and his clothes were filthy. The dirt he'd tracked in on his shoes from outside was part of life in Panama, and the office was swept regularly, but he didn't feel comfortable ruining his boss's expensive-looking upholstered chairs. He was moving back and forth like a caged bear at a circus when Bell was shown into the inner sanctum.

"How'd you know?" he growled as soon as the secretary closed the heavy door.

"That it wasn't sabotage? As I explained to the Colonel, the Red Vipers have already achieved their true goal. There was no need to expose themselves or risk any of them being caught. As to how I knew you'd keep looking? Well, you don't look like a man who does anything by the half measures or accepts the easy answer."

"Tell him what happened," Goethals said. He'd lost some of his tropical tan as the implications of Scully's discovery sunk in —

like he'd preferred this was a Viboras attack.

"Does it have something to do with that crew being the best excavators in the cut?" Bell asked before the mechanic could explain.

Scully eyed him suspiciously, then seemed to accept that Isaac Bell had a knack for pulling the right answers out of thin air.

"It does," he admitted, and retrieved a tobacco pouch and brier pipe from the pocket of his overalls. "Lyle Preston, the team foreman, cheated. He had his guys pull out all the filters from the steam and water lines, he had reinforcing clamps on some of the system's weak points, and he reshaped the dampers to create a massive draft through the firebox. I never caught on to any of this stuff because he'd have his boys change it all back before we did our scheduled inspections."

"What does this mean?" Bell asked.

"He could run temperatures and pressures a lot higher than the machine was designed for in order to make her run faster than any of the other ninety-five-tonners down in the cut. He was a good operator, for sure, but the modifications meant he could raise his bucket and swing his boom faster than anyone else." Scully said this from behind a sweet cloud of pipe smoke.

"Does this mean the stone got in on its own?"

"I had a team pull all the screens at the depot where we fill the water trucks and tank cars. They get inspected regularly, but we weren't due for another week. One had a puncture large enough for that stone to have slipped through. Had it gone into any of the other shovels, the onboard filter would have caught it. Seems fate didn't like Lyle Preston messing with my machines any more than I do."

Goethals said, "Great job, Jack. Thanks for the report."

"Yes, sir." Scully gave Bell a look that was an odd blend of malice and respect.

When he was gone, Goethals pulled a whiskey bottle and a pair of mismatched glasses from a desk drawer. He splashed some liquor into each, and Bell had to lean across the big desk to accept the drink.

"A lot of the guys down here get used to drinking Caribbean rum. Too sweet, for my taste."

"Couldn't agree more," Bell said to the back of Goethals's head.

He'd turned in his seat to gaze out the window. It was just dark enough that all he could see was the reflection of a middle-aged military man who'd made a million decisions and countless sacrifices and who was beginning to pay for them all.

"Logic tells me," he said without turning back, "that just because you were right about the shovel accident doesn't mean you're right about everything else."

"That's correct," Bell agreed. "But it should give you insight into how I operate and provide a foundation of trust between us."

The Colonel finally turned to face his desk. Bell noticed the creases on each side of his mouth had deepened and the bags under his eyes had grown darker. "If you're right about Talbot controlling the Vipers and that he stopped the attacks when I gave him permission to use his boat on the lake . . ."

He couldn't finish the thought.

"Talbot ordered the attack on Pedro Miguel to push you into approving his operation when his attempt to kill Senator Densmore failed."

"Had I said yes a day earlier . . ."

"You can't blame yourself, Colonel," Bell told him. "That act of barbarity is on Courtney Talbot and no one else."

"But . . ."

"No, sir," Bell said firmly. He couldn't let Goethals be paralyzed with guilt. "You had no way of knowing how the Viboras and

Talbot were linked or the cause and effect of their actions. Those men died that day because Court Talbot murdered them to fulfill his obligation to Otto Dreissen. You played no role in that whatsoever."

Goethals was quiet for a moment. Bell knew to let him come to his own peace.

All right, then, Goethals said to himself. It was all the convincing he needed. He looked Bell square in the eye. "Where does this leave us?"

"It leaves me needing to explain one more facet to this affair, one that is very personal. Dreissen had my wife kidnapped the other night."

Goethals's eyes widened, and he grew very still.

Bell continued. "She was abducted off the SS *Spatminster,* far enough from Panama for the captain to carry on with the voyage rather than double back here to inform the authorities of her disappearance."

"How do you know that? The *Spatminster* lacks a wireless."

"Otto Dreissen showed me a photograph of her this morning. She was holding today's paper while a man off camera was pointing a pistol at her head."

"My God. Have you gone to the police?"

Bell chuckled humorlessly. "I was in a

police interrogation room when Dreissen showed me the picture and told me if I didn't stop sniffing around, he would kill Marion. There's a detective named Ortega on Dreissen's payroll."

"Do you know where they're holding her?"

"I suspect on the support ship for the dirigible they used to snatch her from the *Spatminster.*"

"Dirigible?" Goethals scoffed.

Bell feared another dismissal coming. "I know how this all sounds, Colonel, I really do. But logic and local lore bear me out. If the *Spatminster* had been close to Panama City when Marion was kidnapped, the captain would have turned around, agreed?"

"Yes. I know him. Malcolm Fish. Good man. Why wouldn't he think she fell overboard? Happens all the time, and there's no need to report anything until the next port of call."

"Marion had two roommates on the voyage back to California. In order to abduct my wife, the kidnappers would have needed to deal with them. Were they murdered and dumped? Doubtful. Most likely, they were tied up in their cabins and weren't reported as missing until one of them worked her way out of her restraints."

Goethals didn't look convinced.

"Also, a ship's porter or purser had to have been compelled by force to tell the kidnappers which cabin was Marion's. Again, I suspect that man was bound and gagged rather than murdered. Had there been three murders, plus the kidnapping, Captain Fish probably would have returned here. Since he didn't, he's no doubt pressing on. While I'm not sure where the closest port is to him now, I guarantee he'll make contact once he's there."

"Southern Mexico, I'd guess. Let's say I believe you. Why do you suspect an airship?"

"Speed. Once Dreissen decided he needed leverage over me, Marion was long gone. Another boat wouldn't have been fast enough to reach the *Spatminster* and return to Panama in time for him to show me the photograph. A seaplane was the other likely option, but I've heard rumors about locals seeing and hearing a cloud that hums."

"I've actually heard talk of that myself," the Colonel admitted.

"How else would you describe a Zeppelin if you had no idea such a machine existed?"

" 'A cloud that hums,' I should imagine." Goethals looked to be on the verge of believing until he shook his head. "This seems too byzantine, Bell."

"No, sir, it's simple. Dreissen couldn't take the chance that my amnesia would fade and that my investigation would expose his plan."

"And what part does an airship play in that?"

Bell wished he had the answer, but he didn't. That piece of the puzzle was still missing. "I don't know for certain. They are smuggling items either into the country or out."

"Good God," Goethals shouted, before checking himself, and then in a conspiratorial whisper asked, "This doesn't have anything to do with Teddy Roosevelt's visit, does it?"

"Not for starters," Bell said. "The first attacks by the Viboras took place months ago, long before TR announced his side trip here."

"Oh, yes, of course."

"But it's an unfortunate coincidence, at the very least."

"I thought all you detectives don't like coincidences."

"We don't at all, but that doesn't mean they don't happen. Still, I'll want to review your security measures for his visit."

"It's already been worked out that he won't set foot in Panama. He's being taken from his ship on a specially rigged flat-bottom boat that will climb the three locks at Gatun and then tour the lake for a bit while a luncheon is served and then it's right back out again."

"That's good," Bell said, wishing the former President would heed his warning and stay the hell away. He realized the best he could do was wrap up this whole thing in the couple days he had left. "Back to our business at hand."

"Yes. Umm, Talbot doesn't know you suspect him, right? He's back out on the lake now. Why don't we snatch him when he returns to Gamboa and — what's that phrase? — 'sweat it out of him.' "

"He might not come back. He might leave with the Germans, and I, for one, want to know what he's up to out there."

Goethals blew out a frustrated breath. "You've presented me with a lot of allegations with no real proof or possible solutions. What's your point with all of this? What do you want?"

"I want my wife back," Bell said simply. "And you can help. A few months back, a pilot named Robert Fowler flew from the Pacific to the Atlantic in a biplane fitted with pontoons."

"Yes, he took along a photographer."

Bell nodded. "Sam tells me the plane is still here. As it turns out, I know how to fly. The airship has a vulnerability. They need a large open area with a tall vertical mooring mast in order to dock. They wouldn't have cleared a place to land out in the jungle. Too much time and manpower, plus they had to resupply the craft during its transatlantic crossing — the world's first, by the way."

"A ship," Goethals guessed, eyes brightening.

"Exactly. They have a support ship in the waters off the coast. If I can find it, I can rescue my wife because that's where she would have been taken. I bet Dreissen is there too. And if Talbot is smart, when his role is fulfilled once all of this is over, he'll leave Panama with his German boss. I need your permission to borrow that plane so I can see this through to the end."

32

The atmosphere in the wardroom was one
of smug self-satisfaction. The job was almost
completed, and despite a few minor glitches,
mostly the interference of Isaac Bell, it had
gone well. Otto Dreissen had just arrived
with Court Talbot. They'd linked up in
Colón and were motored out to sea for the
rendezvous.

Two other men in the room — other than
the steward, who was smoking, and Dreissen's ever-present servant, Heinz Kohl —
were both in the Imperial German Navy.
One was the captain of the support ship,
named for Otto Dreissen's daughter, *Dagna.*
The second was Max Grosse, the captain of
the airship *Cologne.* Grosse had the distinc-
tion of commanding the first transatlantic
flight, as well as being the man with the
most hours aloft in Essenwerks's airships. A
former pilot for Count Ferdinand von Zeppelin, Grosse had switched companies when

he learned of the vast superiority of Essenwerks's dirigibles. There was a fifth man there, also dressed as a civilian, but he was addressed as "Major."

He nonchalantly draped one leg over the other as he slouched deeper into one of the chairs around the ten-seat oak table. "It is too early, just yet, for the champagne. Two more mines should still be placed, since we were provided a surplus. While not necessary according to our calculations, they will boost the shock wave that will dislodge the spillway from the rest of the Gatun Dam."

"English, please," Talbot reminded him.

"Sorry, Court," the Major said, grinning. "Too much German in my English."

Talbot frowned. He was being mocked for a linguistic mistake that had almost blown both their covers. "Go to hell."

The Major gave him a dead-eyed stare. "When this is over, I would very much like the opportunity to prove that you are not as tough as you think you are."

Talbot shot to his feet. "Let's do it right now."

Dreissen said, "Enough." Then he noticed the Major had pulled a Luger pistol from beneath his coat. "Put that away."

As a precaution to protect his employer, Heinz Kohl had also pulled his weapon, a revolver, he kept secreted in the small of his back.

The two naval officers were astute enough to step back. There was no clear chain of command, at present, and though Dreissen was a civilian, he owned the airship the German Navy had been testing for the past few months under a lease agreement. The American was just a mercenary in their eyes but he had been vital to their operation. The Major outranked the two Captains, but he was Army — Sektion IIIb, to be exact.

That was the intelligence arm of the German General Staff — spies. No traditional soldier or sailor worth his salt held anything but contempt for those in the espionage business. It was within the purview of liars, thieves, and assassins, not a place for an upright gentleman of noble character. Which is why it came as no surprise the Major was quick to escalate a simple clash of egos by brandishing a pistol.

"I said enough," Dreissen repeated. "You two want to fight it out, do it on your own time."

"Of course, Herr Dreissen," the Major said with a sugary smile and holstered his gun. Talbot sat down without saying anything.

Dreissen turned his attention to the two

military men. "I'm concerned that time is running out. Roosevelt will be here in a couple days, and we have two more charges we can plant. While I understand they are supplemental mines not necessary for our success, I would still like the extra insurance they represent. The weather has delayed too many of our flights, and I can't chance not completing the task tonight. Captain Grosse, I understand you fly with only one mine at a time. Can the *Cologne* carry two?"

Grosse stroked his mustache, an exact copy of the Kaiser's. "We have the lifting capacity, yes, but the ship's controls will be sluggish. If there is even the slightest breeze, I fear we can't navigate her inside the valley."

"So, it's risky but feasible?"

"*Ja.*"

"How about it, Mr. Talbot?" Dreissen asked. "Can your boat handle two of our mines?"

Talbot shook his head. "Weight's no problem, it's the room. The working deck of my boat just isn't big enough for two." Dreissen tried to speak, but the newly minted mercenary overrode him. "But we've got ourselves a good camp out there, with a log dock strong enough to hold the extra mine.

You lower them down one at a time. First onto the boat, second the dock. We head out and set the first one, then use our winch to lift aboard the second."

The airship commander looked thoughtful for a moment. "If the weather conditions are favorable, that would work. The boat and the dock will be side by side?"

"Yes. You wouldn't have to maneuver at all, just maintain a hover. Me and my men can guide the mines using the ropes you've tied to them aboard the ship, like always."

Dreissen was relieved. He'd gambled big and it was about to pay off. Germany was about to gain a great deal of prestige and a stronger financial position with the Argentine government, thanks to his scheme. And soon, the expansionist Roosevelt would be dead, and Woodrow Wilson would likely be reelected in a few years. Foreign affairs did not interest him, meaning Germany's future plans would face little challenge from the United States.

As for himself, he figured his exile to the backwaters of the world was at an end. He would return to Germany and accept a place in the Kaiser's inner circle of advisers, steering weapons contracts to the family business. And, he thought, it might actually be enjoyable living at home with his wife and daughters, for a change, and maybe it was time to try for a son.

No matter what, Dreissen knew, he would find a way to enjoy the fruits of his ambition.

He roused himself from his musings. "Court, what about after the last charge has been placed?"

"I'm not going to risk Bell figuring out my role with the Viboras. His amnesia was a godsend, but if he remembers anything, then I'll spend the rest of my life in federal prison. No thank you. My men have all been paid, so I'll drop them near Colón, from where they'll head back to their own villages. I'm going to sink my boat and use the skiff to get to town. I'll get on the first ship out of here and make my way to Brazil. I've got contacts in Rio, and, with the money I've earned, I figure I'm set for life."

"Major?"

"Once I set off the mines, I'll head back to Panama City, keep up my cover for a week or two more, then fade away. I'm sure Sektion IIIb will have another assignment for me in short order."

Talbot said, "I know I'm hitching a ride on the *Cologne* back to my boat tonight, but you'll be busy, and I'd really like a tour. Working under that beast this past week has got me real curious about what makes it tick."

"I can't see why not," Otto Dreissen said. "Captain Grosse?"

"Of course." He gestured to the waiting steward.

"I'll sit this one out," the Major said. "I'll get some sailors to get me back to shore in the gig. Good luck to us all."

The steward moved from the back wall, where he'd been standing, and went to a side table, where he picked up the heavy brass lighter everyone had shared to fire up their cigars and pipes. He inspected it carefully to see there were no hot bits of flint inside the mechanism and then placed it in a metal box that he then locked with a key from a fob he kept in his pocket. Then he went around with a brass vase filled with water and made each man ceremoniously drop in his stogie or pipe waste, which hissed as the smoldering tobacco was extinguished. He shook the vase to make certain all trace of fire was doused.

This foul mixture was then dumped in a glass jar whose mouth was sealed with a screw-on lid.

Only when this bizarre ritual was completed did he pull open a door that sealed the *Dagna*'s smoking lounge. "One last thing, and this is not negotiable, Herr Talbot. There are no firearms allowed on the *Cologne.*" He held out a hand for the holstered Webley revolver.

Talbot thumbed open the leather safety strap and pulled the gun clear. He reversed it and set it in the German Captain's palm.

Moments later, the men reached the main deck. The sun was high in a cloudless sky and made the sea's gently dancing waves flash like mirrors. The heat was kept in check by a steady breeze coming across the decks from the east. Because the *Dagna* was a civilian vessel, her hull and upperworks were painted white, with an accent of deep maroon. She flew Germany's civilian flag rather than the distinctive naval ensign. At present, the smoke that normally coiled from the single funnel aft of the wheelhouse was being diverted using a series of electric fans through special vents below the water-line. It looked like the stern of the ship was wreathed in misty tendrils from melting ice. The system was far from efficient, but it guaranteed no spark or ember ever reached the deck.

There were no open flames in the kitchen, everything was cooked using electric coils, and none of the sailors had any metal on their uniforms that could cause a spark. The ribbons adorning both Captains' tunics were sewn-on cloth facsimiles of their real commendations.

The reason for all these precautions was the seven hundred thousand cubic feet of highly explosive hydrogen floating above the *Dagna* inside the gas cells of the mighty dirigible *Cologne.* The airship's hull over-shadowed its smaller support vessel as it floated above it with its nose locked to the mooring mast on the ship's aft deck. That spindly structure resembled an oil derrick or a miniature Eiffel Tower and allowed the airship the freedom to pivot around as the winds changed direction. The *Dagna*'s fore deck was taken up with the boilers, pumps, and other apparatus for separating the fundamental elements of hydrogen and oxygen from seawater after the salt had been filtered out of it.

The *Cologne* was just over five hundred feet in length and almost fifty in diameter. She wasn't perfectly cylindrical, the support girders between the multiple ring frames visibly stretching her waterproof skin so it looked like the hull was made of dozens of long panels. Clinging to her underbelly were two forty-foot gondolas. One, just aft of the nose, was for the command crew, including all bridge and radio room staff. The second could be configured either for passengers, to enjoy a sightseeing tour of the countryside, or as the payload bay for ninety hundred-pound bombs. The two gondolas were accessed from inside the hull by a long corridor lined with bunks for off-duty personnel on which to rest.

Power was supplied by four Essenwerks's straight-six Cyclone engines, each producing two hundred forty horsepower. The motors were in separate pods attached to the hull and accessible during flight by the team of mechanics. They burned the revolutionary *Blaugas* rather than a liquid fuel like gasoline, saving the airship considerable weight. In normal flight, the *Cologne* cruised at forty-two knots but could accelerate up to fifty in an emergency. In all aspects, she was superior to Count Zeppelin's namesake dirigibles. Rather than the multiple wing-like control surfaces that Zeppelins employed, the *Cologne* had a single cruciform tail for the elevators and rudders.

While the topside of the hull was doped silver to help reflect sunlight and prevent heat from expanding the hydrogen gas, her underside, for this mission, had been daubed in matte black, which made her, effectively, invisible from the ground at night.

She dwarfed all but the largest ocean liners, and the fact that she could fly at twice their speeds made her all the more impressive. The transatlantic flight to Panama proved the concept that regular air service was not impossible. The need to refuel and top off the hydrogen bags during the crossing made a mid-Atlantic rendezvous with the *Dagna* a necessity, but in the future a landing field could be established on the Canary Islands as a permanent solution to that problem.

Captain Grosse led them up the scissor stairs inside the mooring mast framework, returning salutes from two young airmen descending to the main deck. A third crew member guarded the entry hatch at the very front of the dirigible. He too saluted and let the party pass.

Just inside the door was the mechanical lever to release the locking pin holding the airship to the mast. In front of them were stairs that descended gently and followed the curve of the airship's bow section. From there, it was eighty feet back to an access ladder that rose to the control gondola. During normal operations at an airfield, the mooring mast was much lower, and the gondolas could be accessed at ground level via regular doors.

The airship's cockpit was a utilitarian space, with exposed wires and alloyed structural frameworks punched through with holes to reduce weight without sacrificing strength. The view outside was a two-hundred-and-eighty-degree panorama. There were two main control wheels, one for steering the ship left and right, the other to control altitude. Other controls mounted on panels were for ballast and venting hydrogen during flight. There were speaking tubes connected to the mechanics' ready room to call for more or less airspeed. There was ample space for five, including a seat reserved for the Captain.

A tight corridor ran aft from the cockpit along the gondola's left side. It linked several curtained-off spaces. One was for the airship's wireless set. It was little more than a cramped cubbyhole with room for a single man and his gear. There was a lavatory, which was merely a seat with a hole to the wide world below, and three private rooms with cots for the officers. Writing desks could be folded down from the wall in each cabin, and uniforms and other gear were stored in bins under the narrow bedsteads.

Next came another short flight of stairs up into the hull of the airship, and a tunnel stretching back to the second gondola. There were a pair of ladders midway down the tunnel that gave access to the forward engine nacelles. At the end of the tunnel was yet another ladder. The rear gondola was larger than the control cabin and, for this trip, left almost completely empty except for a large winch and cable suspended over a door with long piano hinges in the cabin's floor that could be opened. Next to it was the "cloud car." The contraption resembled the cockpit of a wingless aircraft with a blunt yet still-aerodynamic nose and small fins at the rear.

"What's this?" Talbot asked. "Looks flimsy."

"It is far sturdier than it appears," Captain Grosse said, displaying more than a little pride in the floating oddity. "It is an observation platform that we can lower from the ship. From it, a man with a compass, binoculars, and the speaking tube to the control gondola can act as navigator while the ship remains hidden in the clouds."

Left unsaid was the observer's more militaristic role of bombardier when the airship turned into a weapon of war.

"You Germans think of everything," Talbot remarked. "When Otto told me his airship had a winch strong enough to lower the mines, I never thought to ask why. Darn clever, is what I thought."

"This is how we located the *Spatminster* without the ship spotting us. We remained in some high clouds while our observer below scanned the seas. We will need to leave it behind to accommodate the second mine."

"That brings up the question of the woman stashed in the chain locker." This came from Captain Blucher, the *Dagna*'s commanding officer. "What is to be done with her?"

The men all looked to Otto Dreissen. The industrialist remained silent for several seconds, his face a stony mask, his icy gray eyes unreadable.

"I believe it is too late for her husband to stop us, at this point, so killing Mrs. Bell accomplishes nothing and serves to antagonize him further. She's seen nothing but the inside of her blindfold and the inside of a metal storage locker. We will release her at our next port of call."

"That would be Kingston," Captain Blucher said. "We need some supplies for the hydrogen generator. I believe there is an American Consul in the city."

Talbot said, "Which means Bell will head there from Panama to fetch her. But if something happens to her, I hope you go deep underground, Mr. Dreissen, because Isaac Bell is going to come after you like a just awoken grizzly bear."

Fowler-Gage Seaplane

33

"You're sure you can fly this thing?" Sam Westbrook asked when the warehouse doors were fully opened and daylight shone on the wood and wire and canvas sculpture that was the Fowler-Gage biplane.

"Oh, yeah," Bell said with longing in his voice. He couldn't wait to take it up.

The fuselage and wings were yellow fabric over a wooden frame, and it looked far sturdier than some of the other planes Bell had flown. The eighty-horsepower Hall-Scott V8 motor was a veritable beast behind the big seven-foot propeller. The original landing gear had been replaced with a pontoon that jutted out ahead of the engine and prop. Two small outrigger floats were attached at the wingtips. The entire plane sat on a wheeled cart so it could be towed down to the water just east of the Authority's administration building.

R. G. Fowler was painted on the fuselage

in large black letters.

"And you get so much as one bug splatter on her, I'll make sure that Mr. Fowler sues you into the poorhouse." The speaker was none other than Jack Scully, the Authority's chief mechanic.

"Not to worry, I've got plenty of flight time under my belt."

Scully coughed from deep in his lungs and spat. "Can't believe Goethals went along with this. If it weren't for a shipping error, she'd be crated up and on her way back to the States with Mr. Fowler and his photographer, Ray Duhem. This is the first plane to fly coast-to-coast across an entire continent, you know."

"We're aware of that, Mr. Scully," Bell said with fraying patience.

It had taken all his skill to get George Goethals to allow Bell to borrow the famous plane. Goethals had wanted to send ships out to find the dirigible's support vessel, and Bell had to convince him it would take too much time. In the end, the Canal Administrator had conceded the point but got Bell to promise that he would only pinpoint the ship's location so that an armada could then go after it.

Bell had lied the whole time yet felt no guilt. He was going to rescue his wife and no scruples were going to get in his way.

Scully obviously loved machines. He could fix any equipment the Canal Authority had, from the steam shovels and locomotives all the way down to the rotary fan that sat on the desk in his office. Because of this love, he'd spent a great deal of time with Robert Fowler, the plane's owner and pilot, during the practice flights in preparation for the hop from Panama City on the Pacific Coast to Cristóbal on the Atlantic.

He had arrived leading an old swaybacked horse by its reins. A quartet of five-gallon gas cans were hung from its leather cargo saddle. The animal seemed used to this work and stood quietly while the mechanic unloaded its burden.

"Westbrook, make yourself useful," Scully began. "There's a hand pump on the bench over in the corner. Grab that, and there should also be a bunch of specialized wrenches in a cloth roll. I need them to tweak all these rigging wires. They've gone slack since Mr. Fowler took her across the isthmus."

"Got it."

"Bell, might as well get into the cockpit. That's the fuel tank there on top of the upper wing."

Isaac noted that Robert Fowler was always

prefaced "Mr." but he was just "Bell."

The biplane's open cockpit was little more than a pair of seats, one in front of the other. The pilot sat behind the passenger, and the controls consisted of a foot bar to swivel the rudder and a stick for his right hand to control the elevators that controlled the aircraft's pitch. The motor's water-cooled radiator was directly in front of the passenger's seat. Bell assumed the photographer had taken his shots out the side of the cockpit.

Sam Westbrook gave the bundle of special wrenches to the mechanic for the exacting job of adjusting the tension of all the rigging wires, which, basically, held the plane together while it was in flight. He handed up the rubber hose connected to the hand pump. Bell unscrewed the filler cap to the teardrop-shaped fuel tank and inserted the hose. Sam unscrewed the cap of the first can, plunged the other end of the hose into its gas, and began to pump the mechanism midway between the two ends.

"Sit yourself down," Jack Scully said. "You get a lot more leverage that way."

Sam took his advice, and gasoline was quickly flowing up into the plane's tank. While he siphoned all four cans into the plane, Scully walked around it and played the rigging wires like a professional harpist. He strummed each wire and listened to the twang it produced and tightened the turnbuckles until he heard the right note and pitch.

He may not have liked Bell or the thought of this flight, but he paid the plane professional attention as someone who loved it. At least, that was Bell's fervent wish. Though he knew how to pilot a plane, rigging one properly took experience he just didn't have.

Scully tinkered with the engine for another ten minutes after finishing with the wires. He added oil and checked over all the valves and made certain the radiator was topped off.

Only when he was satisfied did they fire the motor. It lit on just the second crank and roared like a lion. Even with chocks holding the wheels of the trolley the plane was sitting on from moving, the plane itself felt like it wanted to take to the air. Bell couldn't keep a smile from his face despite the significance of this flight.

He choked the engine to silence, after a minute's test, and the prop juddered to a stop.

"Any chance I can talk you into taking me?" Sam asked as Bell jumped down from the cockpit. "Four eyes are better than two."

"I might as well be straight with you now," Bell said when Jack Scully was out of earshot. He was hitching the trolley carrying the plane to the horse so it could tow it out to the water.

"What do you mean?"

"I lied back in Colonel Goethals's office. It's a big ocean out there. I don't stand a chance in hell of finding that ship. Needle in a haystack would be a piece of cake by comparison."

"If not there, where are you going?"

"That's what I was doing all day in the map room. Old Jeremiah Townsend and I picked the two most likely spots Talbot would rendezvous with the airship. I can fly there in under two hours."

"And then what?"

"Wait for the Zeppelin to show and follow it back to the ship."

"Clever, Mr. Bell. So why not take me?"

Bell explained. "The more weight the plane carries, the more fuel she burns. I'm going to need every drop of gasoline if this is going to work."

Bell pointed to the one-man canoe he'd secured to the lower wing. "Plus, I'm bringing that."

"You never explained why."

476

"We identified two likely places. I have to assume Talbot loiters in the area while he's waiting for the Zeppelin's night flight. I can't get too close in a noisy airplane. When I check out the valleys, I'll land out of range and paddle in. If I find no evidence that Talbot's around, I fly off to the other site and do the same thing. With luck, I'll get an idea what they're doing and then paddle back in time to follow the airship."

Sam nodded. "Makes sense."

"Just stand by the phone in your office. I'll call as soon as I reach Cristóbal and give you the coordinates as best as I can figure." Bell suddenly remembered something. He handed a note to Sam. "I need you to wire the Van Dorn office with these instructions."

Sam read the couple lines. "What's 'OTJ'?"

" 'On the jump.' Everyone at Van Dorn knows if I add those letters that it's a priority job. If the response comes back in the affirmative, you have to prevent President Roosevelt from coming here, even if he is just staying in the Canal Zone."

"What's this about?"

"Coincidences are the opportunist's playground."

"Huh?"

"Just send it. And mind what I said about

Roosevelt."

Jack Scully finally stopped griping when Bell climbed back into the floating plane and announced he was ready. He wore a pair of motorcycle goggles Sam had borrowed from a company dispatch rider, and he'd worked a pair of Ohropax wax-and-cotton plugs into his ears. While the engine was loud, what he really needed was protection from the pressure of wind shooting into his ears at fifty miles per hour. He knew from experience that it grew painful after only a few minutes.

The mechanic led the draft horse and its winged cargo across the parking lot and down the shallow embankment to the canal's entrance channel. The day was virtually windless, the water was like glass. The horse had little trouble towing the biplane on its wheeled cart. Without hesitation, Scully entered the water, and the horse plodded along in his wake. The trolley was soon submerged, as the horse dragged it deeper, and all at once the airplane floated free.

Scully turned around to lead the horse back to dry land. Sam took the reins, and Scully returned to the water once more to hand-start the Hall-Scott engine. This time, it fired on the first throw of the prop.

Seaplanes don't have brakes, and this one didn't have an anchor, so as soon as the engine caught the Fowler-Gage started creeping forward. Jack Scully was forced to dive out of the way of the deadly prop. He came up, sputtering. Bell was already well past him by now, so the mechanic didn't see the grin on his lips.

With no wind to worry about, Bell opened the throttle to its stops, working the rudder bar with his feet to keep the plane headed in a straight line. He noted it was a little rougher than taking off from an airfield, and its speed built slower, but as he accelerated, the controls began to feel lighter in his hands. The wings were generating lift.

Despite the canal's calm surface, the ride grew rougher and rougher, and for a moment Bell thought the plane was going to tear itself apart. His hand was just reaching for the throttle to scrap the takeoff when the pontoon lifted clear, and things smoothed instantly. Bell pulled back ever so gently on the stick, and the biplane responded smartly. The nose came up, and he was climbing into the cloudless sky.

He circled back when he reached about five hundred feet to throw a wave at the tiny figures standing at the water's edge. Sam waved, and Bell threw him a salute. Bell felt no more remorse lying to Sam than when he'd lied to Goethals. It's why he didn't talk about his plan within earshot of Jack Scully. The gruff mechanic would have known right away Bell was pulling a fast one because the Fowler-Gage didn't have anywhere near the range needed to go chasing after the airship.

Bell looked for Scully and saw he was on foot and heading back to the garage with his horse walking with its head down behind him.

Bell turned the aircraft to the northwest — a quirk of the canal is that one travels eastward to get from the Atlantic to the Pacific — and settled for an altitude of about a thousand feet. He could feel the drag the pontoon exerted on the airframe. The nose kept wanting to drop, and that meant he had to keep constant pressure on the stick in order to stay level.

He was soon over the Culebra Cut. Steam and smoke rose from around the excavators, which still looked mammoth even from that altitude. He spotted a steam shovel that was sitting idle and knew it was the one destroyed in the accident.

He got a better sense, from up above, how the sides of the canal were terraced like rice paddies in Asia. Also obvious were the massive landslides that continued to thwart the construction effort. Bell was put in mind of King Canute trying to hold back the tide.

It was only from high up that he got a sense of the scale of the project. The cut stretched for some eight miles and sliced through the heart of the continental divide, laying mountains low as it went. The uncountable tons of rock pulled from it didn't just leave a scar but also a testament to man's vision, ingenuity, and tenacity.

He flew over the earthen plug, which prevented the rising waters of Lake Gatun from inundating the work site and the town of Gamboa, and the mighty discharge of the Chagres River, its water the color of milky coffee as the spring floods had not yet abated.

Without warning, the plane plummeted as though the air holding it aloft had dissipated. Bell swallowed the seed of panic and calmly let the nose drop to pick up airspeed. He descended far faster than he'd expected, but, at five hundred feet, he'd dropped below the odd pocket of extreme low pressure. He assumed it had something to do with the Chagres River and how its rapid current slowed when it entered the turgid lake.

Moments later, he was back up to one

thousand feet, and the plane was purring like a kitten. It was far superior to any of the aircraft he'd flown before, especially those with a pusher engine where the prop was behind the wings, as opposed to the tractor design of this one.

Bell crossed over the broad expanse of Lake Gatun, the sun's dancing reflection like a constant companion as he flew. There were no markers of any sort in this part of the country. Eventually, channel buoys would mark the shipping lanes, but for now there was nothing but rising water and impenetrable jungle. If Bell had to put down, he'd be hard-pressed to make it back to any sort of civilization. Had he drifted more easterly, he could have followed the side-by-side tracks of the Panama Railway and flown over some of the new bridges installed to raise the rails above the lake. However, his prize was farther west, where there was nothing.

He had his map at the ready inside his jacket pocket.

An hour and a half into his flight, Bell finally spotted a landmark he'd memorized earlier, a particularly steep-sided island rising from the lake. This was the well-documented mountaintop on the topographical map, and he'd impressed himself that he'd flown straight for it relying on dead reckoning alone. There were other islands around it, as Bell knew there would be.

The area he wanted was still about ten miles away, up a long, narrow inlet that had once been a valley. He carefully scanned the water below for any sign of Court Talbot's boat and his crew of mercenaries. He also watched the horizon for the cigar-shaped airship. It appeared he had the sky to himself.

He flew on for a few more minutes until he found his first target. This was the less likely of the two spots he and Townsend had determined. The valley seemed tight, though the hills weren't as high as at the second location. Seeing the inlet, versus studying it on a map, Bell came to the quick conclusion that the site wasn't suitable at all. It was far too narrow for an airship to operate in with any margin for error. Taking one of those behemoth flying machines into the guts of the valley was tantamount to suicide.

Bell decided to skip it and continue on to the primary location.

The flight time was only another ten minutes, and he dropped altitude as he approached the second flooded valley. The hills were tall enough to hide an airship yet far enough apart that the ship had maneuvering room between their gentle slopes. One remained poking up in the middle of the inundated valley as an island, which could screen him from view of anyone farther up its reach. It would be a perfect place to stash the plane, so he dropped more altitude and prepared to land.

Taking off and flying an aircraft was never the difficult part of the sport, it was the landing. The pilot had to time altitude, speed, and throttle control to the second. Make a mistake, and you overfly the field or, far more common, you crash to the ground. Sometimes you walk away and sometimes that's where you die. Bell knew the risks and was as comfortable landing in an open field as a paved runway. But he'd never landed on the water before.

In principle, it should be the same as at a proper airport but there were differences. The valley was so narrow that Bell couldn't orient the plane enough to land into the wind, he'd need to crab it in against the crosswind. And there was a bit of a chop to the water. He had to time touchdown on the back of any wave rather than the front.

He reviewed everything in his mind before dumping more altitude and lining up the nose with the island. When he entered the valley's throat with hills rising up off both wings, the crosswind intensified, forcing Bell to put more and more pressure on the rudder bar. He eased back farther on the throttle, drifting the biplane closer and closer to the surface. He knew he couldn't land if the nose was pointed too far into the wind because the float wouldn't slice into the water but instead crash across it.

He sank lower still, the lake flashing just a couple feet below him. Just as he was about to land, he released pressure on the rudder, the plane swung sharply, then he touched down with the float pointing in the direction of travel exactly. It was a perfect water landing in tricky circumstances. Speed bled off so quickly, he had to goose the throttle a little to taxi close enough to the island so he could unload the canoe and tow it under cover.

34

Over the past week, *Cologne*'s crew had become experts at night operations above Lake Gatun. The ship soared over the coastline well north of the dam that held back the waters. There was no beach, just mangroves and jungle, and not a soul for miles around. They were at seven thousand feet in a moonless sky and completely invisible. From the ground, it would look like stars were winking out momentarily when the airship blocked their light with its enormous body, then the twinkles would return as the dirigible glided serenely past. The engines were throttled back to a low rpm. Their sound was no more than a hum to any animals below who happened to hear it.

The jungle was dark and featureless, yet somehow a malevolence reached up from its depths. This was no place for man and yet man had come to tame the land and cut a channel through it between the two seas. The tropical forest had fought the incursion with heat and rain and storms and disease. As Court Talbot looked down from his lofty perch high above the canopy, he felt a superstitious dread that the jungle had not given up the fight.

The Captain had forbidden him from the control gondola for the voyage, explaining that he'd be in the way of normal flight operations. He was to remain in the rear cargo hold for the duration, wedged in between the two enormous underwater mines. With him were two airmen, one who had a bandaged hand. Talbot guessed it was from an accident aboard the ship and had no idea that it was Marion Bell's handiwork.

Talbot was also stripped of his Webley, but he had a two-shot derringer backup in his front pocket. And there were plenty of guns at the camp, should they need them.

The three men stared out an open window as the *Cologne* floated over the jungle. The air up there was cool and pleasant, and the Zeppelin was cruising slow enough that the wind barely ruffled their clothes. For the first time Court Talbot could remember in all his years in Panama, he wasn't fending off clouds of insects.

Like some dramatic stage effect, the jungle

was suddenly awash in silvery light. The Captain had timed their arrival to coincide with the rising of the moon over the Atlantic horizon. The foliage below remained a monochromatic black, but very quickly they could see where the jungle gave way to the glittering lake.

The giant airship turned northward as it crossed above the lake. The countless islands dotting its surface were easily spotted in the moonlight. They remained dark drops of matte black on the water's shining surface. Thirty minutes of slow cruising later, Captain Grosse maneuvered the dirigible above the narrow inlet that had once been a valley. Hydrogen vented with a sibilant hiss to bring them lower over the water yet still high enough to clear the few remaining isles.

An electric light shot up from the darkness below. The airship was almost directly above Talbot's workboat and the dock and camp his men had made for themselves. They'd heard the airship's engines and were guiding her to their exact location. More lifting gas was vented until the huge craft drifted lower still until it entirely filled the sky for the men down on the lake. Mooring lines tumbled from the dirigible's bow. When they'd been tied off by Talbot's crew, the light blinked several times, a prearranged signal.

"Ready for the ride of your life?" one of the hoist men asked, his English only lightly accented.

Judging distance at night was notoriously difficult, but Talbot didn't think they were below three hundred feet. "I suppose."

As the safety harness was double-checked, the second lift operator opened the floor panel. The opening was the size of a large area rug, and the darkness seemed to rise up through it from below. The airmen called it *die Tür des Teufels,* "the Devil's Door."

The hook was snapped onto the metal ring that was part of Talbot's harness. The operator flashed him a thumbs-up, and when Talbot returned the gesture, the cable drum rotated backward to lift him off his feet. For a moment, he swung like a pendulum over the abyss, and then he was falling out the bottom of the airship and through the humid night air. He remembered to flip on his flashlight to signal the winch operator. The trip took only a few minutes. As he neared the ground, he began clicking his light on and off. The operator slowed his descent so that he slipped though the jungle's topmost branches with barely a leaf's rustle.

Talbot felt hands reaching for him as he

came to the dock. It was Raul. Talbot killed the light to stop more cable from falling down around his feet. Apart from their looks, Raul wasn't much like his dead brother, Rinaldo. He didn't take any pleasure from life. Even before Rinaldo's murder, he rarely laughed or let himself have any fun. Talbot and Rinaldo spent countless hours drinking and carousing, stuffing as much joy and debauchery into every day they lived. Not so Raul. And he'd grown even more withdrawn following his brother's death. He'd only agreed to fill in as a member of Talbot's crew because of the promise he'd exact his revenge on Isaac Bell.

He'd desperately wanted to drive the truck that slammed into Bell's vehicle at the edge of the Culebra Cut. When Bell had driven to Gamboa, Raul had been behind the wheel, lying in ambush and ready to strike. But dumb luck saved Bell on that leg of his journey. Rather than a lone vehicle, on the road from Panama City, an entire convoy had approached his position. He'd scrambled to roll the log off the road and watched, crouched in the grass, as Bell trundled past, having somehow integrated his tanker truck into a convoy of cargo haulers.

Raul was forced to return to Gamboa at the tail end of the convoy and sneak aboard the workboat while Talbot kept Bell distracted. Another member of Talbot's band of cutthroats had gone out to finish the job during Raul's interrogation and buried the evidence under the avalanche. The Panamanian was actually relieved when word got out that Bell had survived. It gave him the chance to make the death far slower and more painful.

The machete he carried was made from a truck's worn leaf spring, sharpened to a razor's edge on a grinding wheel. Its weight made it the ideal blade for hacking through thick jungle. He was eager to see what it could do to a human limb.

A sudden gust of wind made the *Cologne* spin and strain against her mooring ropes. The ropes snapped branches high overhead as the airship twisted around. A spray of leaves and twigs rained down from above. The big Essenwerks engines changed pitch as Captain Grosse backed the hovering airship against the wind so once again it was directly over the boat and adjacent dock. The gust intensified into a steady four knots from the east.

The dock they'd constructed over the water was a simple affair, with a split-log frame lashed to the trunks of trees that had been drowned when the valley flooded. The frame was decked with rough-sawn planks. These men came from fishing villages, mostly, and knew how to use the jungle to their advantage. The dock was as sturdy as the main wharf in Panama City.

Up the hill from the dock, the men had cleared underbrush to make a camp, with enough room to make a fire and hang their hammocks. It was far more comfortable than sleeping aboard the workboat. They'd brought a slew of mismatched chairs and rigged up an oiled-canvas tarpaulin to keep out the rain. Someone had even fashioned a crude sign and nailed it to a tree. The six men who made up Talbot's crew had named the camp the Vipers' Den, in honor of their recent exploits.

"Look sharp, everyone. We're bringing down two of the bombs," Court Talbot called out. "Tonight's the last of it. We set the final charges, and the Red Vipers disappear for good."

None of the men gave any real indication that they'd paid any attention until Talbot added, "Oh, and you all receive your pay in good gold coins."

That brought a lustful cheer from their throats and turned their eyes bright with greed.

Raul Morales gave Talbot a cancerous

492

look. Talbot held up a reassuring hand. "You get your brother's full cut and my guarantee that Bell won't leave Panama for as long as it takes for the Germans to get to Jamaica. They kidnapped his wife."

A burst of light from above was the signal that the sailors on the *Cologne* had positioned the first of the one-ton mines over the bomb bay door and were ready to lower it. Talbot flicked his light twice to tell them they were ready. A few moments later, the mine materialized, out of the dark, over the men's heads, two lengths of rope dangling from it like a jellyfish's tentacles. When it was low enough, men reached up to grasp the ropes and heave so that the deadly package swung enough for it to touch down on the edge of the dock. The wood creaked under the burden but held fast. One of Talbot's people climbed on top of the square explosive device to unhook the cable so the second one could be placed on the boat.

The men had done this so many times by now that the job had become second nature.

The wind picked up a little more speed, prompting an increase in power to the four Essenwerks motors. The propellers' steady drone changed to a higher pitch, which forced the men working under her floating bulk to raise their voices to be heard.

Once his man was clear of the heavy steel hook, Talbot used his flashlight to signal the German flight engineers to retract the wire and send down the next bomb. The hook quickly vanished into the night. He called over to Raul and handed him a key dangling on a leather thong he kept hung around his neck. "Do me a favor and get me a spare pistol from camp. The Germans wouldn't let me keep my Webley. As if I'd fire it inside a tube more volatile than a stick of dynamite."

Raul didn't reply, but he flicked on his own light and crossed the deck to take the short trail up to their camp.

At first, Raul Morales didn't understand what he was seeing. The moon was hidden behind some clouds, so the light was just about nonexistent, but it looked like a figure moving around the camp. It made no sense because everyone was either on the dock or the workboat. He slowed his approach, crouching low. His machete was in his hand without him realizing he'd drawn it.

He and Rinaldo had grown up around violence. Their father used the machete as a teaching tool, going so far as to cut off a finger of one son's hand when he'd taken a canoe out without permission. Raul had killed his first man when he was barely into his twenties. The man had been poaching the family's fish traps, and Raul had felt the punishment fit the crime when he'd harpooned the thief in the chest with an iron lance. Rinaldo had always been the flashier one, the dreamer and schemer. Raul had been content to stay in their old village as long as those around him knew not to cross him.

The few who tried did not live to regret their decisions.

He was ten feet from the figure when he realized that the intruder was systematically searching the camp. There was nothing to find, a few boxes with food and cooking utensils, spare clothes, fishing gear, and a sixty-pound lockbox where Talbot kept their wages and a spare pistol. He didn't want to leave the box aboard the workboat in case they were caught planting the bombs and had to abandon it.

Just as he threw on a burst of speed to catch the intruder unawares, the clouds parted and the moon's glow played across the man's profile for a moment, before he turned back to his clandestine search. Raul went from calculating hunter to berserk savage in an instant.

It was him. Bell. The man who'd murdered his brother.

He abandoned his flashlight and ran at Bell as silently and as intently as a big jungle cat whose prey has no idea it's about to die. Bell finally sensed the onrushing attacker and turned to meet the man. He barely recognized Raul Morales because his face was twisted into a mask of uncontrolled rage. The whites of his eyes shone all the way around the irises, and his mouth was open in a silent scream full of hate.

Bell had been watching the camp since early afternoon. Rowing in from where he'd stashed the seaplane had been easy enough, though he did cross paths with an anaconda that swam past him and saw a number of crocodiles sunning themselves on the shore and a couple using the power of their mighty tails to swim. None thought enough of the canoe to investigate, which they could have torn apart with ease.

Locating the camp had been easy, for the men had been grilling some poor creature they had shot out of the trees, and the woodsmoke and smell of cooking meat had carried far down the flooded valley. Bell had pulled to shore a good quarter mile from Talbot's men and went in on foot, moving at a snail's pace so as not to give away his presence. He'd watched them share their meal, noting it was a small forest pig they'd killed. Afterward, one man stayed awake to clean and oil his rifle while the others had rolled into their hammocks for an afternoon siesta.

Bell kept an eye on the sentry, fearing he would patrol the boat. But he didn't. As soon as his weapon was reassembled, he pulled his hat over his eyes and fell asleep on the low camp chair.

These men were thirty miles from the nearest town, nestled in some of the densest jungle on the planet, so it came as no surprise they hadn't worried about an ambush. The isolation made them feel comfortable.

Too comfortable, Bell thought.

He left them to their naps and crawled over to the dock. There he found a cache of five-gallon metal cans. Most were empty, but the smell of the gasoline they'd contained tainted the air. Bell filled three of the containers with river water and screwed on their caps. He swapped out these with three of the neatly lined-up cans still filled with gas in case anyone took inventory. Two of these he set aside and the other he carried onto the workboat. He gained access to the engine compartment from a hatch under the crew's quarters.

It took just a few minutes to plant his makeshift bomb. He cut a narrow strip of cloth from the hem of his shirt and soaked it in gasoline. He then used it as a wick, from the motor's open ignition point down to the gas can he'd been able to conceal in the bilge space under the engine's mounting bracket. The space was dark, and even with a flashlight it would be difficult to see his booby trap. And the compartment reeked so strongly of fuel already, he wasn't concerned that the smell would betray the open can of gas.

He crawled out and closed the hatch. He stayed low and peered over the workboat's gunwales to see if anyone at the camp had gotten up. He saw no movement, so he legged over the gunwale and made his way off the dock, picking up the two fuel cans he'd set aside for himself. He returned to his canoe and stashed the thirty-pounders in the footwell.

It would be awkward paddling back to the plane but essential if he was going to follow the Essenwerks airship. He recalled seeing the cans on Talbot's boat the day he interviewed Raul pretending to be Rinaldo and had factored their presence into his plan. He returned and found a spot close enough to the camp and dock to hopefully glean some information as to their actual intentions.

Since he didn't see anything around that looked like it had been delivered from the giant Zeppelin, he assumed they were smuggling matériel into the Canal Zone. Learning what, exactly, was one of the reasons he was here.

He waited, without moving, as the sun went down and the moon rose. The men had roused themselves at dusk, finished eating their bush pig, and talked and joked until a sound emerged amid the background hum of insects. It was the beat of four large propellers thrashing the air as the massive dirigible wended its way up the valley, and when one of the pirates shined a flashlight into the night sky, it came to hover over the camp, and two thick ropes fell from the craft's conical nose.

Bell felt a small sense of triumph at deducing that Otto Dreissen had used an airship to abduct his wife. It had been a wild theory but correct nevertheless.

Once the mooring lines were tied down, Court Talbot was lowered to the ground. Bell heard him say a few words to his men, but he was speaking in Spanish, leaving the detective frustrated and no closer to the solution to this mystery. The only thing he recognized was "Viboras Rojas." Then from the airship's black belly came the steel box. It was perfectly square, and featureless in the uncertain light, roughly six feet to a side. Bell didn't know its function and finally settled on it being a cargo container. He followed that mental thread, which made him consider that the Viboras were real after all, and the Germans were supplying them with weapons smuggled in aboard the airship.

He crept from his hiding spot. He had time to speculate later. With Talbot and his crew occupied, Bell slipped into their camp to search for clues, unconcerned about any sounds he made because the the airship's props filled the sky with noise.

Bell was well aware that someone approached the camp as he was halfway through what felt like a fruitless search, but he didn't have time to hide. He pulled his boot knife moments before the man rushed into the camp.

Raul charged straight at him, machete held high for a chopping sweep that could sever Bell's head from his neck as cleanly as a farmer chopping the head off a chicken. Bell reversed his grip on the knife and threw it when Morales was four long paces away. The blade sank hilt-deep under his right arm where the pectoral muscles met the rib cage. The arm dropped instantly, but momentum carried Raul another two steps before he fully realized something was very wrong.

His arm wouldn't move, so he quickly grabbed the machete with his left before it dropped to the ground. He felt no pain.

Raul saw his opponent was no longer armed and leapt for him, sweeping with the razor-sharp machete so that Bell had to leap back to keep his guts from being spilled. Raul kept up the attack, swinging the blade in cutting arcs that forced Bell to keep retreating. Raul was as good with his left hand as he was with his right. He adjusted his grip, in order to use the blade more like a fencing foil than a saber, and stabbed at Bell, extending just enough to slip the machete between Bell's ribs and into the branching arteries and veins around his heart.

Any good knife fighter knows the margin of victory is the width of a blade.

Bell spun as Raul committed himself to the change of tactics, like a matador getting as close as he can to the horns of the bull. He physically brushed against Morales as he went around, reaching blindly over his shoulder to pull his knife from the man's

501

chest. Twirling like a flamenco dancer, he spun and plunged the dagger into Morales's left kidney. Even as Raul opened his mouth to scream, Bell clamped a hand over it. Blood gushed from the chest wound because the knife had severed the major vessel that fed the arm. He held the man as his life drained from him and slowly let him slump to the ground, the sightless eyes glinting like two poker chips in the moonlight. Bell wiped his blade clean, looking over and seeing a second steel box about to touch down on the workboat's aft cargo area. None of the men saw the silent fight.

Morales had a key looped around his neck. Bell pulled it free and used it to open the little safe sitting close to the most comfortable-looking chair in the clearing, obviously Talbot's. Inside was a chamois sack filled with coins heavy enough to be gold, a .38 caliber short-barreled revolver, and some papers. He took it all.

Keeping an eye on the work going on on the dock, Bell dragged Raul Morales's corpse a short distance into the bush in case anyone else returned to the clearing. His blood was already being absorbed by the jungle's black soil.

Bell went back to his original hiding spot. The second box was fully down now and its braided cable about to be detached. Court Talbot was at the stern, making sure the box was properly centered so its weight didn't cause his boat to list. He motioned to one of his crewmen and the man climbed up the stairs to the bridge.

Satisfied with the placement, Talbot nodded to the man perched atop the container to unhook the crate from the airship. When the hook swung free, Talbot sent two men to untie the mooring lines from around the thickest trees they could find and finally signaled the hovering dirigible that it was free. Its engine beat changed seconds later, and the airship began to glide away.

As much as Bell wanted to rush back to the seaplane to chase it down, he had to wait to make sure he'd stopped Talbot and hope he could find the dirigible during its flight back to its floating base. He had already deduced its likely whereabouts and thought he could intercept her before it got there.

If he was wrong, then he'd gambled with Marion's life and lost.

35

The jungle's nighttime cacophony resumed as the airship flew away, down the valley, and the roar of its engines and whir of its propellers slowly receded. The men busied themselves around the boat for a few more minutes, including topping off the tanks from the spare cans. Bell was relieved he'd thought ahead, because they'd poured in the water as though it were gasoline. Five minutes after the airship had gone, Talbot realized Raul had not returned, and he bellowed his name several times. When he still didn't return to the boat, Talbot gave an order to a man in the pilothouse and jumped down to the dock, taking long-legged strides toward the camp.

Unseen in the pilothouse, the crewman with the most mechanical experience took a firm grip on the crank next to the helm, which was connected to the engine below through a set of gears. He gave it a solid shove.

The fumes had built to a volatile level inside the enclosed engine room, meaning Bell's wick wasn't necessary after all. The very air itself was explosive, and the moment the ignition kicked on it all turned to flame. The hatch blew off, and a column of fire rose through it like the Gates of Hell had opened. The pressure from the explosion blew the door off its hinges and shattered the glass in a couple portholes, tongues of fire shooting from them like cannons.

That's when the five-gallon gasoline bomb Bell had left behind detonated. The bridge rose six feet off the deck and came apart in a spray of wood and steel that peppered the water and scythed through the jungle. The fireball rolled fifty feet up into the canopy of trees, lighting up the scene in stark relief.

The men on the boat were so close to the blast, their insides were turned into so much jelly, and they died instantly. Bell saw Court Talbot launched into the air when he was struck in the back by the concussive wave. There was a chance he was alive, but a very slim one.

The workboat started to sink immediately, even as its deck was awash in flame. The dock too started to burn, and very quickly the few remaining gas cans went up in a successive string of bright explosions. Bell was close enough that he felt the heat of the conflagration on his face.

Just as the workboat and its cargo slid beneath the water, and all the fires were extinguished, the night shattered again as two tons of experimental high explosives inside the naval mine went off in a sympathetic detonation.

Bell was fifty feet away when it happened and still found himself flying through the air for a moment before skidding back to earth, his ears ringing from the acoustical onslaught. He looked back to see everything had been consumed by the blast, the wreckage of the workboat, the dock, even the camp, ceased to exist. Trees had been blown flat in a wide circle of boles, and, farther out, everything else had been stripped of its foliage, leaving naked stems jutting up in a field of smoldering debris.

Bell lurched to his feet, shaking his head to clear it. He staggered back toward the site of the explosion but quickly saw there was nothing to be gained. Around him was nothing but utter devastation. He was about to head off again when he spotted Talbot's hat lying on the ground next to a burning shrub. It felt heavy when he picked it up.

When he turned it over, he saw why and dropped it immediately. It still contained the top of Courtney Talbot's skull.

With no need for stealth, Bell jogged back to the canoe and launched it onto the lake as soon as he'd crammed his legs in around the two cans of gasoline. The oar he'd chosen had a blade at both ends, like a kayak paddle, so he could stroke with an efficient rhythm that had him gliding along the lake's calm surface at a good pace. Occasionally, he saw the eyes of some creature on the shore, reflected in the moonlight, and heard others splashing in the water, but nothing paid him any heed.

No matter how fast he dug his oar in the water, he felt the Essenwerks airship was getting farther and farther away. Even though the airship had left the camp by flying northwest, Bell was certain that their support ship lay to the east, past the busy Port of Colón. With so many ships coming into Panama from the Caribbean and America, the waters west of Colón saw a tremendous amount of seaborne traffic, while, to the east, there was virtually no shipping at all. He was certain their base was there. He figured the dirigible would make a beeline to open waters, from its inland rendezvous, and then curve around Colón at roughly twenty miles from shore.

Bell reached the hidden seaplane much faster than his outbound journey, and would have passed it, had he not jammed some sticks in the water as markers before locating Talbot's jungle camp. He eased under the overhanging branches that had shielded the plane and bumped gently against the central float. He retrieved the two cans and, hunched over, crawled out on his knees and set them on the float. He also dragged the lightweight canoe up and lashed it back where it belonged.

He hadn't remembered to bring a funnel, so he spilled almost as much gas as he managed to pour into the aircraft's tank. The smell made his head spin, until the wind blew the fumes away. He had secured the plane to a tree on shore with a length of cord he'd tied inside the cockpit as a brace. He didn't want to repeat Jack Scully's ignoble scramble away from the prop once it started to spin.

Using the oar, Bell paddled the seaplane from its hiding spot and turned it so that the nose was facing the lake and its tether was fully stretched. He primed the engine with fuel and set the ignition before climbing out onto the pontoon so he could spin the propeller. It was difficult to get much leverage standing right in front of the wooden prop, and it took five attempts to fire the motor.

It died by the time he had jumped in the water and swam under the wing to climb up into the cockpit. So he altered the throttle's setting to run at a higher rpm and climbed back around the engine to stand on the pontoon once again. This time, it took only three hard pulls to crank the motor to life. It ran louder and faster, thanks to his adjustment, and he had enough time to return to the cockpit and sit, in his sodden clothes, while the engine warmed.

After a few minutes idle, Bell untied the tether and began to taxi the seaplane away from shore. Bell used the foot bar to swing the nose until it was pointed down the valley and toward the open lake. He eased the throttle to its stop and felt the familiar sense of exhilaration as the aircraft gathered speed.

Because he was ready for it, Bell didn't think his second water takeoff was as rough as the first. The plane shook as it neared rotation speed, yet not so much that he considered ditching the attempt. The vibrations ceased the moment the pontoon rose out of the water and he was airborne once again. As soon as he had enough altitude, he turned northeast and continued to climb. There were so many variables to factor in his attempt to find the airship, but he really knew it would come down to luck. And altitude. The higher he went, the farther he could see.

He was at five thousand feet when he crossed over the lights of Colón. He could easily see the massive locks, lit for work to continue around the clock. President Roosevelt was due in a couple of days and they needed the locks functioning for his inaugural trip up from the Atlantic Ocean to Lake Gatun.

Bell was frozen to the core. It had been eighty degrees when he'd taken off and at least a quarter of that temperature reading had been lost by climbing so high. And his wet clothes leached heat from his body, so that he was shivering in the cockpit.

He flew on. He had no choice. Marion was in danger, and there was no force on earth that could stop him.

He guided the plane out to sea and kept scanning the water below for moonlight reflecting on the dirigible's skin. Bell knew enough about airships to know her topside hadn't been doped black. It had to be a light color, to absorb less heat from the sun. While she was impossible to see from the ground at night, from above she should shine like a beacon. The moon was high and almost full, so the sea shimmered like mercury. Darker spots on its surface were caused by clouds blocking the light. Away from the moon's aura, the night sky was full of stars.

If the mission weren't so dire, Bell would have found the view magnificent. All his attention was focused on finding the airship, however, not on the natural beauty of the scene below. He scanned all around, straining his eyes to catch the unnatural deviation in light from a large man-made object.

Bell wasn't certain about the seaplane's range. He'd needed two hours to cross the isthmus and guessed the tank still had some gas in reserve. He'd been aloft for an hour already and assumed it would take him at least forty minutes to get back to Colón. His window of flight was closing rapidly, and as the minutes ticked away, his anxiety rose. He didn't care about himself. It was Marion's fate that gnawed at his conscience.

He passed his self-imposed deadline without making a sighting. He knew he'd guessed correctly. The airship had to meet its support ship in these waters. He kept on, his neck and eyes in constant motion as he scanned either side of the aircraft and ahead through the whirling propeller blade for an otherworldly shimmer to mark the dirigible's location.

His faith withered as more time slipped through his grasp. He slid close to despair when he saw he'd passed his deadline by ten minutes. Even if he found the airship now and followed it back to its base and he rescued Marion, he likely didn't have enough fuel to make it to shore, let alone all the way back to Colón. He realized the decision had been made without consciously thinking about it. He never planned to turn back at all. He was going to keep searching until the last drop of gasoline had sprayed into the engine, and, even then, he'd keep looking until he had to dead-stick the plane in an ocean landing.

A minute later, he spotted his quarry. The airship was much lower than his plane, maybe only at a thousand feet, so it appeared small from his perspective, but there was no hiding its torpedo-like body knifing through the air. Bell dumped altitude and speed and was soon at a thousand feet and slightly behind the lumbering Zeppelin. The air was so much warmer that he felt the circulation returning to his hands, giving them back their normal dexterity, and he no longer needed to clench his jaw to keep his teeth from chattering.

He looked far ahead and spotted the beam of a searchlight that hadn't been there moments earlier. It was a signal from the ship to guide the dirigible home. Bell realized that when the Zeppelin came in for its final approach, all eyes would be on it, and the noise of its engines and props would drown out any sounds he made.

He banked left and added some more power. He flew a wide arc around the ship, keeping far enough from her so they wouldn't hear the buzz of his Hall-Scott motor. He went into a holding pattern as he watched the airship slowly approach its marine tender. It seemed to take forever, but, really, it was only a few minutes.

He thought about how he would have to improvise his escape, then admonished himself for worrying about something so far into the future. He needed all his wits to land the plane on the open ocean under the noses of the German crew. He hadn't allowed himself time to contemplate the vast quantities of explosives potentially smuggled into the Canal Zone either. That was a problem for . . .

Bell snapped himself back to the present. The airship looked close to the tender now. He had to land. He eased back on the throttle and let the nose fall away. He'd waited too long, so he gave it more power for a few seconds. Soon enough, the ocean reared up under the pontoon, making waves under the aircraft, at what seemed a break-neck speed. From a few thousand feet up, it had looked like a sheet of mercury. Now it resembled the hide of a living, breathing creature whose skin rippled and heaved in unreadable patterns.

The Zeppelin was almost to the metal mooring mast. Bell could see the bright glow of lights aimed up from the white-hulled ship.

He cut more power as he came in to land aligned with the vessel's bow. Anyone keeping watch would require the keenest of eyes and the best of luck in the world to spot him, but the odds of detection weren't zero. He edged off more of the throttle until the engine felt like it was almost idling. The speed dropped quickly because of the drag of the heavy pontoon, and the nose of the aircraft kept wanting to drop. Water still flashed under the wing with the apparent speed of a whitewater cataract.

Bell pulled back on the stick ever so gently. The nose came up, and then the wings suddenly lost lift, and the plane stalled just a few inches behind the long ocean swell it pushed in front of it. She had kissed the water as gently as any landing Bell had performed and slowed in the dramatic fashion of all seaplanes. He'd done it. He'd snuck in right under their noses. The ship was just a quarter mile away, and he was down safely.

He killed the motor and pulled the plugs from his ears. Despite its distance, he could hear the airship's motors as it made its final approach. His entire body was stiff when he climbed out of the cockpit, every joint protesting being set in motion again. He crouched down to untie the canoe and launch it on the plainly gentle waves. Now that he'd landed, he realized it was his imagination that made the swells appear tsunamic in size.

Checking that his .45 was secure in its holster, Bell slid into the canoe and started rowing for the ship, the sea surging placidly under his near-invisible little craft.

36

The *Cologne* slowed dramatically, barely making any headway against the wind, as she inched closer and closer to her mooring mast. When the tip of the nose passed over the *Dagna*'s stern rail, a rope was tossed down to the waiting deckhands. Like handlers guiding a reluctant elephant at the circus, the men coaxed the airship to the mast. For his part, Captain Grosse feathered the engines with the mastery of an orchestra conductor.

Additional lines were dropped from the airship, and soon the first rope was fed into the electric winch at the top of the spindly mooring mast. The huge dirigible then was drawn in those last few feet so that a locking pin could be rammed home inside the coupling between mast and ship. The engines were cut. The *Cologne* was so large that barely a tenth of her length was above the tender's deck. The rest extended out over the Caribbean.

Swiftly approaching the tender, Bell could hear the men cheering at the end of another successful mission.

He paddled next to the German ship and found she'd dropped anchor. He quickly tied the canoe to the anchor chain and wedged it against the hull. He was hidden from above by the flaring of the ship's bow. He figured an hour was enough time for the crew to finish performing their duties and settle in for the night.

During his wait, the wind shifted, and the airship pivoted around the mooring mast like the world's largest weathervane.

When the hour had passed, and Bell couldn't recall hearing anyone stirring on deck for at least thirty minutes, he climbed the chain as carefully as he could to prevent it from rattling. At the top, he paused, listening. All he heard was the lapping of the water against the hull and the background rumble of machinery deep within it. He shinnied up a little higher. While his thighs burned clamped around the chain, he refused to hurry.

The landing beacon had been long extinguished, and other than the red navigation light on the ship's stubby bridge wing, the ship was only illuminated by the milky glow of the moon and stars. Bell spied a lone sailor with a rifle slung over his shoulder meandering by, then heading toward the stern. Once he was out of sight, Bell legged over the railing and crouched in the darkness for a minute.

He reached the main deck without incident. He walked aft, finding cover wherever he could — winch windlasses, air funnels, the tarp-covered lifeboats. At a pair of glass and metal doors, he successfully worked the handle of one and stepped inside the superstructure. The ship had electric lighting, but the bulbs were dim and spaced far apart.

Logic dictated that Marion was likely being held on a lower deck. He found a stairwell and climbed down. At the end of a hall, bright light spilled from the galley's doorway. He heard someone working in there, scouring pans after a late meal served to the Zeppelin's crew. He passed a dozen closed doors — cabins, no doubt — and came to another flight of stairs. The next deck down, the lighting was even dimmer. It was warmer too, closer to the engine room. He passed more closed doors and almost missed the one with a lock hastily welded to the latch to prevent it from being opened from the inside.

He tapped on the door — shave and a

haircut, but only the first part — tap-tap-taptaptap-tap. He did it again. On the third try, the room's occupant tapped the final bit. Marion hated it when Bell did that, so of course he made it one more of the secret codes and language they shared.

He gently lifted the latch and opened the door. Her lips were hot on his, and her arms around his neck felt like they would never release and let him go.

"Are you okay?" he asked her when she came up for air. Her hair was lank from the heat and humidity, but her eyes were clear as always.

"I'm fine. The Huns didn't dare touch me. I owe you an apology, though."

"Me? What on earth for?"

She gave him her most impish grin. "I didn't expect you'd rescue me for at least another twenty-four hours. Sorry I underestimated you."

"Quite all right," he said breezily. "You couldn't have possibly known there was an airplane I could borrow."

She turned serious and earnest. "You know about the great big balloon of theirs, right? That's how they nicked me from the *Spatminster*. They boarded from a rowboat that they lowered from the balloon. I was blindfolded but could still tell what was going on."

"The balloon is called a dirigible, or rigid airship, and you and I are going to hijack it."

Marion looked dubious. "With just your pistol?"

"And my charm." Bell smirked. He then explained. "The airship is filled to the gills with hydrogen, a very explosive gas. They won't risk me firing the gun, so hijacking it when they take off in the morning should be a snap."

When they reached the deck, Bell noticed immediately that the wind had picked up. He saw too that lights were shining at the top of the mooring mast, when before they had been out. If bad weather was brewing, it made sense that they would take off and try to fly around the storm.

"Are we too late?" Marion asked when her husband went quiet.

"Not sure." They would be discovered if he tried to launch a lifeboat. The airship was their only ticket to safety. "Come on."

There was no one at the base mooring mast, so they climbed up it. The higher they went, the more noticeable it became that the *Dagna* was rolling in the roughening seas. The wind also seemed to have picked up speed. Bell heard men below him and placed a hand at the small of Marion's back to impel her to climb faster. One of the airship's engines coughed to life, a loud blat that cut across the howl of the wind ripping through all the rigging.

"I'd say we're just in time."

They raced up the last few switchbacks of stairs. On the platform at the top of the mast, a sailor monitored the thick hose that was pumping water into the *Cologne*'s ballast tanks. Bell flipped his .45 and clipped the man behind the ear with its grip. His skull had to be extra-thick because rather than collapse into unconsciousness, he clutched the wound with one hand and sprung to his feet to confront Bell.

Bell struck at him again, harder this time, but the sailor blocked the swing with an arm. Bell threw a straight left that flattened the man's nose and caused blood to flow. The sailor was dazed, and so Bell finished him with a strong kick between the legs. When the man doubled over, Bell gave him another rap on the back of the head with the butt of the Colt automatic.

The men coming up from below were only a few landings away. Bell turned to the airship's entrance hatch as another figure emerged from the craft's interior. The light was streaky with shadows, so no one saw any faces, but the newcomer recognized the prisoner and assumed the man with her was helping her escape. Heinz Kohl lunged for Bell, swinging with a left cross from what looked like too far away.

Bell had recognized the bodyguard's tactic and ducked back quickly enough that the man's leather-gloved wooden fist missed his nose by an inch. Kohl was so used to landing his first blow that he was hyperextended. Bell slid in and fired two rabbit punches to the kidneys before dodging as Kohl swung his prosthetic arm like a club. Bell popped back up, hitting Dreissen's bodyguard with a straight right to the nose, but the old brawler was ready and bowed his head so that Bell's fist ended up caroming harmlessly off the man's forehead.

Kohl swung again. Bell trapped the artificial limb between his chest and arm and turned sharply, yanking Kohl off balance enough for Bell to loop a length of the chain railing ringing the platform once around Kohl's wrist and kick him on the outside of the knee hard enough to collapse him to the deck. One more kick sent him off the platform and dangling above the deck by the straps holding his once deadly arm to his shoulder.

He pointed Marion to the hatch. "Go."

There was a small vestibule just inside the airship, and a flight of stairs that would lead down to the keel and allow access to the gondolas. On the wall above the hatch was a large, red-painted lever held in place with a brass pin. Bell pulled the pin and heaved down on the lever, using all the weight of his body. The locking mechanism that held the airship to the mast slid free, and the great ship immediately began to rise. The filling hose ripped from its mount in a spray of water. Bell had to grab a handhold on a bulkhead close by and wrap an arm around Marion to keep them steady as the ship arrowed into the sky.

Wind blasted through the open hatch.

"It wasn't like this before," Marion said, her voice an octave higher than normal. "What's happening?"

"Not enough ballast water. The captain needs to vent hydrogen to get us neutrally buoyant."

Bell shifted to give Marion access to the handhold. He then pulled the hatch closed.

"What the hell have you done?" Otto Dreissen bellowed as he charged up the stairs.

The .45 felt like it leapt into Isaac's hand, and the German brought himself up short.

Dreissen sneered, then said, "Fire that thing in here, and the last thing you see is your wife turned into a human torch."

"Then I advise you don't do anything stupid to make me want to pull the trigger."

The airship lurched hard as it continued to rocket heavenward. Metal struts creaked and moaned at the unprecedented strain they were under. All three were forced to remain where they stood, clutching to railings to keep from being tossed around. Bell felt like he was back in the tanker truck as it was being overwhelmed by the avalanche.

"How are you even here?" Dreissen demanded.

Bell had to practically shout over the metallic protests the ship made as it climbed higher still. He couldn't understand why the Captain hadn't vented more gas to slow its perilous rise. "I had a plane. I followed the airship back from its ill-fated rendezvous with Court Talbot out on Lake Gatun."

Marion gave a little choked gasp at hearing Talbot was involved in this plot.

Dreissen absorbed that news and asked, "Ill-fated? What happened to Talbot and his men?"

"I didn't realize the fire I set on their boat would cause one of the two underwater mines you'd delivered to explode. Whatever it is you're up to is finished, Dreissen. You lost your bombs."

"On the contrary, those last two explosives were an extra bit of insurance. Talbot and his crew made multiple runs every night, ferrying my mines from their jungle camp. They've already wired and submerged enough mines to suit my purposes."

Bell hadn't expected that, though he should have. He'd forgotten that while he'd lost days battling amnesia, Talbot and company had been hard at work. "At the Gatun Dam?"

Dreissen smiled because he knew he'd just rattled the Van Dorn investigator. He paused as if contemplating not answering, but decided that at this juncture there was no harm in gloating. "Near enough that the shock wave generated by the detonation will collapse it. The lifeblood of the Panama Canal, the water of the Chagres River, will once again rejoin the Atlantic Ocean. My engineers estimate it will take a year to replace the spillway and any of the dam that has eroded away, and another three to five to refill the lake."

"Nice fantasy," Bell said, "but it'll never happen. I know who your gunman is, and he won't get anywhere close enough to detonate the mines."

The German shook his head as if he'd caught a child in a lie. "You can't possibly."

"The only person I told about Marion leaving on the *Spatminster* was Tats Macalister. He's your man."

Bell knew he was right. Dreissen would make a terrible poker player. His nostrils had gone a little white, and his eyes shifted down and to the left. Some of the arrogance seemed to leave Dreissen's puffed-out chest.

Bell continued. "He's too good at playing the English dandy to be one of your employees, so I'm going to guess he'd be military intelligence. I forget what you people call it."

"Sektion IIIb," Dreissen said, shocked. "He's a Major."

"And the final blow to your plans is, I had an investigator canvass all the hotels in Milwaukee, looking for the name Dreissen. I know you have a brother based in New York. You and Talbot had to accelerate your plans when word leaked that TR was coming to inspect the canal, and I mean leaked even before I was called in by his political party. You wanted to complete your brother's mission from two years ago. He was the hand pulling the strings to have Roosevelt assassinated by John Schrank. One of our detectives who was there at the time and saved Roosevelt's life knew that Schrank's uncle worked for Essenwerks. You and the

German government are terrified that he might become our President again."

Dreissen didn't deny it.

Bell continued. "When my colleagues discover your brother was in Milwaukee on the day of the failed assassination, I have arranged it so that Roosevelt is prevented from coming ashore, and your shot at blowing him up is over."

"All very clever, Herr Bell. Your insights and deductions are quite accurate. My government does not want him in the White House, nor do we want the United States to have the power to control maritime commerce of the Northern Hemisphere." He let out a dark chuckle that was soon drowned out by the howling wind. "But you are wrong about one critical detail. My brother didn't feel the need to stay with him all the way to Milwaukee. He left Schrank, and the psychologist who kept Schrank drugged and deep in his sick fantasies, in Chicago."

It was like being gut-punched. He'd figured it all out, but it wasn't going to prevent a catastrophe.

Several tense minutes went by. The air grew cold and thin. Their breaths condensed each time they exhaled. The airship's ascent didn't seem to be slowing at all. A loud bang caused Marion to scream. Bell was growing more concerned, and even Dreissen's expression darkened.

"Why haven't we stopped rising?" Bell shouted.

Wind then found a weak seam in the airship's canvas skin and tore open a flap that allowed icy air to rush inside the envelope and fill the stairway with racket.

Dreissen said nothing.

Another bang, and the dirigible shuddered like a ship caught in a storm at sea. More wind filled the stairs, and the massive bags of gas that kept the airship aloft fluttered and chaffed against the wires and braces that held them in place. Metal screamed as it was pushed to the very breaking point.

Marion began panting to get enough oxygen, and Bell felt himself growing lightheaded. He had no idea how high they'd gone but it felt like he was standing atop some of the mountains around Denver. The dirigible began a corkscrew motion that made them feel weightless at times and the shrieks of tortured metal became banshees' wails.

"Since you're trapped, I will deal with you after this crisis is over." Dreissen began to climb down toward the control gondola along the airship's keel, lowering himself hand over hand with his feet barely touching the stairs' treads.

Marion's lips had gone blue and her hands were as white as porcelain. They both gulped air like fish trying to get enough oxygen into their lungs while their breath wreathed them like smoke. The vapor became frost whenever it touched an ice-cold aluminum support strut.

What followed a minute after Dreissen's disappearance deeper into the ship was utter chaos. There came a huge rending crash somewhere aft of the nose section. The wind suddenly grew into a hurricane gale. Marion's scream was drowned by the roar. Metal screeched and tore. The nose suddenly pitched upward, leaving the pair dangling in space and then it swung through several loops, spinning like a dervish. Debris filled the air while the gas bag moaned like a wounded animal as pressure within its envelope rose and fell.

And then everything seemed to stabilize. Bell looked down the stairs and along the central hallway only to see black sky. He didn't understand what had happened. And then the main section of the dirigible revealed itself. It was dropping away from the nose, its backbone snapped. The airship had torn itself apart midway between the entrance hatch and the control gondola. The nose section remained buoyant, the single remaining gas bag providing more lift than the structure's weight. The bags in the rest of the airship had erupted through multiple rips and the broken craft now hurtled earthward.

A pocket of escaping hydrogen met the spark from the one motor that was still chugging away. The explosion was like all the light in the world had been concentrated on that one spot. Heat and fire reached up, and had the fifty-foot section of nose been closer it would have been consumed by the fire and added its own explosive gush of flaming hydrogen to the mushrooming pyre.

When the initial blinding flare faded Bell could see the *Cologne*'s burning husk falling away like a meteor trailing a flaming tail.

The nose section stabilized so that its peak was pointing upward with maybe a couple degrees of tilt. Bell and Marion had proper hand- and footholds and were relatively safe for the time being as the dangerous ascent had reversed itself. Their makeshift balloon was drifting downward as tears in the envelope allowed hydrogen to escape at a steady pace. Soon enough the air began to warm and thicken as they dropped. They soon could breathe normally.

"Are you okay?" Bell asked his wife.

"I'd be better if your rescue plans weren't always so cockeyed."

"Not always," Bell said in self-defense. "But like you like to say, I'm always either at the right place at the wrong time or the wrong place at the right one."

She recognized her words. "So long as you're not at the wrong place at the wrong time. What happens now?"

"Don't forget this is my second time in this predicament. As more gas escapes through what must be by now multiple tears in the envelope, we'll drift back to earth like a couple aeronauts in a balloon. The gas seems to be venting at a slow enough pace to make our journey leisurely and hopefully coming to a soft end."

"How far out to sea were we?"

"Not sure, thirty or so miles if I'd have to guess."

"Can we drift that far?"

"World record was just broken last year. They went for over twelve hundred miles."

"Please tell me it was in a leaky torn-up airship?"

"Special-built balloon, sorry to say."

"Like I said, cockeyed," Marion said in a teasing pout. "Next time whisk me away in one of those or don't bother coming for me at all."

Bell couldn't help but laugh at the absurdity of their situation and his beloved's ability to make light of it so easily. Having come so close to death, most people would have broken down in tears, but not his Marion. She was probably already trying to work out how to film such an escape as this for her next motion picture.

The hatch was only ten feet above where they clung to the superstructure. Bell mapped out a climbing route and used handholds or the circular cutouts in individual support beams to clamber up to it. He forced open the hatch. Because they were drifting with the wind, he was met by an absolute silence, as profound as an empty cathedral. He studied the horizon but saw nothing. The nose rotated ever so slowly, eventually giving him a three-hundred-and-sixty-degree panorama. There was no indication of land or distant lights. He wasn't even sure if they were heading toward shore.

He climbed back to his perch next to Marion. They talked about their adventures since they'd parted at the dock near Panama City. She was jealous of his flight. She would have loved to have gone along and filmed the canal from the air.

Every half hour, by Bell's wristwatch, he climbed up to see if any landmarks were visible and every time he climbed back to report they still had the world all to themselves. He estimated they were at an altitude of three thousand feet and knew the air would be uncomfortably cold if they weren't in the tropics.

As the rising sun rouged the eastern sky Bell caught sight of land, or more accurately the creaming crests of waves breaking onto a beach. He shouted triumphantly.

"Land?" Marion yelled up to him.

"I see a beach. We're too high, though. I think we're going to drift right past, and then it's nothing but jungle for fifty miles until we reach the Pacific."

"We could try for the transcontinental balloon record," Marion suggested, half joking.

"Now who's cockeyed?"

The stairwell and hallway connecting the entry hatch to the gondolas had a solid metal decking but the walls and ceiling were nothing more than thin cotton cloth stretched between structural columns and spars. Bell cut through a wall with his boot knife to expose the shiny outer skin of the enormous hydrogen sack. In a million places it bulged through the mesh netting designed to keep it in place. Because they had sunk even lower into the atmosphere, the pressure against the giant bladder was building faster than it could vent. Bell didn't know how long it could go before it burst and he feared it popping like a child's rubber balloon when he pressed into it with his knife.

The blade sliced cleanly and he felt a rush of invisible hydrogen blow past his arm out the open hatch above his head. He cut more and more holes, reaching as far as he could without actually climbing out onto the bag. When he felt himself getting woozy from breathing more hydrogen than clean air, he ducked down below the cloud of leaking gas and breathed deeply to clear his lungs and mind.

Having filled his lungs to capacity, he climbed through the hissing gas cloud to poke his head out the hatch to determine if they were sinking at the proper angle. It took a few seconds to estimate they would land in the shallows just behind the breaking waves. Perfect.

He rejoined his wife inside the hull. "We should climb down as low as possible so we can jump into the water before this thing hits. It likely won't explode, but it weighs a ton, and I have no idea which way it's going to tumble."

"Makes sense."

"Just take your time and move slowly."

"Right."

As careful as possible, the pair made their way down to the scarred area where the airship had torn itself in two. A slip now would be fatal. There was nothing at the end of the corridor except a hole that looked down to the sea from a thousand feet up. They moved like mountaineers, always making sure they had contact with both hands and a foot, or both feet and a hand. Or, as sailors always say, "One hand for yourself, one for the ship."

Closer to the bottom, the destruction was extreme, with torn metal struts wrenched out of position, cables and wires dangling, and the airship's ripped outer skin flapping in the gentle air currents wafting through the improvised balloon.

The walls of the hallway had been torn away too, so the entire fifty-foot-diameter support ring was visible. It was held together by dozens of girders and braces, looking like a veritable forest of burnished aluminum, suspended high above the Caribbean. Below hung torn longitudinal beams that would have linked the ring to the next ring. The whole structure was very unstable, trembling like it was rubber. Some beams bent like tree branches as the ring twisted and warped. Overhead, the gas bag was a huge, almost translucent sphere held captive by its spiderweb of netting.

A few feet below Bell, Marion stepped out onto one of the thicker beams to make room for him when he reached the bottom. An arm suddenly crossed her throat and choked off her startled scream.

"I told you there was no place you could go," Otto Dreissen shouted up to Bell as he wrenched Marion off her perch and dangled her over the edge of the thousand-foot drop.

37

"Isaac," she said, gasping, her eyes wide with terror.

Bell didn't hesitate or even consider that, if he missed, he would fall past the pair below him and plummet to his death. He leapt down and landed on a girder about seven feet from where Dreissen held his wife's life in his hands. He landed on the narrow beam and teetered for a moment before finding his center of gravity. He stood and whipped his pistol from its holster.

"Shoot me and she dies too," Dreissen said.

"Drop her and you die," Bell countered. "We're at an impasse."

"Not quite. My advantage ends when we near the ground, which makes this one quick negotiation. Your life for hers, Bell. Jump or I drop her."

"And die before she hits the water? Is it worth it?"

"You go or she goes, Bell. Now."

"Sorry, Marion."

"What?"

Bell fired and hit Dreissen in the shoulder. He reeled back, releasing Marion. Rather than fall straight down, Marion spun in midair and dropped only a few feet before stopping short. She hadn't been idle while Dreissen held her hostage. There had been a bunch of wires at her feet still attached to the airship's frame. In full view of her husband, Marion had twisted her feet into the tangled rat's nest of wires. When he dropped her, she'd merely tumbled headfirst and now dangled by her ankles.

Dreissen leapt away, clutching his shoulder yet moving from beam to beam with the agility of a mountain goat. Bell ignored him. Holstering his pistol, he raced to the spot where Marion had vanished. He'd seen what she was doing, understood the risk she was taking, and didn't know if her plan had worked. He dropped flat and looked over the beam and saw the soles of her shoes just a few inches from his face. He started to reach for an ankle and haul her aboard when suddenly some of the connectors securing the wires to the ship popped free, and she dropped a few more inches.

She screamed his name. He could see the

wires digging into her flesh as the weight of her body caused them to tighten. The bundle quivered with the strain, and she started to slip more. He reached down farther, got his hand around her ankle again, and lifted her as high as he could. Marion was able to reach for a beam and twist herself around enough to transfer her weight from her husband's arm to the strut.

"Are you okay?" he asked. "That was a crazy risk."

She quickly started to untangle the snarl of wires so she could stand. "I didn't see any other way out of it. Did you?"

"No."

"Where's Dreissen?"

Bell looked around. He didn't see him. There were dozens of girders that the German could hide behind. He could have reached one and climbed it like a ladder. Bell checked for a trail of blood but saw no spatters. He looked down at the ocean scrolling by beneath them. They had only another hundred feet to go, and he could tell by the water's change in color that the seafloor was shelving up to the beach. "Don't know, don't care."

Marion got the last of the wires from around her ankles and stood, making sure she held on to a beam for support. She had a good head for heights, but having struts only inches wide to walk on would make anyone feel acrophobic.

He kept watching the ocean, waiting for their makeshift flying machine to drift low enough for them to jump. He heard something rattle high above them and thought that Dreissen might be trying to climb out through the entrance hatch for some reason.

He looked back at the water. The color was shifting from blue to turquoise, and the beach was only a few hundred yards away.

"Ready?" he asked and took Marion's hand.

"Always ready to take the plunge with you."

They leapt together and fell the fifteen or so feet to the sea, plunging deep into the tropical water. Marion came up first and had wiped and cleared her eyes by the time Isaac surfaced at her side. He gave her a quick kiss and looked up.

The loss of their roughly three hundred pounds combined gave the remaining gas bag less weight to keep aloft, allowing the nose to begin rising again, and as the dirigible came to the beach, it encountered warmer air that hadn't yet been cooled by the Caribbean and it began to rise higher still.

"Isaac, what if he gets away?"

Treading water, Bell pulled his pistol. He tried to keep as steady as possible, though it was next to impossible. Then again, at this range, and with such a large target, he couldn't miss.

The first four shots didn't have the desired effect, the fifth hit an aluminum girder at the right angle, liquefying a tiny amount of the metal. It dripped onto the hole in the gas bag and ignited its fabric with just the tiniest of flames. The little dollop of fire was almost snuffed out by the wind, but then it caught, steadied, and grew. Hydrogen began to gush from the smoldering hole and at first just about overwhelmed the fire. Then it reached the combustible ratio with the air.

All at once, the last of the *Cologne*'s hydrogen erupted in a towering midair explosion that looked as though the sun was rising in both the east and the west. Flames in shades of yellow and orange and magenta swirled and spun high into the sky as the airship's envelope and the gas cell were consumed and metal framework began to soften. It sounded like they were standing inside a tornado.

Bell and Marion ducked under the waves as a wall of pressure and heat raced out from the epicenter of the blast. From below the surface, the explosion looked like the Portals of Hell had opened above. They resurfaced in time to see the skeleton of the nose crash into the jungle just beyond the beach and collapse like its rigid struts were nothing more than putty.

The pair swam for shore, where the fronds of some palm trees had caught fire as the remnants of the wrecked dirigible smoldered.

They dragged themselves above the tide line and let themselves fall into the sugary sand. Bell immediately rolled up onto one elbow so he could look at his beautiful wife. "I believe you made mention of Dreissen escaping. Do you think that a man who threatened your life should expect his to last?"

"Not even for a second." She caressed his cheek and gave him a flirty little smile. "You know, we should get out of these wet things. Give them a chance to dry in the sun."

Instead of readily agreeing, which he always did, Bell stood and held out a hand to pull her to her feet. "I would absolutely love to, but we have to find a way back to Colón and warn Goethals. We have only two days."

"But everything you said about knowing

Tats Macalister isn't who he claimed to be?"

"I knew who he wasn't, I didn't know who he was. I never told anyone about him. I didn't understand Viboras Rojas's plan or his role in it until I saw they were smuggling explosives. Teddy Roosevelt is about to sail into a trap."

Bell Crashes the Party

38

The pair began walking up the beach. Bell knew the direction to take. What he didn't know was how far it would be. They had landed east of Colón, but he had no idea how distant. And factoring in their drifting flight further complicated things. At best it was twenty miles, at worst fifty. At least there was a nice sandy beach to walk on. Usually, the jungle came right down to the ocean in dense mangrove swamps filled with crocodiles and teeming with malaria-laden mosquitoes.

And they weren't going to starve. When each wave receded, tiny bivalves blew telltale bubbles from beneath the wet sand. Isaac and Marion plucked them with ease and slurped them straight from the shells as if oysters at a fine restaurant. The juices saved them from the risk of having to drink any water from the countless streams feeding into the Caribbean.

Three hours after the crash, luck smiled upon the couple in the form of a native longboat being paddled by six men. The boat was just beyond the breakers, and the men stopped rowing when they spotted and heard Bell and Marion waving and hollering to them. They spoke amongst themselves for a moment, then waved the duo over.

"There are no cannibals here, right?" Marion asked as they walked over.

"If there are, we're not going to enjoy dinner," Bell remarked, and they waded out to the bobbing craft.

The men were shirtless and shoeless and wore skirts of grass around their waists. Their wrists were adorned with bracelets made of leather and glass beads and bits of animal bone. They were Kuna Indians, one of several indigenous tribes that inhabited the isthmus of Panama. Their double-ended canoe was a massive tree that had been hollowed out. Bell guessed it would have taken years to fashion the boat and assumed they were used for many generations. At their feet were baskets filled with fruit and dried fish. A collapsible rack for drying fish was stowed aboard, as well as a seine net of woven braided twine.

Marion asked if any of the natives spoke Spanish. The navigator sitting at the back of the boat rattled off several long sentences, and Marion tried her hardest to understand, but there wasn't a Spanish word anywhere in his speech.

"*¿Tu no hablas español?*" Bell asked, one of the few things he'd learned to say since arriving.

The navigator grinned. "*Si, no hablo español. Mi padre lo habla.*"

"I think I get it," Marion said. "He doesn't speak Spanish, but his father does. "*¿Tu padre habla español?*"

The man grinned again and nodded vigorously. "*Mi padre lo hablo.*"

They made room for the couple, and as soon as they were settled, the men spun in their seats and began paddling again.

"No," Marion protested and pointed behind them. "We want to go that way."

"Colón," Bell said. "We want to go to Colón. Do you know it? Big city."

"Isaac, what are we to do?"

The navigator tapped Bell's shoulder and pointed ahead. "*Mi padre.*"

Oh, I get it, Bell said to himself, then spoke to Marion. "They're taking us to see his father. Their village must be past where we crashed. If we're going to get their co-operation, we need to be able to communicate. Let's go along for the ride."

The men were small in stature and slenderly built, but a lifetime of paddling had given them surprising strength. And their teamwork meant not an ounce of energy was wasted. The boat covered the three hours of walking Bell and Marion had put in in just two, and they kept on for another two hours before the men turned toward the shore where a narrow valley ran into the ocean. A cluster of huts had been built on its western side along a small river that ran from the highlands. Behind the village lay several acres of cleared and cultivated land. Smoke from cooking fires hung over the village, and when the longboat got close enough, children could be heard playing close by.

Bell hopped out of the boat with the other men to help guide it through the surf and pull it up onto dry sand.

Most of the villagers stopped what they were doing and came to see the newcomers in a bubbling, smiling mob. They were not so cut off from civilization that they hadn't seen white people before, but it was an oddity, especially because both Bell and his wife had blond hair. The younger women and girls, in colorful dresses made by them, ran their fingers through Marion's tresses and tittered like little birds.

The pair was eventually led to the center of the village and given water from a gourd. By this point, both were thirsty enough not to care about purity, but it appeared clean and fresh, and so they drank their fill and then each ate a barely ripe plantain. The children lingered, but the men and women went back to their tasks. An old man came out of one of the huts. His hair was coarse and white, and his mouth contained only a couple teeth. When the blanket wrapped around his shoulders slipped, they saw each of his ribs and the bony sternum where they connected in the center of his chest.

Marion greeted him in Spanish, speaking slowly and loudly, assuming his hearing was poor. The man replied in his native dialect, smiling and drooling just a little.

"Apparently," Bell said, "this isn't our boatman's *padre.*"

Bell looked around for the paddlers and realized they weren't there. He left his wife and returned to the beach. The boat was gone. He spotted it out on the open water, heading back the way they had come. He cursed. This was wasting time they didn't have.

"What's wrong?" Marion asked when she saw the look on his face as he marched back into the village.

"The men took off in the canoe. We're stuck here until they come back, I assume with the man's father."

In most situations, Bell had the patience of a saint. Or a sniper. This wasn't one of those times. The afternoon wore on. They were fed some cake, made on a cast-iron griddle, and a stew made from vegetables native to the area. At sundown, they were shown to a hut where rough blankets had been laid on the grass floor.

Sleep eluded them both. The bedding was infested with bedbugs, and, for Bell, the thought of Teddy Roosevelt dying while he was stuck in this primitive place was as galling as the bloodthirsty parasites.

He was up before dawn and strode down to the beach. The sun was a tangerine smear on the horizon, and the waves came in black but turned to cream when they broke. There was no sign of the large dugout. Bell rattled off a string of curses aloud that would have made the saltiest sailor blush.

Marion had come up behind him without him noticing. "I'm going to have to go to confession just for hearing you curse."

He grinned, abashed. "Sorry about that."

"No boat, I see."

"We never should have gotten in it with them."

They spent an idle day in the village. Bell offered to help out with chores, but no one would hear of their guests doing any physical work. He ended up spending most of his time pacing the beach like an Army sentry and watching the horizon for the returning mariners.

They finally rowed into view at three in the afternoon. Bell was so anxious that he waded out up to his chest to pull them to shore. The sixth man in the canoe was of mixed Spanish and native blood and wore a black shirt despite the heat. The white collar at his throat proclaimed his profession. It wasn't the navigator's father who spoke Spanish. It was his priest.

"Hola," the man greeted Bell and made short introductory remarks.

Bell gave his standard reply afterward. *"No hablo español."* He pointed to Marion, who waited on the beach. "She *hablo.*"

"I also speak English," the priest said. "I am Father Marcos."

"Isaac Bell." They got the boat beached, and Bell shook the padre's hand. "This is my wife, Marion. Marion, this is Father Marcos."

"Hello."

"How did you two end up here? Naa wasn't sure. He just said you were stranded

552

on the beach. Was it a shipwreck?"

"In a manner of speaking, yes. But it wasn't an oceangoing ship. It was an airship, like a Zeppelin. Father, I don't mean to be rude, but we need to get to Colón as fast as possible. I don't know if you are aware, but our former President Teddy Roosevelt is visiting the canal tomorrow."

"Oh, yes. The whole town is talking of nothing else."

"Wait. What? Do you mean you just came from Colón?"

"Yes, that is where my church is."

Bell groaned in frustration. "I told them that's where we wanted to go yet they brought us to their village instead."

"Dear me. I'm so sorry. I visit here once a month to minister to these people."

"Doesn't matter now." Bell brushed aside his anger. "There's going to be an assassination attempt on the President's life while he's visiting. We need to get back to Colón so I can warn him. I'm kind of a policeman."

"Dear me," Father Marcos repeated. "Colón is an eight-hour journey from here, and I'm afraid they won't want to make it tonight."

"I can pay them, once we're back to civilization," Bell said, not wanting to sound like he was pleading even though he was. "Anything they want."

"It's not that, Mr. Bell. The men need a night's rest. Bringing you here and fetching me from Colón nearly killed them."

"Dawn, then. We have to leave at dawn." Leaving at sunup would put them in Colón around one. While he didn't know what time TR was scheduled to transit the Gatun Locks and cruise the lake, Goethals mentioned a luncheon in the President's honor.

"Yes. I will speak with Naa and make him understand the importance of this trip."

They met on the beach an hour before first light. The five paddlers, plus Bell, Marion, and Father Marcos. Marcos offered to remain behind to lighten the boat, and Marion insisted on doing the same. Bell didn't like leaving her behind but understood every extra pound in the canoe slowed them down.

"You'll be okay?"

"I'll be fine," she assured him.

"I'll borrow or steal a steam launch as soon as I can. With luck, I'll have you back in Colón in time for dinner. Father Marcos, could you please ask Naa if we can make for the canal's entrance rather than the Colón docks? With TR's visit, I suspect Colón will be a madhouse."

"That's a good idea. Downtown was packed with visitors yesterday." He exchanged a short conversation with the Kuna Indian. Naa caught Bell's eye and nodded to show he understood.

Bell fished something from his pocket. It was the chamois sack that Court Talbot used to pay his men. In it was about a hundred dollars' worth of coins. He opened it so they could all see the gold in the light of the torches several of them carried. He gave it to Naa.

"*Gracias,*" he said.

"No. Me *gracias* to you."

Bell kissed his wife good-bye and helped launch the dugout into the dark waters of the Caribbean Sea. The men rolled into the canoe, each took up a paddle, Bell included, and they began to stroke. It took Bell a few minutes to get into the natives' rhythm because their strokes were a little shorter and choppier than he was used to. Soon enough, though, they were gliding across the water at a pace he wasn't sure they could maintain but prayed they could.

Into the fourth hour, Bell felt like he was going to die. His shoulders and arms ached with an unholy fire, and his spine felt like it had been fused into one solid, unbending bone. His eyes stung with sweat and the need to squint against the relentless glare of the sun. He couldn't draw enough air into his lungs, leaving him light-headed. Water from the gourds they carried was warm and barely made a dent in his thirst, and the smoke-dried fish they ate left his mouth coated with a pungent paste. The only bright spot on the grueling journey for Bell came an hour earlier, when they'd paddled past the Fowler-Gage biplane, which had drifted into the ensnaring tendrils of a mangrove swamp. He vowed to tow it to safety when he returned to rescue Marion.

His companions were showing no difficulty at all with the voyage. They dug their paddles into the water at a rate and tempo that seemed mechanical. They were silent, unflagging, seemingly built for the very task they were performing and no other. Bell could only marvel at their strength and stamina.

They started seeing other boats a little over five hours into their ordeal. They were fishing vessels out of Colón, and, in the far distance, smoke hovering along the horizon indicated the presence of big steamships heading to or from the busy harbor.

Twenty minutes later, they rowed past the city itself. They had cut a full half hour from their regular time. Bell finally let himself relax and set down his paddle even as the other men kept up their machine-like strokes. He had to rest his body. He didn't know what was coming his way and he needed to be alert and loose. He rolled his shoulders and massaged his hands to return feeling to them. The new calluses oozed clear fluid.

They turned into Limon Bay, and up ahead was the beginning of the canal, a long, slender artificial channel that led to the three gigantic chambers of the Gatun Locks system. Naa and his men didn't slow. They stroked at the exact pace they had started with.

Closer still, Bell saw the open mouth of the right-hand chamber, the one used for vessels transiting up to the lake. The left chamber for ships exiting the canal was closed. A long, low seawall jutting out into the channel divided them. That meant a ship had gone up and was presumably still on the lake. He would have heard an explosion of the size needed to take out the dam from a dozen miles away. He wasn't too late.

Bell pointed to where he wanted the dugout maneuvered down the right side of the seawall, and Naa steered them in.

They drew closer still, and the huge chamber began to loom over them. A thousand feet past the open gates were the closed doors leading to the middle lock. At this distance, and from the channel's surface, they looked like the entrance doors to the lair of some mythical Titan. The seawall was on their right, while on their left was the still-natural-looking shoreline, with newly grown grass and even a strip of beach.

It was low tide, so the lock's walls towered thirty feet above their heads, the concrete as thick as any fort's in the world, maybe thicker. He'd seen these chambers several times now and still couldn't believe their scale.

Bell didn't want to enter the chamber itself. It was literally a dead end with the far doors closed. There was a small platform just outside the gates and rising from it were iron rungs embedded in the cement wall. He pointed, and Naa and his men aimed the canoe for it. They dug their blades in the water to slow to a stop at the last second, and the wooden craft kissed the platform without a sound.

"*Gracias,*" Bell said and slid over the gunwale and onto solid ground.

He climbed the ladder as quickly as he could, the hot iron aggravating his already damaged hands. When he popped up on top of the high lock's wall, he startled a worker in white overalls who'd been working in the engine compartment of one of the little locomotives they called mules that were used to tow ships through the locks.

"Hey, you're not supposed to be here," the man said indignantly.

"I don't have time to explain, but Roosevelt's life is in danger. Have they come through?" The man hesitated. Bell grabbed him by the collar. "Answer me, dammit."

The worker's eyes went wide. "Yes. A few minutes ago. They should be exiting the third chamber any minute."

Bell ran. Each lock was a thousand feet long, a little over three football fields. And each was roughly thirty feet higher than the one before it. In all, a ninety-foot climb. Bell had given himself only thirty minutes' rest after pushing his body for five hard hours and yet he ran. He'd come too far to fail now. For the mules to function, their tracks had to climb a steeply graded hill between each chamber before the path flattened out again. Bell staggered when he hit the first of these concrete rises, but he threw himself at the task and powered his way up and soon found himself running along the length of the middle lock, with a second daunting slope up ahead.

His heart raced, his chest ached, and his

mouth was full of saliva. He ran on anyway, hoping the boat carrying the President was still in the third lock, stuck in place, while water filled it to the same level as the lake beyond.

Bell hit the second rise, where the path along the middle chamber transitioned to the upper one. His feet felt floppy, his steps unsure, but he kept at it, churning his legs to climb up to the final lock.

When he reached the top and could look down the length of the chamber, his heart sank.

Because the lake was still filling, a regular ship couldn't yet transit the locks. There wasn't enough water in the upper chamber to float a vessel with a standard keel. In order to fulfill TR's wish, Goethals had had a pontoon boat constructed, with a few dozen metal barrels welded together and a wooden deck laid over them. Two men operated outboard motors at the stern, while the rest of the ungainly craft was shaded by a bright white canopy under which the former President would lunch with local dignitaries while a brass band, standing on a dais between the helmsman and guests, belted out some jaunty rags.

The odd, rectangular boat was now at the far end of the chamber, and the gates were about to open. Usually, the deck of a ship transiting the canal would be at or above the height of the lock's walls, yet, with the lake so low, the special boat sat twenty feet below where Bell stood.

To Bell's right, a short distance away, was the concrete spillway of the Gatun Dam, and somewhere close to its face was a massive charge of explosives. The boat needed only to exit the chamber to put itself in danger.

Bell ran harder than ever. He would not fail.

The distant gates continued to yawn open, driven by surprisingly small motors due to their impeccable balance. Bell pulled his .45 and considered firing it to get people's attention but realized it would have opposite the effect he wanted. They would want to flee into the perceived safety of the open lake. He looked to his right again and saw a figure crouched on the lake's shore pulling up something from below the surface. Though the man was screened by a thicket of tall grasses, Bell thought he saw a detonator with a T-handled plunger next to him.

Macalister.

The range was so extreme, and Bell was breathing so hard, he'd never hold steady enough to fire, yet he had to take the shot.

He stopped and hunched slightly in a two-handed grip that had become more instinct than intention. He estimated the range at a hundred yards and knew the bullet would be seven inches below his aim at that distance.

A round was already chambered, and so he cycled through all eight bullets as fast as he could pull the trigger, denying Macalister any time to duck behind the cover of the copse of trees farther up the bank. As with a golfer who always aims for the cup on a par 3 yet inevitably misses, there are still tales told at every country club of someone sinking a ball in one shot. Isaac Bell hit his shot. He saw a spray of blood blow from the spy's body and he collapsed onto the ground.

Bell paused, his chest heaving. Was it a kill shot? Was this nightmare over?

Seconds trickled by. Macalister slowly lifted himself from the muddy lakeshore, appearing to be favoring his left arm. He tried to haul up more of what had to be electric fuses attached to the mines but lacked the strength. Bell saw him turn his attention to the detonator.

He started running again. The gate at the end of the lock was fully retracted into slots in the chamber walls, and the two mules on either side pulled the pontoon boat forward. The band was so loud, and the distance too great, for anyone to have heard the shots. The gawky raft's nose peeked out of the chamber when it paused for the mooring lines to be recovered.

Bell pushed harder. White water formed under the vessel's flat transom as the two men operating the outboards gave them gas. All Bell heard was the throb of the band — a tuba, a trombone, a showy trumpet, and a snare drum. The boat was under way, moving slow, slower than Bell at the moment, but it would accelerate, and TR would surely want to investigate the spillway. He'd be right over the bomb when Macalister touched it off.

Bell ran past the electric locomotive without giving its operator a glance. The pontoon boat was out of the chamber now and beginning a starboard turn toward the dam. Bell was twenty feet from the end of the chamber wall. The boat was twenty feet below him and pulling away. The calculation was simple physics, though, when he committed himself, Bell didn't run the numbers.

He reached the end and threw himself off the lock, hurtling through the air and plummeting toward the boat. It was a very long fall, long enough for him to regret it, before he hit the tent canopy and smashed down onto the trombonist, hard enough to break the musician's collarbone, and then crashed to the deck, where Bell's right leg broke below the knee in a sickening snap he heard over all the other sounds.

Pandemonium erupted as people fell or were pushed over in the wake of Bell's landing in the middle of their party. A few of the ladies screamed in fear, while the men shouted. Bell found himself being trampled by a stampede that had nowhere to go. Someone kicked his broken leg, and he bellowed in agony. That pain jolted him. He managed to throw himself into a vacant chair and pull his .45. He changed out the empty magazine and fired three quick shots that stopped the crowd in their tracks.

"Back up the boat," he shouted. "We are all in danger. There's mines set in the lake. We have to turn back."

"Do as that man says," a high but commanding voice said. "On the jump."

The two motormen responded immediately, and the boat came to a stop and started going backward again. It tucked itself behind the mouth of the lock chamber wall just as Tats Macalister realized he wasn't going to kill two birds with one stone. Teddy Roosevelt wasn't going to die when the dam blew but he'd at least be a witness to its destruction.

The explosion was huge, a guttural expulsion of force that sent water flying to the heavens and waves to rival tsunamis across the lake. The blast seemed to suck the very air from people's lungs and topple them to the ground. It did all those things and more.

But it failed to accomplish what was intended. The spillway was impervious to the explosion because Macalister had only fused together two of the enormous explosive devices when Bell had opened fire and had then lacked the strength to add all the other wires to the detonator. With only two of the bombs exploding when he'd pushed down the plunger, the underwater pressure wave that beat against the dam was no more than a puff of wind to the solid structure.

It took several minutes for some semblance of order to return to the people on the pontoon boat. Most were shell-shocked — by the blast, and by their own deaths' close call. One passenger, however, took it all in stride. He was polishing his eyeglasses when he made his way over to where Bell sat, panting with pain and exhaustion.

"Isaac, dear boy, what the devil are you doing here? And what was that business with the explosion? Reminded me of my Rough Rider days."

Bell smiled up at his father's best friend. "Hi, Uncle Ted." Roosevelt hated being called Teddy. "It's a long story, but if you find me a drink, I will tell it. But first we need to capture a German spy."

39

Bell instructed the boatswains to beach the motorized raft close to where an unconscious Tats Macalister lay partially in the still-roiling waters of Lake Gatun. Workers from the lock lined its length, gesturing and pointing at the water and the prone figure. TR's security people had taken control of the barge and had everyone positioned to exit it and head straight for the safety of the nearby lock. Bell had cautioned them that there were literally tons of unexploded ordnance in the lake.

While a doctor probed Bell's leg and splinted it with a slat from a folding chair and strips torn from tablecloths as a temporary cast, Theodore Roosevelt loomed over him, his eyes alight with the prospect of more action. "German spy, you say? Never much cared for the Huns' aggression. Mark my words, they're spoiling for a fight."

"I agree," Bell said and sucked air through

his teeth as the doctor cinched the cast tight. "This was a preemptive strike."

"Timed for my visit?"

"Lucky coincidence for them. Gave them a second crack at you."

"Wait, what? Do you mean . . ."TR's voice trailed off, and he touched the spot on his right side where the bullet had become encysted against his rib cage.

The men at the motors had almost zero experience maneuvering their odd craft, so they approached the shore with an abundance of caution, edging in so slowly that when the hull made of barrels hit the shore, there was barely a bump, yet precious minutes had trickled by.

Bell was anxious about Macalister's condition. He hadn't moved since the explosion and hadn't responded when Bell had shouted his name. Isaac kept his .45 caliber in hand but had to drape one arm around TR's broad shoulders and the other around one of his security agents the Canal Authority had assigned. Bell's leg couldn't take even a tiny amount of weight. The three men approached Macalister while the rest of the luncheon party was led away. He lay facedown. There was a ragged hole punched through his shirt high on the left side of his back that was surrounded by a corona of blood. His chest moved. He was breathing.

The former President and the agent lowered Bell to the grass at Macalister's side.

"Tats," Bell called out. "We're going to turn you over. Brace yourself."

Covered by the black Colt, the guard rolled the German spy onto his back. Macalister moaned and opened his eyes. Bell tapped his hip with the toe of his shoe. Macalister turned his head. It took a few seconds for his eyes to focus. There was bright, oxygen-rich blood at the corner of his mouth. He'd been hit through the lung.

Bell and TR exchanged a look. They both understood the wound was fatal.

"Rather tight spot I'm in, eh?" Tats said with a pained smile and that charming accent of his.

Bell said nothing.

"How did you know it was me? No way you recognized me. I planted those reeds for just such an event."

"I knew it was you because you were the only person I told that Marion was leaving the day she did. Felix and Jorge Nuñez knew she was leaving, but not when. You relayed that information to Dreissen and he sent the airship out to kidnap her from the *Spatminster*."

"That all?"

"No. There was something from the night we met. Court Talbot had asked if you were returning from Colón. But he said 'from the Colon' and then laughed it off as a language mix-up. It wasn't that at all. He screwed up his homophones. You hadn't been in Colón, the city. You'd been on the *Cologne,* the airship. I saw a file labeled that in Dreissen's office, which made me remember the incident even if I didn't understand its significance."

"I hadn't thought anyone had noticed. You are good, Detective Bell."

"Let's cut to it," Bell said sharply. "Court Talbot's dead. Otto Dreissen too. The airship blew up over the Caribbean, and your bombs failed to crack the dam or kill President Roosevelt. It's done, so stop playing at being the English fop. Dreissen confirmed you are military intelligence. He called it Sektion IIIb. How about it? Are you going to come clean?"

Macalister coughed, and fresh blood bubbled at his lips. "No. I am not. For all you know, I'm an English anarchist who wants to see the world burn. Whatever Dreissen told you is hearsay."

Roosevelt moved over so that he was standing above the prostrate spy, his great head silhouetted by the sun so that

Macalister had to blink and squint to see the man properly. "How about Milwaukee?" he asked. "Are you going to deny it was a German plot to keep me from a third term?"

"I am," Tats said, mustering the last of his reserves. "But I will say the Fatherland is much better positioned with Wilson in the White House. You are a bit of a loose cannon, Mr. Roosevelt."

TR grunted. "At least tell us your name. I will see to it that you get a proper burial."

He chuckled, and a little more blood spilled from his damaged lung. "Let's keep it 'Lord Benedict Hamilton Macalister.' Sounds so much better than my own name, you know. Bell, you bested me. Well played, old man, well played indeed."

Bell said, "It was never a game. I wasn't playing."

The German spy didn't hear him. He was dead.

Roosevelt and the guard helped Bell back to his feet. He'd gone pale under his tan, and fresh sweat oozed from his pores. The pain was evident in his eyes.

"We need to get you to the hospital over at Ancon," the guard told him.

"And I will come with you," TR said. "I can delay my departure for Brazil for a day.

Least I can do for the man who saved my life."

"Actually, Uncle Ted, can I ask another favor instead?"

"Of course, my boy. Anything."

From that day until her very last, one of Marion Bell's favorite stories was of the time she was rescued from Panama's "fever coast" by none other than the original Rough Rider himself, Teddy Roosevelt.

ABOUT THE AUTHORS

Clive Cussler was the author of more than eighty books in five bestselling series, including Dirk Pitt®, NUMA® Files, Oregon® Files, Isaac Bell®, and Sam and Remi Fargo®. His life nearly paralleled that of his hero Dirk Pitt. Whether searching for lost aircraft or leading expeditions to find famous shipwrecks, he and his NUMA crew of volunteers discovered and surveyed more than seventy-five lost ships of historic significance, including the long-lost Confederate submarine *Hunley,* which was raised in 2000 with much publicity. Like Pitt, Cussler collected classic automobiles. His collection featured more than one hundred examples of custom coachwork. Cussler died in 2020.

Jack Du Brul became a #1 *New York Times* –bestselling author by cowriting Clive Cussler's fan-favorite Oregon® series, which has become a fan favorite. Du Brul is also the writer of the bestselling novels featuring Philip Mercer. Du Brul lives in Vermont with his wife.

The employees of Thorndike Press hope you have enjoyed this Large Print book. All our Thorndike, Wheeler, and Kennebec Large Print titles are designed for easy reading, and all our books are made to last. Other Thorndike Press Large Print books are available at your library, through selected bookstores, or directly from us.

For information about titles, please call:
(800) 223-1244

or visit our website at:
gale.com/thorndike

To share your comments, please write:

Publisher
Thorndike Press
10 Water St., Suite 310
Waterville, ME 04901